Paul Beardmore has nursed an [...] was eight. While at Leeds Unive[...] the stage review, and he subseq[...] naval officer, arts administrat[...] copywriter and publications m[...] throughout Europe and the Far East. Born in Farnborough, he now lives in London with his Belgian wife and two children. *The Jazz Elephants* is his first novel.

THE JAZZ ELEPHANTS

PAUL BEARDMORE

AN ABACUS BOOK

First published in Great Britain in 1991 by Scribners
This edition published by Abacus 1993

A CIP catalogue record for this book
is available from the British Library.

ISBN 0 349 10249 X

Printed in England by Clays Ltd, St Ives plc

Abacus
A Division of
Little, Brown and Company (UK) Limited
165 Great Dover Street
London SE1 4YA

Chapter 1

Rumpus Pumpus leant against the outside wall of the elephant house, raised his trunk in the form of a question mark and sniffed the damp air.

'Rhinoceros,' he said, in a dull, final tone that sounded like the closing comment on all the problems of the universe.

'Rhinoceros.' And he lowered his trunk, closed his eyes and entered into torpor.

Meanwhile, Finta Fanta was a few metres away in the compound and was kicking blithely about in the hay that had been put out for her. First she kicked it one way up the compound until she came to the moat; then she picked up a bunch of it in her trunk and threw it up in the air; and then she watched it fall straight to the ground again. There was not a breath of breeze on this cold, damp day at the end of February.

Finally she kicked it all into a heap against the elephant house wall and ate it.

'Not bad,' she murmured, 'as London hay goes. Goodness knows where they get it from. Always tastes like rhinoceros food, baby fodder, with none of those interesting woody bits that add zest to an elephant's breakfast.'

Rumpus Pumpus was only a trunk's length away and on hearing the word 'rhinoceros' he opened one eye. Perhaps serious elephants don't open both eyes just to talk about rhinoceros.

1

'Did I hear you say "rhinoceros"?' he intoned.

'Yes, my Rumpus, yes indeed,' mashed Finta Fanta through a mouthful of mushy hay.

'You do understand,' said Rumpus Pumpus, 'that I've got nothing against rhinoceros but . . . but don't you find they smell rather strong?'

'Well, since you mention it,' munched Finta Fanta, 'I do actually and . . .' munch, myam, scrosh, squelch, swallow, 'and what's more, I think this hay we get is really more rhino hay than elephant fodder. Sort of thing my father would only eat when he had trouble with his teeth.'

'Exactly,' put in Rumpus Pumpus.

They stood without talking for a few moments; but with a very knowing look in their eyes. They viewed the day, grey and misty and damp. An occasional flipper flap came to their ears from the seal pool. A sheep baaed over towards the perimeter fence, beyond which was the green grass of Regent's Park. Across the path, just beyond the moat and wall of their own enclosure, a couple of kangaroos and a wallaby hopped laconically across their compound; but with no joy in their jump, rather as if their springs were run down.

'I can see you're thinking,' said Finta Fanta and raised her eyebrows in an expectant gaze. After a pause, Rumpus Pumpus spoke.

'Do you know, Finta, the zookeepers and cleaners, and especially the old elephant keeper, are all very nice in their way, and I wouldn't like to disappoint them or hurt a hair on their heads, but when all is said and done, this is no life for beasts like us. We need freedom and fresh air,' he cast an eye towards the rhinoceros enclosure, 'and a chance to keep company of our own choosing.'

'Couldn't agree more, my old Rumpus,' said Finta Fanta. 'Let's see if we can get sent back to Africa and then we can join up with the old herd again and meet old friends; and get back into the good, honest life of the savanna and eat trees and fresh grass,' Finta Fanta was getting quite carried away, 'and wallow in water holes and tramp the great plains and . . .' but Rumpus Pumpus cut her short.

'Sorry Finta. But it wouldn't do.'

'What do you mean, "It wouldn't do"?'

'I mean it wouldn't work,' explained Rumpus Pumpus. 'I've thought about all that. First of all we'd have to ask them; the keeper and so on, I mean; and then they'd know we could talk. Then we'd become scientific curiosities and we'd be studied and observed and all sorts of things like that and they'd never let us go. Secondly, we had a good life on the savanna with the herd, but, look at us, Finta, we're not like the rest of them any more. We don't like the sedentary existence here and the boring diet and some of the neighbours, but we do rather like discussing the finer points of life. And when there's a thunder storm or a snow storm, well, it's comfortable to be inside and be waited on and not have to forage for yourself.

'Then there are all the people. Do you know, we'd miss them? We'd miss discussing them between ourselves and seeing what the latest fashions are. We'd miss the intellectual challenge of piecing together the acquired wisdom of humanity from their conversations round the elephant house. Just think of what we've learnt listening to the crowds. Why, when we came here we didn't even know we were pachyderms, let alone that we had close relations in India, wherever that is, who are tamer and smaller than we are. Do you remember that guide who went on and on for ages about mammoths and mastodons and all our ancestors? Why, back in the herd, they wouldn't even know how to talk. And as for what we've learnt off ice-cream cartons and dropped newspapers: it's a

3

revelation we could only share with humans. Though I must say,' he added, 'I don't understand that pink one very much.'

'Well then, Rumpus, we'll just have to stay,' said Finta Fanta. 'After all, summer will come, there'll be warm days and green trees to look at. And the swifts and swallows will be back and they smell of Africa.'

'True,' said Rumpus Pumpus. 'But so does rhinoceros, in a way.'

Finta Fanta gave a chortling little trumpet and swaggered off to the pool for a drink. She quaffed a few trunkfuls and squirted a bit behind her ears, which always helped her to think. Then she sauntered back to where Rumpus Pumpus was standing. He was chewing a bit of hay and looked forlornly at a trolley of crunchy cattle cake that was being taken across to the cows near the fence. He wondered what it tasted like. It looked very interesting.

'So what do we do?' asked Finta Fanta.

'Escape,' said Rumpus Pumpus.

'Cor!' said Finta Fanta.

'Escape,' said Rumpus Pumpus.

'Rumpus,' began Finta Fanta, although rather warily because she knew he normally thought through what he suggested, 'what would be the point? We both know we can walk down into the moat, I can kneel down and you can walk out across my back and over the wall, then pull me up after you. Like we did that night we wanted to read what it said on the front of our enclosure. And we could kick the perimeter fence down like a couple of acacia trees on the savanna and be in Marylebone Station within the hour. But what do we do then? We'd just be rounded up and herded back, and people would come and photograph us and they'd keep us inside till they'd dug the moat deeper and we'd be nothing but a sensational story for the newspapers. Imagine it, animals of our intellect reduced to titillating humans on a piece of litter!'

'It depends how you do it,' said Rumpus Pumpus; and his eyes took on that cold and knowing look which Finta Fanta understood meant great thoughts, and great decisions.

'The key to it all,' explained Rumpus Pumpus, 'is people. Since we can't really go back happily to the savanna, which anyway has poachers, hunters, game wardens and the like, to become wild life, we'll have to live in the world of people somehow. Now the problem with a straight breakout like the one you've just described is that it puts everyone against us. In other words, it will make people feel that we're against them. We'll be seen as ferocious and unrestrained vandals from the African plains, hell-bent on busting out of the humane care of one of the world's greatest zoos.' Finta Fanta smiled, but regained her serious composure as Rumpus Pumpus arched his towering brow.

'As I've said, talking to people at this stage will only take us from being zoo creatures to laboratory animals. We'd become suitable subjects of study. No, what we've got to do is to find a way that will let us slip out quietly when no-one is looking and then try and somehow find a place, not against humans, but in company with them.

'It'll be risky, we still don't know how we'll succeed but what it boils down to is that we've got to sneak out, not bust out. In fact it's not so much sneaking out, it's sneaking in. Sneaking out of captivity and sneaking into the world of people.'

This time Finta Fanta arched her brow and pursed her lips.

'How? My dear young Rumpus, how?' she trilled.

'Tunnel,' said Rumpus Pumpus.

'I see,' drawled Finta Fanta, and threw another strand of hay up into the air. It floated down in a zigzag, carefree sort of way and, as it fell, she said, 'We just dig a sort of long hole one night and then saunter down it and out into the world of people. Is that it?'

'Not quite,' said Rumpus Pumpus. 'I think, in fact, it may take a little longer than one night.'

And if any visitors had been looking at the two elephants from over the moat, like most spectators do, they would have seen them put their heads very close together as if they were stroking or caressing each other's cheeks. They might have heard a gentle scuffing of their hides rubbing together; but they wouldn't have heard the whispering that was going on between them. The whispering that seemed quite exciting at times as they shuffled their legs about in the cold. They even seemed to jump a bit for joy, bouncing on their hind legs. Onlookers would have made gooey noises, thinking it was all simple affection and elephantine devotion. They wouldn't have seen the wide-eyed excitement of Finta Fanta, the sort of wide-eyed excitement that you only see in someone listening, and listening hard, to an enthralling plan being laid out before him. And they wouldn't have noticed that when dusk came at around tea-time and the elephant keeper came to herd the two beasts back into the elephant house, that each of them, in a very elephantine way, had, at the corner of the mouth, a happy, beaming and rather superior smile.

That night, Rumpus Pumpus and Finta Fanta removed from an unconsidered corner of the elephant house a handbag that someone had once left idly around the enclosure and whose potential the two pachyderms had immediately realized. It contained the usual assortment of personal belongings, tourist maps, a mirror and make-up and other items which the elephants now exploited. With delicate tips of tactile trunks they opened the bag and removed from within a sheet of paper, an envelope and a ball-point pen. With a little effort and following the model of letters printed in the newspapers, they wrote the following letter to *The Times*:

Sir,

Following the Monarch's most gracious initiative in offering Regent's Park as the setting for the forthcoming national sculpture competition, 'The Evolution of the Elephant', organized by the London Zoo, I would like to use your columns to add my own contribution and further publicize the event.

Let me first say that this must be an opportunity and challenge to every art student in the country. Surely no college can refuse to send at least one competing team. And how enlightened to show the elephant and his ancestors not just as individuals dotted around a sculpture park, but as herds and family groups apparently browsing from the trees and verdure. Yet more enlightened is the decision to make all sculptures double life size in order that the smallest and most ancient ancestor, *moeritherium*, should be too big to encourage theft or vandalism; all sculptures thereafter needing to be in the same proportions, of course. The final stroke of genius for the project is that the sculptures be made of raw London clay. Not only does this add a beautiful local element to the entire undertaking, it will also tax the artistic merits of the nation's young sculptors and produce a true winner worthy of the final award.

I mentioned above my own contribution to the enterprise. As a dealer in high quality natural materials with great experience in argillaceous sediments . . .

('Remember those glorious wallows in the clayey waterholes of the savanna,' moaned Rumpus Pumpus wistfully.

'Aaah,' moaned Finta Fanta in agreement.)

. . . I am delighted to supply all the necessary clay quite free of charge. Deliveries will begin before the end of the week.

It only remains for me to wish all contestants the best of luck and to look forward to a sculpture extravaganza of the most awesome proportions.

> Yours etc.
> R.P. Claycart
> Founder, Natural Materials
> Supplies Association

With some difficulties the elephants folded the letter, got it into an envelope and applied a stamp. They did this quite easily by picking it up on the damp tip of a trunk and pressing it gently to the dampened envelope. The next morning they waited in the enclosure until they saw a decent-looking citizen coming in their direction. At that moment Finta Fanta dropped the letter over the wall just in front of the notice on the enclosure.

'My, my,' muttered the decent citizen when he came up to the notice. 'Someone's dropped a letter. Addressed and stamped too; I'll pop it in the post for him.' And he did. And a couple of days later, it was printed in *The Times*.

Chapter 2

A butler with a long nose, on the instruction of an equerry in a black suit, placed a beautifully ironed and correctly folded copy of *The Times* with the letter page uppermost, on a gold salver and carried it on upraised hand through the corridors of the royal palace. The butler led the equerry down passages with crimson carpets, past paintings with gilded frames, up staircases in sweeping spirals to a landing in a high and private place. The butler looked at the equerry. The equerry nodded. The butler knocked twice on a very private door. He paused for a moment of decency and then led the equerry into a darkened bedroom: a warm place, soft and comfortable with the sound and aroma of slumber and snooze.

The butler put his hand on the silken cover of the moving mountain that topped the gilded bed that touched the silken carpet; and gave a gentle, a very gentle, shake.

'Ah, hem,' he coughed lightly, '*The Times*, Your Majesty.' The Monarch opened one, tired, bleary eye and saw a long, long nose; then a golden plate and then a crisp newspaper. The Monarch nodded almost imperceptibly and the butler put the paper on the bedside table. The gold plate made a dull clink as it was laid on fine Venetian glass. The butler stepped back to await instructions and the equerry stepped forward to do his duty.

'Your Majesty,' he purred, 'there is a most interesting

9

letter in *The Times* today. I fear we will need clarification just to handle enquiries that are bound to follow.'

'Humph,' said the Monarch quietly.

'Does Your Majesty remember the reception for The Zoological Society of London, last week?'

'Humph.'

'It seems that certain people are under the impression you would like to hold a sculpture exhibition in Regent's Park. Er, "The Evolution of the Elephant".'

'Your Majesty did appear to become a little confused towards the end of the evening, if I may say so. It couldn't have been what you were talking about to that spirited group by the window that overlooks . . .'

'Humph . . .' somewhat louder this time. 'Equerry?'

'Yes, Your Majesty.'

'What am I supposed to have promised? And please be brief. Remember I had a reception with those people from the Scottish Office last night . . . and you know what they get up to.'

'Er, quite so, Your Majesty. To be brief – a competition, open to the nation's art colleges, to build double-life-size sculptures of the elephant and its evolutionary forebears . . . er, in Regent's Park.'

There was a short pause and a little noise that could have been a chortle or could have been a snore: 'Sounds like the best idea I'm supposed to have had in years,' murmured the Monarch, a note of self admiration overcoming the underlying drowsiness. 'Get it organized, will you, equerry?'

'At once, Your Majesty,' said the equerry. And with a smile on his lips and a spring in his tread, he led the butler from the bedroom. The door closed as the sounds of slumber resumed and the black suit descended the sweeping staircase, followed by the long nose on a wryly shaking head.

The following day the newspapers were full of the forthcoming competition. The equerry, an experienced man who knew his Monarch, had had the plans outlined before the end of breakfast and the palace press office fully briefed before the phone began ringing at nine o'clock on the day the elephants' letter appeared.

Invitations winged their way to the nation's art colleges. The President of The Zoological Society of London, having been personally congratulated in such glowing terms by the equerry, for his hand in evolving the idea with the Monarch, beamed with delight: even if he couldn't quite remember that sculpture competitions were what he talked to the Monarch about at the end of the reception last week. He sketched in little herds of mastodons, groups of *platybelodon*, stampedes of *gomphotherium* and parties of browsing *mammuthus* all over his desk-top map of Regent's Park.

Finta Fanta and Rumpus Pumpus were chewing their way through breakfast, side by side at the mighty trough of the elephant house. They usually stood together like that with their heads to the wall when they were inside because then they couldn't see the rhinoceros across the concourse and the smell of hay was sweet under their trunk tips.

Their keeper came in with a portable radio to keep him company. He began washing down the floor and clearing out. The elephants, he knew, rather liked a bit of music and the sound of voices, so he propped the radio on the manger and whistled along as he went about his sloshy, happy, business.

So it was that on the ten o'clock news of a misty, chilly day late in February, Finta Fanta and Rumpus Pumpus heard of the forthcoming sculpture competition. A sparkle lit their eyes, a tiny trumpet escaped the trunk of Finta Fanta.

'We start tonight,' whispered Rumpus Pumpus in her ear; and the elephant keeper scrubbed on quite unaware of the plan that had been hatched and would swing into action that very night.

At the end of the day, after the elephant keeper had herded Rumpus Pumpus and Finta Fanta back inside the elephant house, he gave them each a pat on the trunk and a warm 'Good night' as usual, and went home to his family.

When all was quiet in the zoo and darkness complete, the two elephants quickly fiddled the catch of their door and moved silently out into the compound. Rumpus Pumpus went first, and wandered down into the moat where he crouched low. Finta Fanta walked gently over his back and out over the moat wall. Once there, she turned and helped him up. A heave and he was out. Finta Fanta leading, they made their way through the damp darkness, up the gentle slope to the Wolf Wood.

Although it was quiet and clammy and dark, as always in a big city there was the deadening sound of distant traffic, the faint light of distant street lights and the lighting in the zoo itself that enabled an animal to see; but left shadows as big as elephants.

The pair reached the Wolf Wood. With a couple of practised trunk twists they were through the gate to the enclosure, shutting it carefully behind them and making for two large trees. The wolves smelt fresh meat and bounded up to investigate; but when they saw the size of the dish, quite lost their appetites and slunk away with disappointed little yelps.

Finta Fanta and Rumpus Pumpus each quickly ripped a tree out of the ground. They shook the earth off the remaining roots, devoured the tasty twigs with those succulent, tightly furled winter buds and crunchy sticks and tore off the larger branches. The wolves were very impressed and slunk even further away. The elephants carried the two great trunks back to their enclosure and laid them across the moat, remembering, of course, to secure the Wolf Wood on their way out.

'Perfect, my Rumpus, perfect,' whispered Finta Fanta. 'A delightful little bridge just for us.'

'Now for the real work,' murmured Rumpus Pumpus.

Together, they crossed back to their compound, went into the house and braced themselves for mighty effort.

The floor of the elephant house was made of thick, reinforced concrete slabs: as were the floors of all the pens in the building which gave on to the large central gallery where the public strolled in opening hours. Opposite the elephants, across the public promenade, were the rhinoceros stalls where one bleary-eyed monster looked on with all the interest of which he was capable.

He saw Finta Fanta and Rumpus Pumpus take up position at opposite corners of one of the concrete floor slabs next to the wall. The slabs, he noticed, were truly enormous. Quite large enough for a couple of rhinos to stand on. Then he saw Rumpus Pumpus press on his corner of the slab with both his forefeet, lean forward with all his weight and, indeed, even lift his hind feet off the ground for a moment in a kind of headstand so that the concrete slab came under the most extreme of pressures. As Rumpus Pumpus rolled back, so Finta Fanta rolled forward and pressed with all her weight on her opposing corner.

The two elephants rocked backwards and forwards in sequence like this until the rhinoceros thought it was some strange kind of ritual; a dance which, in his own little way, he thought quite ridiculous. But after ten minutes or so, each time one of the elephants applied his weight there was a little grating sound; a few minutes more and he could see the mighty slab was rocking just a tiny bit each time the elephants applied their force.

They paused to catch breath; and then both went to the corner by the wall where Rumpus Pumpus had been working. This time, both of them applied their weight on the one corner, then relaxed, then pushed again and so on until finally the opposite corner stood up just two or three centimetres each time they applied their force. They paused for breath again. They both pushed again; but this time Rumpus Pumpus stayed pushing and Finta Fanta slowly removed her weight and then walked quickly round to the corner that was standing proud. After a couple of false tries, she managed to jam the end of her tusk in the crevice at the corner of the slab. Slowly, very slowly, Rumpus Pumpus removed his weight and then quickly went round beside Finta Fanta. He pushed the tip of one of his tusks in beside hers and gingerly levered up a bit. Finta Fanta's tusk came free and she then placed it in the crevice again and levered in turn.

The rhinoceros stood stock still with glaring eye and gaping mouth. Centimetre by centimetre the slab was rising before his eyes. It looked touch and go at times, with little stumbles and enormous endeavour. The effort seemed to go in phases, each phase a little easier than the last and each phase punctuated by a metallic twang as reinforcing rods broke and the moving slab slowly came free of its neighbours.

Eventually, the whole of the edge farthest from the wall had been raised until it showed a black slit along its length. Finta Fanta and Rumpus Pumpus worked their way to opposite ends of the slit. With wriggling and pushing motions of their mighty necks and shoulders they worked their tusks in until they were right under the slab. The two great animals then paused for several minutes. They had their tusks under the concrete and their chins on the floor. They were stretched out, resting, while their tusks supported the prised-up slab.

The rhinoceros batted his eyelids. It shook its head. It was confused and it wondered for a moment if the elephants had gone to sleep. But not a bit of it. When their breathing had returned to normal and their courage was reinforced, they seemed to be bracing themselves for some great, unprecedented effort.

Although their bodies and heads remained close to the floor, the elephants moved their legs up as far as possible to a crouching position and braced themselves again.

Rumpus Pumpus snaked his trunk across to Finta Fanta's ear and whispered, 'Are you all right, young Finta?'

'This is going to be a big effort, isn't it?' she answered with a hint of diffidence entering her voice.

'Think of our freedom,' whispered Rumpus Pumpus, 'and an end to rhinoceros for ever,' he added. Her eyes sparkled at the thought.

'Ready,' he said.

'Ready,' she whispered.

'Right, go!'

He gave the signal. And both elephants pushed with all their might against the floor and heaved upward with enormous force against the rock-like slab.

Nothing seemed to happen. The two animals strained like weightlifters. Though their skin was loose, the pattern of muscles through their forelegs and necks stood out. They gasped, they strained on and on and still there seemed no movement in the slab. Then, quite suddenly, there was a ping as a reinforcing rod broke, then a twang as another went and the slab rose just a few more centimetres.

'Together now,' hissed Rumpus Pumpus. 'Heave!' And they both redoubled their efforts. Slowly at first, then more and more quickly, the slab lifted up with a twinging and twanging of shearing rods and a sound of grating stone like the opening of the trap door on some vast and long-unentered rock-cut chamber. A minute, and it was vertical, a couple of seconds more and it just rocked back to lean against the elephant house wall with a thud that, ever so slightly, shook the entire zoo.

The President of The Zoological Society of London was working late in his office that night. He noticed that at twenty-eight minutes past eleven exactly, he felt a slight trembling and the tea in the cup on his desk rippled a little and then was still. He at once phoned his friend, the President of The Geological Society of Great Britain, and reported a minor earthquake. The latter noted the time and promised to look at the seismometer the following day. Then, with a slight smile on his lips, cursed his old friend very gently, and rolled over and went back to sleep.

Finta Fanta and Rumpus Pumpus now knew that they had won, now knew that nothing could stop them but time. Without pausing to congratulate each other, merely taking deep breaths to regain their composure, they quickly set to. It was late, and they still had three hours' work before them. In a twinkle, they kicked aside the gravel and the rubble under the concrete and with tusk and toe, muscle and will, they began to excavate the floor. They soon evolved a system. One of them stood in the rapidly growing hole and dug out great clods and lumps.

'So lucky for us it's clay here, all pure London clay,' chortled Finta Fanta in a brief breathing space.

The other one picked up the lumps, carried them across the enclosure on trunk and tusk, across the tree-trunk bridge over the moat and dumped them in a rapidly growing pile on the lawn near the wallaby pen, against the park fence. Every fifteen minutes or so they changed places: one digging, one carrying; and so the mound and the hole grew.

By two o'clock in the morning they saw their objectives would be reached. With tired, leisurely, happy movements they dug out the shift's last clods and carried them across the bridge to dump them on the mound. Beneath the floor of the elephant house they had excavated a chamber, sloping on one side to allow entry and exit, that went down into the earth to the depth of an elephant's shoulder. From it led the beginning of a passage which started to slope downwards under the foundations in the direction of the perimeter fence. It was the beginning, a fine and well-executed beginning, planned to the last detail as the elephants' next action showed.

They crossed the tree-trunk bridge and went carefully round the rough mound of pig-sized lumps of clay, smoothing out any trace of elephant footprint or tusk mark. They then went to the elephant pool and drew water with their trunks, hosing down the path between their enclosure and the clay pile. Satisfied that all tracks and traces were gone, they picked up the tree trunks and took them into the elephant house, hiding them in the chamber they had dug. They then turned in the broken ends of the reinforcing rods so that none would stick up from the floor, bending them over with the care, precision and ease with which a benign old man bends his pipe cleaners. Together, they excavated a small hollow underneath the edge of the slab, next to the wall. With trunk and tusk they lowered the slab back into its place. A quick hose-down in the elephant house and all was clean and tidy. Not a thing out of place; and the rhinoceros opposite looking on with a perplexed and worried air as if this world was suddenly too much for it, and full of mysteries it could not understand.

The two elephants then settled down to sleep. Rumpus Pumpus lay out on the floor and Finta Fanta came and rested her head on his neck.

'Well,' chortled Rumpus Pumpus, 'The Natural Materials Supplies Association has made its first delivery of clay.'

And the two of them chortled and chortled and chortled until, with tired smiles on their lips, they chortled themselves to sleep; and didn't wake up till lunch time.

Chapter 3

Grinders' Hall in the City of London is an ancient and venerable building to be found up a small galleyway off Throgmorton Avenue. It is the seat of The Worshipful Company of Bell Founders and Organ Grinders: long is their tradition and magnificent their ceremony.

On the last day of February, unless that day be a Sunday, in which case on the preceding Friday, the Founders and Grinders hold their inaugurations. These are wondrous ceremonies decked in silver, gold, purple and scarlet, chanted in sonorous voices and surrounded in the flowing clarions of clear bells and mellow organs.

This last day of February was a Friday and inside Grinders' Hall the members of the Company assembled for the splendid proceedings to make members of members' sons and consider applications from non-members to become members of this most worshipful body.

The chimes of eleven faded and the sounds of the Great Hall fell near to silence as the ranks of liverymen settled on to their oaken benches. From here and there came tiny creakings as old woodwork moved a fraction under the weight of aged Grinders. Their sighs subsided and against the great stained-glass window at the end of the long, high, rectangular hall, the sound of blustering raindrops, tapping and gusting, made the air just barely live instead of only still and solemn.

It was a scarlet sight, the ceremony, set in the reverence of oak-panelled walls. Tiers of oak stalls, six on each side, rose from the long floor. The entrance centred at one end: heavy oak doors that let in the liverymen beneath the cascades of pipes of the towering organ set above the threshold. Many metres away, at the other end of the hall, was the stained-glass window, rich in red and blue that filled the wall, ten metres or more in height and five or more in width. In front of it was a platform down to which hung eight bell ropes which passed through the decorated oak-panelled ceiling from the bell tower above.

Tier on tier of liverymen sat in solemn silence. Each wore his nacre-tiled, all-weather pagoda hat, beset above and beside with golden dress balls joined to each other by elastic gold string. Their scarlet tunics seemed to fade into the rich lustre of the dark oak stalls and the shadowy light of the hall glinted dully off the octave of miniature organ pipes which each had sewn to his breast. More buttons, more elastic gold string; and each in bell breeches: wide straight-cut trousers coming to just beneath the knee with sewn-in bell plaques to the fore. On legs, embroidered hose; and on feet, buckled shoes. A peal of colour from toe through tufted elbow to fineal dress ball above nacre hat.

Solemnly, one of the number mounted the bell platform beneath the great window. There was a shuffling gleam of mother-of-pearl as two hundred heads turned towards him. The organ started a long, low, quiet tune. The music rolled around the shadowy hall, quiet and rhythmic and private, and mixed with the wind noise and the rain taps from outside to set an atmosphere of deep and quiet expectation.

The liveryman on the platform was the Grand Master of the Company. Magnificently, with solemn gesture and arched eyebrow, he unrolled a parchment scroll before him. The ribbon of a mighty seal dropped from its lower edge: the shadow of meticulous calligraphy showed through to the reverse. In a low, melodious and rolling voice he began to chant the names of all those who were candidates at the year's inauguration.

On and on rolled the voice, forward and forward came the candidates. They came in through small side doors as their names were intoned, or stepped forward from the shadows beneath the organ to meet in a small group at the centre of the stone floor. For them the sight was awesome. The Grand Master calling the roll, the rows of liveried men rising on each side, the total number of candidates as yet unknown to them.

The intonation stopped. The roll was called: fifty-three candidates in all. They glanced at each other. They stood nervous and expectant, dressed in black doublets and black tights with black ankle boots and black skull-caps. They were the embodiment of night, awaiting the dawn of inauguration, if inauguration be theirs.

The music ceased and as its echoes rolled away, the Bell Master and the Organ Master rose in their stalls, the front corner seats farthest from the bell platform, and intoned over the heads of the candidates:

'How many be the candidates?'

The question tailed into silence and the echoes of it chased each other gently through the rafters high overhead. The Grand Master drew breath and in his turn he too intoned, deep, long and final:

'Fifty-three.'

The Bell Master and the Organ Master chanted once again,

> 'How many of us are died,
> How many of us are gone away,
> How many of us cast out
> Since last our gathering?'

The deep, sonorous tone of the Grand Master answered them:

'Six.'

And the candidates gritted their teeth. Their fathers and their sponsors drew breath. Six would be chosen out of fifty-three, forty-seven would be turned away.

'Which six?' intoned the Bell Master and the Organ Master.

A silence fell and the Grand Master turned his back on the assembly and faced the great stained-glass window. The bell ropes fell to each side of him and moved slightly in some unfelt breeze. He raised his hand as if calling upon the story in the window to give an answer.

The window was a field of blue representing a blue sky amongst whose clouds floated the City of London. It was represented as a picture of all its major bell and organ-bearing buildings with sun, moon, stars and a red sunset intermingled with it. Around the outside, the window was framed in the trunks and branches of two tall trees. Their leaves and flowers met at the centre top of the window and visible along their stems were their fruits – oranges to the left, and lemons to the right.

Slowly the Grand Master pointed with the index finger of his left hand on high towards the oranges. Slowly he pointed with the index finger of his right hand on high towards the lemons. Loud as a bell he chanted,

> 'Three to the oranges,
> Three to the lemons,
> Forty-seven rejected,
> These six to be chosen.'

The Organ Master and the Bell Master came down from their stalls. They met at the mid-point between the facing ranks and whispered in each other's ears. The

Grand Master then turned and the two other Masters took up position facing each other at the centre of the hall. They clasped hands right to left and left to right, then raised them to make an arch through which the candidates would soon have to march.

The candidates joined hands and formed an oval, an oval which passed beneath the raised arms of the Bell and Organ Masters.

'Pray, drop hands and face backs,' chanted the Grand Master. The candidates dropped hands and turned to face the back of the candidate beside them.

'So will the selection be made!' intoned the Grand Master. And at this signal the great organ sprang to life with a roar of wind bellowing through feeder pipes and a muffled clatter of stops and treadles as the organist threw his all, across three keyboards of pattering ivory and hundreds of ebony knobs, into the solemn, ceremonial rendering of 'Oranges and Lemons' which the assembled company rose as one body to sing in their strong and united voices:

> 'Gay go up and gay go down,
> To ring the bells of London town.
> Bulls' eyes and targets,
> Say the bells of St Margaret's . . .'

As the song started its slow and rhythmic progress the candidates in turn began their slow and rhythmic progress, moving in a continuous line around the oval they had formed and through the arch of the Music and Bell Masters' upraised hands.

> '. . . Oranges and lemons,
> Say the bells of St Clement's . . .'

roared on the chant at its stately and magnificent pace. Liverymen swelled their breasts and burst the stitching on their ornamental organ pipes to outvoice their neighbours in the mighty sound. Dress balls bobbled and bell breeches trembled as the company sang on with increasing anxiety and anticipation as the first chorus approached.

> 'Here comes a candle to light you to bed,
> And here comes a chopper to chop off your head!'

With the last words of the chorus the Bell Master and the Organ Master dropped their hands like a guillotine and trapped between their arms one black-clad candidate who at once hugged both of them with joy and gratitude. He at least was chosen. The Bell Master leant confidentially towards the candidate as the liverymen waved and cheered. The organ played a fanfare and the Grand Master raised his arm.

The Bell Master whispered in the candidate's ear, 'Oranges or lemons?'

The candidate whispered back, 'Oranges.'

The Organ Master led the candidate to his side, where the candidate placed his hands on the Organ Master's waist and waited for the next rendering of the song.

The Grand Master dropped his hand. At once there was deep silence and the Bell and Organ Masters took up their position as an arch again. The great organ leapt suddenly to life with the procession of candidates once more moving round in their oval, hoping that of all things they would be lucky in this.

Again the liverymen sang,

> 'Two sticks and an apple,
> Say the bells at Whitechapel . . .'

and again at the end of a chorus the arms of the Masters fell and another candidate was chosen. This candidate whispered 'Lemons' into the Master's ear. Like the first, quietly, softly amid the applause and cheering so that none

24

but the chosen and the Bell and Organ Masters should know which line was lemons and which line was oranges.

After three-quarters of an hour of solemn ceremony the Organ Master had three candidates behind him, while the Bell Master had but two. Thus was it come to the most decisive moment. But one place remained, at the side of the Bell Master. A lemon place; yet none but the two Masters making the arch, or the chosen ones, knew it. Amongst the candidates the tension mounted to a fever.

Cold the day, yet they sweated; dry the hall, yet they were moist as with rain; august and dignified the liverymen, yet anxious and uncertain the candidates.

Calculations ran through their brains. The mathematics of pace and music, of rhythm and distance was calculated by them all. As their hopes dictated, they speeded or slowed the procession till at one point the Grand Master called, 'Velocitation!' The organ stopped, the liverymen gasped. 'Velocitation' ran round the gallery like the whisper of a deadly sin. One candidate had artificially speeded the procession by kneeing his predecessor, very gently, in the back of the thigh. But the crime was seen and had to be admitted. At once all liverymen stood and silently pointed – pointed the index finger of the left hand in ceremonial scorn, with ceremonial scowls upon their lips, and the guilty cowered at their glance. He crumpled and sneaked scuttlingly away by one of the side doors; and, the moment it closed, the fingers dropped, the organ boomed out again and the anxious supplicants circulated in suspense.

The chorus approached:

'Here comes a candle . . . '

and a group of some four or five candidates at a few metres from the arch began to hope, began to dare to think that maybe this year their turn had come; and at the last chance they would come good and the membership of the Company would be theirs.

On the other faces, particularly those that passed now under the arch, were graven anguish and despair. Not now, perhaps not ever, would the chance of livery be theirs; hope had come and gone, their knees wobbled and their eyes shed tears and they continued round the oval like mechanical men, with all desire unrequited:

'. . . to chop off your head!'

Like scarlet knives the arms came down and between them stood a dazed, bewildered figure.

The tumult of applause and acclamation died quickly away for there was but one place left. If he chose the wrong fruit, a new round would be needed, all forty-seven would live to try once more.

'Oranges or lemons?' whispered the Bell Master.

The candidate's face went white and his stomach sank within him.

'Lemons,' he whispered falteringly back so that even the Bell Master could scarcely hear. But hear he did and the hall went wild with acclaim as he led the candidate to his side and the selection was complete.

The unchosen candidates were devastated. They collapsed in tears on the floor, a couple fainted outright and many made for the side exits from which, through winding corridors and stone staircases they made their headlong, breathless escapes out of the postern door, and even through gratings in the pediments of buildings, into the wet and blustery day: fleeting black figures in the anonymous obscurity of the grey City on a wet February Friday.

Within the hall a mad scramble of scarlet liverymen took place. They leapt at and over each other in a hectic crowd of agitated splendour, surging forward for the bell ropes to peal out the news of the selection to the world. Already the Grand Master was at the rope of the great bell, working it steadily, up and down, till the deep peal boomed out above them and the lesser peals joined in with a riot of auditory anarchy. The organist was like a heated demon, hopping the red-hot pedals of a purgatorial piano; hands flying as if the very keys burnt his fingers; toes and soles leaping as though his feet were afire. The chosen were lifted shoulder high and chaired round the hall to cheers and calls, and they in delight waved back and raised their arms in joy. All, that is, but one.

He was the last to be chosen and when, as the carollings died down and the newly admitted candidates were taken to the robing room to change for the first time into ceremonial garb, one of his fellows asked:

'Why do you look so sad when the worshipful bells peal for you?'

He replied, 'Because I didn't want to be chosen,' and robed himself with tears streaming down his face, while his fellows took it for a joke and for emotion.

His name was Henri Coulisse, and he came from generations of organ grinders and bell founders. His family only dated back to the Norman conquest so, of course, they were regarded as newcomers to the City and its institutions. In his veins he seemed to carry something of the Latin blood that the Normans had acquired in their stay in France. A blackness of hair, a darkness of complexion, a quickness of eye and a flexibility of movement.

From the cradle he had been surrounded with clarion and glockenspiel, organ concerts in the carry cot, oratorios in short trousers, fugues in flannels and change ringing in adolescence; with all the risings and fallings and bouncings and tremblings of a mixed company of campanologists.

But deep in his heart a spirit of rebellion had sprung up.

A desire unuttered and unutterable that moved in him like an independent force that would not be stilled. It filled his mind as he went through the inauguration ceremony. It obsessed his thoughts as his name was called and, fully robed, but for the nacre pagoda, he walked up the long central passage of Grinders' Hall. The organ played the Grinders' Bell Anthem and at its crescendo and finale he arrived and kneeled before the Grand Master of the Company. The Grand Master called aloud:

'Liverymen of The Worshipful Company of Bell Founders and Organ Grinders, do ye accept our son and brother Henri Coulisse to join us in founding and grinding?'

A deafening chorus of two hundred personal handbells rang out to acclaim assent. And the Grand Master raised from a stand at his side the nacre pagoda with dress balls and gold elastic string that he held aloft and then brought down upon the head of Henri Coulisse to admit him to the Company. But as he did so, just one thought filled the mind of Henri. The long and unassuageable desire to be a jazz trombonist.

Chapter 4

Since everyone at the zoo knew the delivery of clay was coming, no-one seemed very surprised to find it there one morning. A temporary gate was made in the park fence beside the wallaby enclosure, just across the path from the elephant house. The area of grass by this gate was set apart for future deliveries and, funnily enough, no matter how much the sculptors carted off to various locations in the park, the supply was always replenished.

It wasn't at all apparent that a couple of trees were missing from the Wolf Wood. After all, no-one could take a tree without a cacophony of diesel engines and chain saws, so any changes must have been ordered by someone else who dealt with that sort of thing.

The month of March began to slip away. Bevies of art students came to the zoo from all over the country to stake out their statue locations. The put-put-put noise of the zoo dumper-truck was a daily sound as it went from the temporary gate with loads of clay to positions in all the statue grounds of the park.

Every night Rumpus Pumpus and Finta Fanta went to the trap-door slab and stood over the edge by the wall where they had made the hollow under the concrete. As they applied their weight, the other edge bobbed up like a see-saw. One of the pair would go round and jam it, then the other would join him and together they would lift their trap door and begin their nightly labours. They set up their bridge and carried on excavating. Every day they slept till lunch time. Their keeper wondered what was ailing his beloved elephants, why they suddenly seemed so very tired; and he brought in the vet. He ordered supplements of good food, vitamins and protein tablets. With exercise and improved nourishment the pair grew stronger every day and the tunnel went further and faster.

They consulted their handbag with its London guide and its tourist map of Regent's Park and so kept the tunnel straight and in the right direction.

In their first week they had dug out an antechamber big enough to hold a couple of nights' diggings as well as the bridge. Like this they had gone down steeply, well beneath the foundations of the zoo and beneath the drains and sewers of the park.

From that antechamber the tunnel proper started. It was just one elephant wide and one elephant high, leading straight as an arrow out under the park. Once having set the direction, the elephants used the compact mirror from the handbag to keep the tunnel true. If the glimmer of light from the entrance was reflected along the tunnel and could be seen at the other end, then the passage was straight and level. If it couldn't be seen, adjustments could be made till the reflection was visible once again.

They managed to work almost entirely by feel. Every ten metres – the combined length of Rumpus Pumpus and Finta Fanta – they stuck a lump of clay to the wall so that it touched their ears as they walked past. Thus did they know that distance and direction were good.

During April, tunnelling had reached the critical phase. It stretched nearly a kilometre and the elephants could feel that the end might soon be close. At the same time the demand for clay reached its peak as art students descended on the park in their scores, anxious to get their clay on location and their sculptures under way by the end of the Easter vacation. As the little herds of *gomphotherium* began to plant their double-life-sized feet beneath the trees now waiting for the burst of spring, the two *loxodonta*, Finta Fanta and Rumpus Pumpus were at the ninety-fifth ten-metre mark and digging for all they were worth. As students roughed out the sketches of the *platybelodon* group, with shovel underlip and broad-snouted trunk, the two elephants dug on underground, sensing in their mighty bones that the full potential, physical and intellectual, of *gomphotherium* and *stegodon*, would be realized at last in their decisive move for freedom.

At the ninety-seventh ten-metre mark, Finta Fanta, who was digging at that moment, suddenly felt that the clay was wetter than usual. The following night Rumpus Pumpus felt the welcome chill of water, dripping here and there on to his back. He smiled and at the end of that night's digging, when all was delivered and hosed down, he snuggled close to Finta Fanta and whispered in her ear.

'Thursday. Next Thursday should do it. Just think, in a week we'll be free.'

During that week the clay pile by the temporary gate began to grow, which meant that they were now digging faster than the sculptors wanted to cart away. In fact, it seemed the sculptors now had nearly all the clay they needed at their various sites around the park. Finta Fanta and Rumpus Pumpus were excited, it looked as though they would just about do it: the tunnel they had laboured so hard for; and a hundred and fifty to two hundred double-life-sized statues of the elephant and his evolutionary forebears thrown in for good measure.

By Tuesday of that week, they judged the tunnel had gone far enough. That evening and the following evening they dug out a chamber at the far end. It was as high as they dared dig and big enough for both of them to stand in together. They used some of the material from the walls to build up the floor so that the chamber was higher than the general level of the tunnel. The rest of the material they carried out as usual and added to the pile by the temporary gate. The last load had been delivered. The digging was done.

The final metres had been messy: wet and slippery, cold, clammy and uncomfortable. But once they were hosed down and their trap door secured, they rested happy, secure in the knowledge that the heavy work was over, that the plan had held good so far and that tomorrow night, the night of the last Thursday in April, they would be free and their lives would begin anew.

There was a bright moon that Thursday night and not quite full. The wind was blustering and grey clouds tinged with the orange of the town lights sometimes raced across the sky. It was fresh, but not cold. Some trees were in new leaf and others still remained in bud, waiting for May and a burst of real warmth.

For the last time, Rumpus Pumpus and Finta Fanta raised their trap door and got out the tree trunks. They bridged the moat and, taking the handbag that had been so useful to them, they crossed into the zoo. They made their way lovingly past the places and animals they had known for so long. Like young people leaving school, they looked with affection on the institution that had brought them the pains and pleasures of existence for many years, yet felt no regrets at their parting, for it was a place they had outgrown.

The trees wrestled in the wind and the moon made everything a dull, subdued, dark colour. Like clouds of shadow passing through a shaded field they moved silently and certainly towards the clock tower. There, Finta Fanta lodged the handbag where someone would be bound to find it and, she hoped, return it at last to its owner. Then each elephant skilfully removed a drainpipe from the little building. Each took a length of about an elephant's height, but not without regret at causing expense to others. They knew, however, that their presence in the zoo had attracted quite enough money to pay for all of their keep and a couple of drainpipes as well.

With that, they went back to the elephant pavilion, crossed their bridge, and put their drainpipes in the entrance to their tunnel. Then they put their tree trunks in the antechamber for the last time, closed the door of the elephant house and secured it.

The rhinoceros opposite, who was now quite used to the nocturnal movements of the elephants, saw something new. Finta Fanta stood about half-way down the sloping entrance and waited. Rumpus Pumpus gave a last look round, winked at the rhinoceros, and then lowered the slab on to Finta Fanta's back. There was just enough room for him to squeeze in past Finta Fanta. He took part of the weight on his back and then, step by step, the elephants lowered the trap door after them and the rhinoceros, with eyes wrinkled into sacks and bags like an ageing politician's, saw an empty elephant stall, a flat floor and a locked door. They had disappeared. Gone without trace. And in one, gigantic, drawn-out explosion, the rhinoceros farted like a diesel train pulling out of King's Cross station.

Faintly, but quite distinctly to an elephant, Finta Fanta and Rumpus Pumpus heard the unmistakable flatulence through forty centimetres of concrete.

'By Mammuthus himself,' hissed Rumpus Pumpus in the pitch black of the tunnel, 'that lot alone makes the entire exercise worthwhile!'

Finta Fanta tittered: 'Farewell, Crumple Eyes; we sail forth on a fair wind and leave you to a foul!'

Each of them felt about with his trunk until he found his drain pipe, then put his trunk in the end of it and dragged it under his body, between his legs, as he made his way into the tunnel.

Finta Fanta went first and Rumpus Pumpus followed her, silent now and with a sense of foreboding as they went forward in the pitch darkness. The tunnel smelt horribly of dank clay, roots and puddles of stagnant water. The cold, greasy sides seemed to slide clammy hands along their flanks; automatically they counted each distance bump as they went past. From time to time their feet squelched great lumps of clay that had fallen out of the tunnel walls; at about the mid-point the walls on both sides seemed to squeeze them in like the great closing jaws of a cold, gigantic vice. The tunnel walls were starting to bulge and to decay. The structure would not last much longer before parts of it collapsed and blocked.

Though they had walked that way a hundred times before, no time seemed as long and no moments so precarious as these. Some accident, some unforeseen event could spoil it all at this last stage and all would have been for nothing.

Tense, excited, filled with the thrill of freedom and the dread of danger, the two elephants stood at last side by side in the end chamber of their working. They could feel drips and rivulets of water spotting and trickling on to their backs. They slid forward their drainpipes and, by touch, each pushed the end of his pipe into the top forward corner of the chamber.

'Well, my Finta,' said Rumpus Pumpus, 'for all this have we laboured. Whatever happens now, we will have tried our best, and if we do not make it, one day they will find our bodies trapped down here and know at least we tried.'

'That's rhino talk,' quipped back Finta Fanta, alive with

enthusiasm. 'We dug a tunnel, not a grave, and we're going to escape. This isn't heroism, my tusker, this is freedom, now let's make the break!'

They trumpeted and quickly gave each other a friendly biff somewhere on the side of the head – they couldn't see where in the dark – and Rumpus Pumpus, invigorated by Finta Fanta's words, stuffed his trunk up his drainpipe. Finta Fanta felt for his trunk and packed the near end of the drainpipe solid with clay. The seal was perfect. She then squashed a big lump of clay around her trunk about a metre from the tip and rammed her trunk up her drainpipe so that it, too, was sealed in the long, metal tube.

'Ready?' said Finta Fanta.

'Go,' said Rumpus Pumpus.

And they pushed and wormed and waggled and thrust their drainpipes upwards through the sticky clay towards the surface and the night: great tubular drills on the end of mighty trunks.

No sooner had they started to push, than they felt the trickle of water, which was running down the outside of their drainpipes, increase. They pushed and wiggled and bored and shoved, always upwards, always onwards. The flow of water became stronger. First Finta Fanta, then Rumpus Pumpus stood in a cascade falling on to them from above and causing great difficulty in their breathing. It was as bad as they had feared it might be, it could only get worse. Breathing became even harder. Finta Fanta squealed, for a touch of panic crossed her heart as the slurry of clay and water began to pour yet more quickly over her head and shoulders in the bewildering dark. Suddenly she realized that the floor below was soft and her footing was starting to go. She was getting farther from, not nearer, the roof through which they must break out. Rumpus Pumpus turned a little diagonally to shore her up and pushed with all his might against the drainpipe and the roof. Without warning, he quite suddenly felt the end of his drainpipe break free. He pushed it up to the limit, managed to take in one mighty breath through his mouth amidst the falling water and then blew with all his force up the pipe. As he knew, the end of it would be blocked with clay, but his blast shot out the plug like the cork from a champagne bottle and Rumpus Pumpus at least breathed the fresh air of freedom, though still, of course, from within the mud-filled chamber.

How Finta Fanta avoided blind panic, loss of reason and death in what happened next, Rumpus Pumpus never really found out. But if what happened now was an ordeal to test the qualities of elephants, then Finta Fanta had qualities indeed and the ordeal added to those qualities which she already had.

'Breathe in, breathe in, Finta,' shouted Rumpus Pumpus through the din of the falling water. Finta Fanta's fight for a foothold was getting desperate, but somehow she managed one decent breath before she slipped to her knees, lost her drainpipe and became unable to rise again.

Rumpus Pumpus felt her slump down beside him and, feeling the sides and floor of the tunnel all around him turning to a slippery morass, realized he could do nothing to raise her without losing his drainpipe to the upper air. Unable to go back to help, there remained only to go on and break out. Finta Fanta's words 'Make the break!' hammered through his head. He pushed up his breathing pipe and stabbed and dug with all his enormous strength at the roof of the tunnel. Pushing, poking, stabbing, digging, scraping, thrusting, he picked and worked with his tusks all around the hole where the drainpipe disappeared.

Quickly, not just slurry but lumps of clay began falling from the roof. Some splodged on to his back, some went to Finta Fanta's side and he felt her rolling and turning to slough them off. Then without any warning at all, the entire roof of their chamber collapsed and the two escapees lived a minute and a half of nightmare.

At night, Regent's Park is closed. But if you are a canny, hard-up, student tourist and you happen to have an all-weather sleeping bag in camouflage colours, you can, if you're lucky, sneak in at dusk and hide in a thicket where you can pass an undisturbed, if somewhat uncomfortable, night; before getting the train and ferry back to Denmark.

Hans was a handsome chap with a yellow beard, blue eyes, a Danish passport and a camouflage sleeping bag. With the incentive of no money and a ticket home the following day, he exploited his talent for working his way into all sorts of unexpected places and decided that on the fair, if breezy, last Thursday in April, he would give a try to Regent's Park, perhaps by the lake where the bushes are thick, or maybe in some rhododendrons, if he could find them.

Turning off the Inner Circle just after The Home, a beautiful house that he very much admired, he found the path led him down to a bridge across one arm of the Regent's Park lake. He looked around. No-one was to be seen. He jumped the fence to his left and in the bushes, under the trees, beside the water of the lake he found cover which, though far from leafy at this season, was good enough for the night. It was early evening and dusk, he was tired and would have a long day to follow. He crept into his sleeping bag and ate a pork pie and drank a take-away coffee that was still fairly warm. The food comforted him and the warmth of the sleeping bag made him drowsy. As night fell, he drifted quickly off to sleep, waking suddenly in the unearthly silence and the moonlight of the deep night.

What woke him was a splashing, stirring sound in the

lake, about in the middle; and fifteen or twenty metres from Heron Island. His sleeping bag was made for arctic conditions, so he was warm and dreamy as he woke. The splashing reminded him of a big trout on a balmy summer night leaping in the Gudenaa at flies as big as dumbledores.

Then he saw the cold moon and the ragged clouds in the urban sky and realized the buzzings and the rattlings were not the insects of the night but the distant voices of traffic. And his nose felt the chill of April air. What, then, was the splashing? A vole? An otter? Unlikely in Regent's Park. He blinked and looked out over the black water. The fine branches of trees whipped in the wind. The lake was ruffled and disturbed. The lappings of water sounded normal to him, but as he looked across at Heron Island, he saw he was not the only one to have heard something strange. One or two of the trees on the island were dead and their branches had been sawn off short and furnished with nesting platforms for the herons. One or two late-breeding birds were still on their nests. He saw a couple of long necks stick up and turn from side to side like black snakes against the moonlit sky. They too had heard something. They, too, looked at the water.

Suddenly there was a much bigger commotion and what appeared to be a black post stuck out from the depths by about fifty centimetres or so. Hans raised himself on one elbow and goggled in amazement. Surely not the mast of some ancient wreck rising to the surface? He thought of marsh gas and divers and disappearing islands and fishes with funny fins. But these ideas soon left him as the post danced up and down a few times, in a most unfishlike and unbirdlike manner. Then, to his amazement, it made a loud and sonorous pop and projected a shapeless mass of some unknown substance almost vertically into the air. It came down with a flopping splash amid a rain of smaller splashes: all of which watery cacophony brought a chorus of rattling croaks from some of the herons and a bit of scurrying at the water's edge where sizeable ripples caused unexpected discomfort to the little creatures hiding there. Hans gaped. The tube, for he had now deduced that that was what it must be, continued to wobble and waggle in the water and, at the same time sent out a kind of gasping sound. This continued and the movement of the tube became more and more agitated all the time.

Suddenly, bubbles began to burst in the water around it. By now Hans was so gripped by the events taking place that he quite forgot his fear and continued to look on in a kind of awestruck curiosity. The bubbles and the wheezing rattled on for a moment when an almighty splashing crash occurred, like a great wave breaking on a beach. But instead of a wave cascading on to the shore, it looked as if the water around the tube was suddenly pouring through the bed of the lake. It was. Exactly as planned, the two elephants had burst up into the lake to give them the only exit to their tunnel that would leave no trace; and the bonus of a tunnel filled with water which would collapse more slowly, and later, than one left empty.

But what they had not planned was that six thousand cubic metres of water would rush into their earthworks in ninety seconds and that they would be, as it were, in the eye of the vortex. As the roof collapsed, Amazons and Niles, Rhines and Danubes, Hwang Hos and Yangtse Kiangs, Yukons and Limpopos fell upon them from the sky and went roaring down the tunnel in a Brahmaputra of destruction. Clods and lumps of aqueous clay thundered through in the torrent, whilst slurries of stinking mud mixed with the mess to make a frothing, fishy, swampy whirlpool that tore at the bodies of the two elephants and did its best to fling them back into the tunnel whence they had come.

But not a bit of it. The *loxodonta* fought on. Somehow, as the first wave hit them, Rumpus Pumpus locked himself against Finta Fanta and the pair of them held fast as the flood swept over them. The raging waters quickly formed into a foaming whirlpool. Finta Fanta, desperately waving her trunk in all directions to find a grip, broke into the vortex at the centre and managed a couple of gulps of air before the swirling corkscrew knocked it back into the furious eddies of the now submerged chamber.

Back along the tunnel, the water had rushed in, at first forcing out great air bubbles that Hans saw bursting on the surface like the evidence of a submarine sinking with a broken hull. But as the tunnel filled, the air was compressed back to the tunnel entrance and woke every rhino in the elephant pavilion with a sudden start as the pressure forced up the elephants' trap door, which thus let the stinking air out in a great whistling gasp which, as it subsided when the pressure slackened, was terminated by a mighty slam as the concrete slab, at first forced up, then fell back three or four centimetres into position. On and on the water rushed. Finta Fanta felt the violent, cold torrent encapsulating her whole body like a mighty grasping hand with icy fingers. Her breath was almost at an end. Although everything around her was the colour of deepest mud, she began to see white spots before her eyes. She couldn't keep the muck from out of her trunk and her ears were flogged and battered by the current and its load.

Then abruptly, the current let up. The foaming centre of the vortex closed and turned like a grinding wheel whose handle is let go. Ever slower and slower, until Hans, now standing up and starting to wonder if the whole whirlpool hadn't been just a bad dream, saw the froth disperse and blow away in the moonlight leaving that original waving pole. And he now realized the water level at the lakeside was down by some thirty centimetres or so.

In the elephant house, the sighing of escaping air died down; none of the inhabitants realizing that only a couple of metres under the elephants' trap door was now a pool of water; a well, that one day someone would be very surprised to find.

Hans almost thought the show was over; and was about to turn back to his sleeping bag in fear and confusion when suddenly, with a cough, a splutter and a sort of ferocious snort, a second tube appeared beside the first. But this tube was flexible. In fact, against the silver streaks of moonlight on the water of the lake it looked as though it had a pair of lips at the end, rather like an elephant's trunk.

Half walking, half swimming, spluttering, coughing, wheezing, gasping for breath, the two elephants scrambled, floated, swam, struggled out of their tunnel and broke surface in a mighty eruption of mud and water that ran off their backs in the moonlight like liquid silver into a cauldron of molten metal. With tusk and toe they dragged themselves clear of the entrance. Rumpus Pumpus threw aside his drainpipe which disappeared into the depths.

The water now came only half-way up their bodies. They stood for a moment or two just breathing and recovering from the emotions of the moment. Then, without a word, they hosed each other down with their trunks, getting the muck out of their ears and eyes, wiping off their tusks and rinsing their tails.

When all was clean and eyes were clear, when their trunks picked up again the wild, dull breeze of the April night spiced with the stirrings of spring, they raised their eyes to the sky. Never had the moon, so calm, so cold, looked so friendly. Instead of a heavenly body, floating free outside the confines of their zoo, it was now a companion in freedom and they joined hearts with it as members of existence, belonging to no-one but themselves and sharing their belonging with all that was and all that was free.

As the breeze blew on and chilled their backs, they made for the shore, Heron Island their destination, and there they came out of the water and went in amongst the undergrowth. They plucked a few branches for a snack and then snuggled down close together in the bushes for warmth and rest. Above and around them the trees and bushes hid their form. They would have liked more cover than the largely leafless plants could offer, but as it was, the amount sufficed and, if anyone did make out their shape the following day, they only took it for a mound of earth and thought nothing of it. The herons gulped and swayed their necks, and stood and flapped their wings at the newcomers. But they only croaked on their nests until they saw they would be safe, then settled down as if elephants often stopped to pass a night with them.

Less calm about it all was Hans, who looked on in disbelief as the two elephants hid themselves on the island. He too looked up at the moon and wondered where on earth he could be and what on earth he could have seen. Everything had been so unbelievable and so unreal. And now the lake looked just as it had when he arrived, although the water level was a little lower. The trees blew in the wind and the cream walls of The Home could just be seen, pearl-like in the moonlight, through the bushes. What had he seen? Was it a pair of elephants emerging from a whirlpool or was it the penalty for eating pork pie and drinking take-away coffee just before going to sleep? What could he do? Who should he tell? There would be police or security men around the big houses in the park. Then he thought of their questions to him. And why had he been in the park? And didn't he know there was a sculpture competition on with half-finished statues of elephantine beasts all over Regent's Park? Hadn't that inflamed his imagination in the night? And wasn't he a vagrant, and weren't the police cells a good place to sleep off the effect of whatever he had been eating, drinking or otherwise taking? Oh no, not the police, not publicity, not questions. Better a lifetime wondering and a long walk to the station tomorrow morning; a pre-paid trip back to Denmark where he could think about it all at leisure. And that, to his eternal credit, is what he did.

'I thought,' murmured Finta Fanta, 'that we were going to push our drainpipes out into the air, work them about until a controlled flow of water was coming in around them and then, after half an hour or so, when the tunnel and chamber were virtually full, break out the last bit and scramble up to the surface.'

After a very long pause during which Finta Fanta nestled her head even more comfortably on to Rumpus Pumpus' neck, Rumpus Pumpus said sombrely: 'Yes, that was really the idea, wasn't it? But then, I suppose, freedom is full of surprises.' And they both drifted off with a gentle snore.

Chapter 5

On the first Friday in May, unless that day be more than sixty-four days from Inauguration Day, in which case on the preceding Friday, The Worshipful Company of Bell Founders and Organ Grinders celebrate the Burst of Spring.

This is done in the Guildhall Square where the twenty-four most junior members of the Company form a band and play, strictly regardless of weather, the three hour dirge to the death of winter on muffled handbells and de-harmonized harmonium, followed by the Burst of Spring: a one-hour glockenspiel and barrel organ fantasy which terminates on the fourth stroke of five p.m. by the clock of St Lawrence Jewry.

Full ceremonial dress is worn and, afterwards, tea is taken in Grinders' Hall. It was enough to make Henri Coulisse vomit.

As one of the newest entrants he was amongst those due to take part in the Burst. But this ceremony dogged him so, its very forms and formalities made him shudder: its prospect was like treason. An act of treachery against himself for the sake of nothing but a single millenium of family history.

However, a millenium of family history, no matter how short, weighs heavy on a young Grinder, and when he rose from his mahogany bed on the morning of the fateful Friday, he could find no way to refuse his participation to his parents. He breakfasted late, some time after his father, Claud, had set off for the office.

The elder Coulisse went daily to General Catastrophe; in which venerable City insurance house, beloved of The Worshipful Company of Founders and Grinders, he occupied the post of Equipositor in the Claims Equilibriums Department. He loved this work dearly and saw all of life in terms of its demands and procedures. A moral man, he had brought up his family, especially his wife, to adopt the ethics and ethos of equiposition. In turn, his family honoured and revered him, so that from his earliest age, Henri was quite sure in his own mind that he would be a jazz trombonist.

This conviction had impressed itself on Henri, when, saturated as he already was with bell concerts and organ recitals, he heard a trombone played by a clown. As is the way with clowns, the performer had first let the instrument fall to pieces, then tripped over it, then knocked off his partner's hat with it, then half drowned as his partner poured water down it, then plucked a fish out of it, and finally abandoned by his partner, crying in sadness and frustration at his inability to perform, climbed to the top of an unsupported ladder and, balancing there in precarious safety, played Humpty Dumpty as the crowd roared with laughter and Henri Coulisse sat in sadness with tears rolling down his cheeks. Tears because the music was played perfectly, and only the clown, and Henri Coulisse, knew it.

Only an equipositor or a Founder and Grinder could laugh at the clown who played perfect music on a wet trombone. Bit by bit, Henri had collected pocket money, saved money given for birthday presents and made pennies dealing in old bits of gold elastic string. He got a self-instruction manual for the trombone out of the library and sat through the concerts and recitals with rapt attention; not, as his parents thought, and as he let them believe, intent on taking the way of the Founder and Grinder, but intent on transposing in his own mind the music that he heard to music for the trombone. Drifting off in endless dreaming variations of long jazz solos in tight little clubs and theatres that smelt of spicy food and throbbing life.

Eventually, he saved enough and bought a trombone for himself. He hid it in the corner of his walk-in wardrobe with the mouth in a pile of old socks and the tubing stuck up a pair of horrible tweed trousers that hung from above it.

Amongst his former school friends, amongst acquaintances, in the freedom of Saturday afternoons and on whatever evenings he could get away, he slipped out of a life of equiposition and into a world of jazz. A world he knew everything about but of which he could only stand at the borders and hope some day to enter.

The equipositional view of life is quite inimical to trombones. So Henri had taken the expanded polystyrene that was left over when his father had had the bathroom insulated and, one weekend, when the rest of the family was away, he had completely lined the walls in the wardrobe with it and papered it over to look exactly as it had before. No-one noticed the wardrobe was just a little smaller, no-one noticed the door was five centimetres thicker. And from then on, Henri had just enough space to sit on a small stool in the corner of that closet and practise his trombone, far into the night or at any time when he would not be missed, without anyone but himself being able to hear, without anyone but himself knowing that his life had two sides which, where he was concerned, were far from equally poised.

If a certain equilibrium was exhibited in a strange muffled, shuffling variation of his own invention that he often played to himself and thought of as the 'Claustrophobia Creep', it was certainly absent from his wild rendition of 'Well, Git It'. Anyway, in the end, the closet always brought on the blues; not the soul-searching heart-rending blues of impossible love and unlovable people, but the quiet muted music like 'Sobbin' Blues' with which he could sign off and stand up, staggering out to his room and, as often as not, late at night, to his bed.

At about the time he entered the Founders and Grinders, Henri had struck up an acquaintance with a large, bald man in a health-food sandwich bar in Soho. The man was wearing a bluey-grey suit and a pale-blue tie and, surprisingly for someone dressed in some ways so conventionally, he looked quite at ease in the bar and was known and accepted by the proprietor and the other clients. Henri sat opposite him and started to talk. He was a jazz pianist, an old hack of many bands and background sessions, and in the course of the conversation Henri began to enter a world he had only guessed at before. The tapes and the records he listened to through headphones acquired not just the character of performers but a history and a society; a way of doing things as well as a result of what was done.

Henri probably knew everything theoretical, biographical and historical that could be learnt from books on the subject of jazz. But talking to the man in the blue-grey suit was like being touched by jazz itself.

'If you're playing with strings,' he used to say, 'always take your tone from them. In hot, fuggy jazz clubs they don't stay in tune more than five minutes. They can't follow you but, even if you're leading, you can follow them.'

Or he'd gulp his coffee and dab the froth off his upper lip. 'No fizzy drinks in the breaks if you're playing brass,' he said. 'Wind from the stomach makes quite the wrong sort of noise.'

Once, Henri reached for a slice of treacle tart. 'Make that your last ever,' said the man. 'Lose your teeth, lose your lip. No crown will ever give that trombone of yours the same tone as your own original tusks.'

And the last time they met. 'Look at me,' he smiled, 'never been a star, never been a band leader; but here I am still in the business and still holding my own. Know why?' Henri was tempted to guess at some secret of technique and trick of the keyboard when the man chuckled and said, 'Because I never spent the money till the cheque was cleared.' They both laughed at that and Henri went his way a world the wiser.

Henri met the man perhaps half a dozen times. They never arranged it, but Henri was able to get away from home on a Saturday afternoon, nobody really knowing where he was; and his feet always took him to Soho where he lapped up what jazz could be found there at that time of the week. This was precious little, but each little a pearl to be prized. The last time Henri met the man was about a fortnight before the Burst. Three days later the man died and Henri found out about it from the sandwich bar owner. The two of them went to the funeral together and there, at the end of the service they talked to the world of jazz, for it seemed no-one had gone far through life in that world without meeting the pianist in the blue-grey suit.

And so, talking at a funeral, Henri met James Daley whose band was to play at a place called The Splurge next Friday night, the night after the Burst, and needed a trombonist and perhaps a couple of trumpeters too. Henri volunteered on the spur of the moment, without knowing how he would get away from the equipositor, but he would find a way and he would have his session.

So, that morning, Henri breakfasted late. The flat in St John's Wood, where the family lived, had been very expensive but in spite of that managed to be quite homely too. Henri felt set apart from that homeliness. He was eighteen and supposed to be an adult, but in some strange way it seemed that founding and grinding was designed to keep you forever a child. A child to the dual parents of equiposition and liveried ritual. He wanted neither in his heart of hearts. And though the timing would allow him to play in the Burst and later at The Splurge, in truth the former would quite destroy the spontaneity of the latter and he found the day becoming for him a crisis. A crisis which would decide much and be the resolution of much tension, felt over much time.

Henri finished the braised kidneys and downed a coffee. With a long face, which his mother took to signify his appreciation of the honour of the Burst, he went and gathered together his handbells. He checked their muffles and closed the lid on the pair, held top and tail in a black case lined with blue velvet. Into his livery case he managed to pack both his liveried uniform and his jazz clothes. His trombone he put into its own black case, rightly guessing that his mother wouldn't notice a third case beside the other two. He moaned and mooched in his bedroom for a while, then got his mother to call a taxi. He said he would lunch at Grinders' Hall to give him more time to change afterwards. The taxi came and off he went, his mother promising to see him in his splendour before the Guildhall. He wasn't so sure. In fact, he wasn't sure of anything; and so he just said goodbye and settled into the back of a taxi with relief at being out of the house.

The taxi turned into Hanover Gate to cut round the Outer Circle of Regent's Park on its way to the City. By the time it had done so, Henri was in a fury of indecision. Negativeness towards the Founders and Grinders piled upon negativeness, until he finally felt shut in, furious, and heading in entirely the wrong direction. He didn't know what he wanted, but it wasn't the Burst of Spring and it wasn't in this direction. He needed to breathe, he needed to think.

'Stop!' he said to the taxi man: the command of his voice surprised him. The taxi came to a halt in the Outer Circle near Clarence Gate. Henri paid the man off, struggled out with his bags and into the park. He was a strange sight; a young man with a worried look on his face, dressed in a black suit and carrying three voluminous black cases, stumbling into Regent's Park. It was more the sort of thing one sees outside a hotel. Had anyone really been looking, they might have thought they were seeing some terribly high class dosser, or a tourist who had somehow got himself wrongly directed to Regent's Park instead of Park Lane.

However, Henri struggled and manhandled and tripped the bags on round the Outer Circle, then cut through a gate in the hawthorn hedge and into the park proper. He thumped himself down in a turbulence of unhappy indecision on a bench overlooking the lake. He could see a couple of islands in the water that stretched away before him and, to the right, the woods that surrounded The Home.

'Trudge fudgewick!' he said, for want of anything else coming to mind. He shuddered in an unendurable aversion to the Burst of Spring.

'Shan't,' he said to himself. 'Won't!' And then, aware that that was a bit childish in its way: 'Time for me to get to grips with jazz.'

He suddenly realized how ludicrous it was to love jazz and play it only in a soundproofed cupboard away from all humanity, and to hate founding and grinding and to do it in the full regard of the public. It was inconsistency that amounted to hypocrisy and he laughed a little and shook his head.

'Forget the Burst,' he said, and he did. He turned his mind to The Splurge. He must be there to warm up at six o'clock.

Chapter 6

'Finta,' said Rumpus Pumpus, opening one eye, 'we can't stay here, you know.'

'No, not for very long, can we? I suppose a couple of days is the most we can spend here. Once the news is out that we're gone, I suppose they'll be looking everywhere for us. Though, on the other hand, if my theory is right they won't be looking for us round here at all. I just wish we knew.'

But the elephants were unable to make any immediate decision now they saw what their position was. They had their plan of course, but planning from a street map is a different matter from acting in broad daylight when the lie of the land is plain. They rested all morning, then Finta Fanta's gaze fell upon Henri Coulisse, resting uneasily on his seat and surrounded by black boxes.

'What a look of youthful despair . . .' murmured Finta Fanta. 'I wonder what's in the boxes. Clothes perhaps; or maybe musical instruments. They look a bit like those boxes the brass band carried when they came into the zoo for that performance of *Noye's Fludde* or something.' She murmured on and Rumpus Pumpus turned his head till, in between the leaves, he could see Henri, too.

'Don't know,' said Rumpus Pumpus.

'I think,' responded Finta Fanta tentatively, 'that he looks lost, lonely and . . . well, not unhappy but uncomfortable. Wouldn't you agree?'

'Sort of like a lost chord,' rumbled Rumpus Pumpus.

'Exactly,' said Finta Fanta. 'Shall we find him?'

Rumpus Pumpus thought about it. It might be a good idea. Finta Fanta's instincts were very good where judging people was concerned. But the fellow might be just an unhappy tax inspector. He favoured caution.

'Let's just watch a moment,' said Rumpus Pumpus.

The elephants watched and Henri twiddled his thumbs. He smoothed the top of his trombone case with his hand and he gave his livery uniform box a kick which, though not destructive, demonstrated a certain distaste for its contents.

They could see he didn't much like whatever was in that box and they could see him musing about it; though in that strange and frustrated manner still.

Henri opened the box and took out the head pagoda on top. He couldn't believe he'd ever seriously worn such preposterous gear. He never had, seriously. He put it on the seat beside him and eyed a waste-paper basket at several metres' distance. Out came the bell breeches and the elephants almost heard Henri chortle as he looked at them, not knowing what to do.

'Do you know what I think?' said Rumpus Pumpus. 'I think he's a clown. And do you know what else I think? I think clowns work in circuses and . . .'

'. . . and so do elephants!' tooted Finta Fanta.

'Unfortunately so,' said Rumpus Pumpus. 'But perhaps, for once, the misfortune of our species could be used to our advantage.'

'It is a chilly prospect,' said Finta Fanta, 'but I think a little swim may be in order.'

Rumpus Pumpus nodded gravely, and very slowly they started to crawl to the water's edge in the direction of Henri Coulisse.

Though an elephant is a substantial animal, it is

surprising how small it can make itself. In addition, its colour is an excellent camouflage in most outdoor surroundings. Erudite as they were, Rumpus Pumpus and Finta Fanta thought of themselves as being of a hue called 'Powdered Savanna'. Cynics and those with anti-elephantine sentiments would call it 'mud and dirty water'. No matter; they blended with the mud they slid upon and made scarce a ripple as they launched themselves, crouched to the ground, down the slope of the island, into the lake. Gently, so gently, they pushed themselves forward through the water: only an eye, a trunk tip and a sliver of back showing. It might have been a pair of funny logs blown by the wind. Certainly no-one stopped to gaze, and those that saw assumed it was a strange tree trunk and went upon their way.

'Jazz,' said Henri firmly to himself. 'And all that goes with founding and grinding can go into the rubbish bin!'

He gathered the livery together and, with it bundled in his arms, began to stride to the litter bin which was at the water's edge. As his hands raised to throw the uniform to its death, Henri suddenly felt his ankle held firm, as if by a very strong hand. He was forced to take a step back and, looking down, saw his leg was in the coils of what looked like a mighty water snake slithering out of the lake. But before he could scream and struggle, another snake, which now showed itself in fact to be some sort of muscular tube, rose from the depths and rested its extremity on his shoulder.

'Now don't worry,' said a soothing, calming voice like a pleasant echo from a warm cavern somewhere in the bowels of the lake bed, 'just you take your costume and wander along the lake shore, past that bandstand there and up to where that fence is – where the gardens of that house come down to the water. We'll meet you there, unless of course, you'd like to miss the chance of a lifetime?'

Henri hadn't got the faintest idea what he wanted to miss or what he wanted to get himself into. He was frightened, but then in a way he was frightened of dumping his grinding things and frightened of dedicating himself to jazz. Another fear, a physical fear, was no novelty and, in a way, concrete and manageable as the unknown was not.

'All right,' whispered Henri. 'Where the fence meets the water.'

He was released at once and the trunks slid back into the depths. Henri was aware of some vast bulk swirling and moving in the deep. It looked rather like an elephant. Bits of it broke through the surface from time to time. There must be some sort of submarine mahout, a diver in charge, who had spoken. Some college of the avant-garde was building its elephant statues under water and using living models to do it. He didn't know; but picking up his bags, he went to where the fence met the waters.

By the time he got there he realized that whatever it was in the lake, there were two of them. In amongst the branches of the trees which spread out over the water on the far side of the fence, Henri suddenly saw a domed head and a pair of eyes break the surface. Then another head broke the surface. Without a doubt it was two elephants; and not a human to be seen in their company. Henri looked at the heads quizzically, half expecting to see a diver emerge beside them. No diver emerged.

'Look around,' commanded Rumpus Pumpus in an urgent whisper. 'Make sure no-one is looking at us.'

Henri was flabbergasted. There was no doubt about it, the elephant had spoken. There was either some sort of trickery going on, or else he had stumbled on something rather remarkable. As someone who wanted to disappear into a life of jazz and music, he wasn't sure he wanted to be remarked, either. Yet there was no doubt the elephant sounded earnest; and Henri sensed that all three of them might, in their own ways, be fugitives. His actions showed this. For while taking in the incredible nature of his position he was doing as the elephant asked. He was looking round, setting down his bags and sitting on them as if wanting to contemplate the lake and its islands. One or two heads were turned his way – people who had noticed some swirlings in the water and his rather hurried walk. But he looked at his watch and cast an eye to the sky and looked at the trees and made out he was feeding ducks and the heads turned away again to look at more interesting springtime phenomena than a sedate young man with a lot of suitcases.

'No-one's looking,' said Henri, without looking in the direction of the elephants either.

'Sure?'

'Yes,' hissed Henri.

'Certain sure?' came back two whispered questions.

'Positive,' said Henri.

Very smoothly, with the delicate poise and perfect balance of pachyderms, the elephants waded out of the water and disappeared into the undergrowth not more than four or five metres from Henri.

Approaching the fence, Rumpus Pumpus extended his trunk and quickly brought Henri's bags into the bushes.

'Still no-one looking?' asked Finta Fanta. Henri quickly checked.

'No,' he said; and Finta Fanta wrapped her trunk round his waist and hoisted him in amongst the trees where the strangest little meeting in the history of Regent's Park took place.

'Now, don't be alarmed,' said Rumpus Pumpus, 'but, you see, we've just escaped from the zoo; I would say from prison because it is really a prison, but the people there are so nice and well meaning you couldn't really call it that; and we need a bit of help. Now you're a clown and so a chap who's used to elephants and can see things from our point of view so . . .' Henri interrupted him.

'A clown?' he said. 'What do you mean? Greasepaint and one-wheeled bicycles and all that sort of thing?'

'Yes, that's right,' said Rumpus Pumpus, 'and . . .'

'But I'm not a clown! I've never been to a circus in my life . . . well, only once or twice when I was a child, when I saw my first trombone; and then I was so frightened by the lions I never wanted to go again.'

'Frightened by lions,' mused Rumpus Pumpus. 'How strange; nothing to be frightened of there, you just pick them up in your trunk and toss them . . . Oh, I'm sorry,' he said, suddenly realizing that Henri hadn't got a trunk. 'Yes, of course . . . these things are frightening when one is very young.'

'Look here!' burst in Henri. 'I'm not a clown and I'm not interested in being a lion tamer and I don't know what you're going on about.'

Finta Fanta thought she'd better clarify matters: 'You see,' she pointed out in a very gentle voice, 'it's your fancy dress; and that looks like a trombone case and so we thought . . .'

Henri's gaze followed Finta Fanta's to the open clothing case and the things he had been about to throw away. Anger rose up in him.

'What! Clown costume! That is the historic livery of The Worshipful Company of Bell Founders and Organ Grinders and you call it a clown's costume!'

'Well,' replied Finta Fanta, quite unruffled, 'it does look rather like it, doesn't it?'

Henri held his breath and looked the impertinent elephant in the eye. He glanced at the livery, a velvety red heap pouring out of an open case. One of the organ pipes sewn into the tunic made a moan as a breeze passed through it. A slight smile came to the corners of his lips.

'I suppose it does, rather,' he said. 'You probably wouldn't know much about that sort of thing,' went on Henri, 'but it's a livery. A ceremonial dress of a livery company: The Most Worshipful Company of Bell Founders and Organ Grinders, in the City of London and . . . and really I'm supposed to be with them this afternoon for some infernal ceremony that dates back to fifteen thousand years before the beginning of time but,' and here he took his future by the horns and wrestled it into submission in a way he would never have dared to before, 'but I'm running away to be a jazz musician.'

The frank admission of what he was doing amazed Henri. Playing trombones in secret and appearing to be a scion of a worshipful company was one thing, but to throw down the gauntlet to the world and actually be a jazz musician was quite another. To his surprise, the world, in the shape of two wise elephants, accepted him and his challenge without a murmur. No sooner said than done; and done because it had been said. Henri was amazed at his own temerity and encouraged by his acceptance.

'My goodness me!' intoned Rumpus Pumpus with an elephantine combination of gravity and levity. 'Do you know we're running away to be jazz musicians too!'

'Are we?' said Finta Fanta, a little confused.

'Yes, my Finta, we are two of the finest trumpeters the world has ever known, are we not?'

The logic of it all dawned on Finta Fanta like a revelation.

'But of course,' she trilled, 'no-one trumpets like an elephant.'

'And no-one trombones like a Coulisse,' joined in Henri.

He embraced their trunks in both arms and the three of

them patted and praised each other at the good fortune of their meeting and promised to set off together to make their way in the world as jazz musicians, come what may.

Chapter 7

Now, that morning at the zoo, a certain amount of confusion had set in. When the elephant keeper found the elephant house locked and the elephants gone, he assumed the vet had got them for a routine check-up and had forgotten to tell him he was taking them that morning. Now a routine check-up on a pair of elephants takes an enormously long time and, of course, by the time you've scrubbed their tusks and trimmed their nails it's almost tea time. So the keeper had the elephants' fodder sent round to the vet's clinic. But since the vet was, in fact, in the middle of a complicated operation on an ocelot, and in no position to talk to anyone, his assistant assumed it was the coarse fodder for the zebu cattle who had been having intestinal problems and routed it on to them. So the fodder disappeared and the zebu waxed fat and it wasn't till the elephant keeper phoned through to the vet, in the middle of the afternoon, to ask when his charges were coming back that he began to wonder seriously if something were not amiss.

But under the trees at the edge of the lake confusion was giving way to planning.

'Fellows,' interrupted Finta Fanta, 'it's good to find ourselves amongst friends, but we need to press on and do something. We've got to make a start in the world, and at the same time make sure we're safe from zoos, livery companies and the like.'

She was, of course, right. They couldn't stay congratulating themselves in the trees in Regent's Park for ever.

'Well,' said Henri, 'I've got to be at The Splurge by six o'clock. I'm meeting James Daley there before my first session with the band, starting at eight this evening.'

The elephants cleared their throats and looked at Henri.

'I suppose we might persuade him to try out a pair of trumpeters, too,' said Henri. 'I think he mentioned something like that to me.'

'Then we shall go and see,' said Rumpus Pumpus with an air of authority. 'Any idea how we get over to Soho without being seen? Because I should think the police are out looking for us by now and a pair of elephants wandering around the West End will be sent back to the zoo in a jiffy.'

Henri thought for a while.

'Oh, I don't know,' he said. 'In fact you two have already told us how we're going to get there.'

The elephants looked on, proud but bemused.

'Where do you hide a leaf?' said Henri, citing the old riddle.

'In the forest,' came back the reply at once.

'And where do you hide an elephant?'

They thought a bit. 'In the zoo,' said Rumpus Pumpus with a note of disgust.

'Not quite,' replied Henri. 'In the circus, I should say. In the Henri Coulisse Soho Jazz Circus,' he proclaimed. And then, passing Rumpus Pumpus his nacre hat, said, 'Try that on for size.' And Rumpus Pumpus put it on. And he looked for all the world like a frivolous beast out on a frivolous pursuit.

It was the work of only a few minutes for Henri to don his livery, tie his bags together with belts and gold string

and sling them pannier-fashion across Rumpus Pumpus'
neck. He gave each elephant a hand bell to swing in his
trunk and set up his trombone in his hand.

Finta Fanta knelt down and Henri mounted her neck.
Rumpus Pumpus went to the fence and gently bent it to
the ground. They passed out of the wood and on to the
lakeside grass. Rumpus Pumpus carefully bent the fence
upright again, back into position. Then, Finta Fanta, with
Henri Coulisse on her back, took the lead and, with
Rumpus Pumpus following, they burst into a bell-
accompanied trombone rendering of 'Blaze Away' and
headed, like a circus parade, for the park gates.

To their surprise, the other people in the park showed
relatively little interest at first. They must have thought it
was a student stunt in connection with the sculpture
contest, or else just showed that common embarrassment
at the sight of gaiety which is the normal emotion of
people caught unawares by other people's fun.

But soon the little group left the confines of the park,
passed into the Outer Circle and then, by way of Allsop
Place into the Marylebone Road. Now, on the corner of
Allsop Place and Marylebone Road are the Planetarium
and Madame Tussaud's. Two tourist traps of the first
order which, in the spring time are packed with European
youth by the coach load. A disorderly array of assembled
people set to goggle at the wax effigies of the famous and
at the wonder of the heavens. But synthetic stars and
synthetic people are nothing beside live elephants and a
red-hot trombone.

As the make-believe circus parade approached the
queue, one or two heads began to turn. As the music
reached them, more and more heads turned until the
pavement was lined with goggling youth, laughing and
pointing and pleased as punch that the circus was coming
to them. Some thought it was a sideshow put on by

Tussaud's, some thought they were buskers, others circus elephants out for an airing. The music rose, the music fell, the bells jangled and the trombone blew, the crowd clapped and laughed and called in a dozen different tongues. On a sudden impulse, Rumpus Pumpus clamped his bell between his teeth and, putting up his trunk, whisked the hat off his head and held it upside down to the crowd. Coins were thrown, money jingled against the nacre and, as they rounded the corner to head eastward, Rumpus Pumpus passed the hat up to Henri who pocketed the money and, laughing, gave the hat back to Rumpus Pumpus.

'Well,' he called, 'no-one can say we're not professional musicians now!' And they all laughed and trumpeted and lumbered on, slowing the traffic with elephantine dignity.

'Your elephants?' queried the vet. 'Haven't seen your elephants all day. What's the matter with your elephants?'

'Nothing as far as I know,' said the elephant keeper into the telephone, 'only, it's just that they aren't there.'

'Aren't where?'

'Aren't in the elephant house.'

'Well, they can't have got out. They must be somewhere. Someone's got them.'

'No-one's got them. Look, can you meet me at the Head Keeper's office in five minutes. If anyone knows where they are, he does; and if he doesn't, he ought to know right now . . . if you see what I mean.'

'Sort of. See you there in a moment or two.'

At the Head Keeper's office a right little to-do broke out. They thought this and they thought that and they phoned here and they phoned there and the vet and the Head Keeper got angrier and angrier and in the end both turned on the elephant keeper and shouted:

'You've gone and lost your elephants!'

Then the vet scurried off to treat the zebu for the effects of ingesting elephant fodder and the two keepers with their heads hung very low indeed directed their steps towards the office of the President of The Zoological Society of London.

When they had insisted sufficiently that they really did need to see the President, and at once, his secretary sat them down and then, with an air of concern, showed them in when he returned pleased and puffed out from a walk round the park to see how the sculptures were getting on.

He said the elephants must be somewhere, they must have fallen into the moat or somehow got into the rhinoceros enclosure, or maybe they were being used to give children rides or to move tree trunks in the playground.

No, they said, none of those things. And not even a fresh footprint in the compound; let alone a footprint on the grass or ground of the zoo. But the President would not be persuaded. He would go and see for himself.

It was the end of the day and the spring light was beginning to mellow as the President sauntered over to the elephant compound. The last stragglers had left the zoo and a kind of uneasy quiet had settled over the place. He experienced a growing feeling of anxiety as he realized it really would be rather difficult to lose two elephants. He took a key from his pocket and opened the elephant house door. He wandered in. Sure enough, there were the rhinos smelling like . . . well, like rhinos always do; and there was a gap where two fine African elephants were missing. He went round into their pen, through the keeper's door. In a funny way, he almost expected to see them there once he was in the pen himself. But he didn't. The door to the enclosure was firmly locked. The other beasts stood or lolled about as usual in the other pens looking on to the central area. He patted the walls, he looked up to the ceiling. He jumped up and down on the floor. No unusual sound, no lack of solidity, no chink in the universe through which two elephants might drop. He pondered, and he pondered. Suddenly he noticed that he had been staring intently at the rhinoceros opposite, without realizing he had been doing so. And the rhinoceros had been staring at him, on the contrary, quite as consciously as a rhinoceros can. After a long pause the President murmured:

'You know, if only you had a brain, I have a feeling you could tell me something.'

The rhinoceros twitched its ears and, whether by chance or design the President never knew, slowly nodded its head.

'Pah! Must be some sort of student prank,' scoffed the President and turned to the keeper's door. In a similar mood, apparently, the rhinoceros turned to its hay.

But while zoo officials were to scurry here and there in confusion, the procession of the elephants went as if it had been planned for months. It was the time of year when school holidays, Easter fairs, foreign visitors and sculpture competitions were coming into people's minds. They turned to look at the little procession with an air of glee, a flicker of amusement, a passing smile and then went on their way with a bounce in their step and a lightened heart. Some people just looked the other way in feigned boredom or embarrassment. People with children delighted in the chance to be children again themselves and laugh and point and shout and clap and get a sonorous blast from Henri's trombone in reply.

It was Henri's plan to plod along the Marylebone Road, turn right around Park Crescent and right again till they came to Portland Place. There he knew they could go left into the small streets where the fashion houses have their offices and from there, slip across Oxford Street into Soho with a minimum of fuss.

As usual on a Friday afternoon, the traffic on the Marylebone Road was jammed just about solid. The elephants held their trunks up to keep breathing above the exhaust fumes as far as possible. They threaded their way through the cars as daintily as an ant through a gravel path and came to the head of the queue at the traffic lights by Park Crescent.

Now, Metropolitan Police Sergeant Apta Dapta had been born in Assam and knew a lot about elephants. Indian elephants of course, but elephants none the less. At the moment, however, he was sitting in a police car at the head of the queue at the traffic lights at Park Crescent. His driver, Police Constable Monica Sullivan, looked in the rear view mirror and saw the procession coming up behind.

'Couple of elephants and a clown coming up behind us,' she remarked to Sergeant Apta Dapta in a matter-of-fact voice.

'Well, that's all right, so long as they're not loitering,' said the Sergeant and lowered his window to lean out and take a look.

Sure enough the little convoy was weaving its way through the stationary cars in the traffic jam and coming up on the outside lane, on the driver's side of the police car. Police Constable Monica Sullivan wound down her window and took a look, too. Henri's heart leapt to his mouth as he realized the whole impromptu procession might end up in a magistrate's court charged with obstructing the traffic rather than escaping to freedom through audacity and music.

'Audacity and music,' he thought to himself. 'It's worked up to now, it'll work again, with any luck.'

With that he gave PC Monica Sullivan a couple of bars of 'Alexander's Rag Time Band' and then called out to her:

'Are you the patrol sent to supervise our right turn into Park Crescent?'

'No, we're from the Vice Squad. Is there supposed to be a patrol getting you through this right turn into the Crescent?'

'That's right,' said Henri.

'Blooming Traffic Division fallen over again,' said Sergeant Apta Dapta, getting out of the car.

At this moment the lights changed and the two inside lanes of traffic moved forward. The two outside lanes were now completely blocked by the police and the elephants.

'Wait till it's red again, then, and we'll get you through,' said Sergeant Dapta. 'Nice pair of tuskers, if you don't mind me saying so,' he added.

Rumpus Pumpus nodded sagely, although he wasn't too sure he liked the term 'tusker' at all.

'Goodness knows what Traffic are up to,' he continued. 'Now, in Vice we're a bit more efficient.'

The lights went red again and the policeman walked into the middle of the road holding up a commanding hand to stop the traffic that was about to cross the Marylebone Road. Police Constable Monica Sullivan drove the police car forward to the middle of the junction to make their intentions certain.

'Right you are,' shouted Sergeant Apta Dapta. And Henri Coulisse, Finta Fanta and Rumpus Pumpus sedately made their right turn into Park Crescent, waving at the motorists, waving at the police, taking the world in their stride. A final wave to the Sergeant as he got back into the car and drove off towards Euston while the little procession continued towards Portland Place as if it were the most official event in town.

'Bluffed our way through that one all right,' said Henri with a sigh of relief.

'Mmm,' said Finta Fanta, raising her trunk to his ear, 'not so bad, not so bad at all.'

When they arrived at Portland Place, they turned left as planned. Henri stopped tromboning and they went sedately on their way through the narrow streets making a series of right and left turns until they approached Oxford Street along Wells Street. There they toddled across into Berwick Street and Soho, causing little stir indeed amongst the crowds, too intent on shopping to notice an elephant in their way. Henri used his trombone once in the manner of a car horn, and an inattentive mother pulled back her pushchair from the gentle weight of Finta Fanta. The sleeping child inside never stirred in his dreams and the little group of musicians disappeared into the maze of streets and lanes that make up smelly old Soho.

'I hope you know the way,' said Rumpus Pumpus somewhat grumpily, getting his trunk up by Henri's ear.

'Oh, indeed I do, in fact we're very nearly there,' said Henri; and as he spoke a most colourful and appetizing sight hove into view.

Berwick Street divides into two parts. The northern part which gives into Oxford Street, is a shopping thoroughfare with all sorts of likely and unlikely shops offering all sorts of goods and entertainments. About half-way along its length however, Noel Street joins it from the west as does Broadwick Street, a little further on. All the traffic is siphoned off into these roads. Berwick Street, from there, continues south as a shopping street for food and clothes; but also as a street market for fruit and vegetables, effectively closed to vehicles. Both sides of the road are lined with stalls which, depending on the season are bulbous with broccoli, cluttered with cauliflower, piled high with peaches or awash with apples. Crowds fill the pavements, eyeing produce and comparing prices. On the road and between the stalls, pile upon pile of crates clutter up the gangways so that people push and shove to get past and the ground is stained with the juices of trampled fruit and veg.

Vendors' voices fill the air. They cry out wares, bargains, prices, jokes and running commentaries on the weather and the buyers. Porters shout to mind your backs and crack down stacks of crates on to the roadway. And the odour, oh, the odour, the slightly rotten, slightly tangy, slightly cabbagy, slightly fruity, slightly sweaty, slightly succulent, full and overpowering odour of the place! It springs fresh from the fruit and veg of the stalls and springs stale from the wood of the barrows and the imitation grass of the displays. It springs deep, ancient, yeasty from the gutters and the drains and it rolls down that market road like the heavy wind from Ceres' horn when the full load of autumn drops into the late season's warmth.

The sellers are hard-faced with bulging aprons and heavy woollies. Hatted against the weather, red-faced with the wind, bawling cockney right and left. The buyers are locals: from houses, flats, restaurants, pubs, clubs and cafés, eyeing the day's wares with a view to this evening's customers, or to dinner. Or they are local workers, shop assistants from Oxford Street, typists from Wardour Street picking up the week's fruit and veg or just a take-away banana for tea.

There's a pub that's full; and men stand drinking pints on the pavement in front if it. There's a coffee bar where people sit at the window watching the free show of mankind the merchant, busy before their eyes. A whiff of beer and a sniff of coffee waft into the scented mix. For anyone with a nose, this street is a voyage of sensual discovery. No-one has noses like elephants.

At the junction with Noel Street, Finta Fanta and Rumpus Pumpus stopped in their tracks and sniffed. They closed their eyes and raised their trunks and drew in the air as if they were only at this moment surfacing from the lake in the park. After a long, a very long, pause, Rumpus Pumpus said with a deep air of nostalgic finality:

'Zanzibar!'

Finta Fanta replied with:

'Do you know, I suddenly feel very hungry.'

Their path led through the market and slowly they made their way towards the busy stalls where, fortunately, the lunchtime crowds had subsided leaving a throng of people all over the road but at least some hope of wading slowly through them to their destination.

As they began to enter the crowd some people looked up dismayed. The beer drinkers took an interest and yet other people carried on shopping as if nothing had happened. Those familiar with Soho do after all develop a marked ability to look the other way as a reaction to the most remarkable events upon the streets. So Finta Fanta snaked out her trunk and whispered in the ear of a young unshaven man carrying a case of cabbages down the middle of the road.

'Excuse me please, could you walk to one side?'

' 'Angon, dear,' he said, half looking over his shoulder to reply. 'Just let me get the crate out the way . . ' and his eyes opened in wonder and horror. For they had caught sight of a thing that looked like the end of an elephant's trunk and they had travelled up it till they had come to something that was indisputably an elephant's tusk and continued till they had settled on something that was probably a circus clown.

'Oh,' he carried on, ' 'At's a relief. Thought the elephant spoke, like. Ha!'

Henri remained silent.

'I did,' said Finta Fanta coolly.

'And what's more,' said Henri, suddenly seizing a

70

chance that he saw opening up before them, 'if you give her a cabbage, she'll speak to you again.'

In nonplussed astonishment the man let the box of cabbages drop. Still half wondering whether he was being made a fool of or not, he took one of them out and held it up to Finta Fanta's mouth. She opened it and he tossed the cabbage in. She crunched it, she munched it, she chewed it and she swallowed.

'Not bad,' she said, 'not bad at all. And if you give one to my friend here,' she indicated Rumpus Pumpus with a casual wave of the trunk, 'he'll talk to you too.' Almost mechanically the man tossed a cabbage into Rumpus Pumpus' mouth. He munched it and he crunched it, he chewed it and he swallowed it and then he spoke too.

'Not bad. Tell me, what are you going to do with that case of bananas over there?'

'Not my bananas, guv,' said the man in rather a faint voice. Then, finding his costermonger self again roared at the stall holder:

'Gissa casa nanas anal showyera talkin efalent.'

'Dah!' came the scornful reply.

'I tellya if ya gissa casa nanasal showya talkin' efalent. Gospel.'

' 'Ee aint kiddin',' threw in one of the beer drinkers from outside the pub door.

'Go on 'en, George,' said the stall holder, still rather mistrustfully, 'but if it ain't a talkin' efalent, you give me two cases Monday.'

'Ryechar,' said George; and Finta Fanta and Rumpus Pumpus elegantly proceeded to demolish the contents of a case of bananas, while, by now, a small crowd was gathering round them in their own right rather than around the stalls.

'Excellent,' said Rumpus Pumpus, 'quite excellent.'

'Indeed,' added Finta Fanta, 'I think I still prefer our

large African plantains but all in all these South American substitutes aren't all that bad.'

The crowd laughed, cheered, gasped, patted the pachyderms and made wise comments to Henri. And so it was that by skilful remarks and a certain natural showmanship, Henri ambled the procession through the market to Tyler's Court, their immediate destination and the location of The Splurge. Their progress had that air of a pair of gourmets wandering through a mighty banquet, picking at their favourite delights and passing grave comment upon them. By the time they turned into the alley, the two elephants had had a feast of kings and a few bags of miscellaneous fruit and veg stowed away for the future as well.

They waved a genteel goodbye to the crowd and pushed between the stalls into the narrow passage of Tyler's Court. There, on a low doorway in the covered path, between towering brown and white glazed tile walls, rising like a gorge on either side and roofed over at the ends by the many-storied buildings, was an unlit neon sign. It said 'The Splurge' and, dismounting from Finta Fanta, Henri massaged a certain soreness between his legs and then with unexpected confidence went down the steps that formed a little well and pushed the buzzer on the entry phone.

' 'Lo,' came a curt and distorted voice from the little loudspeaker. Behind the words were a lot of chaotic drum and piano sounds and a bit of bass mixed in somewhere. It was like getting a phone call from where a party's going on. The caller is very deep inside; and you are very far outside; and rather nervous and alone.

'Henri!' shouted Henri. 'Henri Coulisse. The trombonist. And I've got a couple of trumpeters too.'

'Oh, great. Come in.'

The door lock buzzed and Henri went in. There was an

austere entrance hall with a sort of box office on the left. Behind that a set of stone steps turned up through the stair well and disappeared overhead. There was apparently some sort of stone landing above, for he could hear the sound of footsteps clattering on the floor and after a few seconds James Daley skipped into view, coming down the stairs with a springy gait and the theme of some jazz riff still buzzing on his lips.

'Good grief,' he said, seeing Henri, 'just popped in from the circus, have you?'

'I suppose you could say that,' said Henri, a little diffidently.

'I thought you had a couple of trumpeters with you,' said James.

'Yes, they're outside.'

'Well, bring 'em in,' said James giving Henri a sideways look as he went to the door and flung it open.

'I'm afraid they're a bit too big to come in that way,' said Henri.

James Daley was getting rather curious by this time. First, a fellow who had seemed the essence of sobriety turned up looking like a clown. Then he left his friends outside and, finally, he said they were too big to get in. He half laughed and stepped through the door, springing up the two steps that led down to it from the alley.

Henri heard a sort of incredulous gurgle from outside. Then in a flat, nonplussed voice:

'Lovaduck!'

Chapter 8

At a great, symmetrical, mahogany desk, placed exactly on the centre line of the symmetrical, white stone, Victorian-Gothic building of General Catastrophe, sat Henri Coulisse's father, looking straight in front of him along the very centre line of the courtyard outside, balancing a problem in his mind as he drummed inaudibly on the desk top with both hands: one either side of the blotter which was centrally placed and minutely aligned on the top of the desk before him. The phone rang. It was his direct line. That outside ex-directory line which only those who had attained principal status were permitted. The handset sat on the back right-hand corner of the desk, symmetrically opposite the identical handset on the back left-hand corner of the desk which gave the exchange line and the internal telephone. The phone continued to ring. Breaking his personal symmetry, he raised it to his ear:

'Catastrophe,' he stated flatly.

'Claud, is that you Claud?' came the imperious voice of the Grand Master of The Worshipful Company of Bell Founders and Organ Grinders. 'Giles here, you know.'

'Claud Coulisse? Yes, Claud Coulisse,' he said, answering the question by asking and answering his own question. 'Is that Giles, or is it someone else?'

'Yes. Look, I'm getting a bit concerned about the Burst. Young Henri hasn't turned up. They should all be in the robing room at twelve and ready to march to Guildhall by twelve thirty. Well it's nearly five past twelve now and there's no sign of him. Thought he was going to grab a bite here beforehand, too. Are you hiding him over at General Catastrophe?'

'No, Grand Master, no. I expect he had some hitch at home. I'll just give Elspeth a buzz.'

'No need. I've already done that. Apparently the young gentleman left in a taxi over an hour and a half ago. You know what the form is if he doesn't show, don't you?'

Claud Coulisse did know the form. He knew it only too well. It was exactly four hundred and thirty-one years since a similar thing had happened and brought down upon the Founder in question a lasting notoriety in the annals of the Company. This was the stuff of long discussions, late at night amongst the innermost quorum of the Company's Bench of Guardians of the History of Founding and Grinding. Already Claud Coulisse, a pale man by complexion, was whitening like an old sheet at the onslaught of bleach; except around the collar, where he was reddening like a fire bar at the onslaught of the current. His eyes swam a little and he felt disequilibrium coming on. Like a balance master faced with an excess overload, he panicked at once and locked the scale solid.

'Oh, he's stuck in a jam, I dare say. He'll arrive any minute now: don't take it out on him too much, will you old chap?' But this was bluff. In his heart of hearts Claud knew that Henri wasn't in a traffic jam and might not even be within earshot of the Great Bell itself.

'Let's hope so,' said the Grand Master. 'At twelve thirty sharp we march with a blank file if we must. At that point, the consequences must be faced. I'm afraid this phone call is Due Warning under the Articles. The Bell and Organ Masters are at my side in witness.' And a black-clad clerk scribbled with a quill on a parchment in a corner of the office.

'Oh, I don't think they'll be summoned for witness.'

'Well, Claud, we must hope not. Good luck, Claud. We must robe now.'

'Thank you, Giles. I'll be across to watch the Burst, of course.'

'Of course. Goodbye.'

The equipositor was freezing and aflame; fearful and hopeful; resentful and yet, in some very distant corner of his mind, perhaps a little admirative too.

The Grand Master put down the phone. He looked the Bell Master, then the Organ Master sternly in the face. Their jaws set, their eyes hardened; they picked up their robe bags and, gravely nodding their heads, made their way to the robing room with a most deliberate tread.

In twenty minutes they were robed and in the Great Hall. The Neophytes milled before them, adjusting nacre hats, setting dress balls at just the right angle.

'Be formed,' boomed the Grand Master from his platform. A huffle and shuffle of feet was heard and a phalanx of young Founders and Grinders took shape before his eyes. In their midst a blank file was left and, as it came to be apparent, a hush fell on the company there assembled.

'Call forth the contumacious Grinder,' intoned the Grand Master.

There was a pause. A pause that seemed to last an hour. A pause in which every neophyte in the ranks looked sideways to his partner and sideways to the doors. Even the Bell Master and the Organ Master looked to the entrances, half expecting a precipitous bustling rush at the main entrance beneath the organ, a roaring invasion, a door-banging arrival, a flustered apology and a sigh of relief from everyone.

But there was no sigh of relief. There was no entry at the last of all possible moments. And the Bell Master called in a clear, final voice:

'Coulisse.'

'Inscribe for pursuit,' called the Grand Master. The Clerk, dressed in black at the Grand Master's side, scribbled with a quill and left by the robing room door. The door closed with a muffled tap and the members assembled, settled into a mood of resignation, ideal for the three hour dirge they would soon be playing.

Robed and inspected, the neophytes broke ranks and collected their instruments, reforming in the court outside. There, flanked by Bell Master and Organ Master, they went forward through the lanes and byways of the City in a slow march termed Ceremonial Dress Ease. To all but a Founder and Grinder it looked like a dignified, formalized shambles paced out to the rhythm of the death-slow tremolo of the deharmonized harmonium. This instrument was carried on a bier at the centre of the formation, its framework of dark-red and gold poles borne on the shoulders of the eight most even-heighted marchers. The deharmonizer, who played the instrument, was chosen for his lack of weight. He sat white-faced and haggard, precariously perched on his gently rocking stool, pumping with ceremonial dread the black slabs of the foot pedals to give the discordant note, perfect only in its shambling monotony.

By five to one, the group was formed up before the Guildhall. At one o'clock precisely the dirge began. The occasional chilliness, occasional cloudiness, occasional sunshine of the spring day cast fickle moods across them, yet in honour to the years they churned out their muffled dirge and the melancholy sound groaned on and on.

Now, the Clerk, who had noted the Due Warning and had inscribed for pursuit, had, after blotting his documents and lodging them with the secretariat, whispered to his friend, the Company's chauffeur. The chauffeur waited near the Guildhall to do the Company's bidding, and other chauffeurs and their cars waited for other dignitaries who came to hear a little dirging and pass a word with onlooking Founders and Grinders. Chauffeur whispered to chauffeur and chauffeur dropped dignitary and picked up important person. Hints and words were exchanged, eyebrows were raised, news travelled. Within an hour, unusual numbers of very prominent people were dropping by the Guildhall square to see, for the first time in four hundred and thirty-one years, a blank file in the Burst of Spring. Oh, malediction!

'Lovaduck,' said James Daley in a flat, nonplussed voice. 'What is this?'

'Well, actually, these are two jazz trumpeters,' said Henri. 'Great performers,' he added.

James Daley was about to say something. Didn't quite know what to say and was about to laugh. But it wasn't a laughing matter either.

'You're not serious,' he said, gathering his wits together and trying to make sense of the situation. 'I mean, you know, are they going to hang about out here in the alleyway? And I was more or less relying on you turning up with a trumpeter, not with a joke. What am I supposed to do now?'

'Perhaps there could be a few problems of space and so on,' said Henri, 'but don't doubt the trumpeters. These are born trumpeters; quite literally born trumpeters.'

'Ah, hem.' Finta Fanta coughed gently and raised her trunk. Despite the noise coming down the alley from the market and from the traffic in Wardour Street at the other end, they could hear a rhythm of piano and bass floating down the stairs of The Splurge and into their ears. It was the unmistakable sound of 'Don't Get Around Much Any

More'. Finta Fanta lifted up her trunk and began to play the trumpet line: a little hesitantly at first, but with increasing confidence. James Daley was thunderstruck. Then he listened and gradually forgot who was playing and felt only the sound itself. He even closed his eyes and, with that, his foot began to tap.

'Mmm. Not bad, not bad at all. Rather good, great, keep it up, keep it up.' His head began to move to the rhythm and an enthusiastic smile began to spread across his face. The sound was a trumpet and no doubt about it. But it seemed to have a delicacy of control no normal mortal could obtain. A personal quality a bit like the talking trumpet of the muted mouth; but unlike it, in as much as the mute was but a single variation of a sound compared to this set of variations applied with all the subtleties of a million valves, or of a single voice.

Suddenly, the music stopped filtering down the stairs. The players above had stopped and James opened his eyes from his reverie and was genuinely shocked to see the elephants still there, and Henri at their side.

'Okay,' he said in exasperation, 'okay, it's good. But I can't do it. We can't get an elephant in there,' he indicated the door, 'and anyway, is it house trained?'

Rumpus Pumpus snorted in disgust and turned away. Something began to dawn on James Daley.

'Hey, did he understand what I said?' he asked slowly, not believing his deduction.

'Of course I did,' said Rumpus Pumpus.

James Daley, who had been looking at Henri, shot a glance quickly sideways to fix on the elephant. He still couldn't believe his ears.

'You're not a ventriloquist, are you?' he said to Henri.

'Of course I'm not,' said Henri, looking James Daley in the eye.

'Of course he's not,' said Rumpus Pumpus and James

Daley snapped his head back to look at Rumpus Pumpus yet again.

'You are!' he accused Henri, getting exasperated and hot under the collar.

'Mr Daley,' said Rumpus Pumpus, in that imperial tone of voice which doesn't allow humans much room for doubt about intentions and facts, 'we rather thought you needed a trombone player, and here he is. We rather thought you needed a couple of trumpeters, and here we are . . .' James Daley's head turned slowly and disbelievingly towards Rumpus Pumpus. It was evident that talking elephants weren't really what James Daley wanted to see. It was evident that he would rather some trick was being played, and the world put back in its safe ways where trumpeters trumpet and elephants lurk about in zoos. But he had to turn his head and, indeed, he could see a movement on Rumpus Pumpus' lips, an expression in his eye, and movements of the tusks to bring home points that showed without a doubt, that Rumpus Pumpus spoke. '. . . we rather thought a few details about size and species would be as nothing to our undoubted capabilities; yet you seem reticent. Come now, let us join forces and find answers, not throw up problems all the time. You see,' he said snaking his trunk out to James Daley's ear and whispering through it with closed mouth, 'we can even speak in the most personal whispers when we need.'

Finta Fanta skilfully brought James round to their point of view by adopting the attitude that he had agreed completely to everything Rumpus Pumpus had said, whether he was actually going to agree or not, and therefore enlisting his help in the solution of the minor difficulties that now faced them.

'You know, that roller shutter in the wall there . . .' said Rumpus Pumpus indicating a black roller shutter that obviously covered some sort of goods entrance from the alley into the same building as The Splurge, '. . . looks as if it's just about big enough for Finta Fanta and myself to squeeze through. I imagine we could go in and out that way and find some large space in there that would be comfortable enough.'

James Daley thought a moment and measured the beasts with his eye.

'Look,' he said, 'if you can fit in there, I'll give it a try; though goodness knows how you get into the clubroom – and I'm not buying your food. It so happens I've got the key to that shutter because that's the way we get the drum kit in and it's easier for the double bass, too. In there is a store room that gives out into the light well. It doesn't seem to be used very much – belongs to some clothing company or other – but it doesn't belong to us or go with the club at all. So if they turf you out – cheerio.'

'Oh, let's give it a try,' tootled Finta Fanta. 'We can be very persuasive, you know, if we need to be.'

James Daley looked slightly askance at Finta Fanta, then disappeared back into The Splurge to get the keys. Henri took the baggage off the elephants and put it in the foyer at the foot of the stairs. James Daley was soon back, hot on his heels the two other members of his band.

'Oh, aren't they gorgeous,' drooled Sady, a strong-featured, dark-haired girl with a fringe, rather in the manner of someone doting on a pet dog or a pair of podgy babies.

'You look pretty cute yourself,' quipped back Rumpus Pumpus with a twinkle in his eye. This remark set the relationship, all of three seconds old, on an entirely new footing.

Sady gulped, blushed, murmured rather faintly, 'Oh, I see . . .' and then cleared her throat and gathered her thoughts and said, 'I play keyboards. What about you?'

'Trumpet,' said Rumpus Pumpus. 'Finta Fanta plays trumpet too.' Finta Fanta gave a toot to prove it. 'And my name's Rumpus Pumpus. Our friend here is Henri Coulisse, trombone.'

'Yes, James told me about him. Er . . . my name's Sady, Sady McCabe.'

'Shake a trunk,' said Rumpus Pumpus imperiously. Sady shook each trunk in turn.

'And this is Pete Davis,' said Sady, introducing the other member of the band who had come down from above. 'Bassist,' she explained. He shook Henri's hand and the elephants' trunks and greetings passed on all sides. Henri rather liked the look of Pete Davis, tall and dark and strongly built, but rather reserved in manner and gentle in speech; he at once detected the makings of a friend.

While the introductions were going on, James had unpadlocked the roller shutter from inside and now threw it up with a deafening clatter that echoed through the covered parts of the alley and up between the close-packed buildings at the centre where the footway was open to the sky.

Finta Fanta looked perkily through the opening. Inside was a large storage space, empty but for a few cardboard boxes on one side. A roller conveyor stretched diagonally down the far wall from an opening in the ceiling to the left. In front of it was a door that went through to the foyer area. The place had an air of emptiness and dustiness about it. It was the same size as the elephant pen at the zoo; but perhaps because it was empty and silent in such a busy and crowded part of London, it had the atmosphere of a calm haven about it, not at all the feeling of a prison.

'Looks all right,' she said with a feeling of relief and happiness in her heart. 'Let's see if we can get in through the door.'

She squeezed down, breathed out and pulled in her

flanks. With a low shuffle that gave the curious impression of a vast body trundling forward on rollers, her head and shoulders went in quite easily. The delicate part came next: for the widest part of the body had to go through the doorway at the same moment as she turned across the narrow alley to ease through at right angles to the wall. Within a few centimetres of success, she stuck. After a moment or two's wiggling – in as much as an elephant can wiggle – she came out the way she had gone in and snorted with frustration.

She looked along the alley. An idea struck her. She walked a little way past the opening and then, drawing in her sides, backed into the doorway. Like a shopper pouncing on a parking space, she swung back into the warehouse. Turning her head, rather as the front wheels of a car turn to line up the vehicle, she reduced her length enough to glide gracefully backwards into the space where, once arrived, she snorted and smiled with success and Rumpus Pumpus remarked, 'Very neat, my Finta, very neat,' before following her example and joining her in the cavernous room by swinging round at a curving, squatting turn that brought them together with a feeling of safety and of being united once more in their own private space.

'Have you got the padlocks?' Rumpus Pumpus asked James. He put them just inside the door.

'Stand clear!' shouted Rumpus Pumpus and with the cacophonous clattering that always accompanied it, pulled down the shutter from inside and declared himself officially, if only temporarily, at home.

The others took their bags and baggage up to the clubroom which, the elephants soon realized, was directly over their heads. In fact the roller conveyor that went across the wall of the store room ended at a hatch that went through their ceiling to the floor of the room above.

The clubroom had been a second level of store-house and was almost identical in size and proportion to the room below. Very quickly the elephants noticed that there was another shuttered door like the one they had come into from the alley.

This door was in the back wall of the building, diagonally across the room to the right from the doorway by which they had come in. It was closed and secured by bolts, not padlocks. After looking round the room, nosing its cardboard boxes, peeking through into the foyer, lifting the trap door at the end of the roller conveyor and giving a shock to the company above, they turned their attention to the roller shuttered door at the back of the building. Finta Fanta had it unbolted in a trice. Rumpus Pumpus raised the shutter with a deft tusk stroke. It darted up, noisily indeed, but a little less so than the shutter that opened on to the narrow alley.

Through this back door was the light well: a yard the size of a netball court surrounded entirely by the backs of the buildings whose fronts faced the roads beyond. To reflect as much light as possible into the back windows of the buildings, this well, like so many others in London, was lined with white tiles, grey and cracked with age, but still, in the early spring afternoon serving their purpose well enough as they allowed a momentarily blue sky to reflect down into the pit a cool radiant light that seemed almost like a haze in the air. At about the level of the fourth or fifth floor, the tiles ceased. Above them several more stories of dusky yellow brick lined the oblong of sky that stood directly above the elephants and extended to their left behind the backs of the adjacent buildings.

'Rather mournful, don't you think?' said Rumpus Pumpus, wandering out with some skill from the door.

'A fish's eye view of the sky,' said Finta Fanta. But they nodded wisely to each other. It was a place in the open air, beside a place out of the rain. They could live there, they would be all right.

'We're going to survive. And the zoo isn't going to get us back,' said Rumpus Pumpus. They shook each other's trunks in pleasure. They warmly rubbed each other's sides with glee.

They poked around in the light well area for a few minutes, sizing the place up, looking through the various barred windows at ground level, which were mostly store rooms. Then they turned and looked at the back of the building they had just left. It was dusty, white-tiled and drab like the rest; but Rumpus Pumpus immediately noticed something right above the door out of which they had come. It was a double door of the same size as the one they had just left. Above it was a joist extending from the side of the building. Evidently, the way of getting large objects to and from the upstairs store, which was now the clubroom, had been to hoist them from the light well on a tackle rigged to the joist.

'You know,' said Rumpus Pumpus, 'the end of my trumpeting trunk would go up quite nicely into that doorway: and that doorway, I think, is the clubroom door.'

'Let's see,' said Finta Fanta. She picked up a short length of gutter that had evidently fallen from above and lay disregarded in the light well.

'Bonk,' it went against the first floor door.

'Ah!' came a shocked screech from the room behind.

'Bonk bonk,' went the gutter.

'Ah! Ah!' came the shout.

There were scuffling and unbolting noises and the doors were cautiously opened inwards and Sady McCabe looked out at them. Behind her, the elephants could see that the band platform on which the musicians played had been built in the same corner of the room as the doors. Beyond it they could just see a table top or two and the upside-down bottles above a bar on the far side of the room.

'A slightly beery, slightly smokey smell, I perceive,' said Rumpus Pumpus as he ran his trunk up into the room and gave a quick toot to establish his presence.

'Never thought of opening them before,' said James Daley from somewhere in the unseen depths.

'Well,' said Finta Fanta, 'the problems are over. One of us can accompany from here and the other from the roller conveyor hatch if you like. Or both from out here. We won't need to get up to the clubroom at all.'

'They're right, you know,' said Pete Davis, suddenly very assertive and very enthusiastic. 'They can do it from out there. And this little jazz band will be unique in the world. So long as they can play' – Finta Fanta snorted inaudibly – 'we'll be famous in a flash.'

The others went silent for a moment as his words sank in. A rather bizarre joke was becoming, against all their expectations, a very strange reality. Pete looked suddenly abashed; but, as he looked round at the others, he saw a change of mood take place. Here was a band that had been trying to get by without brass and that had made up every excuse in the world to do so, suddenly transformed to full power. An air of confidence settled on them: all they needed was practice. He took on their confidence himself and James began to organize things.

Rumpus Pumpus and Finta Fanta went back into the building. The two elephants then set about making their residence comfy. They hooked some old cardboard boxes out of the corner of the room and found a pile of old felt under the roller conveyor. With this and an old carpet they had found in the light well, rather damp for the moment but soon to dry out and fluff up, they arranged a habitation quite as satisfactory as the one they had had in the zoo, and infinitely more personal. There was even a manhole cover in the light well that dropped straight down to the sewer. Henri threaded a loop of wire through the hand grips for them so that they could flick the lid off with a touch of the trunk and so had their own private lavatory. Water was available from a tap over an old pot sink in a corner of the warehouse: it was heaven, heaven on earth; and as they were to find out soon, a heaven in which they were for a short time to live with ease, off the fat of the land.

For his part, Henri was settling in well in the clubroom. He made up for his missed lunch with some sandwiches the others had left on the bar. Then threading his way through the tables, all covered in red and white checked table cloths, made his way to the stage which was in the corner by the hoist door and unpacked his trombone. He perched on a stool, the piano to his right, the big double bass of Pete on its side to his left and music stands and saxophones on a rack in front of him where James held forth at the front edge of the stage. He felt nervous but free and unfettered. He no longer needed to make sure that the slide didn't foul his dinner jacket hanging in the line of play. It wasn't stiflingly hot and crampingly claustrophobic. He could just pick up his instrument and play; and he did. The others nodded as they got ready. It seemed Henri was going to be all right; but they'd know in a moment for sure.

James Daley ran up and down some notes on the saxophone, Sady McCabe tinkled a bit on the piano and gave Pete Davis a D to tune the double bass. They all tootled away privately for a moment and then James tapped on the high hat and brought them to order. They were without a drummer but it didn't matter too much. He raised an eyebrow to ask Henri the question. There was no need to talk. Only one question was possible in the situation.

' "Georgia Pines",' said Henri. And with a nod from James, off they went. That old trad number rolled along, with no drums and with James none too sure of its form. But Henri knew it, and that's what mattered. He came in and played, and for the others it was like an influx of energy. Not that he was brilliant, not that he was bad, but that he was a trombone player and that added the element the band had lacked until then.

As the trombone passage came to an end, Sady McCabe took up the lead on piano. As she came to the end there was a splitting crash but, as they realized what was going on, the band still played and in came the trumpets.

Hearing the session in progress above them the elephants had gone to the trap door by the roller conveyor and pushed it brusquely open. Putting their trunks through into the clubroom they joined the band and the session warmed, then heated, then took off; and the empty clubroom rang to the sounds of a new-found band, a jazz band quite unique, whose fame would surely now be founded. They rolled along through 'Musk Rat Ramble', had Sady dancing at the keyboard to 'St Louis Boogie' and swayed in easy swing as 'Hard-Hearted Hannah' tumbled from their lips and fingertips and filled the empty room with their own unruffled private joy.

The sound wound down. The players relaxed and quickly they went over the programme for the evening. When it came to the question of the elephants there was the problem of trunks. They gave a marvellous sound, a liquid, living note when it was wanted; the shriek from the savanna when that was more appropriate. What was inappropriate was having these sounds somehow coming from flexible hoses that poked in at a trap door or apparently through a door in the wall. Everyone was happy with the sound but uneasy about its source; and no-one seemed to want to really broach the subject. Henri felt responsible and thought about it for a moment or two.

'Those trunks,' said Henri, 'are a bit of a problem. If people see them they won't believe their ears. We'll have to hide them or something.'

'I was thinking that, too,' said James. 'Perhaps we could stretch some fabric over the trap door hole, and over the hoist door, and the elephants could trumpet through it.'

'Not likely,' came Finta Fanta's voice from the trap door, 'the sound would all stay outside. It would be awful.'

'What about miking them up?' suggested Sady. 'They could perform in the warehouse and we'd get them up here over loudspeakers.'

'Of course!' said James. 'But there's no need to mike them up, is there? We can just put a speaker cabinet near the trap door and another near the hoist door. Take out the speakers and the elephants can trumpet through the empty cabinets from outside. Higher fidelity there could not possibly be.'

Everyone saw it as the solution. Amongst themselves, they had quite a few contacts in sound studios and clubs in the area. A few minutes phoning and Sady drummed up a couple of disused speaker cabinets that someone had been wanting to get rid of for years. By the end of the afternoon, a speaker cabinet stood on the raised band platform with its back to the hoist door. In that door was now a hole and an enterprising elephant could easily introduce his trunk into the empty cabinet and play away to his heart's content. A similar cabinet had its back to the trap door in the other corner. They let the trap door back and nailed a piece of carpet over the hole, leaving a corner of it free. Thus one or another enterprising elephant could thrust his trunk through there, into the back of the cabinet, and the trumpet duo was complete.

'Georgia Pines' again, 'Freight Train', 'Pennsylvania Six

Five Thousand'. Henri impressed them with a beautiful trombone solo for 'I'm Forever Blowin' Bubbles', adding a sort of saucy sprightly acceptableness to what might have been a hackneyed old number. Somehow he didn't yet quite have the confidence to give his 'Claustrophobia Creep' an airing; but with the trumpets of Finta Fanta and Rumpus Pumpus, 'It's All Right With Me' swayed unitedly along in a dreamy harmony that warmed the spirit and brought it joy.

The elephants made 'I've Got The World On A String' into their own special number, doubling up the trumpets and smoothing out the sounds. And so the practice ended, confident smiles all round, confidence above all in each other: no-one to try and work round, no rhythm freaks, no-one on a lone ticket to solo fame. They were ready, the crowds could come, they gelled as a band. And they were hungry.

It was well towards the end of the afternoon now. They decided the numbers they would play that evening and broke up for a rest before meeting again at half-past seven. The bar staff were arriving and making up snacks and salads for the evening, putting a biting edge on the band's hunger. Sady and Pete wandered out to find somewhere to eat.

Suddenly Henri realized that he was likely to have two very hungry elephants on his hands and, what was more, they were likely to be on his hands at least over the bank-holiday weekend. No-one was going to turn up in the warehouse till Tuesday at the earliest and maybe they'd be able to stay beyond that with a bit of persuasion. But food, what about elephant food?

He went down to the warehouse and was going to discuss the matter with them when he saw a barrow in the foyer. Doubtless the bar staff used it for moving crates around; but it suddenly reminded him of the food they had been given in the street market outside.

Henri bounded upstairs, slipped on his nacre hat again and took up his hand bell. Grabbing the barrow he trundled it through the door and tugged it up the steps into the alley. He pushed it along, clattering and clanking to the entrance and out into the street market that by now was starting to pack up for the weekend. Henri started at the northern end of the market.

'Food for our elephant friends!' he cried, ringing the bell and pushing the barrow forward down the middle of the road. He recognized the costermongers they'd spoken to earlier.

'Any food for our elephant friends. Cabbages, fruit, potatoes, lettuces, tomatoes. Support four tons of elephant with half a crate of veg!'

They recognized him at once. One immediately gave him a crate half full of cauliflowers, someone else filled the empty half with ripe bananas – nice now but they would be rotten by Tuesday. Henri saw this could all end up as a very good thing, and indeed it did. Before he was half-way along the street, the barrow was full and he took it back to the elephants' store-house. A couple more journeys and the street was covered. What was more, there was a stack of vegetables in the store-house to keep the elephants going till Tuesday at least, if not till Wednesday. Not all of it was on the point of going over-ripe and some of it, if a bit unpresentable, was at least edible for several days to come.

The elephants hooted with pleasure when the goodies arrived and when, a few minutes later, Henri found a sack of brown rice in the little kitchen behind the bar, their diet was assured. A kilogramme ball of cooked rice, a couple of cabbages and a few kilogrammes of fruit are a meal for an elephant. Berwick Street market had taken them to its heart and Soho had given them a haven.

Chapter 9

The President of The Zoological Society of London sat at his desk, hunched over his digital telephone and with a heavy finger pushed thrice upon the number nine.

'Can I have your number please, caller?' said the strong, female voice at the end of the line.

'I'm afraid I want to report . . .'

'Your number please, then I'll put you through to the service you need.'

The President began to get a little irate; but humbled himself before the inevitable and read out his number and his extension.

'Fire, police or ambulance,' said the strong lady.

'Police,' said the President with more than a hint of guilt in his voice now. He briefly explained the monstrous loss.

'Transferring you now, caller,' replied the voice and there followed a buzzing and whirring and some conversation and then a policely voice said:

'Police.'

'Oh, I . . . I've . . . Officer, I've lost two elephants and I'd like to report them missing.'

There was a silence at the other end. The sort of silence that happens when someone is taking a deep breath. Someone was taking a deep breath. But the President was too consternated to pick this up and, prompted by the pause, carried on:

'I don't suppose you've found them already have you, officer?'

'No, sir,' came the very firm reply. And then with a tone that betrayed near-superhuman mastery of emotion:

'Would you give me your name please, sir. I'll phone you right back on the number you just gave.'

The President gave his name and blushed to the roots of his hair. He put down the phone and a moment or two later it rang. He lifted the receiver and gave his name.

'Er . . . your elephants, sir,' came the policely voice. 'Could you give me the details please. Er, you know, I didn't really expect to find anyone at all on this number. This might be quite an unusual case . . .'

The President described his two elephants and a kilometre or so away in Albany Street Police Station, a large sergeant filled in an entry in the incident book in a large copperplate hand. Then he detailed off a constable to go round to the zoo.

At the zoo, of course, the constable drew a blank. A little man in a grey suit with a black briefcase accompanied him: a forensic scientist who was small and quiet and, though obviously flesh and blood, somehow almost invisible. He was the sort of little man that can enter a room without noticeably opening the door, spend an hour in company and relate everything that was said; yet no-one would recall his name or his face and few would remember his presence. He floated round the elephant pen while the constable talked to the keepers. He examined the pathway and the clay heap and the securings on the temporary fence to the park. He dusted a bit of aluminium powder around and almost raised an eyebrow at times. With a torch, for it was nearly dark now, he examined the moat and the wall. Finally they all went to confer with the President.

The forensic scientist gladly accepted the offer of a cup

of tea. He sipped the pale brew appreciatively, examining its mixed aromas for evidence of blending beyond his previous knowledge. Confirming its quality he put down the cup and, ignoring a slurp from the nearby constable, explained the results of his observations.

Nothing he had found, he explained unobtrusively, suggested the abduction of the elephants by anyone outside the zoo. But his fingerprinting had turned up a novelty which he had yet to decide upon, but which seemed to suggest the following. The elephants were rather more in control of things than the zoo staff seemed to imagine. He had detected a recurring kind of print that was new to him but which, he quickly realized, must have been the trunk print of an elephant, the print of its tactile tip. Now the trunk prints suggested to him that the elephants had been able to get out from their enclosed pen into their compound at will. The bars and the fittings of the pen also bore trunk prints which suggested not sucking, or the trunk equivalent of licking or other animal-like behaviour, but rather manipulation and investigation. He concluded that, in fact, if the prints weren't made by elephants, he'd have suspected the kind of investigation which prisoners make of their cells.

The discussion turned to the intelligence of elephants and the forensic scientist had less and less to say. An atmosphere of suspicion began to fall on the elephant keeper. Nothing works quite like conspiracy when you're trying to break out of gaol, went the thinking, this was beginning to look like an inside job: and a certain elephant keeper was the man who might profit from it. The Head Keeper pondered, the President surmised. Had they been sold to a circus for a princely sum? Had they suddenly been whisked off to a wild life park with a helping hand from within? Or, heaven forbid, were they carted to the cannery for onward shipment to exotic restaurants and canine suppliers, after necessary breaking of bulk?

No evidence, no proof, no real leads. The police went back to issue a description of the missing property and the zoo staff went home for a worried weekend: to be spent in part back at the zoo looking for clues; and to be spent in dark recrimination and mistrust of colleagues.

Since no-one had actually reported any stray elephants, Albany Street Police Station rather took the view that the poor beasts had been carted off somehow and would either never be seen again or might possibly be ransomed. With this last thought in mind every effort was made to keep the disappearance secret. The zoo staff were sworn to silence.

A discreet search was made of Regent's Park but a blank was quickly drawn as the few thickets and borders large enough to hide elephants were quickly searched. Some of the more successful groups of student sculptors were tactfully asked to what extent they modelled directly from life; but this only revealed extensive lists of skeletal dimensions and a few complaints that the zoo elephants hadn't been on display on Friday and could they please be let out into the compound again.

So it was that Police Sergeant Apta Dapta didn't get to know about the disappearance until the following Tuesday. He went through the routine circulars and, banishing in a flash the memories of his pleasant bank-holiday weekend with relatives in Bradford, saw the astounding report that two elephants had gone missing from the zoo the previous Friday, with no apparent sign of foul play. At once, he was on the phone to Traffic who confirmed his suspicions.

'Dapta, Vice,' he said on being put through.

'Don't tell me,' drawled Traffic, 'you need the whole of London connected to a one way system to stamp out kerb crawling forever.'

Dapta ignored the professional cynicism with lofty scorn.

'Were you responsible for the Marylebone Road on Friday?' he said. 'The right turn into Park Crescent.'

'Yes.'

'I've got news for you,' said the Sergeant. 'Have you seen the routine circulars this morning: that one about elephants?' Traffic made a few words of assent.

'Well, a pair of elephants made that right turn on Friday about lunch time. I know. I held up the traffic to let them do it. The clown who was with them said it was all arranged with Traffic, so I took his word for it since you often have your little administrative problems.'

'Not guilty, Sergeant Dapta,' came the response. 'Looks like you've got a confession to make to Crime.'

Sergeant Apta Dapta put down the phone, thought for a moment and then rang Crime. The officer at the other end breathed a sigh of relief. At last, a lead; enough information to start making discreet enquiries. They were starting to be afraid they might have to go public to get any information at all. But now they had a description: a good description from a man who was a trained witness and knew elephants to boot. And they had a new mystery: who was this clown? Surely they were the same elephants, the coincidence was otherwise too great. Yet . . . the zoo said their elephants were not trained to carry clowns and march through traffic and such-like antics. A doubt lingered. The affair looked stranger than at first. After all, no ransom demand had been received. Motive was still largely missing.

Sergeant Apta Dapta went over to Albany Street and gave all his information to the officer in charge. When he left, the feeling was growing that this elephant case might be something rather strange. The sort of case that makes reputations, or else ruins them.

An officer in plain clothes made some discreet enquiries. He asked the commissionaire at Madame Tussaud's, he asked the gardeners in Regent's Park, he asked the church warden in Langham Place and he asked the road sweepers north of Oxford Street. One or two had seen something – why yes, had seen a pair of elephants and a clown – playing a trombone if they remembered rightly. Heading they didn't know where, coming from somewhere they didn't know, either. But a day's work on foot gave the detective a picture that he had a certain pleasure in reporting back to Albany Street.

Strangely, no-one in or around the park had seen the elephants, he was able to report, so they had no certain knowledge where they came from. The first definite sighting was at Madame Tussaud's whence they appeared to have wandered off down Portland Place, with the help of Sergeant Apta Dapta and Police Constable Monica Sullivan, and became lost in the network of streets full of fashion houses and betting shops just north of Oxford Street. He'd tried a few people in Soho, but Soho takes a very special kind of policing that Albany Street doesn't normally get involved in. He'd met with the usual combination of deafness and blindness that people in Soho normally seem to suffer from when interviewed by the police. In Berwick Street market he could have sworn that there was a wry grin on a face or two and a touch of rather too forced humour when they ribbed him for seeking elephants in a market with scarce room for a cat to squeeze through.

He concluded that he had his suspicions about Soho. He concluded too, that Vice were the people to deal with on that score. So after their conference and with no new leads from the zoo, they phoned Sergeant Dapta again and said that maybe his role wasn't over. A suspicion lingered that the elephants were somewhere in his territory and this needed local knowledge and a delicate touch to confirm.

'Aaaah,' said Sergeant Dapta with a broad, mysterious

smile, 'so Vice will have to help after all. I'll set my men on to it now. Put out a few feelers, look up some reliable contacts. Leave it with me for a day or two.'

So they left it with him for a day or two; and Sergeant Apta Dapta set up his listening post to gather the chit-chat and rumour of secretive Soho.

In the Guildhall square the clock of St Lawrence Jewry struck four. The deharmonized harmonium stopped. The muffled handbells clonked to the ground. The clock struck a fifth time. A jangling and tingling echoed through the square as the neophytes picked up their glockenspiels. The player of the deharmonized harmonium rose from his instrument and turned to the barrel organ behind him. With a signal from the Organ Master, the barrel organ began to grind: with a signal from the Bell Master, the glockenspiels rang out. The fickle weather shuffled some clouds in front of the sun: spring was come.

Around the square were many dark coats with incy little velvet collars behind the neck. Worn by stockbrokers, financiers, would-be stockbrokers and would-be financiers and barristers presumptive to the head of chambers. A brolly or two tapped the cobbles and in the ranks of the upper crust of the City world there was a genteel coming and going. This or that important man came to do his Founder's duty by watching the Burst for a moment or two. He would mingle with the sturdy knot of quality always tight around the Grand Master and, having passed a word or two with that gentleman, and commented on the conduct of favoured neophytes seen as protégés, would consider duty done and would go his way, back to finance house, bank and stock exchange.

Towards this gentle seething, a thin, tallish figure with a dark hat began to wend his way. The throng was around the glazed entrance opposite St Lawrence Jewry; and this figure approached around the side of the Guildhall square, keeping close to the walls and uncertain in his manners. His coat was of a perfect grey, his socks of a perfect black. His shoes with a perfect shine, his face with a perfect frown. It was Henri's father, Claud Coulisse. Eagerly his eyes searched the ranks of the neophytes. With terrible confirmation they fell upon the blank file; and nowhere was Henri to be seen. With more certitude now, but with even greater despondency creeping through his heart, he approached the Grand Master's knot of acolytes. For the first time in his life he found that he did not brush shoulders with them because, with no obvious sign and no obvious effort, a discreet space was left about him in the crowd. Polite nods there were many towards him, but spoken greetings none. He approached and greeted the Grand Master. Instead of a greeting in return the Grand Master said straightforwardly, and with no humour: 'Yes, of course,' then turned and talked to others as though his social duty was thus quite liberally fulfilled. It was. The father had thus confirmed his worth: his son was confirming his worthlessness.

Claud Coulisse had to linger, to last the distance, to stay the course. His honour demanded it and, despite deep feelings of disequilibrium, he did it. Many a chauffeur smiled from across the square, many a Founder smiled inwardly and sensed his great anxiety and heartbreak. The pleasure of men on the way in at the prospect of a man on the way out. But fifteen minutes or so ticked past. Gracefully he sidled back around the edges of the buildings. Gratefully he turned and walked back to General Catastrophe. There he slumped into his leather chair and with a sigh of relief but also a presentiment of horror, had his secretary bring him a cup of orange pekoe: a cup of very strong orange pekoe, on an inlaid tray with brass-bound handles.

He sipped and moistened his bone-dry mouth. He was in social shock. The afternoon's work ran by in thoughtless routine. To his relief he was before long in a taxi and thudding his way back to St John's Wood.

The drumming engine coincided with his thudding thoughts. Henri; when he met Henri; a confrontation, a facing of fact that had long been postponed and long grown grave. Where was he, and what did he think he was doing, embarrassing and disgracing his father and family like this? After a thousand years of Founding and Grinding, a family is just beginning to build up some esteem in the Company: all to be thrown aside; he had no second son to take his place.

He came into the flat and undid his double-breasted coat. He hung his hat to the left of the coat stand and put his umbrella to the right and then placed his coat on a hanger and hung it centrally between the other two items. It did not hang quite straight. He straightened it, and turned to greet his wife. They passed their normal words of welcome and then he asked if Henri was home or, alternatively, if he wasn't. He wasn't.

The afternoon and evening took on a waiting air. Sherry was drunk in expectation; later, dinner was taken with a conspicuous empty place at the table. An atmosphere of repressed fury entered the air of expectancy. Claud and his wife passed cold formalities of conversation and neither dared mention the absent son. Dinner was cleared – coffee and liqueurs passed. Bedtime began to approach and the equipositor at last began to explore his predicament with his wife:

'It would probably be better, wouldn't it, if at least one or the other of us was up and about when Henri comes home, don't you think?'

'It might be better, dear, mightn't it?' she replied.

He thought that it might, rather than might not, and

that perhaps she might prefer to go to bed in case he had to wait up a long time. Which of course he shouldn't, as Henri should come home at a reasonable hour. However, as he was being unreasonable today, perhaps the hour of his return would be unreasonable too. That was probably a reasonable thing to expect. Although it might not be.

On balance, his wife agreed. 'But I think there could be something good to see on television,' she said. 'Perhaps a drop of brandy would calm us both and we could enjoy the old film or whatever it is. Perhaps it might be better to be relaxed when he arrives, or not?'

Silently but certainly, Claud could only agree. He went over to the drinks cabinet and poured a pair of brandies while his wife found the right old film on the television and they settled down to mellow their emotions.

Goodness knows what the film was about. Mrs Coulisse watched it, pecked her husband on the cheek and delicately went to bed. He poured himself a brandy and watched the news, and then something else and put the heating up a little as he felt a bit cold. Finally he switched off the television and sat down. His mood was changing from anxiety to a kind of warm despair. His chair was very comfortable, and the brandy had been very good, and it was nicely warm. And as surely as the Burst of Spring is punctual, Claud Coulisse slipped out of his worries and into sleep: sprawled in a happy but most asymmetrical way across the length and breadth of his mighty, favourite armchair. The night wore on and he slumbered deep, oblivious even of the dark dreams that turned down in the bottom of his mind. At times a little snore escaped his lips; and his deep, even breathing passed on through the hours of darkness.

Chapter 10

Claud would sleep long in his armchair. Henri wasn't to come back that night, although he sent a Telemessage to say that all was well and he'd see his parents on Sunday morning.

Things at The Splurge were going rather well. On the Friday night they played to a few regulars who stayed even longer than usual and loved, and wondered over, the perfectly synchronized, beautifully liquid trumpets that played through the speakers on each side of the band.

Even by Saturday, the following evening, the word seemed to be getting round. James Daley was booked in for both evenings and on the Saturday most of the Friday audience were back again to hear them play. An unusual event, since, as everyone knows, a Friday audience is almost never a Saturday audience. What was more, for the first time in the short history of The Splurge, the catering broke even, and the band got a share of the total profit: a princely sum worth about a bottle of wine.

'Bonuses!' shouted James. 'Where will it all end?'

Where indeed. This was in fact the very question that began to nag at Henri and the elephants as the weekend wore on. On Saturday afternoon Henri took a chair down to the elephants' room and sat in a corner with a cup of tea and talked things over with them.

'It's unbelievable how well things went last night,' he said.

'Oh, I don't know,' said Rumpus Pumpus, with obvious false modesty, 'we were always confident, you know, and surely you never thought we'd let you down, now?'

'Although you're having me on,' said Henri, 'you're right, you know. I don't think I ever did doubt your abilities and your likelihood of success. It's all gone pretty well and that's a fact.'

'Henri,' trilled Finta Fanta, 'you're worried. Actually I think you're always worried: but what's on your mind? I'd have thought good food, good accommodation and profitable work were all a body needed.'

Henri smiled. He knew Finta Fanta was right, in a way, but it all seemed so naïve in another way. What was going to happen about those wretched Founders and Grinders? He didn't care a jot, that's why he was where he was. Yet in another way he cared very deeply. A thousand years of history, the tradition of centuries, thrown away for a hot night in a jazz club. He thought he had his priorities right, he was sure of it now; but no-one else in his family did. And these elephants! Life in the wild was nothing more than freedom, fodder and fitness. Entering civilization wasn't quite that easy.

'There are some things we all ought to be thinking about,' he said; and sipped his tea and settled back on his chair so that the elephants saw this was something important.

'Go on,' said Rumpus Pumpus.

'Well, as I told you in the park, all that clown gear I've got is really the uniform of an old and venerable society: one of the finest livery companies of the City of London; and, to play here, I've abandoned my chances of being someone amongst them. I've closed a door on them and they'll probably pursue me for it – I don't care if they do – but I'm just realizing now how final it all is. It makes me rather frightened. 'But that's my affair . . .'

'Oh, it's ours too, you know,' said Rumpus Pumpus at once. 'Without you we wouldn't be here; and, I venture to add, without us, you might not be here yourself.'

'No, I'm sure I would be here without you,' replied Henri thoughtfully, 'but companions certainly did help.

'What we've got to consider now is how you two are going to survive in the long term. I get the impression you'll be all right here for a couple of weeks. I didn't hear anything about your escape on the news this morning: the costers in the market all seem to think the thing is good fun and are on our side. So it looks as though the police don't want to publicize your disappearance and no-one round here's going to tell, if we ask them not to.'

'Why should the police be interested in us?' said Finta Fanta. 'We're not criminals. I thought you weren't allowed to keep anyone locked up against his will. The police should be after the zoo more than us.'

'No,' explained Henri. 'They won't be after you because you've done something. They'll be after you because you belong to someone, because you're somebody's property.'

'That's slavery!' bellowed Rumpus Pumpus indignantly.

'Well, of course, in your case it is,' went on Henri. 'But I'm afraid the law hasn't caught up with animals of your ability and integrity. After all, you realized that yourselves when you tunnelled out instead of politely asking if you could go.'

'True enough,' said Rumpus Pumpus. 'We would have become laboratory curiosities. No fit role for a thoughtful elephant.'

'Now, what we've got to do is somehow make you into legal persons. Like that you needn't hide any more. You can go about freely and lead your own lives.'

'Um, Henri,' came in Finta Fanta. 'Forgive me asking, but isn't a person a person? After all, people are quite happy to accept that animals have personalities; and anything with a personality must be a person, surely?'

'Well, that's just the point,' said Henri, and took another sip of tea, 'I would agree with you. But you know what lawyers are . . .'

'Oh yes,' came in Finta Fanta with a trill, 'those law reports in *The Times*. We often used to laugh over those.'

'Lawyers would probably try to say that if an elephant can be a person, so can a pig. So all those who eat bacon for breakfast are accessories to murder,' reasoned Henri. 'The precedent would be too much for them to put up with and so on, and so on.'

'Yes, the law is so tiresome when it's not on your side,' said Rumpus Pumpus.

They fell into a few moments' reverie. Finally Finta Fanta broke the silence.

'Stateless persons!' she suddenly said. 'Isn't there an international charter or some such thing about stateless persons? Can't we declare ourselves persons, on the grounds that we fit all the criteria of personality, and stateless on the grounds that the legal system of no existing state gives us the right to exist as persons?'

'Might well be worth a try,' said Rumpus Pumpus nodding.

'Or,' continued Finta Fanta whose ideas began to flow rapidly on the subject, 'we could apply for citizenship of all the countries we wandered through as new-born calves. That must include half the countries in Africa. If you remember, they were driving elephants all over the place at the time to keep them out of the way of poachers. One of the countries would surely accept us.

'Or why don't we just apply for passports here? After all, we came here because a government department, indirectly, was prepared to pay for us. That must give some basis of citizenship.'

They talked it all over. Apply for this, fill in that; at every step they had to conclude that a photograph would be needed or they would be declaring their presence with no guarantee of immunity from arrest and detention. The whole thing seemed at once ridiculous, frustrating and impossible. Where could they start? What should they do? In the end it was Rumpus Pumpus who summed it all up:

'I think we'd better just think about this one a bit longer and maybe make any discreet enquiries we can, once we've thought a bit more.' Everyone agreed. 'But one thing we can do right away is to play jazz like no-one else on earth. It seems to me that once you're rich and famous you can go anywhere and do anything and people go out of their way to make life easy for you.' This too, was a wise observation and taken to heart by the three of them. The conversation turned to the evening's music, to tales of the zoo and the Founders and Grinders and, before too long, it was supper time and time to get the act together for the evening.

After supper and setting up, Henri went out into the spring evening to take the air before the performance began. It was that hour of gloaming in springtime Soho where light still lingers in the chilly sky but where neon lights the dark recesses of the streets. It has an unreal air about it; as if this kind of light in this kind of place has never been before. Henri wandered back through Meard Street and, through an open window, saw an eyebrow arch in response to his gaze and a long and feminine finger beckon to him. He was neither tempted nor embarrassed, neither outraged nor indifferent. A great feeling of acceptance came over him. A feeling of rightness in being where he was, an acceptance that others were where they were and plied the trades they plied. Vendors of arched eyebrows or Founders and Grinders, they all had their place and were as one to him. Only he was not of them, neither of the one nor of the other. He was a jazz trombonist and, unlike the feeling of Founding and the tremors of vice, there was no conflict there. He could stand up and play. Well, badly, brilliantly, hopelessly; none of it mattered: he could stand up and play.

He came back into the alley from Wardour Street. A small man who had a bald head and wore a grey suit went before him. The man lingered a moment before The Splurge, looked at the extinguished neon sign, then wandered on. The flicker of interest was not lost on Henri. 'A fan?' he wondered. 'Coming back later? Perhaps a policeman, though he looked too short and timid. One of the lackeys of the Founders and Grinders? He looks like the sort of slightly moth-eaten solicitor's clerk they use for jobs like that.' Henri pondered a moment, then went in to get set up for the evening. He didn't forget the little man with the bald head.

And the little man with the bald head did not forget The Splurge. He was a clerk in the civil service and, in his own eyes, he was the failure of the century. He failed to get promoted, he failed to get ahead, he failed to get a girl-friend, let alone a wife, and he failed to see how other people did these amazing things that he wanted but, somehow, never achieved.

Of late he had been working extra hours. He had even gone into the section on Saturday and diligently moved paper across his desk from one tray to another until the one tray was a little less full and the other tray was a little less empty. He had worked hard but without satisfaction; and suddenly had found it was past tea time and left, surprising the security guard on the ministry door, who hadn't even realized anyone was still working there. That seemed to happen quite often.

As age and experience were starting to creep over Mr Sedge, for that was his name, the conclusion became depressingly undeniable that life was somehow passing him by. The aura of working for the government no longer impressed his younger brother who was a mini-cab driver in Edgware. Mini-cab drivers seemed to earn rather more than Mr Sedge. It no longer impressed his parents; for his father had died of a heart attack a few years before and his mother was installed in a nursing home in Bognor: she was, well, mentally poorly now, and didn't always recognize him when he went to see her.

He lived in a one-bedroomed flat in Croydon. Sometimes, in past years, when work as usual had kept him late, he would wander up through Whitehall, along the Charing Cross Road to Oxford Street and, especially when the shops were open late before Christmas or on late-opening days, reward himself with a record, bought along the way. Such were his labours, he knew that he deserved this indulgence; and sometimes would even take a coffee near Leicester Square on his way back to Charing Cross Station.

He did well to recognize his efforts in this way, for no-one else did so. And bit by bit a small collection of records grew in his one-bedroomed flat in Croydon. Jazz records, trad and modern, bebop and ragtime, which he played at a low volume or through earphones so as never to disturb the neighbours. But how he loved them! How he revelled inwardly in that rebellious music. A sort of rhythm and order there was in it, but more than that, a sort of glorious chaos too. There in the middle of the music was something that was lacking in his life and his work. Long he listened to find out what it was and long he laboured at his desk with a half-remembered bar or two of some unfettered refrain to sustain his spirit in a day of passing paper from one tray heaped high, into another near empty.

Well, as he left the office that afternoon with '12th Street Rag' somehow pulling itself into his consciousness, it began to dawn on Mr Sedge that if he didn't go home and have supper, if he didn't button up his coat and wander along to the station, no-one would know, no-one would complain and no-one would find it strange. The idea was quite a shock to him. It was unpleasant in some ways; but in others, rather exciting. It was beginning to dawn on him that, despite his duties and dependences, he was also a free man. This was a strange and unnerving idea. But it filled his mind enough to keep his steps on the west side of Whitehall, '12th Street Rag' having given way to 'Poor Butterfly' that expressed a snatch of sadness in his mood. He found himself crossing Trafalgar Square beside Canada House; and taking the footpath by the National Gallery through into Leicester Square. He could see a film, he could have a meal. Oh, it was impossible to know what to do when all your prohibitions turned to permissions!

He drifted round the streets in a kind of subdued excitement and then was suddenly pulled up short by the anchor of jazz. It was a trumpet and a saxophone in a shop window that reminded him. And also in the shop window were hand bills of the local venues and gigs. The Splurge was amongst them and Mr Sedge, with the anticipation of a child for the pantomime, determined then and there to go. No 'Poor Butterfly' now, 'Boogie Woogie Maxixe' fuelled his growing anticipation with good hard honky tonk. Having found the entrance, he wandered off for a coffee, to return at the appointed hour and enjoy his appointed pleasures.

Mr Sedge had to pluck up a lot of courage to go to The Splurge that evening. But at the appointed hour, he turned up and negotiated the little box office at the foot of the stairs. He went up, feeling a little conspicuous in his suit and raincoat and with a briefcase at his side. But in for a penny, in for a pound, he reasoned; and found himself a little table by the wall whence he had a first-class view of the band and a good line of sight to the waitress as she came and went through the door by the bar. He ordered a lager and a complicated salad. His relief was enormous when he looked at another table some way away and saw that the couple there, obviously much more habitué than he, had ordered exactly the same thing.

Some drink brandy to avoid the workings of their mind. The drug in drink allows escape. Others drink lager to liven up the enlightenment that new mental horizons allow. Such happened to Mr Sedge. After his first couple of pints he was brighter and cheerier than he had ever been in his life. Soon the band began to play 'Musk Rat Ramble' and Mr Sedge slowed down to a steady rhythm of a pint of lager and a small dessert; a pint of lager and an after-dinner coffee; a pint of lager and a small liqueur; a pint of lager and a pint of lager.

At that point he was gay and happy and dancing his fingers on the tablecloth to 'St Louis Boogie' and realized that all his cares had gone. This was revelation indeed. He had always known before that all his cares were in the price of his mortgage and the height of his in-tray; in the condition of his mother and exigencies of his boss. But now, in The Splurge, all was made clear. The cares were, had been, only in his head; and the lovely rhythm of the music, the beautiful call of the clarion trombone, the liquid lilt of the talking trumpets, the beautiful coolness of the sparkling lager had cleared them all away in that 'Original Dixieland One-Step'. He had always thought people became drunk after so much alcohol: but not a bit of it! All became bliss and sweetness and light and the band played on and he hummed to himself and clapped as loudly, louder than any. No, this was the joy of life. Drunkenness? Why, it must be a myth created by killjoys, a story to discourage the young!

Suddenly, Mr Sedge felt very ill. At the same moment, he realized that the band wasn't playing any more and only a couple of tables had people at them and they were finishing off drinks and paying bills. He felt as if his stomach was about to drop between his legs. As if it were the beginning of some awful convulsion that might disgrace him forever. He summoned all his courage and with a sheer effort of will, the convulsion seemed to pass. He looked across the room. It looked less clear now than before, a kind of uncertainty was eating away at everything he could see. The waitress was coming towards him. He sort of beckoned to her and kind of fished in his pocket for his cheque book. Not finding it, he leant forward to grope under the table for his briefcase. He was sure he had had a briefcase under the table at one time and reached out a little bit further. As he did so, the table came up to meet him with quite terrifying speed; and though he afterwards remembered the enormous red and white squares of the check cloth coming up towards his eyes, his head then seemed to pass right through them and everything became black. He closed his eyes and heaved a sigh, and when the waitress reached him she saw a cherubic face laid neatly on the tablecloth and turned towards her. Beneath its closed eyelids and reddish pink cheeks a blissful smile spread across it, and it faced the world without care or wrinkle to disfigure it.

In Soho, the practice of what to do with people in Mr Sedge's condition varies from establishment to establishment. Some places eject them into the street, usually without their trousers, as this serves to remind them that such behaviour is excessive. Other establishments go through the person's pockets and, having found enough to settle the bill and the very heavy expenses of escorting such a person to the road, take their dues, real and imagined, and leave the client propped up among the dustbins. Very occasionally they call the police or an ambulance; but this only when they feel that the former may be looking for the customer or the latter may be needed to prevent the unpleasantness that surrounds a death. In the case of Mr Sedge the subtle interplay of practicalities was as follows. His hand clutched a cheque book and a cheque card that showed every sign of being his own – this is not always the case. He was breathing heavily, deeply and easily and, in a chubby sort of way, looked a picture of fitness. The finances of The Splurge were precarious. The club had only just been granted its licence and involvement with officialdom was undesirable. Finally, and most importantly, Mr Sedge smiled like a Rubens putto eyeing the plump delights of a Rubens Venus. Can one dump a cherub amongst the dustbins? No, there is a heart in Soho and Mr Sedge's smile flew to it like Cupid's arrow.

The bar staff, having asked the elephants' permission, pushed a dozen or so cardboard boxes together in a corner of the warehouse below. Mr Sedge's belongings, including his trousers, were locked firmly in the bar and the key given to James Daley. Mr Sedge himself was borne gently downstairs and, wrapped in a blanket, covered with a few copies of *The Times* and the *Guardian* for good measure, he was placed on the cardboard box bed where he snoozed like a true believer whose sins are, at last, forgiven. Not a soul on the face of the earth, least of all in Croydon, fretted over his unexpected absence.

Henri was learning his trade – the trade of a jazz musician – fast. What does one do at two in the morning when the club closes and one is wide awake, full of the rhythm and the music and thus cannot go to bed? One wanders out with one's colleagues to those other clubs in Soho where such people can drink a beer or a coffee and wind down the emotions that hard tromboning stirs.

The club they wandered off to was in a basement in Bateman Street. A comfortable sort of place well known to James Daley, who had, of course, been introduced to it by the man in the blue-grey suit. It was hardly a commercial enterprise, but a sort of home from home for the musicians of Soho who had nowhere but these places to go when the audience, in their turn, had gone.

In essence it was more or less a single room with a sort of bar in the corner tended by a good-natured-looking girl dressed entirely in black who spent quite as much time sitting and talking with the members as she did serving at the bar. If her conversation was obviously important, people would not interrupt her, but go and serve themselves, putting more or less the right amount of money in the till afterwards.

The clubroom had comfortable sofas, well used but not ragged, armchairs for sitting in in great comfort or for curling up in in nest-like warmth. The lights were low and the conversation murmured and bubbled from three or four little groups of performers dotted round the room.

The musicians propped their cased instruments in the corner and sat in the sofas and armchairs round a coffee table while Pete Davis went to the bar and poured coffees and drinks to order. He brought them back on a metal tray and, picking up his beer, said 'Cheers!' and everyone quietly said the same and relaxed.

'Those speaker cabinets seem to do the trick,' said Pete, and everyone agreed with him.

'Dead right!' said James Daley. 'I think it's the trumpeting that gave us tonight's audience. Quite a few of them were people who came yesterday too. Trouble is, I shouldn't think there's another venue in town that would allow the elephants to play. I mean that could fit them in. Apart from The Splurge it would mean the Festival Hall – and jazz never fills a hall bigger than a clubroom at the best of times.'

Pete disagreed to some extent: 'No, I think the sheer novelty of elephants would get us an audience for a few sessions. The trouble is the novelty would wear off and once we're back to the basic jazz fans there's nowhere else to go.'

'There's always the outdoor scene in summer,' said Sady. 'The festivals and the parks. If we could get the bookings, there's always the seaside resorts too. That could be quite lucrative in its way. Keep us well into the winter anyway.'

The conversation rolled on. For the moment it was clear they would have to somehow stay at The Splurge as a kind of house band. James thought the management there might agree to that as they seemed to be having some success. At least, if the elephants were able to stay, their case would be a strong one.

As the night wore on, the members left one by one. Pete departed about two o'clock and the waitress called a mini-cab for Sady around three. James and Henri chatted on for a while and then turned to the Sunday papers which the waitress popped out to bring in at about three-thirty. Henri noted that the arts pages paid scant attention to jazz and no attention to them. There was the obligatory little paragraph in the heavier papers on the Burst of Spring, but no photographs this year, and no hint of the blank file. Finally he flipped through the news section. How strange; still no mention of the elephants' disappearance. What on earth were the zoo and the police up to?

'Time for me to go,' said Henri to James. 'I thought of going straight home from here but it's too early. I'll wander back to The Splurge.'

'In that case I'll go home,' said James; and they got up and recovered their instruments from the corner and made their way up the stairs to the street.

'Here, take the keys will you. Those are the bar keys: remember all the stuff that belongs to that bloke who's sleeping it off in the warehouse is in there.'

The first light of dawn was in the sky when they said goodbye to each other on the pavement outside the club. James went his way and Henri wandered back to The Splurge to see that the elephants were all right before he went off to his parents' flat. A place he had left what seemed a lifetime, several lifetimes, ago.

The blustering wind had dropped and the clear skies of the previous evening remained to leave a chilly but beautiful dawn, with the sky above lightening and fading out of night into day as the sun somewhere rose behind the buildings and the streets.

In the shadowy ways, odd stragglers wandered home from clubs and bars. Odd taxis trawled the streets touting for the stragglers' trade. A couple of islands of cacophonous din were found in the general silence, where dustbin lorries revved up to compact their loads and the operatives threw heaps of plastic bags into the maw of the rear, feeding its great hunger with the waste of a thousand restaurants.

The light had a hazy, softened quality to it as Henri neared The Splurge. A couple in a doorway in Wardour Street embraced each other closer yet, and in the public ways found privacy and warmth greater than they could get in their lodgings or their homes.

A little police car coasted past. The man and woman inside it glanced at the lovers and let them be; they glanced at Henri, saw his trombone case and coasted on. Soho at dawn on a spring Sunday morning, everyone in his place, everyone at peace.

As Henri entered Tyler's Court, the street lights went out. The end of night passed; the start of day began. He took the key he had been accorded and entered the club, going straight away to the warehouse door which he slowly began to open, not knowing if elephants usually slept late or not.

'Come in, come in,' called Finta Fanta as he began to open the door. Elephants evidently didn't sleep very much, or at least were up and about by half past five or six. In fact, they were at breakfast; crunching their way through a red cabbage and a cauliflower, with one of those rice balls that the restaurant had prepared before closing the night before.

To Henri's surprise, Mr Sedge was sitting up in his makeshift bed and joining in the breakfast too. He was munching a large apple from the elephants' stock, having evidently devoured a grapefruit already; and looked set to round off with a couple of bananas.

'Come in, come in!' echoed Mr Sedge with quite unexpected boisterousness. 'Oh, what a turn up! Ah, you're the trombonist, aren't you? Sit down and have an orange. If you chuck away the damaged bits, the rest is delicious, succulent. Why, you know, I drank too much last night. Yes, I did, I admit it. But it's a funny thing, I don't feel I've got a hang-over at all. Just the contrary, I feel I've had a hang-over all my life and last night got rid of it at last. It's terrible, isn't it? But you know, I was so worried, so terribly worried before – about everything and about nothing at all. It's like the lid coming off at last, you know – now try a piece of this pink grapefruit, delicious – you know, I really can enjoy the world. May seem obvious enough to you, but it certainly wasn't to me. I really, really am allowed to just go out and . . . and have fun . . . isn't it amazing?

'Got to put in a day's work and all that,' he added as an

afterthought, 'bring home the bacon you know, and that sort of thing but, streuth! I'm such an established civil servant that the Establishment itself couldn't disestablish me – and when work's over I can go and play! I never knew that before. Why, I can have breakfast with elephants if I want to! Go to jazz clubs all night long. Oh, thank goodness for jazz and sparkling lager!'

Henri, who had more or less forgotten about Mr Sedge, sat on a chair and laughed. His heart went out to this round-faced little man, sitting up in his cardboard box bed, blanket drawn around his waist to warm his naked legs, the juice of an apple trickling down his chin, and chirping away like a sparrow on a bird-table. Somehow, a shaft of sunlight, reflected from window to window down the light well outside, found its way briefly into the warehouse through the rear window. Mr Sedge positively radiated in return. He greeted it with outstretched arms and a welcoming cry as if it were the dawn of the new age, the light of the millenium.

'Ah, if I did but have my trousers!' he continued. 'Pleasure seems to have had its price. But I'll manage somehow: a small fee for such freedom of spirit,' and he chuckled in a long carefree laugh.

'Oh, no problem,' came in Henri. 'Your trousers are locked in the bar upstairs along with your things. I've got the key. Come up with me now and we'll get them.'

Mr Sedge gathered together the peel and pips that were beside his bed and Henri took them from him and plonked it all in the waste bin near the door. Mr Sedge wrapped his blanket round his midriff like a sarong and, with surprising agility, followed Henri upstairs to the clubroom.

'They're a real find, those elephants of yours,' bubbled Mr Sedge. 'They were telling me about that speaker arrangement you have for the trumpets. Quite ingenious;

and such wonderful trumpeting. I remember wondering last night how you got those trumpets so well synchronized. What's more, you know, yesterday the thought of spending the night with a pair of elephants would have been horrifying. Now it seems, well, so normal.'

'They're not my elephants, actually,' said Henri.

'Oh?' said Mr Sedge; but he detected a note of gravity in Henri's voice that made him wary of guessing further. They reached the clubroom and Henri started to unlock the bar.

'In fact, they are no more anybody's property,' said Henri, 'than you or I are.' Henri found Mr Sedge's belongings.

'I'm afraid,' he said, 'that I'm under strict instructions to get a cheque from you for your bill before returning your trousers.'

Mr Sedge agreed at once. 'Oh,' he laughed, 'but of course. Shall I add something for the breakfast too?' Henri relaxed.

'Oh no, the local market feeds the elephants more or less free of charge,' he explained.

Mr Sedge made out a cheque and quickly got dressed. With Mr Sedge now more conventionally attired, they put on the coffee machine and made a pot of hot and steamy coffee before Mr Sedge patted the lager pump for old time's sake and then went back to the warehouse with coffee and Henri.

Bit by bit Mr Sedge gained Henri's confidence. Putting together the evidence of his eyes and the information of their conversation, Mr Sedge made an inspired guess.

'You know,' he said to the three of them as he sipped his coffee, 'mmm, that's nice. I think you two elephants must be in hiding. Elephants, no matter how articulate, can't just belong to nobody. The world doesn't work like that.

You must have escaped from a circus or a zoo or something – at the very least you're part of a private animal collection.'

There was an embarrassed silence.

'We're actually working on that problem at the moment,' said Rumpus Pumpus. 'In a way you're right. There is someone who claims to own us: but we claim our personalities entitle us to be persons and therefore to be owned by no-one but ourselves.'

'How have you set about making the claim good?' said Mr Sedge, quite sharply and now with a glint of professionalism in his jolly eye.

'Er, well, we haven't,' said Rumpus Pumpus. 'In fact, we were wondering yesterday what to do and how to go about it. It seems almost impossible to do anything about that without getting ourselves imprisoned in some way or other.'

'I see, I see,' said Mr Sedge, rubbing his chin. He took another gulp of coffee. 'You know, I think I might – but only might – be able to help you.'

They all looked at one another – and then back at Mr Sedge. The anonymous little man with the bald head whom Henri had seen the previous evening seemed suddenly a different person. He was firm, solid, cheerful, self-confident, and had a wry grin spreading across his face, almost a laugh.

'Oh yes,' he said, 'it looks rather fun. I'll see what I can do.'

Finta Fanta broke their curious and somewhat mistrustful silence:

'I know!' she said. 'You're a magician: you turn elephants into people.' To her surprise, Mr Sedge didn't bat an eyelid.

'Well, no,' he said thoughtfully, 'not quite. But I do work at the Home Office, on nationality questions

119

mostly, and . . . well, we do sometimes turn foreigners into nationals which is, after all, a much more difficult process.

'I think I could look into it for you,' he continued. 'I seem to remember things like that coming into my in-tray from time to time.'

'It had crossed our minds to apply for citizenship anyway,' said Finta Fanta.

'Ah! No. Er, don't do that,' said Mr Sedge very positively. 'You're of African origin, I take it?'

'Yes indeed,' said Finta Fanta with undisguised pride.

'Mmm,' said Mr Sedge, 'in the normal course of events you'd apply to the Home Office through the Nationality Section at Lunar House. I'm afraid the journey from an African to British nationality via Lunar House can be more complicated than the journey from Africa to Britain via the moon. No, you see, I work here in London with a couple of dozen other civil servants – nearly all of them senior to me, I might add, I can't promise much – who deal with the unusual cases needing decisions at ministerial level. I haven't got much power; but I have got a rubber stamp on my desk with the same address as the Home Secretary on it. At least I can find things out.'

'Are you playing here next Saturday, too?'

'Probably,' said Henri. 'The management are happy with us and we should be able to stay here if all goes well.'

'Then I'll make some enquiries,' said Mr Sedge. He opened his briefcase and took out a notebook and wrote.

'Here's my address. If you're not going to be here next Saturday, give me a ring or drop me a line. Otherwise, I'll see you here at about three in the afternoon, if that's all right?'

They all agreed and Mr Sedge gathered together his things, stacked up his boxes, folded his blanket very neatly and bid them good luck and goodbye for the present. He shook the trunks, shook hands and, breathing deeply, turned and with sprightly step walked from The Splurge and Tyler's Court with a bounce and a bonniness he hadn't known since babyhood.

Henri too, got ready to go. He saw that the elephants had all they needed, then packed up his livery in a bag and stepped out to wend his own way home, slowly, calmly, through deserted Westminster to St John's Wood. At Baker Street Station he bought a Sunday paper and since the day was proving warm for the season he sat on a bench in Regent's Park to re-read the news. And when breakfast time was respectably past and a decent Sundayness had settled on the world, tired but not unhappy, he wandered back to his parents' flat.

Chapter 11

Henri lifted the key and clicked it into the lock of his parents' flat. He tried to turn it but it didn't move: the latch was down and he had to ring. Through the door he heard quick footsteps coming. The door opened and his mother appeared.

'Oh, come in Henri, come in. Where have you been? Thanks for the Telemessage, but what have you been up to? Your father's in the bath. Come into the kitchen.'

He sat down at a table where the remains of breakfast loitered and started picking at bits of toast. He poured himself a coffee and drank it appreciatively as his mother hovered around, very busy with not clearing the table.

'Your father's very worried, you know,' she said as a kind of all-embracing statement that was meant to elicit a lengthy explanation or a prolonged apology. Instead, it elicited the sound of Henri munching toast and an expression of understanding on his face. The expression puzzled her as it didn't seem to show any fear or remorse. She found that a little unnerving but let it pass.

'How long has he been in the bath?' asked Henri. The question rather threw her off balance.

'He's just got in,' she said.

'I think I'll go and lie down for a bit,' said Henri. 'I've been up all night. See you at lunch time. Can you give me a knock?'

'Yes. All right.' And Henri picked up his trombone case

and went into his room, where he snoozed till lunch time.

By then Claud was champing at the bit, anxious to face Henri and try and get some kind of resolution of his anomalous position in the family and in the Founders and Grinders. Claud it was who went to rouse Henri for lunch and, after tapping on the door, went into his room where he saw his son lying in bed with a trombone case on the floor and the curtains half closed. The room had an air of lopsidedness about it that Claud didn't like: the case on the floor; one curtain open, one closed; Henri's clothes on a chair instead of the clothes stand; the air was relaxed and informal, rather like a bedroom in fact. Something needed to be done.

He shook Henri gently.

'Lunch time, Henri. Stir yourself now. Your room's in a bit of a mess. What about a sherry first? Then we'll have lunch. Wake up now: you're back in the family now, you know.'

Observations of this kind trickled out until Henri finally rolled over and opened his eyes. After a while he nodded a bit and eventually, as his father was leaving the room, rolled out of bed and began to dress. He felt tired, but at the same time deeply refreshed. As his limbs came back into action, he felt hungry. Though he had had little sleep, he knew where and who he was; above all he knew what he was going to do. Thinking of his parents, he knew there would be people who might not like what he was going to do.

He drank a sherry with his parents in the sitting room. Claud had rather intended this to be a peace gesture; a kind of welcoming of Henri back into the bosom of the family after he had inexplicably taken fright at the Burst of Spring. It was to be the start of smoothing things over, of getting things back in balance.

'Which one of your friends did you stay with the last

two nights?' asked his mother, not quite able to suppress the anxiety beneath her desire to make it seem as if this was the sort of thing that was always happening. Facts were against her: it had never happened before. Henri's answer was suitably shocking:

'Oh, I spent the nights in a couple of clubs in Soho.'

There was a disbelieving silence and the sherry trembled grievously in Claud's glass. He regained his composure and managed to appear a little joking: 'Rather expensive wasn't it? Or was it?'

'Oh no, they let me play the trombone in the band there. We even got a bonus the second night.'

Another stunned silence.

'You can't play the trombone,' said his mother, seizing on the fact which she thought she could disprove.

'Oh, I've been playing it for a long time. What do you imagine was in that case I brought back with me?'

'That was your livery case,' asserted his mother, trying hard by an act of will to turn it into his livery case even if it wasn't. But it wasn't. Henri's father sensed the confidence in his son's voice: he knew it was a trombone and he could see that Henri knew how to play it. So he changed the subject.

'Well, Henri,' Claud managed a smile, 'I think I can smooth things over with the Worshipful Company. If we go and see the Grand Master in his chambers without a pursuit having taken place, I'm sure we can get the pursuit order rescinded and, after a decent interval, you'll be able to take up the livery again and it'll all become a jolly story in the annals of the Founders and Grinders.'

Now Henri was silent and looked out of the window. They heard a pot boil over in the kitchen and his mother rushed out to take care of it. The men stood awkwardly for a moment, about to say something; then Elspeth called that lunch was ready and they trooped into the dining room and sat in silence before a joint of meat.

As they were pouring on the gravy, Henri said in a mild voice that made it take a little while for his parents to understand:

'I don't think I'll bother with the Founders and Grinders any more. I'll carry on as a jazz trombonist for the time being. It's what I want to do; and if it doesn't work out it'll lead on to something else, I think.'

His father smiled and tried to chortle. His mother took refuge in his father's attempt to laugh it all off. Henri didn't laugh at all. He stayed deadly serious and masticated in a most determined way.

'Nice gravy, Mother,' he said.

Finally Claud made himself clear. In an excruciating little speech, knotted, embarrassed, pleading, threatening, cajoling, heartbreaking to himself, stirring to his wife, serious but irrelevant to Henri, he explained how the family name was being threatened, how none of this could possibly go on, how he could get everything back in place and everything under control and, of course, Henri would be much happier then, wouldn't he? Of course he would. Wouldn't he?

Henri said nothing and attacked a roast potato.

'Well, you'll think it over then,' said Claud, 'and we'll all work it out in the end.

'Look, I expect the Grand Master will be in hall this afternoon, he'll have the business from the Burst to tidy up. Why don't we drop in on him and straighten things out. Make a little homily to him in his chambers. You're rather good at that. He'll like it. Put you back in his good books.'

'I rather would have thought he would have inscribed me for pursuit by now,' replied Henri blithely.

'Well, yes, officially,' said Claud, 'but a lot of his business is underwritten by General Catastrophe and he'll probably see it wouldn't do too much to rock the boat.'

'Tut tut,' said Henri jovially, 'sounds like an unprofessional inducement to me. Pater, I'm surprised at you!'

Claud squirmed like a worm and went just as pink.

'Well, blimey!' he said with uncharacteristic ferocity, 'I've never been so let down and embarrassed in my life! What can I do?' And he stared at Elspeth and she stared at him and a tear rolled down his cheek till he wiped it with his napkin and thrust another gravy-laden morsel of roast into his mouth.

'Sorry and all that, Father,' said Henri after a pause; 'but I won't go back into the Founders and Grinders.' Then with a more serious tone of voice, 'I just couldn't do it. It wouldn't be right. Not right for me, I mean.'

He didn't explain any more but repeated himself from time to time as Claud became more and more uncertain and more and more desperate. Finally Claud lapsed into silence and Elspeth started talking about the dutiful and reverential members of her family down all the ages since the beginning of time and especially her dear grandfather. Finally, in the middle of dessert, the telephone rang.

At eleven o'clock that morning, the Grand Master of the Worshipful Company of Founders and Grinders met the Bell Master, the Organ Master and the Clerk, informally, in the Grand Master's chambers at Grinders' Hall. The Bell Master, a dangerous and innovatory spirit in the eyes of some, ate a croissant.

The Grand Master's brows furrowed. 'What's that you're eating?' he demanded of the Bell Master with a tone of automatic condemnation.

'Croissant,' said the Bell Master nonchalantly and tried not to be reminded of school rules about chewing gum and humbugs.

'It's bent,' accused the Grand Master.

'Most of them are,' admitted the Bell Master. Then he recovered his confidence a little and with several big, flaky crumbs sticking to the moisture at the corners of his lips he continued. 'But you can get straight ones; if you try hard enough.' He looked sideways at the Organ Master who at once came to his aid.

'And ones with chocolate in, and ones that are bready rather than flaky and bready ones with chocolate in, and bent bready ones with no chocolate in but I don't know if you can get bent bready ones with chocolate in because if the flaky ones have chocolate in they're always straight.' It was an impressive little culinary arpeggio which the Grand Master thought it was high time to put a stop to. But the Clerk was feeling a little left out of things and interjected rather clumsily:

'They come from France, Grand Master. In fact there are a lot of them there. I know people who've been to France and . . .'

'Foreign, you mean!' thundered the Grand Master and, scowling at the Bell Master, added meaningfully, 'Might have known it. Now, enough of this; we have contumacy to consider!'

They talked for two hours in low tones over the affair of the neophyte, Coulisse. The walls of the chamber were lined with book shelves on which stood the Proceedings of the Company, the Judgements of the Company and the Occasional Papers of the Company. All were leather bound and gold tooled, brown calf-skin round yellow parchment. Every few sentences of their conversation, appeal was made to precedent and the Clerk got up and scuttled along the shelves, scurrying up stepladders and creeping along the carpet to reach the volumes from the highest or the lowest levels. With each volume came a cloud of dust and a clerkly sneeze and then, on the ancient oak table the Grand Master threw it open with a blast of aged odour and a flurry of croissant crumbs and the three poured over it deciphering medieval Latin and Norman French, de-convoluting eighteenth-century sentences and tutting at twentieth-century terseness. But after two hours, in which the Clerk scribbled references to precedent non-stop with his quill, they ended on a deep decision. The neophyte Coulisse could be pursued unto the ends of the earth. As a contumacious Grinder he would be impugned before the full court of the Company. The penalty, at worst, genealogical transcription; at best, reduction to penury or some other ancient sanction inscribed in ancient archive. As the line of precedent and argument revealed its canons to the aged liverymen and their weaseled clerk in the dark chamber on that fair Sunday, a sense of delight ran through their bones. So absorbed were they in their labours that they dined as they worked. The kitchen sent in cold mutton sandwiches and old Madeira wine. Their eyes twinkled and their hearts beat fast. At last they were to be the prime protagonists in another calf-bound, dusty tome that, a thousand years hence, a black-robed clerk would bring down from a dusty shelf and a Grand Master would throw open at a crackling parchment page headed 'Coulisse the Neophyte: Process for Contumacy'. With joy they sipped their wine, with relish they munched their mutton.

'Nothing like good home fare!' exclaimed the Grand Master slurping his Madeira and casting a knowing eye on the Bell Master.

'Variety and innovation must also have their place in tradition,' offered the Bell Master.

'Ah, but it's tradition finds the place for them,' put down the Grand Master.

'There's place for infinite variation within strict limitations,' tried the Organ Master. 'The organ, Grand Master, the organ, Bell Master: infinite variety within the confines of a strict-defined instrument.'

The Clerk sensed a conversation touching on realities instead of conventionalities and moved to bring things back to safe ground before the Grand Master finished a particularly raucous slurp: 'More mutton sandwiches gentlemen? Good old mutton sandwiches eh, what would we do without them? As a boy, you know, I think it was the mint I liked as much as the mutton. Only later got the taste for the good dark meat.'

The Bell Master raised an eyebrow. 'You know they put garlic on it where the croissants come from.'

'And bend it round in circles too, I dare say,' said the Grand Master.

'But where do you think our contumacious neophyte might be dining?' said the Organ Master.

'There is a chance,' said the Grand Master, a wily old bird when the chips were down, 'that young Coulisse might be at his parents' home. If we could persuade him over, with his father, we'd have him. The problem of pursuit would be resolved and we could get on with the process.'

The clerk looked a little sad as the business of pursuit traditionally fell to him to organize. As there was seldom more than one pursuit in three or four hundred years, the number of clerks who had organized them were well known in Company lore.

'I'll give them a ring,' said the Grand Master and, opening a drawer in his desk, revealed a telephone there on which he began to tap out a number. The phone had to be in a drawer for it was far too modern a thing to be on open display in a grand master's chambers. In the Coulisse flat, the telephone rang.

'Hello!' said Claud Coulisse in a voice strong enough to discourage anyone with a wrong number from continuing.

'Ah, Claud!' said the Grand Master, confident that his position and the circumstances left absolutely no need for him to identify himself.

'Ah,' said Claud, knowing who it was and not wanting to start the conversation.

'Hello,' said the Grand Master.

'Ah!' said Claud and paused. Then he said, 'Hello!'

'Thought about popping over with Henri?' asked the Grand Master.

'I realize it might be possible to do that, mightn't it?' said Claud.

'What about in about an hour or thereabouts?' said the Grand Master. 'We're at the Hall.'

'About that, I should think. I'll ask Henri about it.'

In the Grand Master's chambers the mouthpiece of the phone was covered and a chuckle ran through the group. The Grand Master revealed that Henri was there: he thought he'd soon be coming over with Claud. The Masters nodded and smiled. The Clerk closed his eyes in despair as the opportunity of a half millenium started to slip from his grasp.

Claud put the phone down for a moment and told Henri he thought it would be the right thing to do to pop over to the Hall and see the Masters. Grand Master was on the phone, he'd tell him they were coming in an hour or so. But Henri saw through the ploy his father had fallen for:

'Not I, Father,' he said robustly. 'Once in there, the game's up. They're trying to pull off a pursuit by trickery.'

'Of course they're not,' said his father.

'I'm not going,' said Henri who began to feel the hairs rising on the back of his neck. He looked fixedly at his father who saw it was no time to argue. Claud returned to the phone.

'All things considered,' he said into the phone, 'it's not

really the day for it. Situation's a bit raw. I'm sure you understand.'

'I know,' said the Grand Master, moving the strategy into the minor key, 'we'll pop over to you for a word.' The Clerk's eyes opened again. That was more like it, though still short of a full pursuit. 'Just drop in in an hour or so. That'd be all right, wouldn't it, Claud?'

Claud was relieved at the suggestion. After Henri's stand on the subject he wouldn't have dared to suggest it himself.

'Oh, all right, yes, I should think that will be fine,' he said. 'Yes, do that, if you like.'

The Grand Master scented victory and galloped to the trail.

'Well, I tell you what,' he said, 'we're all ready here, we'll come right away. That's decided then, see you in half an hour or so. With any luck it'll be coffee and liqueur time, I expect.'

The suggestion was like an order to Claud.

'Indeed it will, Grand Master, indeed it will. Look forward to it. Goodbye, Grand Master,' and he hung up the phone.

Claud went back to the lunch table and sat down again. For a few minutes he said nothing and no-one spoke to him. The spoons clinked and rattled over the strawberry mousse. Elspeth made an inadvertent slurping noise and hid behind her napkin for a moment. A feeling of unease began to grow in Henri. He realized that he hadn't really understood how the phone call had ended. Suspicion began to grow in him. His spoon spooned mousse at a slower and slower rate. Finally it rested in the remains of the dessert and he eyed his father, half guessing, half knowing what might have happened.

'Your Grand Master did understand that I wouldn't be across later on, didn't he?' said Henri. Claud looked a bit uncomfortable then said:

'Oh yes, he knows we're not coming.'

The answer rather hung in the air. As if it were the truth and nothing but the truth but yet perhaps not quite all the truth that there was to tell on the subject.

'Was he phoning from the Hall?' asked Henri.

'It did rather sound like it, unless I'm mistaken,' answered Claud.

'What was he doing at the Hall on a Sunday?' mused Henri to himself. 'That old buzzard . . .'

'Henri!' interjected his mother.

'. . . is usually trying to knock hell out of a golf ball on a Sunday,' he confirmed, unaware of his parents. 'He wouldn't give up a clubhouse lunch for one of those dead–dog sandwiches they serve up at the Hall, unless something important was at stake. Even if he could wash it down with free Madeira.'

They lapsed into silence. Elspeth was just starting to say something about respect for the officers of our most venerable institutions when Henri suddenly saw everything very clearly indeed.

'I've been inscribed for pursuit: I must have been if they've followed the rules. The Grand Master was conniving with the others over precedent and pursuit. Oh yes, now I see, they'd want you to bring me to them so they wouldn't have to pursue me. Crikey, you're naïve Father! You've let them invite themselves here, haven't you?' Claud was silent but it was the silence of consent. 'So that you can smooth things over as you think. Don't you see? They'll just bundle me into the back of the Worshipful Rolls and have me tried at the Livery Court before even you could smooth over the cracks in a pat of butter. What's more, if I know that slit–eyed little clerk, they'll be on their way here right now.

'Thanks for the lunch, Mother, I think it's time to get a move on.'

The rest of Henri's mousse remained forever uneaten. His spoon clattered as he pushed away his dish and his napkin ended up wrapped round his chair-back as he sprinted through the dining room door to his bedroom. There he flung open the walk-in wardrobe and heaved out a mighty suitcase. He pitched into it all the necessities of life: sheet music, records, trombone polish, cassettes, books, a collapsible music stand. He upended the third drawer of his chest of drawers into it: the one with all the clothes fit to wear, chucked in a tracksuit and some sports gear, a couple of suits and a sponge bag, clacked the lid down with a clonk and dragged it all to the front door.

He went back to the bedroom, grabbed his trombone and a few pocketfuls of odds and ends, threw his cheque book, savings book and piggy bank into a shoulder bag and dumped the trombone with the other things by the front door. He raced into the kitchen with the shoulder bag and further stuffed it with a loaf of bread, an indiscriminate assortment of tinned food from the cupboard and made for the phone. He was going to call a taxi but as he passed the kitchen window he saw the unmistakable shape of the Founders' black Rolls Royce pulling up outside the mansion block. He rushed out on to the landing and called the lift. The moment its door rattled back he jammed it open with the cased trombone and piled all the other baggage inside. Like lightning he rushed back into the flat, kissed his mother, shook the hand of his amazed father, went back to the landing and dislodged the trombone. He placed it inside, pushed the button to send the lift to the ground floor but got out himself before the door closed. The lift dutifully went down to the ground floor, whence, far below, Henri could hear the sound of the three officials entering the building.

'Take the stairs, Clerk,' ordered the Grand Master. 'Wouldn't do for the young whippersnapper to give us the slip, would it?'

The Clerk clenched his eyes and started the climb. For once the prospect of immortality, a shrine of yellow parchment, outweighed the indignity of being given the rough deal. Henri, however, knew full well that a worshipful company does not survive for a thousand years by fair means alone. So, suspecting their wiles, he leaped up to the floor above his parents' flat. After a few moments there was a bang and a rattle as the lift doors opened on the floor below him. They closed automatically and, as soon as he had heard the buzzer sound from the flat below, he pushed the button and called the lift up to him. The lift doors opened and he hopped in.

'I wonder who all that junk in the lift belonged to,' said the Organ Master as if something was beginning to dawn on him. From several floors below, Henri could hear the weary feet and gasping breath of the Clerk as he toiled up to the Masters. Then the doors closed. Henri pushed the button for the ground floor, and with his foot firmly on the 'no stop' button, he whooshed past his parents, past the Masters of the Company and past the Clerk without any of them knowing what had happened.

Inside the lift Henri slung on the shoulder bag, grabbed suitcase in one hand and trombone in the other and took his foot off the wall button the moment the first floor was past. The doors opened and he hurried out. Quickly, he put down the trombone and whisked a light hall chair into the lift doorway to prevent an immediate pursuit. Then he raised his burdens and walked out of the building, turning away from the Rolls-Royce in case some dead-eyed chauffeur should recognize his going. He got to the corner and turned towards the main road. There, after a few minutes, he flagged down a taxi:

'Soho,' he said, 'Berwick Street.' And he chugged off to the elephants, those who, he now knew, were his best friends in the world.

Claud, of course, had not been convinced that Henri's surmise of the motive for the Masters' visit was correct. It wasn't certain that they wanted to pursue, he thought, and it was incontrovertible that he wanted to smooth over. When he opened the door to them he positively oozed smoothness all over them. Not wanting to betray their motives, they listened to his apologies and scarcely dared to register surprise when he mentioned that Henri had just popped out; and hadn't they met him in the lift? Beneath the surface, however, they were aghast; and had a golf club lunch, rather than mutton sandwiches, preceded Claud's news, apoplexy might have resulted. As it was, Claud enshrined them in the very comfortable sitting room with the smoothest coffee and the smoothest liqueurs. He balanced an argument to them so precisely on the for and against of Henri's behaviour, on the absolute reasonableness of candour, mercy, apology and contrition as sufficient endings to a most unusual chapter of events, that they quickly had no idea of what he was saying and little enough of what to do. The Clerk started to nod off, the Bell Master started to clench his fists, the Organ Master ran through a mental fugue and the Grand Master spoke:

'He is a contumacious Grinder!' In fact, he shouted. Claud's eyes opened wide. He had expected some mercy, some softening of approach. A thousand years of history was, after all, a thousand years of history. But history, at least with the Worshipful Company of Founders and Grinders, is made of hard decisions.

'He must be pursued, you know he is to be pursued,' ranted on the Grand Master. 'You know the rules: you knew them when we talked before the Burst of Spring. That's the trouble with you Johnny-come-lately families with no more than a millenium or so behind them. No ballast. Keep wittering on about mercy and compromise when Atlantis has sunk. Terra firma is no more, Claud: it's the end of the equiposition.

'Now, tell me where he's gone. It's in your best interests now to come clean. Where is the boy?'

Claud muttered something about not knowing, about nothing he knew, about wanting to help, about doing all he could.

'Come on, man, come on,' intoned the Organ Master.

'Talk!' shouted the Bell Master and, as a result of the interchange, the Clerk awoke with a jerk and a snort.

'Oh!' he said shamefacedly and snorted again. Then he tried to bury his head in his handkerchief, blew his nose and peeked out at the others again.

They all fixed their eyes on Claud. A long and steady silence ensued. Claud felt less and less happy and more and more guilty.

'Then tell us what you know,' said the Bell Master. 'Where is he likely to be? Where was he on Friday? When is he likely to be back? In an hour or two? A bit longer?'

The atmosphere subsided a little and, gradually, they encouraged Claud to tell what he knew.

'It gets worse and worse,' muttered the Grand Master. 'It looks like Soho. Clerk, you are empowered to hunt the contumacious Grinder in Soho. Meanwhile,' he rose, drawing the meeting to a close, 'I shall take the necessary steps to get the pursuit authorized for Westminster.'

The Masters drew breath, Claud looked grave and lost; and the Clerk: he just failed to suppress a beaming smile and a deep, long chuckle of success.

Chapter 12

The trouble with affairs of state, as every monarch knows, is that they are so important. Failure to attend to them has a most tiresome habit of causing republics, written constitutions, revolutions and loss of earnings. But there are times, for instance on sharp, sunny mornings in spring when the sky is pale blue and the first buds are breaking, when the daffodils wave above the green grass of the London parks, when the sun shines with a crystalline light, clear enough to make you hook the glasses off the bridge of your nose and breathe the morning, chill with dew; when you wish, oh, you wish you could skip giving assent to a stack of acts, bunk off giving out baronetcies, cut Privy Council meetings and altogether avoid audiences.

Such was this morning. And the Monarch sat up in bed, chin on knees, intermittently sipping tea from a large china cup and listening to the arrangements for the day. The Private Secretary droned on: things to sign, papers to see, a Privy Council meeting, lunch at the Palace, an audience at Court and some time with the children.

'What's the Privy Council got on the agenda today?' asked the Monarch with foreboding and signalled to the maid standing by to pour another cup of tea. The Council had a habit of dealing with arcane matters of great importance and very little interest to the Monarch; and little enough interest to most citizens. But the Prime

Minister sometimes attended and always read the minutes even when absent from the meetings. It was essential to look interested and know what position to take on every item on the agenda.

The Private Secretary read out the list and explained the action appropriate to each. The Monarch sipped and nodded and imagined the windbags on the Council droning on and on while the sun shone through the windows and everyone shuffled from one foot to the other, trying to lessen the leg ache. But the final item arrested the attention.

'. . . and finally a petition from The Worshipful Company of Bell Founders and Organ Grinders to pursue a contumacious Grinder in the City of Westminster.'

'What's that all about?' The Monarch perked up a bit.

'The usual polite request, Your Majesty, from a City institution to formally pass Temple Bar, in other words the City boundaries, in the pursuit of its ancient rights. They sent it over by hand last night. I expect they need it for some urgent ceremonial.'

'Did our William really agree to that?'

'I'm afraid so, Your Majesty. If you recall, rather than lay waste to the capital, King William took the rest of the country by force of arms but negotiated a treaty with the City. He did insist that certain formal rights could only be exercised outside that place with royal permission.

'The petition is quite correctly presented. These things are normally nodded through in a couple of seconds.'

The Monarch thought for a moment. It was a time when all factors needed to be taken into consideration and positive action should follow. The Monarch weighed up the case: it was the first really good day of spring; the sky, through the chink in the curtain, looked as blue as a baby's eye; the sun streamed in wherever it could and London's bird life, such as it is, cooed, twittered and chattered away as if this were the dawn of creation. In a courtyard down below, a dog barked, a happy, jokey yap; and from somewhere down a long corridor came a trill of laughter that made the heart rejoice.

'Instead of nodding it through,' said the Monarch, 'get the top chap from this Worshipful Company of whatever it is to come up here in full regalia and present the petition in person. I should think he'll be as proud as a peacock and flattered to death. What's more, and this is the really important thing, make sure that that stays the final item on the agenda and make sure everyone knows it has to take place at eleven-thirty on the dot. Like that it'll push all the other business through. That windbag of a Home Secretary won't have a chance to hold the floor. Then, Private Secretary, I for once will get a clear half hour to wander through the gardens before lunch on this most glorious day.'

The Private Secretary paused a moment for thought. His mind rattled through the arrangements he would need to make. A smile spread across his lips.

'What a good idea, Your Majesty. I'll see to it at once.'

Two long lines of Privy Counsellors stretched away before the Monarch like an avenue of lounge-suited statues. Each line faced the other and the Monarch, seated on an elegant gilded chair, looked down the room between them to the double doors at the end. The Home Secretary was talking on and on. The Counsellors were shifting from foot to foot trying to ease their aching legs.

'By your leave, Your Majesty,' said the Private Secretary, standing a little aside from the gilded chair, 'we must move to the final item. A petition, as inscribed in the agenda, from The Worshipful Company of Bell Founders and Organ Grinders.'

The Home Secretary, well briefed as to timing,

stopped. The Monarch gave leave. The double doors at the end of the room opened and the Grand Master of The Worshipful Company of Founders and Grinders, nacre hat doffed, bell breeches newly brushed, trod with chamois soled ceremonial slippers along the deep red carpet under the slanting rays of the morning sun. He felt a tear enter his eye as he walked slowly through that silent aisle of the great and the good: he the unquestioned centre of attention, he the subject of all their thought and purpose.

He stopped, a pace before the Monarch who sat with royal dignity. The Grand Master went down on one knee and tendered a scroll secured with a scarlet ribbon, fixed with a blood-red seal. The Monarch took it and passed it to the Private Secretary. The Private Secretary broke the seal with a flourish, unrolled the document with a practised sweep and read the petition in a clear tenor voice that penetrated with deceptive ease to the ends of the lines of Counsellors and filled the room with a pleasant, musical rhythm.

The Private Secretary was one of the very few people outside Channel Islands' courtrooms who read Norman French interlarded with extracts of Anglo-Latin with perfect ease. He stopped.

'What say the Council?' he called.

'Aye!' they all stated in a ragged cacophony of discordant consent. The Monarch handed to the Grand Master the Letter of Assent. The Grand Master stood, graciously backed away four steps from the Monarch, bowed, turned and walked slowly out between the ranks of Counsellors. A faint smile played around his lips; a further tear dampened his eye. He held up his chin and his pace betrayed a slight strut. He was as proud as a peacock and flattered to death.

As the doors closed behind him, the Monarch bowed to the Counsellors and the Counsellors bowed to the

Monarch. With an even tread the royal person left by a side door opened by the Private Secretary and, within five minutes, was tripping through the palace gardens on the first fine day of spring, throwing sticks for the dogs to bring back and bathing in the first real warmth the sun had brought that year.

The Clerk paced up and down in the anteroom to the Grand Master's chambers. Over and over in his mind went the scant facts they had managed to glean from Henri's father. Trombone playing, somewhere in Soho, not home all night; it must be a club, he must be in a band of some kind. In all probability it was impossible to find him; but he would try, he would search till every last stone was turned, and if he didn't find Henri then, he would turn all the stones again because he couldn't let by the only chance for five hundred years.

With a bustle and a flurry and an air of starry-eyed satisfaction the Grand Master returned. His prominent chin and his cold, grey eye seemed for a moment softened by the contact with majesty he had just experienced. He changed into his normal clothes in the anteroom and met the Clerk. On his brow was imperial pride, and unexpected grandeur. He sat down with the Clerk and passed him the Letter of Assent. The Clerk checked its formalities were correct, heaved a sigh of relief and said:

'I shall start at once, Grand Master. In the most discreet manner I shall discover the person of our contumacious brother and report his location to the Company.

'May I add, I think we should be forming the Restitutory Phalanx now: we do not know at what short notice it may need to be called out to exercise our right of recovery under the petition.'

'Of course,' said the Grand Master. 'The Organ Master shall convene it forthwith,' and he tapped the Letter of

Assent with his fingers and dreamt of a long, red carpet between a line of Privy Counsellors, and a royal person at its end.

But the Clerk narrowed his eyes and set himself at once in motion. His moment had arrived and he went, pausing only for a mutton sandwich, to scour the likely haunts of a quarry, hidden without an overwhelming intention so to hide.

Later that same Tuesday, Sergeant Apta Dapta turned his mind to his promise to make some direct enquiries in Soho about such things as elephants and, maybe, a clown or two. It was constables' work really: footing it through the quarter, checking up on the musicians in the theatres and the clubs, working out what could have happened to the livestock. Yet it attracted him. Elephants: he'd known elephants since he was a boy. He liked elephants, he knew their smell and their ways. He had vague memories, as a little child back in Asia, of patting elephants' trunks and watching them being washed in the river and at work in the timber yard. No, for this week, he said to himself, he'd do it himself. He wanted to get back on the ground again anyway. It never did to leave the streets to themselves for too long. People took advantage, criminals began to think you weren't interested. Word got round quickly amongst the vice. No, he'd wear his uniform, make himself as obvious as possible, and just try it for himself on a couple of evenings. He'd start tomorrow; by then he'd have a shrewd idea of who should know what and what was going on with whom.

Straight away he made a few phone calls. He found out which theatres had trombonists playing at the moment; he alerted a couple of observers; he looked at the great street plan of Soho on his office wall and said to himself, 'Now where in all of that do you put a couple of elephants, I ask

142

you? I wonder. I just wonder . . .' and he leant back on his chair and pondered, nodding to himself with anticipation.

Now the Clerk was already ahead of him. By the time he left the tube station at Tottenham Court Road he was licking the last vestiges of mutton from the inside of his teeth, gripping his brown leather briefcase with whitened knuckles and tensed in the heroic model to go and do great deeds.

Sitting in the underground amongst the normal collection of very conforming people he had worked himself up into a fury of indignation at the immoral propensities of the young Coulisse. Merciless pursuit has no justification quite as powerful as moral righteousness; and the moral righteousness of the Clerk was now at feverish levels.

He burst into the air of Oxford Street like a storm-trooper recruited for the purposes of lace making. In other words, an enormous and generalized enthusiasm applied to complete ignorance of how to go about the task.

After a few metres of Oxford Street he plunged left to Soho Square where, finding nothing more outrageous than a hospital and two churches, he continued along Greek Street, disappointed but undeterred.

It struck him, as his progress continued, that his first idea of just walking into the clubs and theatres and asking if a trombonist called Coulisse worked there might not be very effective. Of course he had been through Soho many times, enjoyed its restaurants, visited one of its theatres once, known about it all his life, but he now began to realise that he had never taken the place seriously. He had thought of it as some sort of playground into which he would now dash to find a wayward child. Yet he saw that the people in the streets, the waiters in the restaurants, were adults as he was. If he caught someone's eye, he saw that in his earnest stance and with his businesslike air, it was he who was being weighed up and assessed, not the reverse.

He suddenly realized he was doing it all wrong. Henri would have to eat, that was the basic fact to build on. If he went home and changed into something less conspicuous and spent his time wandering past the poorest eating houses at the most auspicious mealtimes, there was a good chance he would see Henri within a week. He felt sure of it and he wasn't wrong.

For that afternoon and evening he wandered the streets, picking out the places where the locals might eat. There were few enough of them. Off the main thoroughfares, in the streets where studios and clubs clustered, sometimes there would be one, sometimes two tiny cafés. Places where people who knew people met people. The Clerk found perhaps a couple of dozen of them. In one of these he thought, feet aching, head reeling, tired like never before, he would find his quarry. He flopped off home to spend a well-earned night asleep and to return for a Soho breakfast.

He emerged next morning from the tube looking certainly more casual than on the previous day. Nonetheless he would not have been taken for a local, nor for an *habitué* of the place.

Beak Street, Broadwick Street, Frith Street and Lisle Street, D'Arblay Street and Bridle Lane, Romilly Street and Foubert's Place; here or hereabouts were the titchy cafés that spurned tourists and served workers, where credit was reserved to the family but regular customers in hard times qualified for free tea and an extra slice of cake. Some of them, the Clerk found out after his fourth breakfast that morning, catered almost only for Chinese or only for bleary-eyed film editors who staggered out to eat after a night over the Movieola.

At eight in the morning there seemed to be few enough performers. Yet some there were. Studio time being the precious commodity it is, there were knots of actors dressed with an air of studied neglect who lubricated their larynxes before a day at the microphones. They swapped the gossip, they eyed each other over; watched the clock, for nothing put pounds in the pocket more than punctuality.

By midday the Clerk had developed a kind of feeling for the place he was looking for. He knew Henri a bit, he knew his background well; and of all the cafés he could find only three, perhaps four, which felt comfortable and seemed to attract musicians. Over four days he would circulate between the four of them. Like that he would spend each main mealtime at least once in each of them. It would be so easy for Henri to be missed: but he began to feel that a vast problem had been reduced to a manageable one.

It would soon be seven o'clock and the light was beginning to fade. Some people were still leaving offices and heading homeward. Some were diving into pubs. The roads, as always, were blocked and crowded with cars. People dodged out of the Clerk's way on the narrow pavements as he trod steadily along. Other people overtook him, leaping at day's end to the Underground as if it would close in a minute or two. Yet the Clerk noticed that through the bobbing crowd there was a figure that kept about ten paces ahead of him. A figure that progressed at the same steady pace, that turned from side to side to look inquiringly at people and windows and cars and doorways. It was a figure in blue, the dark blue uniform of a police sergeant. It was, of course, Sergeant Apta Dapta; and what struck the Clerk was that the policeman appeared not only to be looking but to be sniffing too.

At each road junction, at each courtyard, each twenty

paces or so, he seemed to turn and sniff the air in a quite unusual manner. When Sergeant Apta Dapta turned off towards Shaftesbury Avenue, the Clerk kept to the back streets and approached the next café on his list. It was one of those narrow affairs with a high, glass-fronted counter on the left as you come in the door and a series of tables with bench seats stretching along the right-hand wall. At one of the tables were five young people of about Henri's age. Two couples sat comfortably opposite each other, while the fifth person, a blond-haired girl with a rounded, short, hair-style and an enormous blue donkey jacket several sizes too large for her, perched first on the end of one bench, then on the bench opposite, changing position every ten minutes or so. In truth, the benches were too narrow for three, so she changed sides each time the buttock in question ached too much: and everyone laughed at the exercise.

The Clerk took a coffee from the counter and ordered a lamb chop and vegetable dish which he calculated to be the item that would take the longest to prepare. He went and sat down with his back to the group of youngsters, facing the back wall with the inevitable mirror on it; but more intent on what there was to hear behind his head. One never knew who knew what about whom; eavesdropping could have its compensations.

'*Gnathobelodon*, I imagine,' said one of the men. 'That's not the one with the shovel underlip, is it?'

'Oh, no,' said one of the women who seemed very confident of the subject in question, 'a great big rubbery underlip in all probability but not a bony shovel – that was *platybelodon* and several others. That shovel underlip was quite a common trait at one point in elephant evolution.'

'Anyway,' carried on the man, whose donkey jacket flopped open a bit to reveal a T-shirt with 'Plastic Money for Plastic Arts – Subsidize a Sculptor' written across it in characters hewn from the living rock, 'our *stegodon* group should take the prize.'

'Well, I don't know,' chipped in the woman with only one buttock on the seat. She was facing the back of the Clerk at this point and he was stealing surreptitious glances at her in the mirror on the back wall of the café.

'I think we might have problems. That *amebelodon* group from Liverpool can't get the wretched beasts to hold together. They either get the clay too wet and end up with a heap of mud, or get it too dry and end up with a heap of crumbs. Double life size is big, you know.'

'Well, I think they deserve all the disasters they get,' said a second woman, squashed against the wall on the same side as the one-buttock wobbler. 'They were trying to depict those poor *amebelodon* conducting an indecent act. For goodness sake! *Amebelodon* wouldn't do that in family groups. And in a Royal Park too!' There was a raucous chuckle and the sculptor in the T-shirt asked:

'Who's supposed to be judging this competition anyway?'

'A committee, I think,' groaned the woman, dressed entirely in black with unnaturally black hair, black pendant plastic earrings and orange lipstick, sitting next to the T-shirt. 'Apparently the President of the Zoological Society is supposed to be judging for something called "palaeontological exactitude"; fair enough, I suppose. Then some landscaping adviser to the Royal Family is supposed to judge for "environmental conformity", i.e. whether it looks nice in the park or not. Fair enough I suppose, since the Royals did stump up the location. But finally, the seventy per cent of points to be awarded for sculptural merit will be awarded by, wait for it, yes, your very own Royal Academy's Sir Danvers Panter!'

'Oh, no!' chimed in the chorus descending to a long groan. Chins hit the table. 'Not anatomy Panter. The man with never a muscle out of place. The nit picker. The man who thinks great sculpture is a medical text book!'

'Enough to make you put your elephants in indecent positions,' drawled the squashed-in woman.

'I've got cramp,' said the percher and changed sides with her back now to the Clerk. 'That's better. But I think we stand a good chance just the same. Once you've got over the sheer scale of the thing it's quite fun. You can't believe the dimensions at first when you rough it out, can you? Then the size falls into place and it's just so much muck-humping. What's the competition like, anyway, apart from Liverpool's heaps of mud and dust?'

'There's a good group coming on near Bedford College, a *palaeomastodon* group. It's one of the Scottish colleges, I think. Of course, they're a smaller species than most so they're farther ahead than average.'

'What about that group from Bradford? They're doing *amebelodon* too, under the trees by the Broad Walk. I think they're terrific. The one they've got more or less finished looks as if it's heading straight for that refreshment booth to shovel itself a ton of ice cream.'

'Maybe, but you want to see their driver with the dumper truck. If he ever masters back-wheel steering it'll be a miracle. Mind you, they got some of the best clay. The last few deliveries were very wet,' said the man facing the Clerk's back. 'But when's the judging supposed to be?'

'Ah, now I've been reading all the small print about that,' said the woman. 'Apparently it's all going to take place at some kind of jamboree in the Park at the end of June. Some members of the Royal Family plus the President of the Zoological Society of London will cruise round the park in a gold-plated Land-Rover, or some such vehicle, with the other judges in tow. They'll talk to all the sculptors, lined up like good little boys and girls before their statue groups, and then judge their productions. All this is supposed to be taking place at the same time as a sort of zoo open day which has a special elephant theme with lots of ethnic input and so on. It's supposed to be a sort of British-sculpture-meets-the-Commonwealth-Institute-on-the-elephant-plains kind of thing. There are going to be all sorts of marquees and such-like in the park and the whole thing will be billed as a sort of Royal elephantasia.'

'Bit ambitious, isn't it?' drawled the T-shirt and donkey jacket. 'Still, if we win it, there's going to be a million miles of film footage and television exposure and goodness knows what amount of coverage in all the art mags. We'd have commissions stacked up like kiln saggars. Quite a dolly prospect, what!'

'Well, yes,' came in the buttock percher, 'but I just wish the zoo'd get the real elephants back on display. They haven't been out for a week now and I can't get that *stegodon* neck and foreleg without some more sketches from the zoo elephants. Goodness knows what they're doing with them.'

'Perhaps the lions have been feeling peckish lately – I know they're trying to make the zoo self supporting . . .' said the man opposite her and they all groaned and nattered on about the latest films and meeting the others in the pub and so on.

The Clerk's lamb cutlet arrived and he set to, slowly and deliberately, not wanting to speed his departure despite the fact that all this talk of elephants and sculpture was the most deadly bore and the most disgraceful use of Regent's Park since siting that abominable zoo in it. Animals – and art students – ought to know their places and stick to them. *Stegodonion* or what not, I ask you!

The café seemed a popular place. One or two more people came in and quickly filled it up. Before long the Clerk found himself sharing his bench with a couple of other customers, showbiz tailors by the sound of it; and by the look of the pins sticking ostentatiously out of their lapels.

As if to spite the Clerk, the tailors started talking about horses and the finer points of colic and such-like disease. He felt the world was turning into a menagerie.

By now the little café was brimfull of people. Plates were clattering around in the kitchen and people at the counter were ordering sandwiches with the discernment of epicures:

'That's a topside on rye with low-fat margarine, one lettuce leaf, a sprinkle of red pepper, no horseradish and just a touch of French mustard.' That was all a bit strange to the Clerk; but after a few minutes it made mutton sandwiches seem rather mundane. He looked round and sliced a boiled potato on his plate. He puddled it in milky gravy and lifted it to his lips. At that moment his eyes caught sight of a figure whom he could see only imperfectly in the mirror in front of him.

In it he could see the aisle between the seats and the counter and beyond that the glass door of the café, through which the street outside was visible. It was a narrow street with a pub and one or two shops on the other side. Just opposite the café was a small clothes shop and someone was on the pavement looking in the window. A shock ran through the Clerk. He couldn't be sure, he was looking at someone in failing light from behind, in a mirror and through a glass door with 'Piping Hot Soup to Take Away' written on it. The street had passers-by who got in the way, not to mention the gourmet sandwich buyer in the café who annoyingly rocked back and forth across the Clerk's view as he waited for a clear sighting.

But the figure across the street looked like Henri Coulisse: and the Clerk was trapped against the wall in this overcrowded café by a bunch of horse-breeding Soho tailors who were beginning to vex him not a little.

Now the Clerk had to act with great circumspection. Alone, he could not be sure of arresting Henri successfully. He needed to find out where he was staying, if possible, work out his routines and habits and then, at just the right moment, send the Restitutory Phalanx to bring the contumacious Grinder back to the City and the Hall.

The Clerk set down his knife and fork, pushed away his plate and interrupted the discussion on whether thrombosis in mares can be misdiagnosed as colic. The tailors, rather grudgingly, let him out of his seat and he made his way along the crowded aisle towards the door. A glance out of the window showed the suspect figure had gone: there was a queue at the till. The Clerk planted a bank note on to the cashier's mat and slipped hastily into the street. The cashier didn't bat an eyelid.

The Clerk looked left and right. Whoever the person was, he was now nowhere to be seen, which meant he must have turned off into one of the two adjoining streets nearby. The Clerk thought it must be the one to the right and walked quickly along to reach the corner and look through the length of a short thoroughfare which had no-one recognizable in it. There was time for the window-shopper to have cleared the street and turned into the parallel way at its end. The Clerk had to make up his mind. Continue and gamble that the man had gone this way, or return in the now slender hope he had gone the other way and would still be visible. He hesitated, then pushed on to the end of the cross street. He was in luck. Some forty or fifty metres along the pavement the Clerk saw him again. Without closing the distance, the Clerk followed him at a leisurely pace and with no difficulty: the man was unhurried and unsuspecting. They drifted into

Brewer Street and then up the steps to the end of Berwick Street.

By this time the shops were closed and it was dusk. The lighting in Berwick Street was not good and the street itself seemed very empty with the crowds, the market and even the cleaning lorries gone. The Clerk was now at the top of the steps and saw that he and the man were almost alone in the street. So he paused to avoid being noticed and the man turned to cross the road, showing his full face. It was Henri Coulisse and no doubt about it! So the Clerk at once turned left into Peter Street to avoid being recognized himself. After a couple of seconds he re-emerged to continue the pursuit; but it was no use. In those two seconds Henri Coulisse had disappeared; and despite fifteen minutes of the briskest walking and searching, the Clerk couldn't for the life of him see where the young fellow could have gone to.

'Colic and *stegodons*!' swore the Clerk; and on a deserted corner slapped his hands against his thighs in a mixture of pleasure and frustration at finding and losing, at approaching but not reaching the goal.

'Tomorrow,' he thought, 'tomorrow this little area will be scoured with my most fine of fine-toothed combs.'

And indeed it was. The Clerk was nothing if not methodical and the next day he returned to look into every doorway, to read the name by every bell-push, to check every café and alleyway and to think himself deep into the mind of the young Coulisse, in order to find there the kind of place he would be attracted to, the kind of place he was staying in. To disappear so quickly, reasoned the Clerk, he must have gone to ground, gone home as it were. He hadn't been in any of the pubs or cafés in the immediate area, so home for Henri was probably Berwick Street or thereabouts.

The Clerk noted the clubs, noted the cafés, noted the

pubs and began to haunt them all. For two days he sipped insipid coffee, ate floury pizza, stood as long as he dared gazing along the streets by shop windows and, above all, stood with a barely touched pint of beer in his hand on the pavement in front of the Berwick Street pub, the King of Corsica. He tried to look like one of the locals drinking his beer outside on the chill spring days to avoid the crush inside; and he savoured the beer with the fruitiness of the Berwick Street air.

On Monday evening his patience was rewarded. Yet, but for close observation, the prize was nearly missed. He had, as usual, been looking mainly at the buyers and the passers-by on the pavement; and at the stalls, so that when a hand barrow clattered out of an alleyway, somewhat to his right and across the street, he didn't pay much attention to it.

It was getting near to closing time in the market and the King of Corsica had just opened. The Clerk, tired but determined, had gone into the bar, not crowded at all at that early hour, bought his pint and wandered out to the pavement to sup it with more joy than was usually the case. His feet were tired and, despite the old brown shoes he was wearing, his toes were sore. He leant back against the wall in a most unclerkly stance: one might by now nearly have mistaken him for a visiting VAT man or perhaps a public health inspector waging futile war against the quarter's less fastidious kitchens.

But he heard a clatter from the opposite side of the street and saw someone with a hand barrow emerge from the alley behind the stalls and the now thinning crowds. He thought straight away that it looked like Henri, yet dismissed the thought as mere coincidence since the barrow showed the man was anything but a Founder and Grinder, even a contumacious one.

At first the Clerk lost sight of the man as he turned to

the end of the street. He must have walked along the pavement, for he passed behind the stalls lining both sides of the road. Now the market is so arranged that the crowds stand to buy on the pavements and the stallholders stand in the road, or beside the stalls. They restock the display from their crates and they sell from the scales at the ends or backs of the stalls. So the pavements are crowded with customers and the road is a little freer, being the passage for people crossing, the standing ground for stallholders and the warehouse for full or empty crates.

The Clerk again became aware of the man with the barrow as he began to approach the Clerk from the far end of the street. But he did not come along the pavements. Instead he was in the middle of the road, glimpsed only from time to time between the barrows and the crowds; with the barking costermongers doing their best to rid themselves of everything they could before the close of business for the day.

At some distance the Clerk saw him stop and ask a question to a stallholder, the man laughed and shook his head. The man with the hand barrow turned and wheeled it across the street. Now the Clerk could see his back. His head was hidden behind a bunch of bananas hanging from the stall covering, the barrow was hidden by the body of the stall. He was asking something of another stallholder. They conversed for a moment, a coin changed hands and the man bent down to load something on to his hand barrow. The movement caught the Clerk's eye; and the face in profile dipped past the gap between the bananas and a delightful young lady negotiating for a pound of mushrooms. The Clerk had seen it, it was Henri, and no doubt about it. This time he would follow him to his lair.

The Clerk took two gulps of beer and then put the pint glass on the pavement beside the wall. By late evening there would be many others beside it. For the moment, it

154

stood there alone, a third of a pint of beer standing as a tramp's temptation beside the wall of the local pub. The Clerk jostled along the pavement till he was opposite Henri. Only three or four metres separated them, but it was a busy three metres, a packed three metres, full of fruit and flowers and veg. People paused and pushed and paid. It was ideal for the Clerk, he could stay so close and never be seen.

Henri, on the other side of the stall, had just loaded a case of slightly ageing-looking cabbages on to the barrow, took the handles and pushed it on a bit more. He seemed to be on familiar terms with the stallholders. When they said 'No' to him, they did it with a 'Not today, try again tomorrow' gesture, and a knowing smile that was noticeably absent from their dealings with the general public. Soon, Henri had accumulated a couple of branches of blackening bananas and a case of what looked like assorted vegetable sweepings that one stallholder seemed to have set aside specially for him. Henri took this gladly but the Clerk thought he did it out of gratitude rather than desire to have the sweepings. For the life of him, the Clerk couldn't work out what Henri was up to. Was he a merchant in second-hand vegetables, a compost collector, a pig farmer? He had no idea: but once the barrow was full, Henri managed to take it to the pavement between two stalls just opposite an alleyway – Tyler's Court – and there he eased it up the pavement and, turning it with some dexterity, trundled the hand barrow into the gloom of the covered alleyway.

The Clerk quickly crossed the street and pretended to size up the melons on the side of a stall. The costermonger's lady bustled up to him:

'Pahnd each,' she said, 'lovely melon aht a season, only pahnd each.' The Clerk shook his head and looked at Henri, now just visible about half-way along the alleyway.

'Okay guv, seventy-five pence to you. Breaks me art but I can see ya knows ya melons.' The Clerk saw he would have to do something to stay where he was and started to fumble in his pocket for a coin. But he turned his head to keep Henri in view and the lady thought he was refusing. He could see Henri knocking with his fist against a roller shutter on the left-hand side of the alleyway. An unseen hand threw the shutter up with surprising force but, from where he was standing, the Clerk could see no-one nor any thing inside the building.

The stallholder's lady leant over confidentially, 'Fifty p. then guv, but don't tell the old man there. Givin' 'em away, I am.'

The Clerk fished a coin from his pocket, which happened to be a fifty-pence piece. He gave it to the lady who threw the smallest melon into a paper bag and shoved it into the Clerk's hands. The Clerk now saw Henri about to enter the doorway with his barrow of veg and quickly nodded at the stallholder and dived into Tyler's Court. Henri was just disappearing into the building; and the moment he did so the roller shutter was thrown down with a rattling crash and the alleyway was empty again. Shadows and noises grew between the buildings and the dim light from the uncovered central section and the streets at either end illuminated the noisy murk only slightly.

The Clerk went up and inspected the roller shutter: it gave no clue. But now he noticed the doorway beside it and saw the small, unlit neon sign, 'The Splurge'. He placed his ear to the door and from somewhere inside he could hear a piano and a bass drum and a clarinet playing an old jazz number, sad and slow.

'A jazz club!' thought the Clerk, 'I have him!' And on the Central Line, on his way back to the Hall from Oxford Circus to Bank, the Clerk scoured that week's issue of the listings magazines. In a deep recess of *Time Out* he found the mention of a new jazz venue, The Splurge, just off

Wardour Street, said to have excellent trumpets and reasonable food. Their jazz correspondent would be reporting more fully next week. Meanwhile, sessions at the following times including Wednesday evening from eight o'clock.

'Wednesday evening, eight o'clock,' said the Clerk firmly to himself. 'We might even turn up early.'

Sergeant Apta Dapta had been having a good week. Never mind about elephants, he'd been imposing the Vice Squad's presence on the streets of Soho again. Find or lose the elephants, the whole operation was well worth while. The good ladies of Meard Street gave him a few descriptions to look out for. The jovial little Italian who ran the grocer's shop said he'd keep an eye open for suspicious furniture lorries – the Sergeant dared not say exactly what he was looking for to everyone – and pressed a panetoni on him. He refused it but detailed off a constable to check on the source of his salami. Unmerited gifts are always a sign of a guilty conscience.

The Sergeant rattled the shutters and tried the doors wherever an entrance or a storeroom looked big enough to take an elephant. He eyed the restaurant menus and talked to the health inspectors: no-one offering large portions of cheap meat, no-one causing farmyard smells for no apparent reason.

Only one point struck him as possibly interesting. In Berwick Street market no-one actually said anything and no-one actually gave anything away but his most long term acquaintances there showed a certain cageyness. They scoffed, a sure sign of knowing something; they smiled, a sure sign of relief on the face of those who are in the know but not guilty; one even winked, a sure sign of knowing nothing oneself but knowing others who know all. Despite these signs, there was no concrete evidence for the elephants and after a couple of days in this manner, Sergeant Apta Dapta returned to the station to think: happy to be up to date with the street news, unhappy to be drawing a blank for his colleagues at Albany Street.

'Back to that old square one,' said Sergeant Dapta on the phone. The constable at Albany Street assented and the two of them arranged to walk round the park again and then try to trace the route. Madame Tussaud's, Park Crescent, Langham Place, back to Soho. Maybe someone in one of the film companies needed to shoot a couple of elephants and had hidden them in Wardour Street before transporting them to a studio somewhere. He rang round the studios; no, there were no elephant films in production anywhere, no walk-on roles for pachyderms.

The Sergeant sat and thought. He sat and thought for a very long time and he remembered everything he'd ever known about elephants and everything he'd ever heard about them: in books, in films, above all from the anecdotes of the sub-continent that still ran rich in his family and were still told by aged relatives in Bradford who, speaking no English, evoked the plains, the mountains and the monsoon for spellbound audiences of those that would listen but knew these things only from geography lessons given by teachers who had never smelt sandalwood.

'That elephant,' thought Apta Dapta, 'he it is you must hunt. That elephant, he it is you must chase. That elephant, he it is you must subtly seek, for with his massy bulk he can gently place his feet. That old man wrinkle-skin, aged as years, aged as man; old lady tusk digger, branch-eater, mango-muncher, hiding in the teak thicket, hiding in the high grass, living in the forest glade, crunching, munching.'

The Sergeant mused, leaning back in his chair in the office. The map of Soho on the wall faded to a blur before his eyes. Its lines became the black shadows of the leaves as the tall sun shines down through the forest. Its white spaces became the dappling of the forest floor, the sun on the tall grass savanna, the shadows of morning light in the cool of the day that will be hot before long. He imagined the sighing grasses, the blowing leaves, the crunching, munching of a troop of elephants digesting their way through wild nature. And suddenly he had it! He leapt bolt upright in his office.

'Three in the morning!' he said. 'The jungle at three in the morning!'

Somewhere in Wardour Street, somewhere in Berwick Street, that's where it was and at three in the morning they'd find it.

The little forensic scientist who was attached to the case, the same who had gone to the zoo, was very dubious about it all. But Sergeant Apta Dapta explained it to him and, when all was said and done, if it worked it would be a coup of the first order in the ingenious annals of detection.

At two o'clock on the Friday morning, the Sergeant and the scientist drove into Soho in an unmarked van. They parked it at the northern end of Wardour Street and the two occupants got out of the front and went round and climbed into the back. There they sat opposite each other in the subdued light and the forensic scientist tuned in a radio. One corner of the van was taken up with an enormous loudspeaker.

'Now,' said the forensic scientist, 'it's all set up just the way you wanted. Here's the speaker: with the microphone I'm using that'll give you a mouse rustle at half a mile. There's a cut-out on it, so it shouldn't give more volume than your ears can stand. There's the cut-out switch. Don't touch it or if I drop the mike you'll be deaf for life. It's a radio mike so I won't be trailing kilometres of cable behind me. For this quality of sound, though, the range won't be that far. There's a lot of steel in these buildings and we'll probably have to be almost in line of sight. We'll talk to each other over the personal radios. You switch yours off unless you want to talk to me: you need all the silence you can get in here. If I want to talk to you, I'll tap the radio mike three times, you'll hear that on the speaker here and then you can switch on your personal radio.'

'Wouldn't I be better off in headphones?' asked Sergeant Apta Dapta.

'Maybe,' said the little man quickly, 'I've brought some; but the frequencies of the sounds you're looking for are going to be best rendered on a thundering great speaker like the one you've got here. Anyway, I hope so. Let's test it out. You'll be interested in the background sounds, not my squeaking shoes or bits of paper blowing in the wind, but deep sounds; it'll be like they were almost lost in the very back of the loudspeaker, if you see what I mean. Use your imagination – you'll have to learn to listen. I'd have brought a sound expert; but you must be almost the only guy in London who knows what he's listening for.'

The Sergeant sat in the van and listened and the forensic scientist, wherever there was a warehouse entrance, a double door, a viewing theatre, a chance of a voluminous space inside one of the buildings, stood or sat and directed his microphone against the window, the wall, the shutter or the ventilators. The apparatus looked like a fifty-centimetre length of drainpipe with a handle branching from the side towards one end. They heard many things and with headphones and speakers glimpsed a world of sound that, boring at first, soon grew in interest and became a shared world between two discreet professionals and the discrete events that take place behind the walls and shutters of Soho between two and four in the morning on weekdays in spring.

A lot of rushing and banging as the microphone changed place. The forensic scientist took up a new position. Rattles, bangs, clinks, street voices, distant cars. Far, far in the background, as if a million kilometres away, a steady, heavy note, like a muffled tap, pause, tap, pause, tap and on and on forever. A great room with a large clock ticking away for no-one.

Another position, clickings and whirrings, someone counting in the far, far distance like the voice of an invisible galaxy, counting the stars. Then quite suddenly, the unmistakable faint jingle of a spoon in a coffee cup, a burble of voices:

'What a shot, what a shot!' just distinguishable out of the blackness of the speaker, the video editing suite clicked and counted, the time-base ran on and on.

Several times they moved the van, several times at each stop they set up and listened. The odd passer-by looked very warily at the scientist and the scientist, fully aware of the passer-by, knew exactly when to stop acting as if he were invisible and exactly when to step forward, pull out his identification card and say:

'Metropolitan police, please move along, sir,' and so clear the ground of spectators. But at three in the morning people looked and went their ways: the clientèle at that hour either avoids the police, avoids identification, or is the police.

The forensic scientist went back to the van and he and the Sergeant switched on the dim lights inside and opened a vacuum flask of coffee that Mrs Dapta habitually made for night-time activities. Despite the hour, the little forensic scientist was alert and intensely concerned with his efforts. The Sergeant related to him the sounds and the words he had heard. The little man nodded and smiled. Sergeant Apta Dapta had a good set of ears; probably better than his own. If what they were listening for was here they'd find it, and no doubt about it. The Sergeant opened the back door of the van just a few centimetres and pulled up his collar to prevent the chill affecting him.

'That's what I like about Soho,' he said, musing out loud, 'it's like no other patch in the country. I know it like the back of my hand. There are fifty crimes being committed within two minutes' walk of where we are now. I know who's doing it, who's doing it where and they know I know they're doing it and they know they've got to be discreet. But for all my acquaintance with the place, someone can still go and hide two full-sized elephants here and I haven't got more than a vague idea of who or where. In one way you know everything, in another way you know nothing. That's why I like it.'

The forensic scientist nodded. 'Last stint?' he suggested. 'Tyler's Court and then Peter Street; then we'll call it a night. The early risers'll be on the streets in an hour or so and once the tube starts running it'll sound like an earthquake through this little apparatus.'

'Last stint,' confirmed Sergeant Apta Dapta.

They drained their coffees and set up their equipment again. The man with the microphone slid into Tyler's Court. They heard more and more of exactly the same. The Sergeant began to dream as he listened. A curious sort of waking dream where he had lost his body and was floating free in space, a faculty of hearing without a body to lend an ear. He was in an upland forest, somewhere a diesel engine revved, a logging lorry or a timber lift without doubt; in fact a lorry-load of hams hauled along the Embankment; there was a movement in the trees, a wind in the grasses of the clearings; in fact the water in the sewers a metre beneath their feet. He was looking for something; he was looking for some thing; something that would appear through the head-high grasses, something that his guide would indicate in the depths of the dark forests all around.

The forensic scientist was pointing the microphone at a large, black roller shutter in Tyler's Court. It was a good prospect and he pointed and waited. Impatience served no end in this most exacting of waiting games. The Sergeant's fantasy moved on. Something moved in the high grasses, too far away for him to see. So meaningful was that slow and gentle movement, yet heavy and intentional that a thrill ran through him. He could almost smell the monsoon wind and the rain dripping from the leaves on to the soft floor of the open jungle. There came a long, low, deep rumbling. In his fantasy the guide put his fingers to his lips and pointed towards a thick clump of tall grass overhung with mighty trees whence came the sound of twigs creaking and the slow mastication of grass and leaves. A long, low, deep rumbling. The sound of the bowels of the elephant, just like the sound of the bowels of the earth.

Suddenly he snapped out of the reverie. A long, low deep rumbling! That was it. He grabbed the radio and in a breathless whisper told the forensic scientist to stay exactly where he was. He'd join him in a flash. And he did.

On thick rubber-soled boots, Sergeant Apta Dapta rushed swiftly and silently along Tyler's Court. He reached the scientist who was standing opposite the entrance to The Splurge, his microphone directed at the great, black roller shutter. The Sergeant stopped listening and started sniffing. He sniffed round the edge of that black shutter like a rose grower in a Persian garden. At first he smelt it just a little, like a hint, a soupçon of smell. Then a little stronger, and finally the shutter wobbled a little and a little warmish draught wafted out. A draught full of animal, full of Africa, full of ecstasy. A draught laden with elephant just as sure as Sergeant Apta Dapta knew a teak forest; this he knew was his quarry. With a gigantic gleaming grin that showed up white in the shadows of the Court he turned to the scientist with both thumbs turned up in a sign of total triumph. Softly, gently, giving no cause for attention, they stepped silently back to the van. The night's work was done. Now they could move to action.

The Sergeant, just like the Clerk, next had resort to the listings magazines which, that week, mentioned The Splurge. Just a couple of lines with a recommendation of the new-tech trumpeting that came from speakers with no apparent indication of how it was all synchronized. The Clerk made discreet enquiries at the listings magazine's offices. Some sort of resident group, it appeared, that wouldn't be changing for a week or two. The Clerk had to be satisfied with that information and trust it was true. He looked carefully at the hours of sessions in the magazine and went into conclave with the Grand Master, the Bell Master and the Organ Master.

Sergeant Apta Dapta, however, had other means at his disposal to ensure that his quarry would not escape. Police Constable Monica Sullivan showed a passion for police work and demonstrated a zeal that was entirely commendable. He would place her in observation of the premises. One person was enough: surely an elephant was not going to get out without being seen. Albany Street agreed that observation in Tyler's Court was better carried out by Vice than Crime. PC Sullivan declared herself most anxious to have a go and so was installed on watch.

There are two ways of watching. You can hide and look at your suspect through a peephole or you can make yourself part of the local scene and stand brazenly, but unsuspected, in the full view of everyone. The bold PC Sullivan took the latter course. Only she didn't stand, she lay. It was but an hour's work to collect a miniature scaffolding tower on lockable, rubber wheels, from the council depot, a few pots of paint and a pair of old overalls and start to paint the ceilings in Tyler's Court. For, at each end of the Court, the buildings facing the main thoroughfares continued overhead and, like most such passages, the ceilings were scarcely well maintained. If needs be there was enough work on the ceilings – cleaning, making good, rubbing down, undercoating, top coating, cleaning light fittings, weatherproofing, to keep her occupied there for a month. And of course, the scaffolding practically blocked the passageway; so, if any unexpected breakout occurred, the police would always know which exit the elephants must head for. But a month's work was not needed: a few days did more than suffice.

Chapter 13

Having got PC Monica Sullivan installed on her back in Soho, Sergeant Apta Dapta convened a meeting at the zoo for that afternoon. He then went to get a few hours' sleep before rising for lunch and taking a slow drive in the patrol car to Regent's Park.

The meeting took place in the President's office. Everyone sat round in an atmosphere of tense expectation, bathing in the relief and the pleasure of success to date; and eager to find out how matters should be executed from then on.

Sergeant Apta Dapta chaired the meeting, though in a most informal way. The others, sitting in the green upholstered chairs around a coffee table covered in the binders and notebooks of the participants, took part as their legitimate interests dictated. The officer from Albany Street sat chastened and attentive, pleased the police had triumphed, sorrowful it was not he. The forensic scientist sat alert but tired, fading as ever into the background. The elephant keeper showed both relief and concern, and the zoo vet a kind of haughty professional criticism, crowning himself as the expert above all experts present. It was the most junior member of the group that spoke first, the elephant keeper.

'What a relief you've found them,' he was saying to Sergeant Apta Dapta.

'Easier than I feared,' said the Sergeant, 'though it was a

166

long shot and could easily have failed. When we thought we'd found the area, we went there and listened for them. Just like I did with my uncle in the sub-continent. We heard the stomach rumblings, thanks to our microphones, of course.'

'Have you actually seen them?' came in the vet, dubiously.

'No,' said the Sergeant, 'but I heard them and, just as importantly, I smelt them. Unmistakably elephants.'

'They might be in poor condition by now,' said the vet, 'why not recover them at once?'

'Two reasons,' said the Sergeant. 'First, an elephant giving out contented stomach rumbles at three in the morning and smelling like a fit and healthy elephant, no hint of faeces or urine, you know, is being taken care of by someone and almost certainly being properly fed.'

'Quite right,' said the elephant keeper. 'That deep belly rumbling in the small hours is a good sign – good as a check up from the vet,' he said; and then looked a little abashed. But the vet looked abashed too: he was supposed to be the expert and here were two lay people with practical experience he couldn't match.

'And second,' continued Sergeant Dapta, 'we want to get the people who are responsible for this. In all probability they weren't there at three in the morning, so I've set a permanent watch on the beasts – a very discreet watch you understand.' Heads nodded all round. 'And what we do now is plan at this meeting how we'll move in and snap the lot of them – elephants, abductors and organizers. A jumbo raid, you might say!' Nobody laughed.

The forensic scientist pulled out a large-scale plan of the area and spread it over the jumble of books on the table. Everyone edged forward to get a closer look and he took them through the facts of the case in plain detail.

'The elephants are in this room, in this building, in this alleyway that runs between Wardour Street and Berwick Street,' he said. 'The room they're in is against the alleyway and gives on to it through a roller shutter door. We've got to assume that that's the way they got in there and the only way they can come out. Now, that entrance is covered. We've got someone discreetly concealed by it all day. She'll call us up on her personal radio if there's any movement. Every night we'll send a customer into the club upstairs. The club's right beside the warehouse and seems to be some sort of new jazz venue. It's possible they've got something to do with it all. The two parts of the building connect inside.'

'Now then,' came in the Sergeant, suddenly grave, 'you want your elephants, and so do we; but we also want everyone who works in that club and, what's more, in the great traditions of Vice we need to make a major raid. The whole area of that club smells of a patch getting out of hand. The costermongers are smiling at each other when the police pass by; there are odd characters hanging around in the cafés attempting to nose out information of their own while trying to look inconspicuous. It needs a really thorough-going police raid in the grand tradition. That'll get you back your goods and get us back in control of the streets.

'The men from Albany Street,' the constable from that station smiled in acknowledgement, 'will form a special elephant unit. They'll need to be supported by you gentlemen from the zoo and you'll have to inform us of any special equipment that'll be needed.

'Vice will go for the people: there'll have to be a lot of us because we aren't sure just what that club's fronting up. There might be any sort of operation in progress in there,' he said in a dark tone.

'The time of the raid is a quarter to six, next Wednesday

evening. Not a normal time for Vice raids, I know, but a time when any of the big businessmen who might be involved would still be there – and may be just late enough for the evening staff to have turned up. We'll confirm it later, but it looks as if that's the time to go for.'

The President rolled back in his chair and looked for a moment at the ceiling. 'How are the animals likely to behave in the midst of all that lot, keeper?' he said.

'If there are no smoke bombs, tear gas or such like antics it should be all right,' he replied.

'Oh no, none of that. That's not our scene at all,' said the Sergeant.

'Whistles?' asked the President.

'Ah,' said Sergeant Apta Dapta. 'Thanks for mentioning that. No whistles, I think. Just a nice quick, quiet raid.'

In essence, the street plan made their decisions for them. As their heads came together over the sheet there was a pointing and mumbling, an explaining and burbling of talk. In summary it came down to this. They would station the scaffolding at the Wardour Street end of the alleyway. They'd block Wardour Street with a police car just to the south of that and totally block Berwick Street market by getting a car down between the stalls in the middle of the road and stopping it there – it would have to be a mini, that one. About twenty uniformed police would then surge into the club from vans parked in Broadwick Street and arrest everyone. In their wake would follow the elephant unit of police and zoo people who would secure the quarry and subsequently lead it sedately back to the zoo. Everyone nodded sagely, it was all so simple.

'Well,' said Sergeant Apta Dapta, 'I think that's it. Have to confirm it all, of course, but that looks like the plan. Any questions?'

Everyone nodded wisely in assent. So simple, it

couldn't possibly go wrong. They all emphasized the importance of secrecy to each other and, relieved and satisfied, went their various ways. For the most part, looking forward with some thrilling expectation to next Wednesday.

In the Great Hall of the Founders and Grinders the Bell Master, with curling lip and critical eye, walked along a rank of the thirty fittest and fastest members of the Company. Their gaze was cold and predatory and his gaze was merciless and sharp. At the organ, the Organ Master played a low and lurking tune, a predatory fugue that would lead to a predictable climax as the Restitutory Phalanx laid hands upon the contumacious Grinder. For several days now they had engaged in heavy bell-lifting to tone their muscles. They had mastered a complicated new peal to perfect their co-ordination. They had learnt rounds to the tune of the de-harmonized harmonium to accentuate their feelings for hate and disdain. They were a worthy wolf pack that did but wait news of the quarry from its scout, the Clerk.

And the Clerk was at that moment emerging from the labyrinthine underground station at Bank, cutting down alongside the windowless bulwarks of the Bank itself, chin jutting forward, pacing, strutting hard, heading for the Hall with the news of the quarry's lair.

As the Bell Master dismissed the Phalanx with a predatory scowl, the Clerk entered the building and made straight for the Grand Master's chambers. In the outer office he went to the filing cabinet and drew out the Letter of Assent: lovingly, he stroked its thick parchment page and ran the back of his finger along the silken ribbon and touched the deep-red seal. He filed it again with a wry smile and knocked at the inner door. There was a creak and a scuffling sound such as occurs when someone who has been lolling back in his chair with his feet up on his desk comes suddenly upright at the prospect of discovery. The Clerk was bidden entry and went in to the Grand Master.

The latter sat at his desk in a grey, pin-striped suit. His slightly beefy face wore a combined air of expectation and guilt: hope that Henri had been found, shame at having lolled in his office with his feet up. The Clerk noticed this facial combination not one bit. But on his own face was written the radiance of success. His wrinkles contorted into a caligraphy of self congratulation, vignettes of pride doodled at the corners of his mouth, dots and crossings of indignation furrowed his brow. With stentorian voice he spake:

'I have him, sir, I have him. As tight as a ferret in a mole-hole we have him, sir, for the taking.'

The Grand Master beamed to see that the Clerk had no suspicion that he was the sort of fellow to loll back with his feet on his desk, day-dreaming of the royal presence.

'The Phalanx must march soon. I've a few calls to make but it could be next Wednesday evening. He's engaged at some kind of jazz club in the depths of Soho and I read in the listings that they have a session on Wednesday with their regular band. He's obviously part of that. Next Wednesday evening it is.

'Is the Phalanx well rhythmed? Is it bell-toned to muscle strength? Are its co-ordinates determined?'

'Relax, Clerk; and well done!' said the Grand Master. 'Your name will be forever inscribed in our immutable annals. Yet, there is the pursuit to come. Let me summon the other Masters and overlook our plans.'

The Grand Master drew open the drawer and with commanding hand tapped out the extension number of the organ loft. Through the earpiece the Clerk heard the Organ Master saying he would come, as a dying breath from the organ expired in the background behind his voice.

He called the Bell Master, by then in his belfry. He too would come at once. Harmonic resonances died into the distance and were abruptly cut as the Grand Master replaced the receiver. Less than two dutiful minutes later, there was soft tapping at the door and the two Masters walked in and were seated in the chambers. They sat expectantly for a moment. The Grand Master looked grave and drummed his fingers on the desk. Then he smiled and said:

'We have him. Clerk has tracked him down!'

It was Clerk's turn to smirk now and the Masters praised him vociferously and slapped him on the back and asked for details. The Grand Master took up the request:

'Details!' he said. 'And a plan of attack. Apparently next Wednesday evening is the time!'

'Indeed it is,' said the Clerk and went on to explain the situation and the programme at The Splurge.

They fell to planning in deadly earnest. The Clerk sketched out on a pad the detailed plan of the streets around Tyler's Court while the three Masters pored over the *A to Z* to get the larger picture first.

'Ludgate Hill, Fleet Street, the Strand?' said the Bell Master, already in his mind's eye seeing the serried Phalanx marching.

'I think not,' said the Grand Master. 'Holborn Viaduct, High Holborn, St Giles' High Street or perhaps New Oxford Street, then Oxford Street itself looks more like it.'

'It does, it does!' said the Organ Master enthusiastically. 'We'll cross into Westminster at Gray's Inn Road, up-battle-casquing to the Gryphons in full march – just think of it, the first marching up-battle-casque for four hundred years or more! From Oxford Street we'll turn down Wardour Street. But then what? We could go straight in at Tyler's Court, into The Splash . . .'

'Splurge,' interjected the Clerk.

'Er, Splurge,' continued the Organ Master, 'and drag him out by the scruff of the neck. Or . . .' he trailed off thoughtfully.

'Yeees?' said the Grand Master.

'Or, we could divide file and send one column round the block to enter the Court from Berwick Street and the others to proceed as just mentioned. Catch him in the pincer just in case he's a mind to bolt for it.'

'Mmmm,' mused the Grand Master. 'A good idea. I think I've one of my own to add to it. After all, it would be rather too much if he should smell a rat and get away. I think we'll invite ourselves to the club and just make sure he doesn't get a chance to flit away first.'

'Not very easy, I'm afraid, Grand Master,' came in the Clerk. 'The timing of the restitution before the performance starts is so that we can move in with the least possible difficulty and away before much of a disturbance is caused.'

'Mmm,' said the Bell Master slyly. 'On the day of the restitution you could stand on watch in the vicinity, at least make sure he's there and let us know if he's not.'

'That would be something,' said the Clerk. 'Yes. In and around the market. In the pub across the road. Up and down Wardour Street. That should be possible. But if I didn't see him we would have to assume he's there and go in anyway.'

'That's a risk we have to take, I think,' said the Grand Master with a touch of oafish pomposity that quickly subsided. 'Now, the strategy.'

They pored over the Clerk's hand sketch and thought of the approach. Certainly the Oxford Street approach was the general line to take; but the detailed arrangements at the final thrust were more open to discussion. The frontal attack – a full phalanx channelled into Tyler's Court, storming the club and restituting contumacy to submission. Or should it be the pincer movement? One prong through the market and the other through Wardour Street, meeting with a steel grasp at the club where the prisoner would be taken.

These were grave matters. Knowing the detailed lie of the land, the Clerk made a suggestion.

'The pub I mentioned in Berwick Street, on the opposite side from Tyler's Court,' he said. 'Its patrons have a habit of drinking on the pavement outside and at the hour of the restitution the pub will be open. Say I and two or three only of the sturdier members of the Phalanx were to take up position there before the remainder made their pincer assault from both ends of the alley. We few could stop any attempt to bolt before the arrival of the pack. At the other end of the alley is a scaffolding which the Phalanx can certainly get past but which discourages exit from that end. I don't think he'd leave in that direction. In any case, setting groups to guard both ends would diminish the splendour of the Phalanx too much. We could hold him up at least long enough for the main body to come up behind and take him. But for those three or four, the full power and glory of the force would not be diminished.'

The arguments weighed heavy with the Masters. They were practical and preserved the traditions of mass onslaught which lay dear in the heart of all genteel Founders and Grinders.

'One problem, though,' came in the Organ Master. 'How would the group of you fulfil the requirement to be in full restitutory regalia? Some of the clientèle at the pub and in the market may not be able to appreciate its significance. If the contumacious Grinder were to see it, it would forewarn him of our coming. You would, after all, have to take up station some little while before arrival of the full force.'

The Clerk pondered a moment. But the Grand Master answered:

'I have it. Overalls! The Special Duties Group may wear

their regalia underneath overalls used as a disguise. They can look like house painters or such-like workmen. I can give the dispensation necessary for disguise.'

The others nodded: it would be cover enough. At the moment of the restitution they could strip off their overalls and take part in the process. They grinned a little wryly, a little cunningly to each other at the thought of secret operations of this kind. An ancient order perhaps; but not afraid to innovate in times of need. Another precedent for Clerk's archive. Things looked better and better.

Mr Sedge came into the office that Tuesday morning like a new man. What was more, the Home Secretary apparently had a Privy Council meeting that day. Mr Sedge did not work with the Home Secretary, of course, but the head man's absence invariably made life easier for the lower orders.

To begin with, the security man at the ministry door did not recognize Mr Sedge and checked his pass most thoroughly. He remembered a more careworn, wrinkled man who often left late and seemed slightly grubby no matter how clean he really was. This man was sprightly of step and looked more as if he'd spent the bank holiday on a healthy walk over the North Downs; which, in fact, he had. But the pass was genuine and Mr Sedge got into work.

Mr Sedge's 'office' was an alcove separated by free-standing division panels from the rest of a vast room, similarly divided, where the lower-ranking members of several special sections worked. His length of service – as opposed to his strict seniority – was apparent in the fact that his alcove included a window through which genuine daylight came – a status and luxury not available to the majority of those who laboured in that enormous open office.

The first sight of his alcove immediately raised a spasm of

painful memory in Mr Sedge. There was his desk with in-tray piled high. His slightly tatty swivel chair was behind it, resting at a random angle, ready to receive him. Beyond that were his two regulation grey filing cabinets with a few piles of files and papers on top of them and a sort of used dustiness hovering around them. It was all brown dividing screens, grey furniture and cream walls. A sort of pasty uniformity that made one feel insipid. No self-respecting cannibal would ever eat these battery bureaucrats. Any premium for free-range humans would be worth the price.

On top of the grey steel desk was a desk tidy whose crevices carried the ingrained dust of ages. The telephone had once been ivory in colour, but now was murked with black, grey and brown mottling: the result of coffee spillages, the thin veneer of that unique office concrete of dust, caffeine and perspiration. Mr Sedge, for the first time in his life, suddenly saw all this for exactly what it was: the cell of the worker bee, a lowly place in the lofty hive; and he smiled at his new perception.

In a couple of steps he was across at his desk and chucked his briefcase into the chair. He gathered up his desk tidy, emptying out the pens, took his coffee-cup place-mat and his in- and out-trays and stalked off to the lavatory. Filling a basin with water, he threw in his desk clobber and then wetted a handful of paper towels. These he took back to his desk and dealt with the phone, the filing cabinets and the window sills. Back in the lavatory he finished his washing up and brought it back to this desk. Ah, what a difference it made to get rid of the muck of ages! This was quite definitely a new start.

He fitted the piles of files back into the sparkling desk trays and breathed a sigh of satisfaction. Now for some action. He pushed the chair back a bit from the desk and put the in-tray files in his lap. There were about twenty of them and normally he would have spent all day reminding himself of their contents, writing minutes on them, completing the dockets and passing them to his out-tray after initialling the circulation list on the front. Today he quickly flicked open each file in turn, saw what it was about, signed it off and plonked it in his out-tray. On one of them he made a two-sentence minute. In the course of the week two of them came back to him for further attention but the other eighteen disappeared forever.

'My my,' chuckled Mr Sedge, 'if only I'd known, if only I'd known.'

Having polished off the day's work before most of his colleagues were even in the office, he turned to his filing cabinets and pulled out three groaning files. One labelled 'Nationality – Special Decisions', another labelled 'Africa – Stateless Persons' and a third labelled 'International Law – Recent Nationality Cases'. He had just spread these around over the top of his desk plus a couple of files of departmental memoranda and Current Rules when the Head of Section breezed by and just glanced into his alcove. That bright spring sunshine was coming through the window and Mr Sedge looked up with an equally bright smile on his face and an air of alert activity that quite took the Head of Section's breath away. He gazed over the top of the screen at Mr Sedge's smiling face, then he noticed the clean and shining aspect of his alcove. Then he saw the out-tray, the out-tray at nine thirty in the morning, full to overflowing. He took a deep breath but it was Mr Sedge who broke the silence:

'Good morning to you!' he chirped.

'Er, good morning, er, Mr Sedge,' said the Head of Section and went to his office very pleasantly surprised but very downcast when he saw the pile in his own in-tray. He wondered privately how long this zeal would last.

Well, suffice it to say that it lasted a very long time and

in any case all through that week in which Mr Sedge went through the routine work like a knife through warm butter and created hours of time that he had never known he had had before, in which he got to the bottom of the problem of the elephants. He flicked through decision after decision, case after case, and found little enough that would really fit. He read the memoranda, the instructions, even the legal text books and found a hint here, a help there, a reference now or bits of judicial opinion then. He even managed to get an animal rights briefing sent over from the Ministry of Agriculture and an endangered species declaration from the Department of the Environment. He had never done this kind of thing before and he could hardly believe that this same desk, between these same screens, by this same window, in this same ministry, could be such an exciting place this week when, last week, it had been a treadmill that seemed grudgingly to turn out meal tickets and just about pay the mortgage.

He was building up a case, becoming a campaigner and he found that the kind of torpid isolation he had previously fallen into was not now a prison but an asset. It meant he had few friends and few expectations upon him. It meant he owed no special debts of allegiance to individuals, it meant that he was not part of one of those departmental boats which others spent a lot of time not rocking. He was his own man, within the context of the Section of course; but his own man doing his own thing and the more he did it, the more he wanted it – legal status for his friends, the elephants. By Wednesday afternoon, he had a lead. By Friday morning, he had a plan.

By three o'clock on Friday afternoon, Mr Sedge's in-tray was empty. He leaned back a bit in the tatty seat and drummed his fingers on the desk top. The arm of his chair, grey and frayed, came into view. He pulled open a drawer in his desk, pulled out a form after rummaging for several seconds, and then indented for a new swivel chair. He could have done that at any time over the last five years but things like that were only now occurring to him spontaneously. The form went into an envelope and into his out-tray. He picked up the phone.

Over the next hour he phoned and noted and tied up the loose ends of enquiries made during the week. By four o'clock he was putting the notes in his brief-case and looking at the clock. For camouflage reasons, he got out a file and put it on his desk, open. At ten past four, the Head of Section breezed out and a sense of relaxation started to exude from the alcoves around him. Now on most Friday afternoons the other members of the Section left as soon as they could and, passing Mr Sedge's alcove, caught a glimpse of him piled high with files and deep in work. They would feel a pang of guilt, followed by a knowing smile and perhaps a weary shake of the head at what they took to be conscientiousness taken to the point of self sacrifice.

By half past four this Friday, the little trickle of departures was well under way. But from the corner of their eyes they saw no labouring bureaucrat set to for the evening, but a clear desk in a clean and tidy alcove: not a sign of disorder and not a sign of Mr Sedge. They felt their pang of guilt, but quite a different guilt; they smiled, but quite a different smile; traditions were being broken and fear clutched a little at their hearts. What had old Sedge discovered that they did not know?

Young Sedge, or at least, rejuvenated Mr Sedge, had discovered that he needed a few maps and diagrams, a few odds and ends for a very special briefing session he was due to make on Saturday. He breezed past the security guard who groused his usual farewell and out into the sunshine and showers of a nippy spring day. By way of a couple of shops he made his way back to Charing Cross and Croydon.

Late the following morning, Mr Sedge washed up his breakfast and went to his wardrobe. He didn't often eat breakfast in his dressing gown and pyjamas but this was probably the first time he had done so without feeling the need of some special excuse. He'd had breakfast in his pyjamas because he felt like it on a Saturday morning. So there!

His wardrobe made grim viewing. Apart from the shirts, nearly all of which were white, it seemed to shade in tones of grey through charcoal to black. Mostly chain-store suits.

'Blimey!' he said.

He started rummaging about in the drawers. After a while he pulled out an old soft shirt that he'd picked up on holiday somewhere, cream in colour, and a pair of slacks. He couldn't decide which awful jacket looked least awful and managed to scramble into a heavy sweater that went less badly than he thought. Yes, he felt more or less right, picked up his briefcase and by way of quite a few clothing shops and a snack in a restaurant somewhere, made his now laden way to The Splurge where he arrived, as promised, at three.

On entering Tyler's Court he was annoyed that the scaffolding at the Wardour Street end seemed to have been placed expressly to make entry difficult. Someone in white overalls was still working at the top, apparently filling cracks in the ceiling. Whoever it was certainly worked slowly and this, coupled with the fact that one hardly ever saw a tradesman working on a Saturday afternoon these days, made Mr Sedge pause and look up with a moment's idle curiosity. He saw it was a woman, which was interesting but not unusual; although she was undeniably somewhat neater, her overalls somewhat cleaner, her hair somewhat more strictly taken care of than he would have expected. This was all taken in in a moment's observation and Mr Sedge passed on to the door of The Splurge. He rang and was let in when he gave his name on the entry-phone. As he crossed the threshold he saw the decorator looking carefully at him from the top of the scaffolding tower.

Henri came skipping down the stairs to meet Mr Sedge in the entrance hall. They exchanged greetings and went straight in to the elephants. The rear roller shutter was up and the elephants were out in the light well enjoying the air and getting what exercise they could.

'Hello, Mr Sedge,' trilled Finta Fanta. 'I'm so glad to see you.'

'I am too,' said Rumpus Pumpus and Mr Sedge shook a trunk all round and reached up and gave Finta Fanta a rub behind the left ear.

'Ooooh!' she squealed in delight. 'So lovely!'

Mr Sedge laughed, 'I wondered if you'd really like it. It's one of those little details I picked up in the mass of elephant literature I've been through this week,' he said. Rumpus Pumpus wrinkled his brow and nodded his head, very impressed.

'Look,' said Henri, 'I'll bring out a couple of chairs and we can talk out here in the air. You'll need your briefcase, too?' he asked; and Mr Sedge nodded.

Now seated and documented, the little group set to to discuss their prospects. Mr Sedge opened the discussion with an optimistic tone:

'Whatever happens, I'm pretty sure there's enough material here to make out a good case on your behalf. Of course, anything can be disputed, but we've got enough to make a good start. In my humble opinion, and it is humble, you've got a chance. Not the slimmest of chances, not the greatest of chances; but a chance. I've seen literally thousands of cases go through my department – that's interesting, last week I would have said "*the* department", now I say "*my* department" – and when all is said and done it boils down to two things. First, the Home Secretary's got to want you in, not out. Second, the case has got to be argued so that it creates no precedent, breaks no precedent and can be presented as humane and just.'

'But how do we know if he wants us in?' said Rumpus Pumpus.

'Oh, that's easy,' bubbled Mr Sedge. 'When it's a question of humans, the thing gets all very complicated. Home Secretaries get obsessed with spies, with political persuasion, with colour, with race, with sex, with marital status, with "pro" lobbies, with "anti" lobbies, in short with all the intricacies of xenophobia in all its vote-catching and vote-losing complexity. It boils down to votes, you see. But if we play our cards right, there is one group against whom there is no significant "anti" lobby and for whom there is a very significant "pro" lobby.'

'Yes, yes . . .' came in Finta Fanta excitedly. 'Which group is that?'

'Animals,' said Mr Sedge. 'The moment this is an animal rights issue, the cards start stacking in your favour.'

There was a difficult pause. The elephants shook their heads slightly and Finta Fanta said:

'It isn't really animal rights we need, you know. We need human rights.'

'Yes, yes, I see that,' said Mr Sedge. 'I'm coming to that one right away. The trouble is that if you're human from the start, then you're illegal immigrants; because you haven't gone through any of the formalities of entry. You could be deported at the drop of a hat, virtually. No, look at it this way, the animal ticket is the entry ticket: the human ticket is the one we need to apply for now. What we should aim for is a special status of something like "animals with human rights".'

The elephants looked dubious but interested. Henri

smelt a rat: the over-ripe odour of a fudged issue.

'An attractive compromise,' Rumpus Pumpus said, 'but how would we know we weren't abandoning fundamental rights for a mere title? We need the rights which our capacities require, not a title in return for behaviour that will be seen as an interesting kind of trick.'

'Indeed, indeed,' continued Mr Sedge. 'What I had in mind was the following. We start from animal status – but very special animal status. Under international treaty you are a protected species.'

'Of course!' said Rumpus Pumpus matter-of-factly, '*loxodonta africana*.'

'Quite so,' said Mr Sedge, 'and, in practice, that means that if we can introduce you into an official nature reserve, you'll be fairly safe.'

'We'd be packed off back to the zoo!' said Finta Fanta.

'Not if you institute proceedings for false imprisonment against the zoo and get a temporary injunction to prevent capture pending a judgment.'

'Sounds a bit thin to me,' said Henri.

'Well, not really,' said Mr Sedge. 'If either the proceedings or the injunction application are allowed to go ahead the legal system will have given *de facto* confirmation that you are to be regarded as persons. The whole law is framed in terms of the rights of 'the person' in these matters. Any judgment is a victory because it paves the way to applications for citizenship, passports, you name it.'

'Then why the nature reserve?' asked Rumpus Pumpus.

'Well,' said Mr Sedge. 'If we designate the reserve a habitat for *loxodonta africana* it becomes a criminal offence to disturb you. It doesn't do anything to your status as individuals but it effectively gives you your freedom while the legal process is sorted out.'

'And who in this country would designate a reserve as a

natural habitat for us?' said Rumpus Pumpus a little impatiently.

'Well, actually,' said Mr Sedge a little coyly, 'the Secretary of State for the Environment.'

'Go on,' said Finta Fanta with rising interest.

'Well,' Mr Sedge explained, 'the Secretary of State for the Environment is empowered to add species to the list of protected animals, especially in designated habitats, which in turn attract special protection. Now it seems there's a nature park actually in London, in the Lea or Lee Valley, they can never decide how to spell it; quite an extensive area of rough ground, reservoirs and playing fields that never got built on because it all used to be a marsh. Well, in there somewhere there's a nature reserve with a number of specially designated species which are going to be added to next week by order of the Secretary of State.'

'Protected species in London,' mused Rumpus Pumpus. 'What on earth are they?'

'Butterflies, mostly,' said Mr Sedge. 'All but one are butterflies.'

'And what's the other?' intoned Rumpus Pumpus. Henri caught a glint in Mr Sedge's eye and paid close attention.

'Er, *loxodonta africana* actually,' said Mr Sedge. There was a stunned silence. 'I got the papers from my opposite number in Environment,' avowed Mr Sedge, 'and then filled them in and sneaked them into a delivery from our minister's private office to Environment's private office.'

'Worth a try, I suppose,' said Henri with a rising appreciation of Mr Sedge's initiative.

'Very much so,' said Mr Sedge. 'All the species can be designated by Latin name only and, you see, the Secretary of State for the Environment went to a state school in Birmingham and graduated in Economics at the University of Keele; he's never learnt Latin in his life. He thinks you're butterflies. Given the *africana* tag, he'll imagine some rare exotic species wafted in on freak winds from the Sahara: but butterflies none the less.'

A smile spread across their faces, then a kind of helpless guffawing broke out and they rocked back and forth and rolled from side to side in helpless mirth. The elephants tootled and trumpeted, albeit gently, before subsiding to a more enquiring state of mind again.

'Maybe we're going to be glad of that possibility if it materializes,' said Henri. 'We probably haven't got much more than another week here. The management won't want to keep us forever as a resident band: we've had a couple of offers from other venues according to James and it's important for us to get around the jazz scene, not just stay in one place. No-one seems to have caught on to what we're using the warehouse for, but someone will soon and then I expect we'll need a new home. As a last resort, that nature reserve could be interesting.'

Finta Fanta and Rumpus Pumpus looked very dubious. They looked at each other and they looked at Henri and Mr Sedge. They didn't really like the sound of it.

'Sounds to me,' said Rumpus Pumpus, 'a bit like all the disadvantages of the savanna – that was a national park too, you know – plus all the disadvantages of the zoo and none of the advantages of either.'

'Oh, I don't know,' said Mr Sedge. 'I've been looking on the map and there are thousands of hectares of space over there. Most people don't realize it. There are hundreds of football pitches, of course, all a bit boring that, but there are hundreds of hectares of rough ground too, including the nature reserve, a river, a canal and several reservoirs. I don't know if you would be allowed in there or not but it's a vast area by zoo standards – there should be lots of rough grazing – marsh, scrub and grass; and some woodland.'

'Mmm, twiggy bits,' said Rumpus Pumpus and licked his lips.

'Let's make a contingency plan,' suggested Finta Fanta. 'We'll work out how to get to this reserve and if we need to do it, we can.'

'I think that's a wise idea,' said Henri. 'You never know what's going to happen in our situation. Heading for protected species status should work for a bit at least, if we need it to.'

Mr Sedge spread out his maps and street plans on the ground and they began to pore over them. The basic route was very easy, if very open. They would either have to pull the circus trick again or go at night, perhaps through the back streets. But they left the details for later. Henri could always guide direct from the map on one of the elephant's backs. And the elephants themselves seemed to have hit on something that interested them rather excitedly, though they showed this only in winks and nudges to each other and a brisk flick of the tail.

'So that's it really,' said Mr Sedge. 'If it's granted, your protected species status should be made official on Monday. At that moment I'll apply for naturalization papers for both of you and the fun and games will start. It's likely to be a long paper-chase but there's a chance of success.

'The main plank in our platform is that you were brought here specifically at the government's request, on a permanent basis. It's a strong position to be in – there's many an applicant at the ministry would like to add that to his application.

'So that's that for the moment. Any chance of dropping in on a rehearsal?'

'Of course,' they chorused. 'We're due to go over a few routines at four. Then we'll take a break till the action starts at eight. Will you be stopping?'

'Why not?' said Mr Sedge. 'Yes, I think I will. But not quite so much sparkling lager this time. Once is enough for that experience.

'By the way, have you noticed that painter in the alley outside?'

'Yes,' said Henri.

'What do you think?' said Mr Sedge. Henri turned his mind to the scaffold and the painter and thought a moment.

'I don't know,' said Henri. 'I hadn't considered it much. Scaffolding's a nuisance, of course: the elephants couldn't get out where that's in the way; but what do you make of it? You seem concerned.'

'Well,' said Mr Sedge, 'that woman doesn't look much like a painter to me. Do you think she might be from the police?' Henri looked a bit surprised. Mr Sedge continued: 'Think of it from their point of view. The police must have been informed that you're missing,' he nodded towards the elephants, 'but there's been nothing in the newspapers, nothing on radio, nothing on television. They've told the news agencies to keep quiet. They're perhaps expecting a ransom note or something like that. But probably it means that they're pretty sure where you are and are working out some way of getting you back. Don't you think?'

'It makes sense,' said Rumpus Pumpus. 'Of course, this part of town must be regularly under police observation. Even if that is a lookout, it may not be for us.'

'That's very true,' said Henri. 'Of course, a lot of people must have seen us on the way here. The costermongers are on our side but I suppose, if we're realistic, the police should have found us by now.'

A silence fell on the little group. For the first time, the impermanence of their situation really came home to them and they began to see how important Mr Sedge's work on the nature reserve might turn out to be. Rumpus Pumpus broke the silence.

'I think,' he said, 'we'd better plan on going to that nature reserve, come what may, a week on Sunday. That'll give us another full week here and a chance to make our names. Then we could play from there – there must be something in that locality.' The others nodded.

'What's more,' came in Finta Fanta, 'we'd better plan several routes and means of making the journey and we'd better do that by Monday; because, if that is the police in the alleyway, they could be planning a raid at any time. Best be prepared.' There was a kind of awesome consent to this idea. Then there was the noise of a banging door opening over their heads and James Daley leaned out of the hoist door and hailed them from above.

'Brasses in position, please; we're ready for the off.' And he added, 'Glass of lager, Mr Sedge?' They laughed.

'A small one,' he replied, 'then it'll be coffee. I'm on my way up.'

They heard Pete Davis' double bass thumping through a few well-chosen chords and Sady McCabe's electric piano run up and down a scale or two. The elephants went to their portals and the two men went up to the clubroom. Soon Henri was trilling his trombone and Mr Sedge leaned back at a table, a glass of lager before him, closed his eyes as the music began and gently drifted through a dream of jazz bliss, sipping in great moderation the joy of his palate and wallowing in emotional immoderation, deep in the stirring rhythms of a better than average jazz band with world class brass.

Chapter 14

At a long table in the Neophytes' Buttery, two lines of young men, pale-faced, apprehensive of the deed to come, faced each other and crunched buttered toast in silence of word and crackle of crumb. Such was the awe of the Restitutory Phalanx some two hours before it marched, that engraved on their brains became the wood sculpted calendar whose oaken letters proclaimed a date that they were privileged to see displayed, but of which others would only read, deep in the annals of the Company in ages long to come.

Some who dared bravado in the face of trepidation smeared a little pale-red strawberry jam on to the fingers of scorched bread which they held. More drank strong tea with little sugar and no milk. Those immersed in the spirit of the moment added much sour lemon juice and set their teeth purposely on edge. A bitter grimace for the turmoil of combat.

Grouped among the seated Phalanx were three of even height and even build whose drink was essence of pure lemon juice alone and whose conversation summarized the acerbic apprehension of them all. The one caught the eye of the other two. He astricted his abdomen.

'Excruciation,' he said, slowly, bitterly.

'Restitution,' snarled the other.

'Wine vinegar,' said the third.

'Gall.'

'Bile.'

'Concentrated ammonia,' came back the third, and the three of them winced in unison, sharpening their hate like scimitars.

The three of them glanced over the others. Their sentiments were general, their appearance uniform.

They wore at this moment their clinging black underwear: tailored cat-suits of the finest jet-black worsted, single garments with long sleeves, long legs and round necks fastened at the back by a cross-laced black silken cord, a second skin tailored at great expense, to be worn this once and never more. To be worn in victory and kept as a victor's prize or to be worn as the vanquished and burnt to black nothingness for shame at defeat.

At the ends of the arms these black bodysuits terminated in open-fingered gloves. The protruding digits raised and lowered toast; and the white napkins contrasted like snow on coal along the lines of their laps.

Their thoughts were turned inward, like a true knight's, to the need of valour in battle, to the need of honour at all accounts, to the doubts of ability to acquit oneself well in the fray, to the details of plans, learnt and to be remembered. The clock came to the half hour. The servants took their places behind the long stools. The Phalanx murmured thanks for their repast in the time-honoured chant, then stepped back over their stools and filed out to the robing room where others waited to accoutre them. As they left the buttery, the servants cleared the plates with deafening clatter and each remembered whose plates he cleared, so that one day he could dandle babes upon his knees and say: 'Before the Restitution it was I who cleared His plate,' and so bask a moment in the glory of the deeds of the valiant dead.

Those who would soon be vying for valour were now robed in full Restitutory Regalia. Aged men, long steeped in the lore of Founding and of Grinding, had striven for the chance to robe these splendoured youths, the flower of the Company's fitness, the muscular young arm of its ancient strength. Slowly each one drew on his damask-broidered sox and thereover squeezed the skin-tight battle-plaqued bell-breeches, impervious to thrust of sword or lance by virtue of the strips of bell-metal double-sewn in eider stuffing deep in the criss-crossed seams of these impervious belles culottes. Thereafter the magenta restitutory tunic, organ-pipe armoured in a brilliant and bedazzling curving breastplate of musical defence. Epaulettes of brass, gauntlets of finest chamois, hardened with studs of cedar wood. Each a pair of manacles hanging from his waspish waist.

Finally the old dressers raised themselves on stools and stood behind their charges. In their hands were casques, new cast, of the thinnest bell metal, which they lowered in ceremony over the neophytes' heads. These coverings of strife and battle replaced the nacre pagodas at times of earnest intent. One dress-ball remained, at the summit, but specially made for these helms of gilded, solid bronze. The sides of the helms descended in graceful curves to the ears whence straight down to the shoulders, where they spread to take support from the lath-tips of the brass epaulettes. With no head inside, each helm was tuned to resonate at its bearer's battle frequency. Just before lowering it to the neophyte's shoulder, the old and wise tapped the flawless bell-metal and the casque descended resonate and true not only to the shoulders, but, in its music, also to the heart and to the soul of each its bearer. The note stopped forever by the process of encampment, then rang forever in the mind of every Phalanx member. The fires of their spirits were kindled; from this time on, the bronze ball headbut was the fear of all adversary.

Robed, they left the robing room and filed to the library

for final briefing. The three whose bitterness surpassed all sweetening dared a whispered comment on these momentous times.

'What privilege to have a special rôle in this affair,' said the first of these young men.

'Indeed, and what a task to overcome our shame at the deeds of our co-founder,' said the second.

The third was obviously of a more practical turn of mind: 'Do you think lemon juice is really enough? I mean it embitters beautifully but wouldn't a good hot chilli make the drive to assure disaster to the contumacious more positive?'

'I do see what you mean,' said the first. 'It would add fire to excruciation.'

'Excruciating fire,' echoed the second; and added dreamily, 'we could go and engulf him in flames like that: the breath of justice.'

'Ah, but due process,' came back the first with wise admonition tempering his snarl. 'Due process there must be: no doom without judgment.'

'I suppose so,' sighed the second, consciously eddying his acid-laden breath across his palette. Then he nudged each companion in turn and passed them a couple of tiny packets wrapped in scraps of linen. 'Bread soaked in vinegar,' he said knowingly. 'Suck at the moment of our quarry's sighting.' They nodded and palmed the tiny packets, gloating inwardly at their unfair advantage.

In the library's central concourse they assembled and stood side by side, row on row as the Grand and other Masters filed in before them and the final talk of tactics and of action followed in its place.

The Grand Master stepped forward and gave them first their general briefing:

'You twenty-four,' he intoned, 'you three octaves of neophytes, you three peals of the mightiest music of the mightiest city in the world: this evening rests nigh a thousand years of our tradition in your hands.

'As you proceed to grasp the discordant note within our order, as your tuned hands seek out to clutch the untuned airs of contumacy, as your measured tread goes out to fulfil with royal wish and olden Company accord, the destiny of our time, remember the spirit of all our times and the centuries of our annals go with you.

'No Founder, no Grinder could ever wish one minim more than to be neophyte at the moment of contumacy. Shame in the very bellows of our organ must call our muscles to the pump; dishonour in the very bell tower of our manse must bring our finest sinews to pull our sweetest sallies. And you young music-men, whose shame it once has been to march in goodly order at the four square sides of the first blank file in four hundred and thirty-one years, to you it nobly falls to abnegate dishonour, to you it nobly falls to rid us of ingratitude, to you it nobly falls to place upon ourselves the first, in all these years' undying archive, of a full-scale restitution.

'Your actions must be one in harmony, a fugue of interwoven effort. Your actions must be rigid-rhythmed, filled with breachless regularity; the variant, inscrutable rolling of a well-timed peal. This peal will hail our greatness in our deeds, this peal will hail your greatness in our scrolls. If some of you excel and merit scrolls, be it so well. But let not one of you be unworthy of the archive. If there be single valour, good; but of all it is the common valour counts. Without the deed of all, the deed of one is lost; without the common will, one will is but a wish. Wishes will not suffice, deeds alone will do.

'Fix now the visage of our hunted vassal firmly in your minds. See the here-suspended picture, mark it well. Chase him. Chase that man down the crowded years of time; chase him to the ends of England, but chase him and take him; take him and bring him here where we in reasoned judgement shall arraign him for his deeds and find our verdict.

'I leave you to these experts for your final brief.' He indicated here the Bell and Organ Masters: 'But first one final, vital ceremony.

'There are some three among you picked and volunteered for special service. They it is shall precede the mighty Phalanx. As you are underway toward the restitution ground, three shall form a vanguard and take post near the place. So installed, they it is shall stop all prior bolting of the quarry. Step forward the Special Duties Group!'

At the Grand Master's invocation three regaled neophytes, the same bitter three, stepped out from the assembled Phalanx. They came along beside the rows of ancient book cases to just below the low dais on which the Grand Master stood. They waited expectantly, robed and hatted, proud and flattered. The Grand Master clapped his hands. Three of the aged dressers entered, one behind another, each with a golden salver in his hands and each with the salver held before him as a presentation of great value and esteem. On each salver was a folded garment and each garment held in offering to the group: the badge or cloth of rank or duty to designate this special force.

'To do this duty,' spake the Grand Master, 'these youths must stand in soiled overall disguise,' a gasp of distaste arose from the band, 'and not just soiled overall disguise; but must do so before a public house in one of the most disreputable areas that our neighbouring city of Westminster has to offer.' At the mention of Westminster an even greater gasp of disapproval arose.

'Step forth,' he commanded to the first salver-bearer. A small, slightly stooping man with silver grey hair shuffled forward, all honour and obsequiousness on his face. From the salver, the Grand Master proudly took, and lifted by the shoulders, a pair of carefully soiled overalls. They dropped unfolded and hung bespeckled with grease and paint before the reverent Phalanx. The suit had been tailor-made for the neophyte in question, professionally distorted to simulate real wear, selectively soiled and aged and randomly bespattered with the mess of hard labour under a special commission to one to the nation's most famous artists. The final product was exquisite in its verisimilitude and could only have been told from the true article under close scrutiny by an expert workman.

The first of the Special Duties Group stepped forward and, with slow and graceful movements, pulled on the overalls above his regalia. A second dresser came forward and removed the bronze helm from his head. He placed it on the now empty salver and lowered on to the neophyte a plastic safety helmet with simulated mud and concrete spatterings and fictive marks of dropped bricks. The disguise was perfect. Only the person inside it was now recognizable as a Founder and Grinder.

With similar ceremony the other two members of the Special Duties Group were disguised, then given bricklayers' holdalls to carry their battle casques, to be worn once cover was broken. Almost in that moment was the bitterness of preparation submerged in the feelings of humble honour which awoke in the chosen three.

'That of all young men of all the world, I it is who lead in the epoch of restitution, is scarce believable,' thought one; while the others thought, 'In this is my bitterness made sweet,' and, 'In my gall, my all.' Their hearts beat, fast and almost unbelieving.

'Once briefed, forth!' declared the Grand Master. 'Of this day will you all be proud when, as old men, the hand of death is near and you recall the glories of your lives.'

He departed to his chambers. Once he was gone, the

Bell and Organ Masters, assisted by the Clerk, turned to the final briefing. With map and chart and much fine wording they traced the route, described the tactics, exhorted the Phalanx to perfection. With trembling hearts, the briefing finished, the Phalanx formed in the Great Hall. They were ready to march.

Sergeant Apta Dapta walked up and down the lines of policemen standing smartly at ease after their briefing, late on Wednesday afternoon. The white collars against the dark-blue uniforms, the flower-pots and flat hats all in perfect order, Metropolitan badges shining in regulation brilliance. With a sharp word of command he dismissed them to their posts. Like well-prepared men, they all went and urinated and then proceeded to their vehicles to await radio instructions. These were not long in coming.

The incomprehensible fuzzy garble of the personal radio crackled and boomed. The operation had started. Slowly, two large vans, each with eleven policemen and a driver, nosed out of the police station. One van was green and the other blue. Not exactly unidentifiable since their load was clearly visible through the windows; but not very conspicuous anyway.

They were followed by a third miniature van, cramped in the back of which were three Albany Street constables, the elephant keeper and his assistant; and the zoo vet. These six formed the elephant unit.

'This is going to be very interesting,' said the vet, nervous and not quite knowing what to say.

'If anyone's hurt my elephants, I'll do him,' said the elephant keeper.

After a little turn around the West End they pulled into Broadwick Street and parked outside the post office where a strategically positioned constable had kept the kerb clear for them. There they waited again.

Sergeant Apta Dapta, once the vans were gone, strapped on his personal radio to take overall command of the operation and then went to the ground floor of the police station to draw his secret weapon. It was an old, black bicycle kept lovingly at the ready in a special bay of the street-level garage. He had had it in Bradford when he first took up a post in the force. It had rattled his bones on those cobbled streets many a night and it had become, across the years, one of his most valued tools in the fight against organized crime. When the vans and patrol cars got stuck hours long in jams, he breezed past on the old black bone-shaker and beat them to the scene. With a little metallic snap, he lovingly unhooked the trouser-clips from the cross bar and put them on his ankles. With a quick check of the tyre pressures and the lights, he straddled the vice bike and pedalled off into Soho. He cruised round the quarter for twenty minutes or so just to be sure all looked well, then pedalled north along Wardour Street, taking care to look into Tyler's Court as he puffed past. Near the northern end he turned left and rode through to join the vans at Broadwick Street. He took out his radio:

'Paint Pot, this is Vice Bike,' he called on the radio. PC Monica Sullivan heard the crackling call sign on top of her scaffold.

'Paint Pot,' she replied.

'Block the Wardour Street entrance. Over,' commanded Sergeant Dapta.

'Wilco. Out,' came back the reply.

She quickly gathered her tools together and took a white and red sign, hitherto hidden amongst her paint pots. It prohibited entry to pedestrians and directed them along the pavement. She scrambled down the scaffold tower and hung the sign on it near the bottom. Then she unclipped the wheel locks and pushed the tower right to the outer limit of the alleyway where it joined the Wardour Street pavement. There she locked the wheels again. Making sure her overall properly concealed her radio, she climbed the tower once more and sat on its top, apparently filling a crack in the ceiling: in reality keeping a sharp eye out for any signs of people leaving.

'Vice Bike, this is Paint Pot,' came back PC Sullivan on the radio.

'Vice Bike,' replied Sergeant Apta Dapta.

'Passage blocked as planned,' reported PC Monica Sullivan. 'The whole of that jazz band that play in the club upstairs have arrived and they seem to be practising. I can hear the odd toot of a trumpet or two. Anyone else who's there must have been there since before I came on station in the morning. Our little bald bloke with the briefcase isn't around but a handcart-load of old veg went in fifteen minutes ago. Over.'

'Good work, Paint Pot,' came back the Sergeant. 'Pity about the little bloke, he might turn out to be Mr Big. Anyway, if the veg is going in, the beasts should be all right. Sit tight and wait for further instructions. Out.'

'Roger. Out,' came the reply.

A few hundred metres away, at the junction of Oxford Street and Berwick Street, a black taxi had pulled up and four men were getting out. They were a strange quartet and it was only with some effort that the driver managed to ignore them properly. Three were dressed in identically soiled overalls, with identically cement-spattered and brick-damaged hard hats. The fourth, although dressed in white overalls and with a cloth cap on, and therefore presumably the foreman, somehow didn't quite have the air of a foreman about him. Perhaps it was the way he carried a briefcase in the most self-conscious of inconspicuous manners. Anyway, he paid the fare and they all walked south along Berwick Street, one behind the other on the narrow pavements, rather like a file of soldiers who had starched their camouflage and so weren't quite sure whether to be on their best behaviour or their worst.

Before long they were dutifully standing near the wall of the King of Corsica, pints in hand, raising and lowering glasses without drinking very much at all. In little furtive whispers they cued each other to take turns in fixedly watching the entrance to the alley.

'Assa!' said the Clerk, with a piercing whisper, for it was naturally he in the cloth cap. This exclamation was a virulent, serpentine version of 'How's that?' expressing urgency, success, caution, danger and surprise all in one. The object of this outburst was Henri himself, whom the Clerk had seen coming out of the alley with his hand barrow; going back, in fact, to pick up a second load of elephant fodder. One of the accompanying neophytes choked on his beer at the outburst, one cringed in fear and the third looked around bewilderingly trying to see what was afoot. The Clerk turned his back on Henri so as not to be recognized and instructed the others to watch him. Henri loaded three cases of old veg on to his barrow and trundled it back to the alleyway, occasionally giving a hello or a nod of the head to stallholders he knew on the way.

They waited and Henri did not appear again. They were assured of their quarry if only their luck held.

While they were waiting, the Restitutory Phalanx had marched. Three ranks of seven stepping in battle gear splendid along Holborn Viaduct and now coming up the rise towards the Gryphons near the junction with Gray's Inn Road. The Bell Master strode before, plainly proclaiming the rhythm of the march with the steady swinging of his legs. The Organ Master came behind, flowing over the road in even-measured ease. Behind them all came the Company's black Rolls-Royce with the Grand Master himself, seated centrally on the cream-coloured leather of the soft rear seat, holding in a white-gloved hand the Letter of Assent. The car moved silently forward at the pace of the Phalanx. The Worshipful Company's pennant fluttered from time to time from the small mast at the forward roof of the car.

As the Phalanx approached the Gryphons, the Organ Master took from his bosom a single organ pipe of about a half-cubit's length. He placed it transverse across his mouth with the air intake to his lips. He gave a single sharp toot. It was a moment all neophytes had waited for for four hundred and thirty-one years. He paused, then gave a double toot and at once the right hands of the left-hand column, the right hands of the centre column, and the left hands of the right-hand column shot into the air and grasped the bronze dress balls at the top of the casques. There was a pause of three marching paces. The Bell Master, then the first rank, drew abreast the Gryphons. The Organ Master gave three toots: as the left foot came down on the next pace, twenty-four casques were upped in unison; perfect, delicious unison; whipped off the heads by their bearers and held straight aloft on arms as true as organ pipes. As the left foot came down on the following pace with a simple sweeping movement, the left-hand column swung their raised arms to the right, the right-hand column swung their raised arms to the left and the centre column stayed with raised arms stock-still. The battle casques met with deafening redound.

Secretaries, clerks and shop assistants scurrying to bus stops and Chancery Lane tube station, stopped and watched a moment as the clang defeated the noise of the traffic. As the resonance subsided they saw the casques turned bell-like above their owners' heads again and, on the fourth marching pace from the redound, descend vibrant in a single vertical motion on to the heads of their owners: once more resonated with the importance of their task, once more steeled to the capture that lay before them.

Onward they marched into Holborn, oblivious of traffic signs, traffic lights and the chaos they caused. No-one seemed to mind very much, so official was their presence it could not possibly be unknown to the authorities. They branched into New Oxford Street and then, with goggling tourists, uninterested motorists and distraught traffic wardens, straight on into Oxford street itself, leaving an unresolved fund of chaos at the junction with the Charing Cross Road. Car drivers obeying green lights stamped on their brakes to avoid mowing down the Phalanx and bus drivers obeying red lights laughed or fussed or waved in glee at the unexpected spectacle before them.

Weaving about between buses and taxis, roared past by motorcycle messengers, buzzed past by bicycle couriers, they passed the junction with Wardour street and prepared to turn left into Berwick Street.

The Organ Master held aloft two half-cubit pipes, one in each hand; and signalled the left turn by dropping the left hand in that direction. They were near their goal; and, in the ranks, the pits of stomachs were churning; and sweat, cold and clammy, was breaking out on the heads of the marching neophytes. Beneath their battle-casques they gritted their teeth and, to themselves, hummed stirling organ themes to steel their quaking souls for the task ahead. Once again the Organ Master held aloft the half-cubit pipes: this time crossed as a signal. When the pipes uncrossed, the long-learnt, long-rehearsed plan for recovery would come into action. The left foot came down, the pipes uncrossed, the Phalanx broke into

Restitutory Trot and from the Grand Master's Rolls-Royce came a horn blast to urge on the Phalanx and galvanize the faint-hearted.

Henri, now a practised hand at manoeuvring a coster-monger's barrow, bumped it down the steps and through the door, which banged to behind him. He trundled it through to the warehouse and stacked the crates in their usual place against the wall. Rumpus Pumpus was just going out into the light well to take up his trumpet position. Finta Fanta was already under the hatch and gently flapping one ear to the tunes above.

'You know that painter outside has completely blocked the alley at the Wardour Street end,' said Henri. 'I wonder if Mr Sedge wasn't right about there being something suspicious about her.' He then left and ran up the stairs to take up position with his trombone. Rumpus Pumpus looked back in towards Finta Fanta.

'Blocked the passage, eh?' he said. She raised an eyebrow and looked darkly at Rumpus Pumpus.

'I think that's a danger signal,' she said. 'Carry on practising but get ready to put our escape plans into action.' Rumpus Pumpus nodded. 'And keep an ear open for sirens, though I don't suppose they'd normally give us the luxury of a warning.'

They both turned to their music and practised heartily. But in the first pause, Finta Fanta threw back all but one of the bolts on the roller shutter to the alleyway and then turned to her trumpeting in a much calmer frame of mind.

Sergeant Apta Dapta looked at his watch. The last seconds reeled off; time to go.

'Block One, this is Vice Bike,' he called.

'Block One. Over.'

'Position. Over.'

'Wilco. Out.'

Four hefty constables, two with da-glo armbands, leapt into action at the southern end of Wardour Street. One grabbed four traffic pylons and plonked them across the road, directing all the traffic into Brewer Street. The other three leapt into the patrol car and followed the last vehicle northward until immediately south of Tyler's Court. Here they slewed the car across the street, blocking it entirely. Two got out and looked important; giving a thumbs-up to Police Constable Monica Sullivan, still on top of her scaffold but busily ripping off her overalls to reveal her police uniform underneath.

'Block Two, this is Vice Bike,' continued Sergeant Apta Dapta.

'Block Two. Over.'

'Position. Over.'

'Wilco. Out.'

And a little police mini turned out of d'Arblay Street and headed south along Berwick Street. As it came to the market, the officer driving it made little taps on the horn to warn the pedestrians of its presence. The pedestrians cleared the busy centre of the road and the mini, barely small enough to pass between the rows of stalls and piles of crates, nosed its way carefully along until just south of Tyler's Court.

The costermongers, some now packing up their stalls, others rubbing shoulders with the Special Duties Group of the Founders and Grinders outside the King of Corsica, cocked eyebrows at each other. A police mini in the market; something was afoot. As the constable from the passenger seat of the mini got out and looked carefully round, dozens of pairs of eyes turned idly away but sharpened nonetheless their observation of events and exchanged warning glances one with another. Unnoticed to all but an experienced few, bundles of notes moved from the hands of costermongers to the hands of costermongers' wives, to be secreted about their persons in the motherly embrace of intimate seclusion. When something was afoot, it was best to spread your risks.

The driver of the mini reported back to Sergeant Apta Dapta that they were in position, then got out himself ready for action in case someone should bolt from Tyler's Court. At that moment, in fact, bolting from Tyler's Court was the last thing anyone really had in mind except, perhaps, the elephants. The Restitutory Phalanx was fast approaching, the police were fast approaching and the band played on. Just for a few preparatory seconds, calm reigned. Then the storm began.

Now knowing that all his men were in position, Sergeant Apta Dapta launched the raid. From the vans outside the post office in Broadwick Street, twenty-five burly bobbies, bursting to leave boot-prints across the unacceptable face of vice in Soho, swirled into the road and dashed in that utterly determined, bustling half-run that all the best policemen seem to develop. Into Berwick Street they poured, heading for Tyler's Court. They kept no ranks but wove their way like flying dark-blue shuttles through the threads and knots of bystanders, who were by now starting to take a semi-professional interest in the whole affair.

But as the policemen were about to rush in amongst the stalls of Berwick Street, the two right-hand files of the Restitutory Phalanx in the full momentum of Restitutory Trot ran into the market as well, barging policemen, costermongers and passers-by in what was now a fury of righteous assault, to break their way through to the contumacious Grinder.

The left-hand column peeled off left through the eastern end of Broadwick Street and then right into Wardour Street. Their job it was to secure the eastern end of Tyler's

Court which, on arrival, they found blocked by Police Constable Monica Sullivan's scaffold tower. At once they started to scramble through it into the alleyway. At this, the two constables at the road block immediately ran forward, uncertain whether to laugh or be harsh with this bunch of oddly clad freaks who seemed to be in danger of disrupting their long-laid plans.

If laughter there was, it was short lived. Three of the Phalanx were just about through the scaffold tower and into the alley when the policemen reached them, remonstrating at the tops of their voices.

The Bell Master, who had followed this file at three trotting paces, turned and faced the policemen with an awesome rage upon his face.

'Right of antecedent pre-eminence!' he roared in a voice that rang clear and hard and brought the two policemen to a halt with its force and indignation. It was hardly the language of ne'er-do-wells; and something in the bearing of this party was indeed haughty and authoritative. What was more, the phrase rang a vague bell in the back of the mind. Like one of those interesting little lawyer's asides during the lectures on criminal practice.

But the policemen shrugged off their doubts and came on, reaching out to grab the Bell Master and the last two members of the Phalanx who were just about to clamber through the scaffold. Quick as a flash the three Founders and Grinders turned on the policemen and with a snap-clang and a snap-chang they whipped their manacles from their belts, snapped them over the policemen's wrists and snapped the other end over the bars of the scaffold. In fury at being hoodwinked by the onset of an educated voice, the police attempted to reply in kind. But they only succeeded in securing their own handcuffs to the scaffold, with no-one in the other end. They were forced to resort to shouting at Police Constable Monica Sullivan to come down and help them. Yet before she could properly call up Sergeant Apta Dapta to tell him what was happening, a commotion at the other end of the alleyway made her turn and wonder even more amazedly what was going on.

A kind of impromptu rugby scrum seemed to be taking place behind a human barrier of three workmen in identically soiled overalls. A foreman in white was with them and they had wedged themselves across the narrow alley, trying to stop a dozen policemen forcing their way in. This would have been hopeless, of course, were it not that the policemen were mixed up with and sandwiched by a cohort of those half-armoured medieval-looking heralds who seemed to be trying to jump and trample over everyone in a heroic effort to penetrate first into the passage.

The Special Duties Group outside the King of Corsica had, of course, seen the two columns of the Restitutory Phalanx trot into the hurly-burly of policemen and run and wrestle their way through the debris of the closing market towards the entrance of Tyler's Court. With commendable alacrity, to be forever inscribed in the annals of the Company, the Clerk had ordered a rush to the entrance of the alley where four, such as they, could block the way to twenty. Grounding drinks and holdalls in a lightning movement they had leapt out between the barrows, across the road, past the police mini and between the other row of barrows opposite, to the entrance of the alley. One of the three in the Special Duties Group grabbed the large imitation grass cloth that had yet to be removed from the stall near the entrance and with a throw, lucky indeed, but nonetheless worthy of a retiarius, had cast the blanket-sized cover over the oncoming policeman. As the constable had stumbled and fallen, bringing down a couple of his colleagues in the process, the Special Duties Group had slipped in and blocked the way: but were now being forced inexorably backwards by the pressure of about thirty people upon them. Snapping out of her amazement, Police Constable Monica Sullivan called Sergeant Apta Dapta on her radio:

'Vice Bike, Paint Pot. Over.'

'Vice Bike. Over.'

'It's all going wrong! There's a crowd of carnival characters and some house-painters trying to bar our way. And they've handcuffed Block One to my scaffold! Over!'

'What? Over.'

'They've handcuffed our blokes from Block One to the scaffold and now they're ringing on the door of the club.'

Upstairs, Pete Davis was sitting one out and picked up the entry-phone by the bar.

'Who's there?'

'It's the barman, I've forgotten my key,' said the neophyte, as planned.

'Okay. Wait a moment,' said Pete Davis. He then told the others, who smelt a rat at once. The barman wasn't due in for another two hours.

'Better go down and see who it is,' said Henri, who put away his trombone and moved towards the trap door which led down to Finta Fanta, just in case. Pete Davis went downstairs.

In the alley outside, Police Constable Monica Sullivan suddenly saw the rugby scrum broken by a particularly burly constable who wielded in his hands a formidable-looking sledge-hammer.

Although, compared to the worshipful companies, the Vice Squad had virtually no tradition at all worthy of the name, one of its primary tenets, amounting to a standing practice if not to a tradition, properly established, was that during a raid, at least one door must be smashed open with a sledge-hammer. Even if nothing was found, it left tangible evidence of the raid and it left visible warning to the neighbourhood. Like Police Constable Monica Sullivan, the sledge-hammer man had seen the neophyte ring the doorbell. He had felt the barrage of the Special Duties Group starting to give and, incensed that such underhand methods as ringing doorbells might be used, burst free of the mêlée with a lung-breaking roar. Heaving the Clerk back against the wall with an elbow very much stronger than that of any City bureaucrat, he dashed for the door with a roaring cry of:

'Stand back!' and 'Follow me!'

Despite the inconsistency of the two commands, the struggling mass appeared to get the general idea because Police Constable Monica Sullivan was able to report live to Sergeant Apta Dapta:

'Wait a moment! Yes! Vice has broken out. Vice is on top. George has burst through with the sledge-hammer, he's running for the door. Those clown characters haven't got any stomach for it, they've leapt out of the way. Here comes George! Oh no!'

'Paint Pot. Vice Bike. What's happened? Over,' urged the Sergeant.

'Vice Bike. Paint Pot. Oh! The door opened! Just as he got to it. He leapt down the steps, swung the sledge hammer and as he brought it down the door opened. He smashed himself on the toe-cap and fell head over heels inside. The clowns seem to have leapt in over him. And now everybody's stuck in the doorway of the club and no-one seems to have the faintest idea what's going on.

'Permission to go and find out. Over.'

'Paint Pot. Vice Bike. Stay put! You're much better off where you are by the sound of it. Is anyone stopping them get in? Over.'

'Vice Bike. No, it's a kind of running riot but everyone seems to be cramming in. Over.'

'Paint Pot. Vice Bike. Right, I'm on my way in myself.

Stay put. Over.'

'Vice Bike. Wilco. Out.'

The Sergeant flexed his muscles, checked his trouser-clips, swung his leg over the vice bike and, with his jaw set firm, pushed away from the kerb by the post office and made for Wardour Street – apparently the only entrance he could hope to get in by.

The elephant unit followed him away, scurrying smartly down between the stalls as planned, following up the vice squad and the chaos; a little band of specialists in the wake of the general charge.

Looking down Berwick Street as he passed the end of the market, Sergeant Apta Dapta could see a large crowd of guffawing costermongers trying to look along the alley which the constables who had been in the mini now sealed off with commendable initiative.

However, as he was pedalling round to the Wardour Street entrance, the brawl in the passageway moved to the foot of the stairs leading up to the clubroom. Pete Davis, having stood back in the recess by the box office as the cartwheeling policeman with the sledge-hammer had come flying past him, now gaped in amazement as a tussling knot of Founders and Grinders wrestled their way to the concrete stairway, somehow simultaneously arresting and being arrested by a more or less equal number of now very red-faced Metropolitan Policemen. Suddenly, Pete Davis remembered Henri had warned him that some sort of violent pageant of this nature might occur to try and get him back in the bosom of the Worshipful Company. Taking a vast lungful of air, he roared up the stairs:

'Henri! It's the Worshipful Company! And half the Metropolitan Police too, by the look of it.' He shouted with a broad grin on his face as he now watched the colourful human wave struggle up the stairs to the clubroom with much gasping and barging.

But Henri needed no second warning. At the first confirmation of the Worshipful Company, he raised the hatch in the clubroom and scrambled down on to Finta Fanta's trunk, dropping the hatch behind him. He struggled along to her neck, about to scramble for the door to the light well, when Finta Fanta checked him with a timely trunk stroke.

'Stay put,' she whispered commandingly. 'It's all worked out. Hang on tight.'

She lowered his trombone to safety amongst the packing cases under the roller conveyor and nodded to Rumpus Pumpus. With a deft swipe of the trunk, Rumpus Pumpus threw back the one remaining bolt holding the roller shutter, threw up the shutter itself with a deafening clatter, turned with remarkable agility and backed out into the alleyway as if he were gliding on castors. Wild panic now broke out amongst the dozen or so policemen and liverymen still trying to get into the club door. They had not bargained with the backside of an elephant bearing down on them in the narrow alley. Under their helmets and battle-casques, their hair stood on end – a most exotic sensation – two of them turned and fled, the others crushed even quicker into the doorway; and one fainted on the spot. Carefully stepping over the unconscious policeman, Rumpus Pumpus backed up until Finta Fanta in her turn came backing out, crouching to get Henri, who was on her neck, under the lintel.

Once in line, facing the Wardour Street exit, the two elephants trumpeted at the top of their voices. Snaking her trunk up to Henri, Finta Fanta explained in a tone of deadly earnest calm:

'Hang on for your life. This is going to be a stampede and I can tell you that's no light matter.'

At this moment Sergeant Apta Dapta arrived at the scaffold and leant his bike against it. Looking at the two policemen manacled to the structure, he went pale with rage:

'What do you two . . .' he started to shout, summoning his most cutting admonitions from the depths of his outrage, when his pallor turned positively white as he looked beyond the scaffold and saw Finta Fanta raise her trunk and trumpet. And with her ears flapping till they touched the walls on either side, he saw her begin what he knew only too well was the start of that dreaded event, the stampede. Police Constable Monica Sullivan screamed and gripped the rails of the scaffold tower with whitened knuckles. The elephant came on and with a crash Finta Fanta thrust her head between the scaffold bars as Sergeant Apta Dapta leapt clear in the nick of time.

The wheel locks on the scaffold tower broke at once; down went the vice bike, up went the manacled constables who, in precarious positions worthy of a circus act, saved their arms from being wrenched off by jumping on to the lower rungs of the tower and being carried along with it.

At this moment the elephant unit entered the other end of the alleyway. With a unanimous shout of 'There they are! After them!' they dashed forward in the wake of the elephants, expecting to calm them down for a docile and triumphant return to the zoo. Such a return, however, formed no part of the elephants' intentions.

As planned, Finta Fanta veered immediately to the right but, as was not planned, there she saw before her the large police car athwart the road. Pirouetting with a most unelephantine suppleness, she swerved to the left, scaffold tower still attached to her head and started north along Wardour Street.

'Left and left again!' tooted Rumpus Pumpus from behind. With the vagaries of such an unpredictable enterprise in view, he had memorized all the relevant pages of the *A to Z* as perhaps only an elephant can.

'Round the block!' he tooted.

Finta Fanta responded with renewed effort and, apparently unable to disengage herself from the tower, picked up speed as she rushed towards the junction with Broadwick Street. At this point Henri regained his wits a little and sat up to see where he was, disengaging himself from the jangling scaffold. At the same moment, Police Constable Monica Sullivan also dared to open her eyes and, of course, could not believe them. Not only was she being propelled through Soho on top of an elephant's tea trolley, but there, staring her in the face was the very man she had seen at Park Crescent abducting the elephants which she was seeking. Like any good policewoman in the circumstances, she arrested him immediately. Leaning over the jangling, jerking scaffold rail, she grabbed Henri's left arm in a complicated-looking wrestling hold and snapped one end of her handcuffs on his wrist. As was now the established fashion in this part of London, she snapped the other end on to the scaffold. At that moment Finta Fanta dived left into Broadwick Street, the scaffold tower actually making the turn on two wheels. The awful sensation of being in the crow's nest of some reeling ship gripped Police Constable Monica Sullivan's stomach; while Henri found himself at full stretch, his feet just retaining their purchase on Finta Fanta's neck and his upper body suspended over the road below from the handcuff above. To Henri's infinite relief, the tower, after cornering wildly for a moment, righted itself and led the stampede once more. But Finta Fanta decided she had had enough of it and, not knowing Henri was handcuffed to the structure, prised her head free with tusk and trunk so that she was now butting the tower along with each running step, making it not only sway but jump up and down even more alarmingly than before.

With a glint in her eye, she saw looming up the left turn

round the block into Berwick Street and, with a final but of her mighty forehead, sent the scaffold tower careering straight on along Broadwick Street, while the elephants turned south along Berwick Street to complete their escape route.

Henri, of course, had no alternative but to go with the tower. He separated from Finta Fanta with a strangled cry and the look of a marionette suddenly pulled off the stage to hang like a pendulum from the proscenium arch. Police Constable Monica Sullivan let out a whoop of triumph as her suspect joined her willy-nilly; but the whoop turned to a scream as she realized that the tower, now let loose of all control, was careering around like the galley tea-trolley in a raging typhoon. Henri and the police constables found themselves whipped around on a most unmerry merry-go-round, turning half circles and back again, full circles and on again while the bumps in the road repeatedly made one wheel or another leap and lurch. The whole tower leaned, righted itself and leaned again in the most unpredictable manner.

But this progress was not to stop unchecked. In the middle of Broadwick Street the iron-railed public lavatory loomed up suddenly in their path like an island in the track of a rudderless speedboat at full throttle. The shock was terrible. A lamp-post fell like a skittle. A couple of motorbikes parked outside were knocked over like dominoes. One wheel of the tower mounted the narrow pavement, throwing the whole scaffold out of balance as it careered into the railing and started to fall like a trellis-work caber about to go head over heels into the roof of the underground lavatory. The slope on the platform became too steep. Police Constable Monica Sullivan, shaken and off balance, fell as the tower hit the railings. But even as she fell, the tower locked itself at a drunken angle and Henri, still suspended by his handcuff from above, reached out and grabbed her by the ankle. With a wrench and a jerk and a final to-ing and fro-ing of the springiness of the tower, all came at last to rest. The two constables slowly unwound themselves from their position in their cage and looked up at the leaning structure to see, suspended from its topmost rail, Henri, one arm above his head in the handcuff and the other being pulled downward as part of a human chain. For, suspended from his other hand was Police Constable Monica Sullivan, legs uppermost, head downward, her nose but a few precious centimetres from the wicked iron spikes atop the railing round the old convenience. She heaved a sigh of relief. And when the bouncing in the structure had stopped at last, the driver of the nearby police van managed to help her down. Soon after which she was able to unlock Henri and re-lock him again in the back of the aptly placed van.

They both slumped on the seats in the back. Her feeling of triumph now strongly tempered with the mercy of gratitude, she closed her eyes and breathed deeply. Henri did the same.

An elephant stampede is a terrible thing. Such mass of animal muscle, such irresistible movement. It is like a living earthquake, an event beside which all other animal things are weak and insignificant. Despite all this, the elephants in a stampede do not really run but adopt a unique kind of accelerated walk so that, despite the speed and the power, there is an element of tip-toeing about it – an odd movement in many ways.

These finer points, however, were understandably lost on most of those caught up in the events. As Finta Fanta rid herself of the troublesome tower, she took the left-hand turn into Berwick Street somewhat wide. Rumpus Pumpus came up on the inside and slipped into the lead, realizing now exactly the route they would have to take and giving Finta Fanta time to recover from her scaffold wrestling.

As he came to the front, Rumpus Pumpus saw Berwick Street market stretched before him and just for a second he had a brief doubt. The stalls were mostly closed now, but stood in the light of the May evening with crates and boxes still piled up about them. Worse in fact: with many a crate and box piled in the narrow defile between the two rows of stalls. And an elephant is a powerful animal and knows its power in its mind and in its bones. And knows what damage may be done in the mere world of men when its freedom and its person is at stake and liberty stands as the prize, over against the penalty of captivity.

Rumpus Pumpus let forth a trumpet blast that stopped the market street dead upon its tracks. Costermongers looked up from their boxes of old cabbages, and pedestrians stopped, transfixed a moment in mid-stride, before turning to view with wide-eyed awe the elephants, paused for a second before some awful rush. The knot of lookers-on, straining at the police cordon at the end of the alley ceased to strain in that direction and turned to look in another: in the direction from which that trumpeting had come. Their jaws dropped like drawbridges, falling to let in disbelief. Their eyes grew like balloons, fit to pop at what they saw.

'Oh . . . oh . . . oh,' murmured a sturdy, but now deathly pale costermonger who had seen service in Kenya and knew the tell-tale signs of elephantine activity.

'Oh . . . oh . . . No!' he screamed. Alone of all those standing there transfixed, he rushed across the road, grabbed the handles of his barrow and managed to turn it and pull it up on to the broader pavement not far from the King of Corsica. Well for him that he did. Woe for the others they did not. For as that lone barrow rattled up the kerb, Rumpus Pumpus and Finta Fanta in line astern and with full power thrusting in their limbs, began the terrifying stampede for honour and for freedom.

On they came. A pile of packing cases flew like woodchips in a hurricane from Rumpus Pumpus' foreleg. A barrow jutted into the road and caught his shoulder. The sturdy wooden framework bounced away in a cracking of timber. The wheels fell off against the kerb and the barrow lurched sideways across the pavement.

Suddenly the seriousness of the situation seemed to dawn on the passers-by and the lookers-on. They dived for cover: ignominious marmots of the Berwick Street savanna bolting for the safety of their burrow doors. Aghast, they saw a second stall, surrounded by packing cases, knocked aside. Finta Fanta's mighty feet came down on the boxes as they slewed all over the road. A tremendous squirt of squashed red cabbage and over-ripe oranges leapt from beneath her and spattered over the cowering drinkers trying to disappear from in front of the pub.

'Aaaah,' they cried in fear and disgust. But the word changed to 'Ayyy', as suddenly they all saw what Rumpus Pumpus had seen at the start of his charge and now realized was an inevitable casualty of the course of action being taken. As Rumpus Pumpus well knew, the police mini completely blocked his path.

Now certain that no-one was inside that doomed diminutive of automotive encumbrances, Rumpus Pumpus came upon it with all the determined attack of a decision long taken being executed at its best. His left forefoot rose from the ground and his great momentum carried it forward on to the back of the car. As his weight swung forward, the car crumpled with a shattering of glass and a crunching of metal that made the onlooking policemen wince with pain. The right foot passed on to the upstanding wreck. The opposite corner collapsed in sympathy with the first and left a sort of metal hillock in the road which one of his rear feet pressed upon and reduced to a pale metallic pimple in the midst of a debris of rubber and glass.

Finta Fanta, following, trampled on in suit. Her passage flattened the remains and, as she kicked the engine section sideways for good measure, the block burst out of the carcase of the car with a heart-rending crash and lay for a second like a scrap of automotive litter to be kicked like a Coke can into the gutter by the insouciant feet of the monster passing by.

The policemen at the alley entrance knew not what to do. Their hands went to truncheons, to radios, to mouths and to backs of necks; wielding, switching, sucking and scratching in an exasperated semaphore of procedural habit and completely inhabitual reflex. Finally, realizing their crowd had dispersed, they turned into the alleyway to make for the club.

Rumpus Pumpus and Finta Fanta stampeded on. To its great credit, the elephant unit, now puffing and panting and positively keeping its distance, followed on foot as best it could. The elephants crashed through a couple more stalls, though avoiding many more, and swerved left into Peter Street where, thanks to Wardour Street being blocked by the police, the narrow way was open to let them pass. Then they turned south along Wardour Street itself, past the pylon road block and the astonished young constable directing traffic in the way, and on and on along the route that Rumpus Pumpus now knew he had to follow to its end, if there was to be any hope at all of some brief independence and an honourable life.

The constables who had turned into the alleyway to make for the club saw, coming towards them from the far end, visibly shaken but still very much in command,

Sergeant Apta Dapta, now heading for The Splurge where obviously the débâcle, which this all seemed to be, would achieve some kind of explanation.

The Sergeant tried to call up Police Constable Monica Sullivan on the radio, but, failing to reach her, pressed on into the club, detailing off the two constables to secure the lower premises and also the roller shutter which the forensic scientist arrived to investigate if need be.

Sergeant Apta Dapta climbed the stair in the club and was already well aware, from before the first step, that there was a furious argument in progress in the clubroom above. As he came through the door he saw the incredible spectacle of twenty or so policemen grappling hand to hand with twenty or so liverymen, all trying to clap handcuffs on each other, arrest one another and warn off the others in a cacophony of authoritarian language issuing from the hailest lungs in the land. Odd constables were handcuffed to drum kits and lager pumps, and odd Founders and Grinders were handcuffed to tables and trap door rings. Policemen were shouting at the tops of their voices for everyone to come quietly, while everyone else seemed to be shouting at the police to tell them they were breaking the law. Everyone seemed to have done exactly the same training, so that the mass of men were in a kind of tense and clanking deadlock in various heaps around the room with no-one actually able to impose himself on anyone else and no-one actually listening to what anyone was saying.

Sergeant Apta Dapta took off his helmet, threw it on the floor in disgust and, in a gesture of supreme exclamation, booted it indiscriminately like a football in the hope it would relieve his own feelings and maybe do something that would break this quite unconscionable scrum. It did. The helmet flew from his foot through the air above the grimacing antagonists and smashed through the light well window with a horrible crash, itself duplicated a moment later when the large plates of broken glass smashed again on to the concrete below.

The noise brought the mêlée to a standstill.

'Now,' screamed Sergeant Apta Dapta. 'Just what on earth is going on?' There was a stunned silence. Then in a calm, urbane and cutting voice from behind his back Sergeant Apta Dapta heard:

'I think it is I who should be asking you that question.' And the Sergeant turned to see the Grand Master of The Worshipful Company of Bell Founders and Organ Grinders standing imposingly behind him in the doorway. From his hand hung down a parchment scroll, more or less unwound by the great weight of a heavy, ribboned seal, which, if the Sergeant was not mistaken, bore the deep embossing of the royal device itself.

The Sergeant was uncertain of what to do. The elephants had manifestly gone, the prime suspect with them. The whole operation had turned into a kind of fiasco with a bunch of clowns, one of whom now waved a very imposing piece of paper under his nose. He turned to the Grand Master and then, quite suddenly, snatched the parchment from his hands and studied it closely. A profound look of scepticism mingled with a profound doubt spread across his face. The face of the Grand Master displayed only towering complacency.

This bunch of comics were evidently not criminals. At least not in the sense of people who steal elephants and hold zoos to ransom for them. The parchment and the bearing of all these people reminded him of a small subheading in the last chapter of the largest book on criminal law that he had ever come across. It simply said that certain quasi-criminal powers had been vested in a few guilds and individuals under the feudal system at the time of the Norman conquest. Virtually all of these had been subsumed into criminal statute during the nineteenth century. With a policeman's eye for a loophole, it was that one word 'virtually' that now leapt into his mind. As if the page of that law tome were open before him, it danced before his eyes and underlined itself a dozen times. Sergeant Apta Dapta thought for a moment and made out he was reading the scroll to give him time. The Grand Master gave him all the time he wanted.

'Under what prerogative do you claim to act?' asked Sergeant Apta Dapta carefully. His memory had served him well, his tact even better; it was precisely the right question to ask.

'The royal prerogative. You have the Letter of Assent in your hand,' said the Grand Master with a nonchalant air. 'We pursue a contumacious Grinder,' he explained. But when this met with a sort of perplexed silence he amplified his statement:

'One of our number who has broken his obligations. Him we are pursuing unto the ends of the earth.'

'Is he here?' snapped the Sergeant, wanting to cut through the superciliousness. The Grand Master cast a doubting eye over the assembly. The only people not in some sort of uniform were the band. Pete Davis was hugging his double bass to protect it from the mêlée, Sady McCabe was peering round the edge of her piano, eyes wide open with alarm and interest. The session drummer sagged on his elbows and looked bored. James Daley looked around in a non-committal way.

'Is he here?' repeated Sergeant Apta Dapta.

'Er, no . . .' started the Grand Master uncertainly, 'I don't think he is. A young fellow, a trombone player: dark hair and slim. Apparently very fond of vegetables of late . . . We've had an eye on him. Name of Coulisse, Henri Coulisse.'

At the mention of trombone and vegetables, the Sergeant

snapped into action.

'Sorry, sir,' he said, 'that's our man, not yours.' Then raising his voice to the other members of the band:

'Let's know where he is. It'll be worth your while in the end!'

They all looked bemused. But a young constable came in on the conversation instead.

'Sergeant?' The Sergeant nodded him to go ahead. 'Sergeant, I saw him. He was sitting on the neck of the leading elephant when it burst out of the alleyway. He was curled up and crouched over the head. But it was him all right. Matched the description perfectly.'

'Get yourselves unlocked at once!' shouted the Sergeant. There was a general scrabbling for keys and bolt croppers – another standard vice squad implement. Three constables were detailed off at once to arrest the remaining members of the band and take them to the police station. Then taking the other policemen, and with various Founders and Grinders hanging on, he rushed out into Berwick Street where he hoped the personal radio would work again and he could find out where the kidnapper and the supposed kidnapped were to be found. The Grand Master and a bodyguard of Founders and Grinders followed him.

As he approached Berwick Street, he became aware of shouts and confusion and a sound of debris being cleared up and moved out of the way. He emerged to see the last member of the elephant unit just disappearing round the left turn into Peter Street. He tried to rush after the fleeing elephants but the crush of people and remonstrating coster-mongers was altogether too strong. What was more, his desire to follow waned at once when he saw the elephant unit was barely able to keep up with the headlong rush. This Mr Coulisse must have given them the slip. He tried the radio yet again and this time it crackled into life at last:

'Paint Pot. Vice Bike. Over.'

'Paint Pot. Over.'

'Paint Pot. Where are you? Over.'

'In the back of the van in Broadwick Street. I'm pretty roughed up; the elephants have got away. Over.'

'Never mind the elephants. I'll get on to Traffic right away. They can hardly disappear and we'll round them up at our leisure. But have you seen the guy who was riding them? Over.'

'I certainly have, Vice Bike. He's here in the van with me, securely handcuffed to the wall.'

'Right of antecedent pre-eminence!' shouted the Grand Master, waving the scroll at Sergeant Apta Dapta. 'Form Phalanx and to the van!' he roared at the Clerk.

'Form Phalanx and to the van!' repeated the Clerk. And the obedient Phalanx, reappearing from their various manacles now formed around the Grand Master and the Sergeant and set off to the vans, obliging a somewhat reluctant Apta Dapta to go with them. Not quite sure whether he was being led or whether he was leading, the Sergeant bustled round the corner beside the Grand Master inside the Restitutory Phalanx, all the way trying to get in touch with his headquarters on the radio. Finally he got through.

'Vice Nexus. Vice Bike. Over.'

'Vice Nexus. Over.'

'Vice Nexus, this is an emergency. Get through to the Commissioner, if necessary the Home Office. Can the Grand Master of The Worshipful Company of Founders and Grinders claim antecedent pre-eminence in the matter of arrest? Over.'

'Roger, Vice Bike. Wilco. Out.' If you've been operating the Vice Nexus radio long enough, nothing surprises you.

At Vice Nexus a young lady picked up the phone to the Commissioner's office. In the Commissioner's office a secretary rushed in to the Commissioner with a note. The Commissioner picked up a very special phone, and in the Home Office a very special person answered it. The very special person picked up another phone and in the royal palace the Private Secretary lifted the receiver and listened.

'Yes,' he said curtly and put the phone down again. Back went the message, from phone to phone, from note to phone, from phone to radio until:

'Vice Bike. Vice Nexus. Over.'

'Vice Bike.'

'Your query, Vice Bike. Answer affirmative. Over.'

'Roger. Out.'

Sergeant Apta Dapta, amidst the Restitutory Phalanx, reached the vans.

'Your prisoner, it would seem, Grand Master,' he said. The Grand Master beamed, the Clerk went into ecstasy.

Between them they piled the Restitutory Phalanx into the waiting vans and commanded the police to take them to their Hall. The Sergeant had not the will to refuse and Henri, so close to escape, was taken in irons to the City where in full ceremonial process he would be arraigned as a contumacious Grinder.

Meanwhile, Finta Fanta and Rumpus Pumpus were making life distinctly difficult for the elephant unit. In fact, the elephant unit was getting farther and farther behind its quarry with little hope now of being able to exercise its calming charms on the supposedly tame beasts who had a will very much of their own.

Having crashed through Berwick Street and broken out of Peter Street, the two animals veered right and headed straight along Wardour Street, then turned quickly left into Old Compton Street which gave them their first more or less unencumbered run. Unencumbered is, of course, a very relative term in Soho. Soho is always encumbered, that is part of Soho. But it is quite surprising how a one-way street, apparently full of cars nosing their way along, around delivery vans and avoiding pedestrians, can suddenly find room for two charging African elephants coming in the opposite direction. Elephants have a remarkable presence; quite enough to create hectares of room in a busy street.

Cars ran wheels up on to kerbs, pedestrians leapt into doorways and motorbikes roared into alleyways. Such is the care of an elephant, such are the quick reactions of those who inhabit this quarter, that scarcely any damage was done. In fact, everyone took it as a remarkable joke, if somewhat frightening; and half expected to see a film crew following up with cameras rolling.

The reality was rather less predictable. Following the beasts, now at a distance calculated to cause the greatest ire to motorists who had just avoided the principal danger, was a funny collection of individuals – three policemen doing their best to egg on a slightly overweight vet in a white coat and a rather bewildered elephant keeper and assistant: all trying to keep the elephants in view and avoid heart attacks themselves. This was no easy task.

The motorists shouted at them to get out of the road; the policemen tried to clear back the traffic as they ran to keep up the chase. But by the end of Old Compton Street, the elephant unit had to concede defeat. The vet tripped and brought down the leading policeman; the elephant keeper jumped over the sprawling bodies but lost his balance and rebounded very firmly off a substantial bouncer watching the free show from the pavement outside his club. The bouncer's reflex was to join the brawl but, seeing the policemen, retreated into his porch and the little group, breathless and utterly demoralized, sat on the pavement and tried to console each other.

The elephants however, now aware of the success of

their strategy, redoubled their efforts and with a resounding trumpet veered right into Moor Street and Cambridge Circus.

The effect of this was the same as breaking out of tight-packed scrub into open savanna. The analogy was not lost on the elephants. As they left the narrow streets of Soho behind, a zest for freedom ran through their bones, their great hearts came into full rhythmic beat and they stormed ahead regardless of what anyone else seemed to want them to do.

Rumpus Pumpus led them straight out into Cambridge Circus where, the traffic lights being for the moment in their favour, they crossed with no bother to the centre of the roundabout and then pushed on into the southern section of the Charing Cross Road without more ado.

Trumpeting their arrival as they went, the traffic, they found, treated them very much as it treats an ambulance or a police car. It pulled aside to let them pass and, by keeping more or less to the centre of the road, they had little difficulty in getting through.

The lady at the whelk stall in Cambridge Circus opened her eyes wide, gave a hasty 'Well I never!' and went on serving whelks. People in the bookshops looked up from their browsings with marked initial interest but soon returned to the reality of literature and away from the fiction of real life. Cabbies cursed, chauffeurs swerved and the elephants trundled loudly on.

Straight over the traffic lights at Cranbourn Street where the Twenty-nine bus was blocking the traffic flow anyway. So they merely overtook it and ran on, tooting a warning and amazing the passers-by. The traffic now got thicker as they began to approach Trafalgar Square. The instant portrait painters by the National Portrait Gallery turned on their stools to take in the spectacle. Their subjects leapt to their feet and pulled out their cameras trying desperately to photograph the incident as an unforgettable souvenir of London life.

The elephants, however, were not pausing to pose. They swept on past Edith Cavell's statue, now finding it easier to force a way through the oncoming traffic on the wrong side of the road because the vehicles on the left were largely stationary in a tail-back from St Martin-in-the-Fields. Cars and lorries swerved and showed their hazard warning lights but, rather than hooting, took avoiding action and carried on their way afterwards. Driving in this part of London is, after all, an obstacle race of outlandish proportions. What did it matter if the obstacle were an elephant rather than a taxi picking up a fare in the middle of the road?

Rumpus Pumpus' mind was sharply focused on the map of the metropolitan streets he had learned and now recalled to memory. There it was! The façade of St Martin-in-the-Fields. He set course by the traffic island in the middle of St Martin's Place, where it gives on to Trafalgar Square. The lights were at that moment against the oncoming traffic and he took the chance to thunder past the southbound queue on the wrong side of the road. The lights changed, Rumpus Pumpus gave a mighty trumpet blast and gained the complete attention of the driver in the leading vehicle – a van – turning north out of Trafalgar Square to meet him. The driver was evidently well endowed with common prudence for, on seeing the oncoming beast, he slowed to a crawl and kept well to the left. The vehicle behind him honked once, saw Rumpus Pumpus, and honked no more.

Rumpus Pumpus crossed the traffic island giving the lights a salutary rattle but doing them no harm and forced on into the square where the elephants mixed with quite amazing ease with the circulating traffic. You may have had the experience yourself: the bigger and more impressive the vehicle you drive, the more other drivers are courteous to you and give you leeway. If you are driving an elephant; which is to say, if you are an elephant, precisely the same holds true. A definite element of deference enters the behaviour of those around you and, of course, since you are not a vehicle, the laws concerning vehicles don't really apply to you, so you can take a few liberties with the normal traffic practices.

The two elephants shot across the eastern side of the square amidst the swirling traffic and dived into Northumberland Avenue with much tooting and trumpeting. This was no more bravado than an essential safety procedure: the pedestrian crossings at the entrance to that road being as usual full to overflowing. The crowd was heaping up, there at the kerbside almost toppling over waiting for the green pedestrian light and a break in the traffic when the elephants bore down upon them. Their hearts were gripped by the wild warning note, mothers clutched children to their knees, grown men hugged their briefcases like comforting dolls, tourists stood back aghast. A colourful group of youths cheered loudly and clapped their hands. Rumpus Pumpus and Finta Fanta stampeded through. The children laughed. One mother fainted.

Northumberland Avenue was simple. Straight along that chasm between ministries and out on to the Embankment. They turned under Hungerford Bridge and the speed of the traffic here took Rumpus Pumpus by surprise. A stream of coaches, cars, motorbikes and lorries thundered past them; wisely he dived for the left-hand lane. A parked coach just beyond the bridge forced them out into the centre lane of their carriageway. A gap in the traffic and they were on the central reservation. Dropping their speed they saw a gap between the oncoming vehicles, crossed the westbound carriageway and took to the broad pavement beside the dolphin lamp-stands and the wall of the Embankment, beyond which was the River Thames itself.

As they saw the water, both elephants let out a squeal of delight. And there in front of them – Rumpus Pumpus could be proud indeed of his navigation – was their immediate goal: Cleopatra's Needle – an elephantine needle if ever one there were.

Now neither elephant particularly wanted to do any sewing; but Cleopatra's Needle marks a most significant place in London. Its unique advantages the elephants now put to their own use. The needle, an Egyptian pylon of great antiquity and covered with hieroglyphics, stands on a short jetty protruding from the walled bank of the tidal river. This platform is but seven or eight metres long, with the pylon at its end. On either side of it are steps going down into the water at high tide, or leading down to the mud and shingle bottom of the river, exposed some four or five metres below, at low tide. To get down on to the jetty one has to cross the wall that runs near shoulder-high the length of the Embankment. To enable the curious to do this, there are stone steps provided precisely for this purpose which pedestrians can scale on the shore side and descend on the river side, on to the jetty; whence most of them then gaze at close quarters at the needle itself or admire the two magnificent sphinxes that lie facing each other just at the top of this stairway. Each sphinx is about twice the size of an elephant; so that when Finta Fanta and Rumpus Pumpus arrived at the scene they suddenly seemed to lose their status as towering monsters and fit into the proper scale of things again.

Walking now, but without hesitation, they started to climb the stone stairs between the smiling sphinxes. In the distance their large ears heard the sound of a police siren, then another somewhat closer. The Sergeant had evidently alerted Traffic and their information was sending them on the trail of the elephants.

Finta Fanta led the way, carefully making her way up the steps that were definitely small for her large feet. She reached the top and carried on, her belly at one point touching the topmost step as she straddled the summit slowly, step by step descending on to the jetty below. Rumpus Pumpus followed and when both were down upon the jetty, they turned left and then gingerly stepped over the low iron railings that topped the further steps which led down into the water.

A small crowd was starting to collect, some climbing the steps behind them, but keeping a prudent distance nonetheless; others hanging over the Embankment wall and goofing unbelievingly at the sight before them. The sphinxes for once must have felt quite upstaged.

In the river, a vicious ebb tide was now well under way. The first steps that led to the water were already bared as the water went down. The greyish-brown liquid swirled all round the jetty, though as they were descending in its lee, the water before their eyes was calm.

The crowd evidently had no idea what was going on. The grade one know-alls declared the beasts to be thirsty and definitely going to drink. Yet Finta Fanta and Rumpus Pumpus had their forefeet over the railings already and would appear to be able to reach the water with their trunks from where they were. Yet still they pushed on. The sirens came closer. Now their forelegs were up to their elbows in water and their hind legs crossed the iron railings too.

The grade two know-alls declared they were going for a bath. They would start to squirt water over their backs soon and probably someone would come and rub them down with a brick. Yet now their fore-bodies and lower heads were in the water. Their trunks curved up above the surface to let them breathe from time to time; and still they pushed on down the stairs.

The water crossed their necks and their hind legs entered in. Down and down they went. Two backs and two tails showing: a bit of back and a bit of a tail. One tail, two tails showing, a trunk and a back. With a great swirl and a motion of submergings the elephants pushed off from the stairs. One police car, another police car screeched to a halt. Four constables rushed up the steps and stopped. As the sirens had fallen silent, two waving trunk tips had slipped beneath the surface and the great grey Thames rushed on into the spring evening as if nothing untoward had happened and no unusual aquatics had taken place.

The crowd stood bewildered and suddenly broke out chatting and describing to passers-by, policemen and latecomers. The policemen looked nonplussed and radioed reports. The sphinxes sat upon their haunches; and they, remembering perhaps the Nile, stopped feeling affronted and smiled and smiled and smiled.

Chapter 15

Imagine if you will, your feelings, when, as a lusty youth, deep in the power of jazz, you are wedged corporally in the back of an ignominious van, proceeded before and behind by a split phalanx of triumphant and vindictive Grinders; then to be roughed with rasping manacle, swung from hand to hand down into the dungeon of the Worshipful Company whose dripping water is for music and darkness for justice. Like Henri, your feelings are undoubtedly perturbed; undoubtedly contorted.

Such was his handling; and such was the night that followed his arrest. But in the back of his mind Henri had been prepared. He knew the Grinders' Hall, its denizens and its ways. Once the prisoner was found unbroken, a little mercy could be coaxed from its adamantine stones. With contacts, a proper offensive could be mounted against the injustice of his position: an offensive disguised as the defence to his contumacy, an onslaught he felt brewing in his breast that would vindicate and free himself from The Worshipful Company of Bell Founders and Organ Grinders forever.

As he expected, at half past seven the following morning the great bolts on his dungeon door were thrown back and a young drudge came in, just visible in the thin, grey light which crept in from a small grill high in the wall giving into an internal courtyard. The drudge placed a small bowl of cool gruel just out of reach of Henri, manacled to the wall. Then he left and threw the bolts back into place with loud crashes on the black oak door.

An hour later the drudge returned and placed the bowl just within reach. Henri still refrained from reaching for it. The drudge went to the door and turned, looking at Henri. Henri looked back at him.

'Smoked haddock,' said Henri. 'Smoked haddock with croquette potatoes and tomato sauce. Half a grapefruit, some toast and marmalade and a jug of coffee; no sugar, just cream.'

The drudge was taken aback.

'Tell the gaoler I stand in jeopardy of purgation through ordeal and claim my right to warrior's nourishment.'

The drudge disappeared and the gruel remained untouched. What the Grand Master had hoped was that a night in the cells would render Henri a meek and abject repentant who would think himself glad to be summarily dismissed from the Company. But what the gaoler's report told him was that this was not the case. Somehow, despite a mere millenium of contact with the Company, his family had imbued him with its rules if not with its practice. The right to purgation through ordeal of all offences still stood in the Company charter. Its execution had long since been commuted to administrative penalties; but the Grand Master knew, and Henri knew too, that purgation through ordeal, still held sway as a right of vassalage for contumaceous liverymen; and the right pertaining to it could not be denied.

The great bolts were thrown back. The gaoler appeared and sloshed across the damp, stone floor to the corner where Henri was manacled.

'I am to ask you what liberty has the vassal before purgation through ordeal?' said the gaoler.

'No liberty,' said Henri, as if trotting out the response in a catechism, 'except the liberty of the Company's premises and the liberty of visits to prepare his case.'

'Thus it is. Forget it not,' said the gaoler and taking a key he unlocked the manacle and Henri took the freedom of the building, and took it well.

He went to the buttery after taking a shower and dressing in some undress vestments and a dressing-gown which he found in the robing room. At a table there was laid a half grapefruit, a plate of steaming smoked haddock with tomato sauce and croquette potatoes. He also ate toast and drank coffee. He leant back and looked at the servant loitering nervously in the door; at the panelling and the furniture and the strong daylight now coming in the windows high above. They were a bunch of tricksters these people. They'd try anything on. Their only redeeming feature was that they gave you your due if you knew your due; and knew how to demand it.

He made his way to the library and then, by inscribing his name in a book near the entrance, reserved for himself one of the small rooms that led off it and could be used by liverymen for private discussions and researches. Once in there, he used the telephone which each of the studies possessed and called General Catastrophe – a private line in General Catastrophe which operated a telephone on the back right-hand corner of a large mahogany desk. The phone was picked up immediately.

'It's Henri here. Hello, Father,' he said, not waiting for a response at the other end.

'Oh. Oh. Uh. Oh,' came the series of strangled noises down the line.

'Hello, Father. It's Henri here,' said Henri again. Quite used to his father's manner, all the struggling and grunting passed him by and he got straight to the point.

'Did you know, I'd been imprisoned at the Hall as a contumaceous Grinder, Father?'

'No,' said his father falteringly. 'But I had guessed it must be you. The newspapers this morning were full of sensationalist stories about an elephant stampede and a police raid in Soho that all seems to have gone wrong. The Company was portrayed in a very poor light by some of the papers. They've reported how someone suspected of stealing the elephants has been kept out of police custody by the Company. Apparently, questions are going to be asked in the House about the residual powers of livery companies. Quite ridiculous. As if everyone wasn't fully aware of our powers and status.

'Was it you, Henri? Tell me it wasn't you,' he pleaded.

'Oh, the bloke taken by the livery company was me all right. That's why I'm ringing you; but I haven't stolen any elephants. In fact, I can tell you nobody's ever stolen that particular pair of elephants – not even the zoo – and I don't think anyone's ever going to. But what's happened to the elephants? Have the police got them?'

'What? The elephants? Oh, oh well, no. No, apparently not. They seem to have disappeared off the face of the earth. Got into the Thames or something – there were some rather amateurish looking pictures in the papers. They've apparently disappeared from view. Drowned I expect, or hidden in some warehouse or other.'

'Terrific!' came in Henri.

'I say,' came in Claud surprisingly, 'you don't know where they are, do you? You know you're supposed to co-operate with the police. It would be a serious offence if . . .'

Henri cut him short. 'I didn't even know they were heading for the Thames. Come to that, was anybody with this pair of elephants or were they running free?'

'Quite free, apparently,' said Claud.

'Then how could anyone know where they might end up?'

'Quite so,' said Claud, realising the truth of the implication but not quite sure he had got the whole truth.

'Anyway, Father,' continued Henri, 'there are important things to be doing. You'll have to take a few days off work and come and defend me against the charge of contumacy.'

'You're indefensible,' said Claud, clearly shocked. 'And take a few days off work? There are claims to equilibrate!'

A couple of weeks ago Henri would have said nothing to this attitude and gone weakly before the court with all his rage showing as no more than humble contrition. But now his rage was in his mouth and, though tempered with the essentials of politeness, its power hissed down the line to his father.

'Anything can be defended,' said Henri with a positiveness to his voice that Claud found quite intimidating. 'But you're the only member of this wretched order of unordained high priests of commerce who could do anything more than put in a half-baked plea for mitigation on my behalf.'

'I had, of course, considered what mitigation . . .'

'Father, I'm not going to mitigate anything. I'm going to defend myself – or you are – and defend myself successfully. Now get over here and let's work out the defence; you know they can start the hearing tomorrow, if they want to, though it'll probably be in a couple of days.'

Claud prevaricated. 'One can't just leave one's work,' he said. 'Who's to equilibrate the *Glory of Old Gaul* case? My secretary is quite unprepared for an absence. She would be shocked. You know that serious-minded people in responsible positions . . .'

'Father. Get over here right away or I shall make an antecedent cross-petition against you for genealogical transcription on grounds of mentorial neglect.'

Henri heard only a deep breathing, becoming more and

more desperate with every breath inhaled in response to his threat. Then he heard a china teacup raised and rattled in a neat and nervous state. In his mind's eye, Henri could see a perfectly symmetrical blotter, spattered with most asymmetric blots of cool orange pekoe spreading outward with uncontrollable rapidity. A pallid voice, the flavour of broken Marie biscuits came back.

'All . . . all right, Henri, all right. I can see a point in it. I'm sure I can. I'll be over soon. One of the research rooms off the library are you?'

'Yes, Father. I'll see you soon.'

By the time Claud arrived, Henri had the desk and the two oak side-tables covered in volumes, tagged and bookmarked at the relevant pages. His mind ran ahead in a hot and hurried frenzy at the case he was preparing and the arguments he was to pursue. Dimly, through the old leaded-glass windows of the door that gave on to the library itself, Henri saw the slow, half-reluctant approach of Claud. The father came and tapped at the leaded panes and Henri called for him to come in. Things had certainly changed in his life. His feeling that it was he who had summoned his father was confirmed at once by a single look at the equipositor as he came in through the door. He was pallid and retiring, unsure and undistinguished. It was the stable equilibrium of a silly sheep fallen into a deep pit. Henri had absorbed equilibrium all right, one could not but do so in his father's household; but it ran through his veins now as the dynamic equilibrium of the tightrope walker, the tense and balanced readiness to act, aware of danger but determined to reach the safety of the other side.

Claud walked in, crossed the green carpet and sort of oozed into the chair on the other side of the desk from where Henri was seated.

'No, come round this side, Father,' he said. Claud came

silently round and sat beside him.

'I've got some ideas,' said Henri. 'I'm sure we can make a case of it; but tell me your thoughts. What do you think we should use as the basis of defence? What do you think is the main thrust of the argument?'

To his surprise, Claud perspired and said nothing. A long and uneasy silence ensued. No idea, no greeting, no flash of recognition or of sympathy passed between them. And then in the wells of his father's eyes Henri saw something that he had never noticed before. Yet it had always been there in one form or another; but always hidden or disguised, never admitted to nor mentioned. It was fear. Fear amounting almost to a terror, fear of all things, fear of life itself. Henri had known it as a dislike of jazz, as a disregard for the circus, as a frowning upon humour and art, as a disapprobation of spontaneity. But now he saw what it really was; it was simple fear. And all this equilibrium, all this lifelong balance and unhurried calm, all this energy channelled to produce a life of unruffled quietude and compromise; all this, Henri saw now, was but a device to hold at bay the fear of life itself with all its accidents and uncertainties. It would keep at a long arm's length the very business of living where disequilibrium was evidently some kind of death. Instead, Henri's idea was of a kind of excitement whose resolution was success and whose loss was the chance to try again.

Claud knew none of what he was giving away: Henri saw it and said nothing about it. But he saw it was the time to stop asking his father for advice and to employ the old man in his own schemes. For the old man's schemes were now redundant, a new lead was needed.

Henri knew Claud's knowledge of the Company, its ways, its laws, its lore and all its rulings, was encyclo-paedic. Just as the Masters and the Clerk had worked at their case in the Grand Master's chambers, so Henri now worked at his in the little research room off the library. He started to ask Claud about this statute and about this custom. He raced to shelf and book case to read the reference and then put back the tome. From time to time he dashed out into the library itself, coming back with other volumes and sheaves of yellowed papers. For every question, Claud had an accurate answer. To every idea and opinion Claud cited the precedent and the practice. Henri's pen flew across the pages of a thick, bound notebook.

Claud's coat came off, neither of them noticed when; Henri's dressing-gown gaped open and his strange array of clothing hung about him like an elegant line of washing. One of them rang down for sandwiches. Plates of mutton buns came up to them to disappear, they remembered not when; and so leave their crumbs for the aged cleaner who, days later, was able to clean them at last from the upholstered seats and the deep-pile carpet. Through the rest of that day and the following night they worked. Claud, at first numb, the threat of genealogical transcription having completely shipwrecked the initiative, later began to warm up as he saw a glimmer of reason in what Henri was evidently trying to do. The warmth had become a tired and grudging admiration by the time day dawned and they realised they must rest. They went off to members' bedrooms and slept some hours there; Henri till midday, Claud a little less. For Claud went quickly home and back to the Hall, to have lunch with Henri, newly roused, bringing him fresh clothes and luxuries like a tooth-brush and a flannel.

Lunch was a sandwich again. Panic had gripped Claud once more in its clutches but, more quickly now, Henri broke down the fear. There was nothing for it. The accused was always obviously going to defend himself in his own way and there was nothing he could do about it. The afternoon wore on and the pace began to slow.

Tomes were returned to shelves and sheaves of papers to cabinets and files. The die was cast. Claud sat back in utter resignation. Henri made a final note and leant back in his chair. He raised his hands behind his head and a smile came over his face. Outside, the spring evening was subsiding into night. Henri thought he saw a bat flitter past the window – probably not, but it didn't matter. The phone rang, and Henri picked it up from the drawer. He listened, acknowledged briefly and returned the phone to its place.

'Tomorrow morning at ten,' he said, 'the process will begin.'

Claud put his head in his hands and shook from side to side. Henri smiled. 'I think,' he said, 'this is going to be a most interesting trial. Well, we're ready. There's not a jot more to do. Supper and bed for me. See you at half past nine tomorrow, Father?'

'Half past nine tomorrow,' echoed Claud and slunk away.

Henri, after a good meal and a brisk, monotonous stroll round the courtyard of the Hall, threw himself into bed and slept like a wintering bear till eight the following morning.

The Great Hall was decked in forensic finery. The Court of the Entire Company was assembled: long rows of deep-mumbling liverymen dressed in their full ceremonial gear, manning the rising tiers of benches that sloped up from the floor of the hall back towards the panelled walls. Upon the stone flags in the well of the hall, transverse benches had been placed, each behind long, transverse tables crossing the width of the floor but leaving a gangway on each side, in front of the tiered stalls above. The transverse tables were littered with bundles of papers and documents. One or two tomes made their appearance there and people sat at these transverse tables also mumbling to each other; but noticeably never mumbling to the occupants of the tiered benches above.

Facing the transverse benches, on the raised dais where the bell ropes hung loosely and in front of the great stained-glass window, were three high-backed chairs of solid oak, but they were padded with scarlet leather and embossed with the Company's arms at the top of the leather insert in the back. To the left of these was a desk of such old and battered oak that its appearance was black. Behind it was a chair of the same substance and colour; both were angled to give the occupant a view of the high-backed chairs and the well of the hall.

For all the bright colours of the liveries, for all the clear light that came in now, despite the stained glass in the window, an atmosphere hung about the hall that was unmistakable in its strength. Had it been visible it would have been like black smoke somehow evenly spread throughout the volume of the air. Like a moral fug it clouded all the light, like an atmosphere of heavy burden pressing into all the crannies of the hall. It was a thing called the assumption of guilt. It was breathed out by all the assembled liverymen, reinforced at every breath. It was a dark joy in all their hearts, a pleasure that they warmed to, to come to those proceedings to see the grinding imposition of the inevitable; and full righteous in its execution.

Yet in one tiny corner, this atmosphere was not breathed out. Two people, one a fully ceremonially clad liveryman, the other a young man dressed in a black silken bodysuit and skull-cap, sat at the first of the transverse benches at its left-hand end. The atmosphere near them seemed lighter; despondency and dullness to be sure, especially from the liveryman; but an alacrity, a fervour and a flexing of the limbs differentiated the pair from all the others. Henri and his father were in place. Proceedings had but to begin.

Amongst the muffled creaks this hall produced, at the moment of those bated breaths, came one from the organ loft above the doors at the opposite extremity of the hall to the Grand Master. None heeded it; but one creak amid an undercrepitation of a thousand others, equally ignored. Yet its emanation was foreboding, had its origins been known.

Into the organ loft crept upon their stomachs the three members of the Special Duties Group, a cold and acid aspect to their eye.

'Keep down!' whispered the first, moving forward beneath the level of the parapet which ran the length of the loft, an ornamental balustrade of pierced oaken foliage above, a low wall of stone below.

'I come,' confirmed the second, apparently transporting some bulky cross upon his back as he crawled.

The third said nothing, for he held a bar of iron in his teeth. They stopped at the centre of the loft, between the organist's seat and the parapet and beneath the mighty pipes that rose nigh to the ceiling above their hidden heads. Stealthily they dared a glance through the pierced oak balustrade down into the body of the hall.

'We shall not be seen,' whispered the first.

'Indeed,' drooled the second, 'they all look toward the dais. Are they not magnificent? Look at their perfect uniformity! Look at the hopelessness of the accused!'

The third member's whisper breathed across. 'Ah, but should that hopelessness be unsure, fortunately our presence will ensure it.' He toyed with the iron bar he had taken from his mouth. 'Our bitterness and bravery in restitution must never go in vain. I think we will ensure the sentence even though the verdict go against us.'

'Look at them,' whispered the first, 'the finest company

in the finest array. My heart swells to be one of them. How theirs will swell if ever he is found not guilty and yet our just initiative succeeds.'

'Indeed, indeed,' came in the hushed replies.

The door to the left of the dais opened and first entered the Clerk in his black, clerkly robes, smirking like a cow in clover; occasionally throwing glances at Henri for when he screwed up his lips in what he thought was disdain. Henri thought it looked very funny. The Clerk sat at the black oak desk and, once in place, reached to the floor and lifted a handbell, ringing it three times in short bursts of one and a half seconds each. The mumblings died away. With a scrabbling, a stamping and a heaving of aged limbs everyone stood up. The three Masters of the Company entered from Henri's right, climbed the dais and sat in the high-backed chairs; the Grand Master in the centre, the Organ Master to his left and the Bell Master to his right. With another creaking clatter everyone sat down again.

The creaks and rustlings died away and everyone composed himself for the opening indictment of the Grand Master. That venerable gentleman, his dress balls wobbling very slightly as he drew breath, made ready to pronounce the charge.

'Indictment!' shouted the Clerk, suddenly rising, sitting, shouting and scribbling all at the same time. The Grand Master composed himself and drew breath again. The indictment began:

'That this Coulisse being duly inaugurated by our proper ceremonies and thereafter called to serve, upholding due tradition before the Guildsmen and others of the City, willingly and wantonly abandoned these his services to take unknown vassalage outside our order and contrary to all fealty incumbent on him, thereby proving in the action what of necessity must ever have been true in fact that his genealogy was unfitting for our Company and thus should be established in its place as unfounded within us or before us and therefore unworthy amongst, by and beneath us and therefore begs transcription to its true ascent, or being proven in the line of blood, purifying through ordeal within the Western Bastion where the setting sun reminds eternally the lying and unworthy spirits come contumiceously among us to right unmanfully their evil and abominating acts deep to our vital spirits, forever of their crimes.

'That the process be executed, judged and fulfilled!'

'Aye!' rang out the voices of the multitude, half rising in enthusiasm as the Grand Master's voice rose to its passionate crescendo, and then subsided to a stamping of feet and a thousand echoed huzzahs, rolling round the room in slow declining noise.

Claud went as white as chalk and sat shaking in his place. Henri leaned back and started to peel an orange. From a brown paper bag he took a lemon and placed it on the table before him. The act was quite improper: but none dared say a word, for the symbolism was perfect.

Eyes strayed up to the fruit depicted in the stained-glass window and back to Henri and his peelings. Finally, ripping the end of the loose peel off the orange, he put it down and picked up a rather ramshackle-looking collection of papers from the table before him.

'What rascal's insolence!' went the whisper in the organ loft. Three sets of lips tightened into hateful sphincters. 'Pass up the bow.'

The second neophyte eased forward the object he had carried. The first took part of it in his grasp: the ancient steel stirrup of a mighty crossbow.

'Look at the ranks in the hall,' said the third. 'They are as outraged as ourselves and feel the burning insult of abuse as we do. Let us ready and fire in one. All will understand; but only we are in a stance to act.'

'Hold on, hold on,' whispered the second. 'Grand Master is no neophyte. Let us let him prove his principle, even though we ready up his sentence.'

With that, the first Special Duty man went into a seated position behind a pillar of the parapet and pulled the ivory snatches of engraved boar's tusk the length of the crossbow's shaft and hooked them, one each side of the shaft, to the crossbow's cord, thick as a man's thumb. He nodded to the second, who was lying down with the bow from his waist to his toes.

'I'll wind him a prosecution fit for fiends,' he murmured and slowly began to turn the twin handles of the moulinet that fell each side of his pelvis at the butt of the deadly weapon.

Henri glanced at one or two of the papers, then rose and addressed the Grand Master. He was suddenly a slim, alert, black knife of a figure in the midst of the decorated cake of all their finery.

'Defend and call witnesses,' he declared, as if he conducted cases like this every day. In a certain way, he might have thought, looking at Claud, he had conducted cases like this every day of his life. The Grand Master nodded assent.

'The defendant!' declared Henri. A hushed titter of voices ran round the hall. The defendant! The defendant as first witness! Under those nacred hats many lawyers were hidden, many a denizen of the Chancery, many a Founder used to grinding the truth out of defence witnesses. One never called the defendant first. Not unless one was very sure. But very sure of what?

Henri went up among the witness ropes. The ropes of the peal hung in a circle to the right of and a little behind the Masters' seats. Witnesses stood within this area and answered their questions with the purity of a bell's note.

For otherwise they were not in keeping, and, impure, were at once condemned.

The Grand Master coughed imperiously. Henri remained looking out over the court. Before him the transverse benches backed away from him one row behind another until above them rose the organ, its vertical shafts apparent between the vertical lines of the bell ropes that surrounded him. With a kind of casual unconcern that was as much pretence as a genuine reflection of his feelings he waited, as complete silence fell, for the prosecution's examination.

He looked askance at the seated Master, at the Clerk, pen poised and an acute vehemence in his eyes. But the silence lingered on a few seconds yet for, in truth, it had not really occurred to the Masters that the case would be defended. With a certain huffing and puffing and gathering together of robes and shifting of position, the Grand Master finally worked out what to do and launched into the prosecution case.

'Are you Henri Coulisse?'

'Yes, Grand Master,' replied Henri warily but politely enough.

'Were you at the Burst of Spring?'

'No, Grand Master,' replied Henri flatly.

'The prosecution case rests!' shouted the Grand Master with a great beam of triumph on his face.

Approving noises rose from the encircling benches, leers of triumph crossed the faces of the assembled members. Some with a legal background arched their eyebrows in surprise: if brevity was laudable, it was unwelcome to them professionally as it tended to cast doubt on one's right to one's fee. The Worshipful Company, however, was certainly not going to pay any fees to anyone, so that the arched eyebrows ended in a wise nodding and the warming prospect of an early lunch.

Henri turned to the Clerk.

'I choose to interrogate myself,' he said, evidently rattling off a procedural formula.

The Clerk raised his backside, still scribbling at the same time, and shouted drily:

'Statement!'

Silence fell in the hall as the court and the audience settled down to listen to Henri's statement in defence of himself. The old buzzards, decked out in their tunics and baubles composed themselves benignly to listen to a long plea in mitigation. They felt themselves altruistic and magnanimous in doing this and quite looked forward to a set-piece speech which they could appreciate and discuss over lunch, trading opinions of its merits and weaknesses, its technical brilliance or its structural faults, all in the certain knowledge that, in fact, it mattered not a jot: the only possible verdict was guilty, and the only possible purpose of defence was entertainment. Henri drew himself up. He gazed around. His father sat up in his seat and looked on expectantly. Henri spoke.

'Surfeit,' he said. Then, 'The defence rests its case,' and left the dais to go back and sit beside Claud and laconically start a gentle meal of oranges and lemons.

'He's going for a nominal punishment,' hissed the first Special Duty member wrestling to keep the steel bow horizontal as its terrible force was flexed. The second said nothing, straining with the moulinet and striving to keep silence as the snatches edged back towards the loose-catch with the stiff bar of cord between them.

'Don't underestimate the subtlety of the Company,' spoke the third. 'We shall be ready if they acquit, to acquit ourselves correctly. But that weasel out of Westminster won't wriggle from our grasp. We have the means to end all his arguments; and no-one in the hall would rather be down there in audience than here in action, beyond the call of duty, if only he had wit to be so.'

The Masters looked sideways at each other, then sideways at the Clerk. And the Clerk, had he been able to slip quietly between the floorboards and disappear without trace from the presence of the Company, would have been sorely tempted to do so. But he couldn't, so instead he scratched away with his quill and at the same time flicked back through a vast book of notes where, to his surprise, he saw the rubric that jogged his memory. He stood to attention like a snake up a drainpipe and said:

'Grand Master, the court must beg you to explain the accused's absence of shackles.'

The Grand Master's memory was jogged too. 'Purgation through ordeal,' he said surlily.

Memories were jogged in the audience and, as legal minds flicked over the pages of the tomes treasured up in their imaginations, an appreciative murmur ran around the ranks; and an anticipatory trembling of dress balls accompanied a turning of heads towards Henri. Henri sat fast, orange juice dripping from the corner of his mouth. Gradually, faces turned back towards the Clerk.

In the organ loft, preparations hastened to an end.

'Quick, quick,' urged the first, 'judgment will be upon him. We must be ready for acquittal; wind, wind!'

The recumbent neophyte strained the moulinet the last quarter-turn and with a little click the twin teeth of the loose-catch sprang up before the cord. He wound back the moulinet and detached the snatches, winding them to the butt and grasping the crossbow by its stock. The third neophyte wriggled forward.

'Let me place the quarrel,' he asked; and lying by the second, lay his iron bar, a murderous-looking shaft flighted with stiff pinion feathers, in the groove along the bow. He nestled its notch to the cord and passed it to the first neophyte. This scion came between the other two, bow to shoulder, and aimed through the oaken foliage, ready to loose at Henri and sink their quarrel through his contumacious heart.

'It's as if the whole hall waits in fear of his acquittal,' breathed the third. 'You can sense the desperation in their hearts. Their coming dishonour, though, will be short.'

'I think we speak for all,' murmured the second.

'Hush,' said the first. 'I let fly on acquittal.'

But there was no acquittal.

'Judgment,' stated the Clerk flatly. The three Masters smirked like foxes in front of chickens. The Grand Master nodded. Each nodded back at him. The Grand Master stood. The entire court stood but for Henri who was pulling a lemon apart. The eyes turned on Henri and he reluctantly shambled to his feet. The Grand Master drew mighty breath. With fire-eyed screech he cried:

'Guilty!'

With a resounding drumming of a thousand feet came back the assent, 'Guilty!' from the company; and the wild, unbelieving eyes roved the chamber for dissenters; but there were none, the doom was done. But an unexpected voice spoke out quite calmly:

'Mitigation.'

It was Claud who had spoken and the Masters' gaze went to him. He stood firm, and repeated, finding now an even greater firmness in his voice:

'Mitigation.'

'Mitigation,' repeated the Clerk, and sat down. The Masters followed suit and sat too. With astounding dignity Claud walked out to the dais and taking his place amid the ropes spoke:

'Mitigation.' He looked round the faces, up to the organ, down to his son who seemed somewhat surprised at this but nonetheless ready to go along with it.

'Surfeit,' continued Claud, 'surfeit is dear to many of

our hearts and indeed holds honourable place at the heart of the ordeal. Several, the record proved, have chosen the ordeal of surfeit.' The Clerk nodded sagely. 'But I wish to take my part in the affair. When a son is guilty, is not the father guilty too?'

Some nodded at this and appeared to admit a certain truth. Others scoffed, inborn evil they preferred and saw it wherever crime was done; glorious livery was not to be tainted by the theories of environment and upbringing used to excuse every excess of modern life: character was what counted, character, which came from good stock and inborn worth and had nothing to do with circumstance and upbringing. Claud, as usual, had weighed the facts.

'Just as there can be no absolute proof of a paternal element in this crime, so can there be no absolute proof of its absence. Searching my heart, I find for my son, for I find in my heart a core of guilt that one way or another I will expiate: and what better expiation than the bearing of the burden the court must place upon the son.

'Figure in your reckonings the punishments he has suffered, and anyway must suffer, regardless of ordeal. Exclusion from livery, what horror that entails.' Many winced. 'Incarceration for a night and, it seems, the need to have spent long days cooped up with wild beasts that lately did escape and make havoc from Soho to the Thames.'

The assembly showed little enough sympathy for the destruction of Westminster; but the notion of being incarcerated with wild beasts had a certain classical twist to it that made some members flinch. Pale glinting of their sewn-in organ pipes betrayed the movement: Claud continued.

'His penance is enough: is done. My penance but beginning. What should it be? I take unto myself his ordeal. Central to the wayward child is spoiling, is surfeit, central to surfeit indulgence to disgust in what one loves. I love this company, its members and its ways. I love this tunic and this hat, this organ and this court. Our tiered justice, step on step of truth, our hallowed ways and hallowed Hall, its passages and bars, dungeons, bastions and butteries, its libraries and stairs, its very walls and grilles, its posterns and its portals.

'And what within these butteries and bars? What shall the ordeal be? An orange and a lemon?' He looked closely at Henri who watched his father with equal closeness, grasping at his intention. But the Organ Master cut in.

'Never. Not those,' he said, 'the fruits of our ceremonies, the desecrated citrus of his own reception to our order. No sin, nor orange nor lemon, it shall not be.' The Grand Master nodded and a murmur of assent went round the hall, hallowing the fruit and reserving their presence from ordeal.

'Not fruit,' continued Claud, 'nor any item of institution, except the informal institution of our current habits. What is our joy? What is the real joy ejected members must be denied? Is it to dance in round? Is it to stand wind-gusted on a hail-strewn day in spring and burst the spring upon the City? The real joy of heart and hearth is the joy of food at the hearth of the buttery. The deep satisfaction of our order is the food of conversation and the interchange of personal wealth, in meaning and information we exchange at the wood fire of the buttery. The memory and mind entrenched in the mellow dowsing of our port, the full and satisfying warmth of mutton sandwiches in the cinder-oven bread of stone-hearthed kitchen. These are our joys; and in ordeal these are the pleasures made to try us.'

The speech brought moisture to the multitude of mouths. Luncheon approached; and a subtle salivation in the peacock ranks anticipated the meal. Stomachs began to churn slowly, desiring comfort of the slain sheep: the deep, rich meat of old ewes spiced and roasted, sunk in the gravy of spit-roasted juice; placed with cream butter in slices of rustic bread, flavoursome like the chaffy whiff of a stone-walled granary. The feeling for food became a fury and their eagle-like, waiting eyes, old men in a frenzy of desire, fixed on the ascetic Claud and jumped ahead of his speaking to the conclusion of their law. He would not keep them from their food on the pretext of sentence: nor disturb the mellow thinking of their afternoon in the recall to hear sentence. Finish now. Finish the legal meal before the real meal and finish the sentence with the meal to come. A symmetry of gastronomic balance, fitting to their legalistic thought and utterly acceptable to the equiposition of Claud now facing them and absorbing in the air their satisfaction in his penance.

'Let our luncheon,' said Claud lightly, for him almost playfully, 'necessarily light for those who labour,' smiles were suppressed, 'be the precursor of the penance. Mutton cased in bread and port in cask, from the ceiling to the floor, stacked in the architrave of the Western Bastion till the purging food has passed the tract of the guilty and the distension of his gut disgusted his crime to himself and all of us.'

This was followed by a kind of worried silence: not altogether quiet like a tomb, but perturbed like the silence of a library, where students, struggling to understand, squirm in their seats to twist their minds to comprehension. They did not understand. But they caught the drift of the meaning and sought in their minds for the substance of the ordeal.

Still cramped in the organ loft the Special Duties Group had no such uncertainties.

'Look at the confusion those two are sowing,' said the

251

third. 'Yet there's no difference with the father substituted for the son. We'll oust uncertainty. Let fly at the father. The quarrel's vinegared, let fly, let fly!'

'No, not if he goes to the bastion,' said the second. 'That's doom enough; not if he goes to the bastion.'

The quarrel pointed now square at Claud.

'Granting the ordeal would save the shot. But with all the hall I'd rather shoot,' said the first.

'Do not grant the ordeal,' they muttered. It seemed as if the hall half heard and many agreed. Certainly the bafflement began to lessen. Then the air of questioning lessened also.

One or two worked it out, then whispered word of their thinking to their neighbours. The neighbours passed it on and finally the ranks eased back upon their pews and looked in admiration at Claud. But the Masters had not the resources of their neighbours. They sat in bafflement and awaited their question. They looked to the Clerk, he raised his eyes from the parchment and explained.

'In effect, Grand Master, the mitigator proposes the manner of ordeal by surfeit. Such an ordeal is, of course, in accordance with tradition and as a self-imposed test no objection can be raised from without. Supersession through illegality does not apply and discharge through proxy is fundamental to original justice.'

The Grand Master wasn't quite sure about all that. Quite what original justice was rather intrigued him and he would have pursued the points of law like a ferret after rabbits if it hadn't been lunch time and slight, uncertain restlessnesses breathed around the hall. He looked to the other Masters. They all three then looked at Claud and then at the Company. The Masters conferred in low voices between themselves and then the Grand Master rose and gave a verdict.

'Ordeal granted!' he proclaimed, and the hall relaxed, confident the affair neared its close.

It was simply too much for the Grand Master. His stomach rumbled to the limit of the organ loft, his spittle drooled on to his chin, he entered into an anxiety of pre-prandial anticipation that brought him and his associates to their feet.

'Port and mutton,' he cried. 'Court adjourned!' And barely sustaining the needed dignity led the Masters from the stage.

'The bastion it is! Fickle chance! Robbed of our greater purpose,' mourned the Special Duties Group; and stood up to shake their fists at providence and at Claud, to make plain the true outcome which a better justice would have given him.

Yet having been so cramped so long, they stood unsteadily and got one arc of the crossbow caught in the oaken balustrade. The first member fell backwards, bringing the other two with him and dropped the bow, loosing prong first, against the organ seat. With rather more power than a blunderbuss, the weapon loosed with the crack of a dozen drover's whips. The quarrel leapt from the cord in a low-pitched, howling whine and smashed into the panelling of the organ where it somehow contrived to short-circuit the control switch and turn the bellows on. The Special Duties Group threw themselves down out of death's way but thus landed on the fan of foot pedals. The organ let out one ghastly wail and a shower of sparks and went dead. The three neophytes scuttled shaken to the dungeon to return their borrowed weapon to the armoury; and reflect with chastened mood on the good fortune of Claud.

The skirmish and screeching in the organ loft, however, was completely covered by the stampede of famished finery, crushing to the buttery and the bars, rushing behind their stomachs to the benches of the refectory; a rumbling, trembling, thronging, banging, stamping exodus of the mighty who disappeared through many doors to leave the hall a scene of emptiness peopled only by Henri and Claud, the swaying sallies and the left-over papers of legal dispute.

Henri and Claud stood for a long time simply looking at each other. For the first time, there was a mutual respect in their gaze as they had never known before.

'Thank you,' said Henri, quite simply and his eyes were moist with the complex emotions which the simple words evoked. His father quite openly cried.

'I'm not entirely sure why,' said Claud, 'but I owe it to you.

'You'll fix the architecture so I can breathe, won't you?'

Henri nodded. They had already discussed the approach to make, should ordeal be the accepted outcome.

'I'll see to the supplies. There'll be enough for a year but I think I'll find a way somehow of getting you out in six months. I can always petition the Worshipful Company.'

They came together, Henri walking out towards the dais from the transverse benches, Claud walking down from amongst the bell ropes to meet him. They shook hands and turning together went slowly off, Henri toward the research room in the library and Claud to deliver himself up for ordeal at the office of the Grand Master.

Once in the research room, Henri picked up the phone and called his mother, telling her the outcome and the sentence. She sobbed a little and was silent. Then said, 'Such is the immutable way of Founding and Grinding. Had my antecedent companies held the doom, the outcome had surely been the same. Let us not be too much in sorrow but dry our eyes and live again. Will you be home for supper?'

Henri said he would not, hung up and then rang down to the kitchen where a chef answered him.

'I'd like six hundredweight of mutton sandwiches, twenty-eight cases of port and a hogshead of water made up and sent to the fourth niche of the sixth floor of the Western Bastion by five thirty,' he said commandingly. There was a pause as the chef noted down. The chef repeated the order only slightly questioningly.

'That's it,' said Henri. 'Get it done right away.'

'Right away, sir,' came the reply. 'What membership number?' Henri gave his father's number and the chef duly noted it. Then Henri ran himself upstairs and through corridors till he came to a landing on the third floor where, had one been unaware of the day's events, one might have thought a mighty grampus had somehow landed puffing and blowing in the stair well. Footsteps, too, became apparent and then a labourer came into sight with a hod on his shoulder full of stone blocks which matched exactly the matter of the walls around him.

'Take a breather!' said Henri.

The man saw something of a smile on Henri's face. He knew that smile. It definitely meant the breather was not to be missed. Henri fished in his pocket and came out with a bank note of high denomination. He placed it in the shirt pocket of the labourer who leant on the hod balancing it as he stood. Henri winked.

'Fifteen to one,' he said. The labourer looked a bit puzzled. 'It's you knocks up the muck, do you?' asked Henri.

'Yeh,' said the man, very interested.

'Fifteen to one,' said Henri. Something dawned on the man.

'Oh, right guv. Yeh. Fifteen to one. Definitely, yeh, fifteen to one.'

Henri pushed another note into his shirt pocket. 'Set that sticking out of the third course near the back wall.' He gave the man a steel knitting needle.

'Third course near the back wall,' repeated the man and winked. Henri pushed a third note into his pocket.

'That's half,' he said, patting the man's pocket. 'Meet me here immediately afterwards and, if all's well, you get the other half.' The man nodded, slung his hod on his shoulder and carried on up the grey flagged stair. Henri relaxed and went back to the library. He stayed there awaiting sunset, looking out of the leaded panes of the window across the stone ramparts and the glass and concrete towers. His thoughts ran on from the trial; he contemplated the elephants and wondered where they were. He suddenly recalled Mr Sedge and the band; he hoped all was well with them. The light was beginning to fade. He cleared up his papers and replaced his books. Slowly, at the dying of the day he made his way to the Western Bastion.

As Henri knew he would, the chef had brought the ordered goods to the designated niche and stacked them there while the bricklayer had begun his task. The niche itself was now almost completely closed. Only an opening the size of a low door was to be seen at the left hand side. Henri glanced in by the light of the workman's lamp and saw that all his provisions were installed as well as a steel knitting needle, invisible to those who didn't seek it, sticking from the third course of stones at the back wall.

Two niches along, there was a window in the bastion and its iron frame cast a long shadow across the grey rocks of the walls. The sun was gone, the sky darkening. With scraping and sploshing the workman turned the last mix of muck on the square spot board near the entrance, now utterly black.

The Masters, the Clerk and one or two retainers shuffled up with Claud amidst them. Now it was come to this there seemed but little to say. The workman announced his mortar was prepared. Claud turned and with a strong, weeping face, nonetheless upright and firm now, shook everyone by the hand in turn, starting with the Grand Master and finishing with the workman. With a sigh he looked at Henri, and a smile passed between them. Then Claud ducked through the little door and, one by one, the workman placed stone on stone, row on row. With a slurping sound he oozed the last stone into the last hole and, where Claud had once stood, there was now but a grey and faceless wall. Not a sound came from within. No-one spoke. As one, they turned and went their various ways.

Some minutes later, on the third floor landing, Henri passed three notes to the workman. They nodded to each other.

'Fifteen to one,' thought Henri.

Chapter 16

When Finta Fanta and Rumpus Pumpus had disappeared beneath the eyes of the smiling sphinx, the police called off their search and tried to make sense of the eye-witness testimonies.

The elephants, however, were tiptoeing gently along on the bottom of the river, occasionally thrusting up their trunks for a breath of air and occasionally even lifting an eye to the surface for a moment to recognize where they were. These fixings of position and gulps of air were discreet and far between however, so no onlooker ever saw more than what could have been a piece of flotsam or the flurry and swirl of the wind-blown water.

The tide was running out swiftly but the elephants had to take things as they were and make the best of them. As they tiptoed out towards midstream they quickly lost their contact with the bottom, touching it only from time to time as they half swam, half ran along the fast flowing stream. The density of an elephant is approximately equal to that of water, so that they behaved rather like submarines. After a good breath of air through the trunk they tended to float just beneath the surface and be carried down by the current. But after breathing out, they tended to sink and would resort to a few paces of a kind of gravityless gallop along the bottom till they upped trunk and breathed, and rose again. It was extremely exhilarating. Not only the cold, zestful, if a little muddy, water of the spring-time Thames but also the feeling of floating in freedom, when normally one carries a weight of some tons upon one's feet.

Once they had reached the middle of the stream, they carried on down in this way. Daylight was going now and Waterloo bridge slipped overhead like a band of darkness on the evening sky. The lights were on all along the Embankment pavements. Skipping and floating and occasionally peeping, Finta Fanta and Rumpus Pumpus floated parallel to them, sometimes eyeing the lit-up metropolis, sometimes jostling to find the swiftest water. They came to adopt a side-by-side formation in which they could keep touch with one another and take full advantage of the swift flow against their broad, combined sterns. The blue and white arches of Blackfriar's Bridge passed above them, the accompanying railway bridges too. Rumpus Pumpus put up an eye and noted with satisfaction the floodlit dome of St Paul's Cathedral, soon passing out of sight behind utilitarian blocks of offices. Past Southwark Bridge and Cannon Street and on and on they floated. Rumpus Pumpus ticked off each crossing in its turn and, after Tower Bridge, settled to the fifteen-kilometre swim with comfort and satisfaction.

As Westminster and the City fell behind, as Bermondsey and Wapping drifted past, the elephants allowed themselves more observation, though they needed very little, it must be said. Few boats or ships moved. What went down river went only a little faster than they did themselves, so tended not to overtake them. What went up river were light craft, small boats, engines straining against the ebb: the tanker barges and the commercial craft awaited the flood out near the estuary. They toddled jovially on.

As they drifted south in Limehouse Reach it became clear that the water was rapidly falling to its lowest levels.

More and more they ran along the bottom, less and less they floated on the flood. At Greenwich Reach they fared well enough in the middle of the stream. Cautiously, they eyed the great ocean-going ships tied at the piers and wharfs. They caught a glimpse of an elegant brick building on a hill, floodlit in the near night.

'Mmm, zero degrees longitude, I should say,' mused Rumpus Pumpus to himself; and on they toddled, backs now showing from time to time like upturned boats. Yet no-one bothered much. Bath tubs and oil drums and bits of piers and occasional vehicles; runaways from wharfs and timber yards are all washed daily down the Thames and, often enough, thrust daily back up it at the turn of the tide. Mostly the elephants kept hidden and, avoiding boats, kept out of the eye of the river police.

As they turned north, Rumpus Pumpus began to look out with more frequency. It was gone eight o'clock now, so that all the working water frontage, where it wasn't derelict wasteland of the old once-thriving port, now left in ruins, was in any case shut up for the night and quiet. Where roads came near the water, car headlights sometimes shone, but mostly the river was bounded by black eyeless buildings with street lights behind them flaring in orange and pale yellow into the night sky.

Rumpus Pumpus caught sight of his landmark: the entrance to the Blackwall Tunnel. Even from the water he saw the flare and reflection of the southbound car headlights as they dropped and disappeared to enter it. And there were the red lights on the power station chimneys and the river curving suddenly to the right. A landing place, he must find a landing place. He nudged Finta Fanta to port, into the deep water that here ran nearer the left bank. They passed the tunnels and the entrance to the East India Dock Basin, past the wharfs and the estuary of Bow Creek that flows into the Thames from

the north. And there, on the Canning Town side, he and
Finta Fanta left the water, which now ran towards low tide
in a much reduced channel at the centre of the river bed.
Slowly, not unhappily, the pair of them walked up the
mud and shingle to the bank of the northern shore. Here,
for one short stretch, the stone walls and jetties gave way
to a hundred metres or so of rough, marshy-looking
ground coming down to the water's edge. Beyond it, not
five hundred metres away, ran the Silvertown Road and
stood Canning Town. But here the elephants nestled
together, slowly drying off and warming each other,
crouched on the elephant-coloured mud just below the
high water mark. By day, a million goofers from the
people of the region and newspapers of the nation would
have spied them out and given them no peace. But by
night, their camouflage was perfect – two elephant-
coloured lumps on the elephant-coloured mud at night,
when the working river was at rest. Not a soul saw them;
and they snuggled down and slept.

'Reminds me of Heron Island,' murmured Finta Fanta.

'Me too,' said Rumpus Pumpus, 'but this time, I know
where we go from here.' And they closed their eyes and
slept.

About their ears the breezy winds played and to them
came the music of the flowing river; ripples and runnings
of flowing water, a soporific sound when eyes are closed
and the dereliction and the sadness of the run-down
waterfront shut out. To the mind, the lapping of the
murkiest water can soothe and calm and comfort.

Something changed in the sounds of the water. The breeze
had dropped somewhat and the sky, always hazy in town,
seemed to be clouding over more. Rumpus Pumpus
stirred. His stirrings alerted Finta Fanta. He opened his
eyes. Down the slope of the uncovered river bed he could

see the water; but it stood now in an indeterminate stance. It was not flowing as before. It was deathly quiet: some traffic murmurs came from well away, but above all it was peaceful, almost watchful.

In the water, Finta Fanta could see the angle of a plastic milk crate floating slowly on the stream. It was turning, more or less steady in its place and she wondered if it were tethered. Then she noticed it was moving slowly, but if anything with gathering speed, in the direction from which they had come.

'Rumpus,' she said. 'Look. The tide's turned.' Sure enough the milk crate was now steadily flooding in on the tide.

'Good,' grunted Rumpus Pumpus. He cast an eye at the sky and his ears heard only the night noises of the city. 'Must be getting on for two o'clock,' he said. 'Time to go soon.'

After a few minutes they stood up and walked the few metres to the entrance to Bow Creek. The wasteland to their right now stood up above the low tide level to more than twice the height of an elephant. Under the shadow of the bank they made their way carefully along and waited by the mouth of the creek. As the tide started to flood, they turned into the creek and, returning to the middle of the stream, began to walk up it with the flood.

Above them, to their right, the rough ground covered in coarse grass stood high and dark. To their left were the packed wharfs and landing places of the warehouses and factories; mostly high up on steel-piled banks, towering way above even their mighty heads. As they rounded the first main meander, the creek turning back on itself, they trudged along with water now only up to their bellies though starting to rise fast. An alsatian, obviously let to roam around the premises it guarded, sniffed them and bounded, barking madly, to press its nose against the steel slats of the fence. Through the spaces between them it saw the elephants and its note changed to a cringing, yapping kind of bark; half warning, half fear. The guard came up to see what was afoot and shone a light around. He found no intruders and could make out no shape clearly in the river below him. He took it for a false alarm and went back to his coffee and his detective novel.

The flood was starting to run more strongly now and the creek deepening. As they passed under the bridge that carried the East India Dock Road, the water was well up their sides. A vehicle or two thundered by to their left where the river swung round near the Blackwall Tunnel approach road.

'My next landmark,' said Rumpus Pumpus as he heard the lonely lorries on the highway. 'If my memory serves me right – and it always does – we should soon come to a lock and from there on it's straight walking.'

Already the maritime creek had become the inland River Lee (Lea). Where vegetation could grow it was apparent, even in the loom of distant street lights, that the banks had lost that roughness of the tidal marsh and had started to harbour stunted alders and the odd briar brake. The river widened and Rumpus Pumpus saw his next goal before them. Like a door, in fact a pair of doors, side by side, with a steel framework of overhead gear above, the lock, which is what he sought, connected the River Lee (Lea), that wandered haphazardly all over Hackney and Walthamstow Marshes, to the canalized navigation river that ran more or less directly along the valley's western side.

As Rumpus Pumpus saw the lock he was astonished at the height of the rise – some six metres or so – and the sheer walls that surrounded it to cut off the tidal river from the navigation way behind. The flash, or widening, of the river by the lock was also deeper. He and Finta Fanta

263

wallowed and swam their way through it and continued upstream, uncertain now how to proceed. Rumpus Pumpus' plans relied on following the navigation way. Beyond the flash they found their feet again and wallowed on in the blackness. They passed under a road bridge and saw the black crisscrosses of a steel rail bridge before them. The navigation way ran beside the river here, some three or four metres in level above it. Between the two was a grass causeway with the towpath on it.

'Ah hah!' said Rumpus Pumpus with satisfaction. His plan held good. On their left the deep-piled sides now gave way to a sloping bank out of the river up the side of the causeway. It was steep and surfaced with flat stone but it looked possible.

'Do you think that slope looks as steep as the moat round our pen at the zoo?' asked Rumpus Pumpus. Finta Fanta blinked a little and the two waded across beside it.

'Nothing like,' she concluded. 'Frontal assault, I should say. If we take it steadily we should be able to climb straight up.'

'You go first,' said Rumpus Pumpus. 'Like that I can push you.'

Finta Fanta started up the steep slope. As her hind legs came to the foot of it, some metre or so beneath the surface, Rumpus Pumpus placed his broad head against her stern and gave a helping push. In two or three careful paces she was up. Her forefeet reached the top and her hind feet followed. She turned, locked trunks with Rumpus Pumpus and with no more effort than she had had, he rose with dignified speed from the water and took his place on the towpath.

'That, my dear,' he said, nodding at the canalized waterway before them, 'is the River Lee,' (Lea), 'Navigation. Look sharp now and follow it up and we'll arrive before dawn.'

And so they did. With great sure-footedness they trod the length of the towpath as the hours of darkness slipped away. Mostly they were simply able to follow the path; but when it crossed the river on flimsy-looking bridges or passed beneath roads and bridges with too little clearance for the elephants, they simply took to the water again. Being a canalized navigation, it was nowhere more than a couple of metres deep; and so they were able to trot ahead against the gentle tamed current with no problem. So they passed under road and motorway, skirted fields and factories and headed generally north-west. They met no-one in those dead hours, walking steadily on, for all the world like a pair of overgrown tow-horses bringing nothing but themselves up the River Lea (Lee) Navigation from the Thames to Walthamstow Marshes.

At Lee (Lea) Bridge Road they had to take to the water again to get under the bridge. It was deep, there being a weir nearby that let an overflow back to the natural river now some kilometres distant across the marshes. But they swam and struggled through it, enjoying its warmth compared to the cold tidal waters downstream and eventually scrambled out near a fallen tree on the eastern side, opposite the dark, black bulk of a corrugated-iron-covered timber yard that smelt of pine and chip-board and, they detected, just a hint of mahogany somewhere.

Before them now stretched a fine, wide path just a metre or two back from the towpath proper. They followed it eagerly, it was good going and the night was drawing on. It must have been between five and six o'clock. A distinct lightness was coming into the sky in the east; but it was a noise, not the light, that made Rumpus Pumpus stop.

'Listen,' he said happily, 'I think we're nearly there.'

In the growing light they could just make out a straight black line as their horizon. From one extremity of it there came an irregular clanking, coming and going in the rising breeze. Then a light appeared and the clanking came clearer and more regular. Finally, the single light was now followed by many and it became evident that they were looking at a long railway embankment stretching to their right across the flat expanse of the marshes, topped by a train rattling its early morning way to Liverpool Street with a cargo of dawn commuters.

'Come on, Finta, we're virtually there,' tooted Rumpus Pumpus and they quickened their step on the good, broad path and headed on. The track crossed under the railway embankment beside the river, under a fine arch of blue Stafford bricks and the elephants found that they had now left football pitches and playing fields behind and had come into an area of rough ground which, after the railway bridge, became even wilder with brakes of alder and willow, marshy ponds and buddleia bushes, reeds and boggy tracks and dryer parts with some hazel and briar.

The light was now growing fast on a grey, breezy day, that looked as if it promised rain. The elephants paused and looked around. 'This must be it, I suppose,' said Rumpus Pumpus. 'I think I could live off the long grasses and woody shoots, don't you?'

'Yees,' said Finta Fanta, a little warily. 'For a while I could.'

They wandered on a little further and then Rumpus Pumpus trumpeted for joy: 'We are there!' he tooted and pointed with his trunk at a wooden sign.

'Home sweet home,' said Finta Fanta and read out the words in a sonorous voice: 'Walthamstow Marsh, Nature Reserve.

'Well, Walthamstow Marsh, bid welcome to *loxodonta africana*, your latest protected species.'

And the two elephants grabbed trunkfuls of grass and began to browse. Slowly, they wandered off amongst the brakes, ponds and trees and were lost to view from the railways and the paths.

Mr Sedge walked with sprightly step up to the news-stand at East Croydon station. Dull and threatening to rain as the day was, his joy at living overwhelmed the weather entirely and he jostled forward for a paper.

He caught sight of a full-page headline on a tabloid – 'SOHO JUMBOS SMASH VICE SQUAD' – and with pounding heart and eager eye, bought a selection of the press to glean what details he could. By the time he left Charing Cross he was apprised of the main facts and almost ran along Whitehall to get into the office and start sorting out the next action. Go straight to the minister? Take the day off and go hunting for the elephants? No-one seemed to know where they were. Go to the police and tell what he knew? But they knew everything they needed to and would hardly believe him if he told them about his conversations with elephants. And what of Henri? It seemed the Founders and Grinders had him under some sort of ancient prerogative. If that was so, he could not hope to talk to him even before the police. And anyway, he knew nothing, other than what was printed in the papers; indeed, rather less.

At one point, Mr Sedge nearly leapt up and made for the door, to rush out and scour the riverside, to do anything that would establish where his friends were and let him help them. But into his mind came the image of Finta Fanta and Rumpus Pumpus poring over the map at The Splurge and planning their moves with great care. He didn't know where they were, but he knew where they wanted to go, and that pair of elephants, he knew, had a marked ability to get where they wanted without being seen by anybody very much – except to enlist help in their own enterprises.

Suddenly, a strong note of steadying deliberation entered Mr Sedge's mind. As if one of the elephants were advising him and telling him not to go running all over the place when a bit of imagination and an addition of swift action should be quite enough to save the day. Mr Sedge made an assumption. The assumption that the elephants knew where they were going and would somehow, by means only they could devise, have got there. He couldn't possibly verify his guess; but having made it, his next action became obvious and immediate.

From perching on the front of his desk he walked round and sat in the seat, then took a notebook from his briefcase. He scribbled out a note and was about to raise the phone when a feeling of caution came over him. It was still half an hour before the time he had, under the departmental rules, to be at work. So he threw on his coat again and went out. At St James's Park underground station he found a phone box that worked and spent fifteen minutes making a series of anonymous phone calls to some very significant people. Within ten more minutes he was back at his desk: breathing space, he hoped, at least a day or two's breathing space, and the news would tell him soon enough if his assumption had been right.

He checked with his contact in Environment if the protection order on *loxodonta africana* had gone through. Finding that it had, he immediately put the finishing touches to two applications for naturalization and two passport applications. He made them up into the appropriate files, added all the dockets urging speed and ministerial attention and then put them in his out-tray. The messenger system would operate in usual clockwork fashion and sparks would start to fly, he judged, at about this time tomorrow morning. He would be ready.

His thoughts then turned to Henri. He put through a call to The Worshipful Company of Founders and Grinders and discovered Henri's trial was probably due for Saturday. Knowing Henri was likely to need every second he could get, he decided to leave him alone till the weekend: but the question of the police involvement worried him. Would Henri face questioning from them and possible charges, along with Mr Sedge, for harbouring escaped elephants? It all seemed a bit unlikely if you knew the elephants were people acting under their own free will. But the authorities did not know that. It made Mr Sedge feel a little uncomfortable.

As the large open office began to fill up, Mr Sedge sensed it was going to be one of those days when everyone was tense, looked a little sideways at everyone else and was at pains to be seen doing everything correctly. As always, this tension filtered down from the private office: the sanctuary of the minister himself, his advisers and his immediate executives. The cause of this tension was, of course, the very events that Mr Sedge was indirectly involved in. A major débâcle with the police, an event seized upon by opposition politicians and campaigning journalists to question the rule of law and slap down parliamentary questions about whether the police, or pageantry, keeps the law of the land. A mighty hunt for convincing excuses and binding precedent was afoot in the upper echelons of the ministry. The hunt followers felt the pace and fury: some roughed in with glee, others tried to hide.

At twelve-thirty sharp, Mr Sedge left his desk and went out for his lunch hour. He bought a selection of tasty sandwiches at the take-away and then slipped into an electrical goods shop in Victoria Street. From there, now the proud possessor of a personal radio, he headed rapidly for St James's Park where, with coat wrapped firmly round him and a bag of sandwiches on his lap, he unravelled his purchase, got the orange ear-pads of the headphones over his ears and, after fiddling two batteries into place, got it working in time for the one o'clock news.

It began to drizzle. The park was empty but for passers-by who scurried quickly under umbrellas and kept their heads bowed. Mr Sedge's umbrella went up too, somewhat uncertainly in the gusty breeze. At least the sandwiches were all right and he munched away at them with hungry appetite.

As he expected, the news bulletin was beginning to clarify the evident confusion of the morning papers; the picture was becoming clearer. A goose waddled out of the lake and begged for a piece of bread. Mr Sedge threw a piece to it. It gobbled and honked. Another protected species in a London Park, mused Mr Sedge. On came an interview with the President of the Zoological Society of London. Obviously everything had to come out now. Mr Sedge nodded in satisfaction as each point confirmed his guesses: it was not clear how the elephants had escaped; it had been assumed a ransom might be demanded so no publicity had been allowed; the Metropolitan Police had done a wonderful job in tracking them down; unconfirmed reports had come in that the elephants were in Walthamstow Marshes. Yes, this did seem incredible and no, he didn't have the faintest idea how they could have got there from Cleopatra's Needle; he really couldn't say whether the man in the custody of the livery company was anything to do with the elephants or not, this person was certainly unknown to the zoo.

There then followed a lot of boring interviews about the rights and wrongs of worshipful companies removing suspects from police custody, the rest of the news and then the start of the news comment section.

Here Mr Sedge's munching slowed again as the programme took in a live interview from the radio-car parked in Walthamstow Marshes.

'Now for it,' murmured Mr Sedge. 'Fingers crossed for the value of anonymous phone calls.'

'. . . and those rumours have indeed proved to be true,' said the reporter from the radio-car. 'The two elephants are here in the nature reserve, to all intents and purposes wandering around, browsing on the grass and the branches as if Walthamstow Marshes were the Serengeti or, perhaps more to the point, Whipsnade. Obviously, the word has got around amongst the local community here but I must stress that police are keeping the general public well clear of the area and people shouldn't try to come and see the elephants.

'Perhaps the most surprising thing here is that literally hundreds of volunteers from a host of environmental, animal rights and ecology groups have descended on the area and are helping the police to keep the public at bay. Fortunately the elephants are in an area bordered by steep-sided railway embankments and the River Lea,' (Lee), 'so it's possible to keep people out fairly easily.

'The ecology groups seem to have been tipped off by an anonymous phone caller at about nine o'clock this morning. It's also been pointed out, quite correctly it would seem, that these elephants are a protected species and, what no-one realized before, this area is a designated habitat for them under the various acts of parliament protecting wild life.'

'Does this mean they're in Walthamstow Marshes to stay?' asked the presenter.

'Well, common sense would seem to say that the elephants belong to the zoo. Although they haven't been positively identified by anyone from the zoo yet, we must assume that these are the elephants which disappeared. But even so, spokesmen for the animal rights and environmental groups here are saying that they'll fight any move to what they call 'reincarcerate' the animals, as they are wild animals under the acts and this is their legally designated habitat. This looks like becoming a *cause célèbre* for the animal rights movement.'

'Is there any indication of how the elephants got to Walthamstow Marshes since they were last sighted at Cleopatra's Needle on the Embankment yesterday?'

'Well, indications are that they got here of their own accord. Footprints have been found at various places on the towpath of the River Lee,' (Lea), 'Navigation and it looks very much as if they must have drifted down the Thames to the River Lea,' (Lee), 'estuary near Canning Town last night and then walked up the river to this nature reserve in the small hours. Just how they did this has yet to be adequately explained.'

'Was there any suggestion that they were accompanied?'

'Apparently not. There are plenty of witnesses to the fact that they took to the water entirely unaccompanied yesterday and there's no evidence of anyone accompanying them on their way here. The whole thing gets more and more mysterious. How did Walthamstow Marshes get designated as a habitat for elephants? How did the elephants know it? How did they manage to find their way here, apparently unaided? The only person who can probably answer these questions is this morning's anonymous phone caller.'

'Is it thought that this anonymous phone caller could be the young man whom the police wanted to question in connection with their raid on Soho yesterday? The young liveryman who had to be handed over to The Worshipful Company of Founders and Grinders yesterday?'

'Well, wouldn't it be nice if things were that simple? But no, the police obviously checked on this but he was actually locked in a dungeon, would you believe, at the time those phone calls were made. Unless someone is working in collusion with him, which apparently seems unlikely, he would appear to have nothing much to do with the elephants at all.'

Under his umbrella in the friendly drizzle, Mr Sedge beamed with delight. Those phone calls had done their job admirably. The news report mumbled on to the legal aspects and the tussle over jurisdiction concerning Henri. It did nothing more than confirm the status quo and bring it into question. He packed up his personal radio and gave it a friendly little pat. Then he eased it into his coat pocket and headed back for the ministry. The goose gave a last honk as a surplus piece of bread came its way; but didn't seem to mind too much when a voracious sparrow made off with a good half of it.

If anyone knows how to question people, make no mistake about it, the Vice Squad does. They've only got to have a suspect for a couple of hours and they'll give you his ancestry for the last couple of centuries, not to mention his whereabouts at the time the incident, whatever it was, took place. Where Soho is concerned, such is their background knowledge of the intertwining vine of relationships that curls in and around that quarter, that most statements hardly need checking independently.

The trouble with the jazz band was that they all told the truth. What's more, working the night through as they did, they all got up around lunch time and were at the peak of their form around midnight. Yet, by this time, the police, healthy, clean-living chaps that they were, were beginning to feel positively dreary. As they left their interview rooms and compared their notes, they resorted to strong coffee and brisk washing in cold water to shake off the lingering tiredness: none of it worked. As the night wore on they went back to Sady McCabe, back to Pete Davis, back to the drummer who'd only come in for that one night and back to James Daley. By this time the police were on their knees with the intellectual effort of questioning and the members of the band were just getting into their stride at the hour of the most spirited playing, at the time of the most rhythmic swing.

At half-past two, Sergeant Apta Dapta called the band before him. Their belongings were returned to them and they were told they were to be set free.

'But I know there's something you're not telling me,' said the Sergeant. 'We'll find out what it is, though, so why don't you just tell us now?'

The four musicians, bright, perky, full of the pleasures of the end of day, a little tired now perhaps but nonetheless looking forward to relaxing, looked at one another. Pete Davis grinned and kept silent. James Daley shrugged his shoulders and smiled and shook his head. The drummer looked genuinely nonplussed and Sady McCabe actually laughed out loud.

'We'd agreed not to tell anyone,' said Sady McCabe, looking at the others. 'Because no-one would believe us. You wouldn't believe us either: but what do you think, band? If they promise to let us go anyway, shall we tell them?'

The others looked dubious.

'Would you still let us go, even if you thought we were being cheeky with you?' said Sady McCabe with a jovial grin on her face.

'It might make me think twice about it,' replied Sergeant Apta Dapta. 'On the other hand, withholding information is an offence.'

'Well then, since we don't want to withhold any information and we're not trying to be cheeky. It's just that you may think we're cheeky because of what we say. We'll tell you.'

The policemen looked on, curious to know what was coming next. Some had grins at the corners of their mouths. The grins dropped like falling bricks when Sady McCabe said:

'The elephants can talk, you know. They're people like you and me. No-one's stolen them; they just, well . . . are.'

The Sergeant looked at the constables and they all looked at each other. A sort of feeling of anger went through them, then one of resignation.

'If they've got their things, let them go,' said the Sergeant. No-one made any more comment. The band shrugged their shoulders and filed off. Outside the police station they laughed and went their ways. Inside the police station, the constables went off duty and Sergeant Apta Dapta checked that the search along the river between Cleopatra's Needle and Blackfriar's Bridge was in proper progress. Then he too went home and wondered what on earth police work was coming to.

As we know, finding the elephants was to cause no problem at all. The problems, in fact, all started when they were found. But Sergeant Apta Dapta, when he heard where they were, clapped his hands with glee, checked that the elephant unit knew what was happening and closed his file with satisfaction. Off his territory and out of his speciality, it could all be left to the good men of the Metropolitan Police at large. With considerable joy he turned once more to good old Vice and considered how to build on the impact of the previous day's raid.

The elephants, by eleven o'clock, had long since caught scent of the small army of people that now surrounded them. Carefully discovering the limits of their terrain they saw bevies of anoraked ecologists and animal rights activists, dotted here and there with blue police uniforms, at all the exits to their nature reserve. At least a couple of people stood guard at the footbridges over the river, and larger groups clustered at the railway arch they had come through. More were at a railway crossing at another corner of their domain, beside a bridge far too low for an elephant to walk through.

It was apparent to the elephants that the police were keeping everyone at a good distance. Several film crews and cameramen were scrambling about on the railway embankments with long lenses and lots of encumbering tripods.

'I think they're afraid of us,' said Finta Fanta when the elephants had made a discreet tour of their domain.

'Yes,' said Rumpus Pumpus, 'not surprising, I suppose. I remember reading in a Sunday newspaper once how someone had gone to Africa and been terribly brave, facing up to lions and gnu and, most of all, the mighty elephant. Do you know, he must have been really afraid of us, because he came all the way from Europe just to shoot us and take our tusks. Trying to increase his strength by capturing some of ours, I suppose. If only he'd known what piffling things lions are and what stunning boredom savanna elephants regarded humans with, he'd never have bothered.'

'I don't suppose he would,' said Finta Fanta. 'If they only knew the lengths that wild elephants go to in order to avoid humans, they'd never feel pursued again. I suppose it's stampedes and charges that make them afraid – we've used that to our own advantage – but can you imagine an elephant being frightened of a stampede of humans, a football match, say? Come to think of it, football matches probably are quite frightening; but then you only have to stay away, don't you?'

'Precisely,' said Rumpus Pumpus, lifting his trunk like a periscope and sniffing at the drizzle-laden air in all directions. 'I say, I sniff someone familiar.' Finta Fanta lifted her trunk and rotated too. They were side by side in a clump of alder bushes, grazing intermittently on the very long but rather dead grass that grew in the small space of open ground between the low trees. 'Smelt him in Old Compton Street last evening,' murmured Rumpus Pumpus, 'and somewhere before that, too.'

'The zoo,' stated Finta Fanta. 'It's the vet from the zoo.' They both shuddered at the thought. Both of them were wondering how to handle it. He had presumably come to take them back. They'd resist: but how far should they go? Should they reveal their speech? Should they go like sheep? Should they try and go elsewhere? They suddenly both turned an eye to each other and said:

'Sedge!' Then laughed at the simultaneous idea.

'What do you think he's doing?' asked Rumpus Pumpus. Finta Fanta was good at this sort of speculation and murmured on:

'Mmm. Our escapades must have reached the papers and the radio; he'll know about our journey to the Thames. He's the one who pointed out this reserve and got it designated a habitat for us. So I would guess he'll do something to make sure everyone knows we're supposed to be here. In fact, you know, I would guess, wouldn't you Rumpus, that it's probably his action somehow that's kept everyone at bay? Just think: no-one stumbled across us and ran off screaming or anything like that. No, the authorities and those others have all turned up apparently knowing we're to be left alone. I think our Mr Sedge might be behind that – he's the only one who could have told them.'

'That does make sense,' agreed Rumpus Pumpus. 'Stay put and see what happens?'

'Well, up to a point, yes. And anyway until tomorrow. But, what about our career as trumpeters? We ought not to let that drop, ought we? We ought to carry on getting into human society and earning our living, don't you think?'

'I do, I do. But I don't think we should leave this nature

reserve till Mr Sedge tells us it's all right. What if we wait till tomorrow afternoon? If we've heard nothing then, we can break our silence and get in contact with Mr Sedge over the weekend. He told us his number and address. He could perhaps suggest something.' They agreed on this, then turned to their munching.

The grey and drizzly afternoon of a May day settled over Walthamstow Marshes. The green leaves, and they were there in abundance now, stood out like salads against their wooden bowls. A single glance showed luscious green everywhere and in whatever they chewed there was an exciting sappiness that only truly fresh plants have when eaten in the full growth of spring.

Two sides of their reserve were bounded by railway embankments: on those the trains clanked by with an intense loneliness above the flat plain of open marsh and scrub; passing from the densely settled region of Hackney, across this tongue of country which pushed south through the grime of London, to the equally densely settled borough of Walthamstow, a minute away but in another world to the valley at its side.

On the third side of their domain ran the river Lee (Lea) Navigation; and on the fourth side were Walthamstow reservoirs, beyond Coppermill Lane – the surfaced remnant of an ancient track that must once have wound a precious dry-shod way through the dangerous bogs, from one bank of the valley to the other.

On a drizzly day to a casual glance, a dreary place of unexciting nature and of stagnant pools. But to an elephant eye, a sanctuary where a pair of kestrels nested on a nearby pylon, swung and hovered, plunged and rose and gave testimony to a teeming life of voles and mice and rats; who in turn were evidence for a host of insects and a forest of undergrowth and plants. Chilly and damp to be sure, but lusher by far than many a tract of savanna. The elephants, all things considered, felt very much at home.

Chapter 17

By half-past two in the afternoon, Mr Sedge had cleared his work and permitted himself a cup of coffee at his desk. Machine coffee in a plastic cup that guaranteed migraine if you drank enough of it; but hot and steamy none the less and therefore acceptable. He fingered the delicate little plastic framework which, like all truly established civil servants, he had obtained at his own expense to hold the plastic cup and provide a handle that didn't burn one's fingers. In the upper echelons of the administrative officers, tea could be taken from white china cups with a gold rim round the top. It is doubtful if it tasted any better than the machine-made coffee.

Mr Sedge turned over in his mind the probable events of the morrow when his nationality and passport applications hit the occupant of the private office. He was sure of his ground, his precedents, his contacts in Environment, everything. But he was afraid of what would happen if he was laughed out of court – in other words if anyone in that office tumbled to the fact that R. Pumpus and F. Fanta were a pair of elephants. Of course, they would have to know in the end: but if the principle of their eligibility for citizenship and passports was established before their species was revealed, they were in a strong position. The reverse, and everyone risked looking ridiculous. He went over the points in his mind again but saw nothing new he could do. He suddenly noticed that his fingers had stopped fiddling with his coffee-cup holder and reposed on the desk, firmly crossed.

The internal messenger came round.

'Just to keep you busy,' he grunted, plonking a pile of dossiers in Mr Sedge's in-tray.

'Ah, I was just feeling like a nice complicated repatriation appeal,' joked Mr Sedge through gritted teeth. The messenger shuffled on, having satisfied the necessity for politeness with his standing platitude.

But Mr Sedge's eye fell immediately on the file about half-way down the small heap. The tag sticking from the side identified it at once as the one he had sent up that morning with the elephants' passport application.

'Dash!' he exclaimed under his breath; and worried it out of the heap. On the front was an informal memo from the acceptance clerk in the private office. He was on good terms with this man, largely because his preparation of documents was always so meticulous.

'Caught you out at last!' ran the friendly, handwritten memo. 'No photos with the passport ap. Pse attach same and resubmit.'

'Double dash!' said Mr Sedge under his breath. He'd hoped to get away with that one. Usually, the last thing they were bothered about was the photos. It was an unspoken point of honour not to judge by appearances: largely because it caused all sorts of trouble afterwards. Just the same, even for an application raised in the special section, they were supposed to be there and he couldn't very well try and palm them off with an excuse. The acceptance clerk was obviously acting on instructions – perhaps there was an F. Fanta somewhere who was a known criminal. The photos would have to be provided.

The alternative would be to drop the passport applications altogether. The trouble with that was that if the passports were granted they effectively conceded nationality and the naturalization papers could be discreetly withdrawn.

'Triple dash!' said Mr Sedge and got up and went out to the coffee machine and took another dose of its harsh medicine. He plonked his cup-in-holder back on the desk in his alcove and slopped sploshes of coffee over the desk surface. This annoyed him at first and he glowered darkly about for a moment. He was blotting up the stains with a paper handkerchief when it occurred to him that coffee-stained photographs might not be too recognizable. He fished out an old bus-pass from his wallet and solemnly impressed the foot of the coffee-cup holder, nicely wet with black coffee, on to the face of it. After a few moments he had a rather bad photograph of Mr Sedge with a brown crescent moon looping across it from one corner to the other. It still looked like Mr Sedge though. Next he tried a bit of painting and managed to make himself look like a kind of Dravidian pirate but, nevertheless, still indisputably a member of the Sedge family and in no circumstances anything other than *homo sapiens sapiens*.

'Is there no race on earth with tusks?' hissed Mr Sedge. He scoffed at the picture, tore it and the bus-pass in two and went back to sipping the remains of his coffee and drumming with his fingers on the desk.

'Elephants,' he murmured. 'Elephants . . . elephantia . . . elephantiasis . . . Ah! Elephantiasis. Now there's an interesting possibility.'

Elephantiasis was a disease of which Mr Sedge had vaguely heard and, in the hope that it made people look like elephants, he fished his dictionary out of the bottom drawer of his desk and looked it up. No luck. It could cause the legs to swell to elephant-like proportions but obviously didn't change the features much or have any exotic dental implications.

His fingers drummed again. Suddenly, his hand leapt to the phone. His principal opposite number at Clive House, the passport office, answered.

'Look, I've got a "special" going through at the moment,' explained Mr Sedge after the usual hellos, 'but the bloke has come down with some weird skin condition that'll make his photograph distinctly inhuman if we try and get it included now. The document's needed urgently, of course. Is there any way a passport can be issued without a photograph?'

'Shouldn't be, of course,' came the immediate reply, 'but if it's a private office job and your minister recommends it, I suppose it could be done. I seem to remember we issued a protected person's one once with a photo but without a name. It was for a shipwrecked sailor who'd lost his memory. Stuck his thumb print on the name line and explained it all on the "Observations" page.

'Come to think of it, the easiest thing to do would be to issue the passport for three months only, stick a thumb print where the photograph should be, explain it all under "Observations" and just do a Form D renewal, changed particulars, when the three months are up.'

'Could you clear that in principle with your head of section and get it to me in writing, if it's okay?'

'Right oh. Ring you back in an hour.'

Mr Sedge spent an anxious hour. It took him nearly all of it to clear the rest of the rubbish out of his in-tray. The phone rang.

'Do as I suggested,' came the reply, 'and it'll be all right – but not more than three months – all right?'

'Fine,' said Mr Sedge, 'thanks, you've solved a big problem.' He put the phone down. 'Three weeks would be enough,' he muttered to himself. He pulled out the dictionary again and checked 'thumb': 'a part or thing', he read, under definition number four, 'like, reminiscent of, or employed as, a thumb'.

'Got em!' he exclaimed, slapping the book closed with enough force to make the bureaucrat across the aisle look in Mr Sedge's direction for a moment. Then he grabbed his coat and umbrella, and prepared a special black briefcase with the royal coat of arms discreetly embossed on the front in gold, then prepared himself to go out on official business – a rare treat indeed to office fodder.

Once outside the open office, Mr Sedge stopped by a door in the corridor and read a notice 'Conference in Progress' with some anxiety. Instead of taking the lift he went down the stairs two floors and listened at the equivalent door on that level: silence. He opened it carefully. Another conference room as he had expected – but empty at the moment. He scanned round it quickly. In the far corner on a side table was the phone he had been hoping to find. This was a call that must not be overheard in the open office. He padded across to the table and rang Environment. A certain Mr Sedge would be coming from the Home Office to officially ascertain the identity of the elephants now in Walthamstow Marshes. They were, of course, the elephants from the zoo; but the ministry had to have its own independent reports for police purposes. Environment, well used to this kind of inter-ministerial formality, assented at once and told Mr Sedge to liaise with the joint police-zoo elephant unit that was currently masterminding affairs in the marsh. Environment forewarned them of Mr Sedge's coming and instructed full co-operation. Mr Sedge set out for the marsh.

It was about four o'clock by the time he was in the street and heading for Victoria Station. He smiled a little wryly to think that his minister was at that moment on his hind legs in the House of Commons defending himself at Home Office questions over the vestigial rights of worshipful companies. To his knowledge, the minister was an honorary member of two or three such companies himself. It would be a delicate dispatch-box dance.

At Victoria, Mr Sedge plunged into the Underground, his post and seniority not being sufficient to elevate him to that class of civil servants entitled to take taxis, let alone staff-cars. He bought a return ticket to Seven Sisters Station and arrived there rather quicker than a taxi, and very much quicker than a staff-car. Following his street map, he cut through several roads of run-down, dubious-looking terraced housing that might have been anywhere in any not particularly desirable part of north London. Via an alley and, as he had suspected from long experience as an adventurous boy, a hole in a fence, he got through on to the tow path of the River Lee (Lea). He followed it along, a pleasant enough walk, though rather muddy. To his left, across the river, he could see the banks of the Walthamstow Reservoirs with Canada geese tugging at the close-cropped grass of the slopes. The river looked dark and far from clean; but the huddled figures of a couple of fishermen loitering under a vast green umbrella suggested its condition was not hopeless, even if not perfect.

In places, the tow path ran past blocks of flats, in others past a timber yard and the back gardens of rows of houses. Huge willows towered over it, their bark a bare, murky grey; but their branches now covered with the tiny reddish-green springtime leaves of May. Some gardens had tulips in, bowing and nodding in the breeze and feeling a little forlorn in the chilly afternoon that threatened to drizzle again, despite a few wild breaks in the cloud.

Soon, Mr Sedge spied a green footbridge spanning the river, immediately before it a boat house that evidently belonged to a rowing club, judging from the ranks of sculls visible through an open door. The far bank of the river was lined with moored cabin cruisers and, checking on the plan, he saw this must be Springfield Marina. This would be the footbridge to cross and, beyond the marina which came into view on the other side of the bridge, would be the marsh where the elephants had set up home.

A bevy of people stood around the end of the footbridge which had evidently been cordoned off by the police. As the area came into full view, Mr Sedge saw that what he had taken to be a caravan was in fact a police mobile control centre. A road which came to a dead end at the footbridge led off to the right. On it were several vans from television organizations and a funny-looking taxi with aerials sprouting out of it. He realized this must be the famous radio car of the news bulletins.

'My my,' murmured Mr Sedge, 'quite impressive, really.'

He went up to the door of the mobile control unit and confronted the most senior-looking officer in sight: a middle-aged, deadly serious-looking type with a flat cap and a razor sharp gaze designed to cut down lies like nettles before the scythe. Mr Sedge took a deep breath, swung his brief-case up before him so that the coat of arms came into view and then worried out his civil service identity card from inside.

'Sedge – from the Home Office,' he said firmly, showing his card to the chief inspector and extending a hand in as grim a welcome as he could manage. The chief inspector relaxed – which is to say he ceased being as sharp as a scythe and became about as welcoming as a lawn mower – beckoning Mr Sedge into the caravan where he was asked if he'd like a cup of tea. Mr Sedge declined the tea but managed to cadge a pair of wellington boots from the police while they checked with the elephant unit by radio to see that they were ready to receive the man from the Home Office. They were. Over the bridge, apparently, and follow the path until you come to the marsh. The elephant unit would meet him there.

'Now,' said Mr Sedge, feeling the strength of character which refusing police tea required, 'the ministry wants me to take a small film crew close up to the elephants so that the public at large is reassured about their welfare. I'm to be responsible for it, not you, and the approach is to be conducted under my supervision.'

There were a few sideways glances amongst the police at this, but 'responsibility' was the magic word. The police acquiesced; and Mr Sedge went out in gumboots and with briefcase and hailed the reporters who were standing about frustratedly in sheepskin coats trying to drum up yet another report from what had become a decidedly static situation.

'Sedge, Home Office,' said Mr Sedge. 'I've come to verify the elephants' identity for official purposes and, if you'd like to, you can send a small camera crew with me.'

They needed no second bidding. Within a couple of minutes the BBC and ITN had turned out a team of three each from the waiting vehicles: a cameraman, a sound engineer and a reporter who imagined he was going along to give his own impressions. However, once the little group of seven were across the bridge and out of sight behind the marina, Mr Sedge gave them an impromptu briefing.

'Now,' he announced, standing under a tree that grew in the middle of the path behind the marina fence, 'we'll meet up with the elephant unit in a minute and go towards the elephants. I have to go ahead alone and conduct my verification. When that's finished, if it's safe to do so, I'll call you forward and you can have a few minutes fairly close up to them; but you must always do as I say, and go away when I tell you to. Now have you got your interview microphones ready?'

The reporters started to explain that they would just get ambiance and sound effects near the elephants and conduct interviews after withdrawing, hopefully with the elephants somewhere in the background.

'Won't do,' said Mr Sedge, beginning to enjoy his role as the solid voice of officialdom. Nonetheless, a little smile played at the corners of his boyish lips as he said, 'You must have interview microphones ready as you approach the elephants. As you will see, the ministry regards this as a matter of great importance: the next hour will be significant for thinking beings everywhere.'

The newsmen began to wonder if Mr Sedge was quite all right when he said this: the gravity of the message, the humour on the lips. They paused a moment but seemed to conclude that, since the only way to their news metreage was via a fool, it was best to humour him. Interview mikes at the ready, the group turned and continued towards the marshes. Within a few minutes they met up with the elephant unit who, from the earth track, lined on each side with deep ditches full of stagnant water, pointed to two gently moving mounds of grey that could be seen about fifty metres distant. Through binoculars which the police lent the newcomers, Mr Sedge saw the top of the head of his dear old Finta Fanta and the unmistakable waggling ears of his good friend Rumpus Pumpus.

The vet in the elephant unit tried to exert his authority by tendering all sorts of advice on elephant danger signals; which way to approach in relation to the wind, and how one should always keep a substantial tree between oneself and the beast. The elephant keeper tried to point out which of the pair was likely to be more dangerous and the three policemen added such conventional wisdom as seemed to be appropriate to accosting elephants.

Mr Sedge cut in, 'Verification is uniquely my responsibility,' he affirmed, patting his briefcase. 'These ditches are going to prevent your easy approach in the first instance: but don't worry. Wait here for my further instructions.' And with that he leapt, without warning, across the stagnant ditch, well over a metre wide; made a precarious-looking skid landing on the other side but, to his own amazement, somehow managed to retain his balance and trudged straight off down a narrow and very slimey path towards the animals without paying the least attention to all the warnings he had just heard.

'Oi!' 'Watch it!' 'Idiot!' 'Come back!' the group started to yell.

'Shush shshsh!' hissed the vet. 'You'll alert them, frighten them!' The little group silenced immediately; but the cameramen hoisted their apparatus to their shoulders and their muscles tensed like dynamic athletes ready to capture the live news metreage of the week – a sedate-looking British civil servant chased off Waltham-stow Marshes by a pair of African elephants. They could feel the headlines pulsing through their veins already.

Long before he'd even peeped through the binoculars, however, Mr Sedge had seen the tip of Finta Fanta's trunk turn towards him and search for a scent as the presence of people had been detected. Before the trunk had fallen again, Mr Sedge had seen the little wave it had given. He at least knew he was expected and could look forward to a good welcome.

The vet flustered around preparing the group to go in and get Mr Sedge if he appeared to have come to grief. The policemen braced themselves with the prospect of heroics. They saw the plump figure slithering along the slimey path with a step that, in the circumstances, betrayed considerable sprightliness and not the least fear. From time to time he was seen to raise an arm or twist his hips to stay upright in the mud, sometimes he jumped or circumvented a puddle and, finally, the path led him around à briar brake that left only his shoulder and head visible, then curved behind a spinney of alders where he was irretrievably lost to view. The backs of the elephants, however, remained visible through the upper branches of the low trees.

The newsmen and elephant unit walked up and down the earth road on the bank of the stagnant ditch in a kind of exasperated tiptoe, craning necks like boys outside a nudist camp, hoping to catch a glimpse of what they weren't allowed to see.

Mr Sedge rounded a tuft of hairy grass and came face to tusk with the two pachyderms who immediately tootled a welcome. Back on the path, the vet turned white and feared the worst. The sound-engineer pulled on a pair of impressive-looking earphones and pointed a long-range microphone – looking a bit like a short length of khaki drainpipe stuck horizontally on top of a handle – towards the clump of alders. Mr Sedge greeted his friends wholeheartedly:

'Hello, hello,' he said in turn to each of them, shaking a trunk here and a trunk there and receiving a pat on the back and a warm embrace from both of them. 'You certainly took to heart all the maps and machinations I talked about the other day. This reserve has been designated for you, all right. You must have realized that by now. You're surrounded by everybody but nobody dares to touch you. What's it like being a major news item?'

'Not too bad,' said Rumpus Pumpus rather laconically, 'but how are things with regard to nationality and status as sapient beings? It's all right here, you know, no complaints, as yet; but we don't want to stay here any longer than necessary. It would just become a rather larger zoo.'

'Yes, of course, it would,' said Mr Sedge. 'That's why

I'm here. You're being left alone at the moment because you're hurting no-one and the zoo's a bit afraid to stand up for its rights and take you back: it hasn't got any transport and feels shamefaced about the whole thing. Finally, the animal rights and animal protection lobbies are insisting you stay here. This is a designated area for you – and since official cruelty to animals is political suicide, people in high places are anxious to keep you safe and happy for the moment.

'I shouldn't really be here at all,' Mr Sedge and the elephants chuckled at this with great good humour, 'but I've managed to make myself the official responsible for identifying you . . .'

'Oh that's easy,' said Finta Fanta, 'I am er . . . myself.'

'So am I, actually,' said Rumpus Pumpus.

'Good,' said Mr Sedge. 'Well, that's got the formalities out of the way. Now, what I really need from you is a photograph for your passports.' There was a short silence.

'Are you serious?' asked Rumpus Pumpus. 'They'll think someone's trying to be funny.'

'Quite so,' said Mr Sedge, hooking his briefcase handle over an alder twig and releasing the catch so that the bag hung open beside him, conveniently to hand. 'So I've told them your skin condition would make photographs misleading at the moment – well that's true, isn't it?' Six eyes glanced at each other a-sparkle. 'And they've agreed to accept thumb prints instead. If we get away with it, they'll issue three-month passports that we can renew as a formality.'

'Oh, well . . . I haven't got a thumb,' said Finta Fanta, rather crestfallen.

'Yes you have,' said Mr Sedge. 'Just reach into that bag and pass me the ink pad, will you?'

Finta Fanta's trunk snaked neatly into the bag, rummaged around for a moment and then pulled out the grey-lidded ink pad which she passed to Mr Sedge.

'. . . "reminiscent of, or employed as, a thumb", says the dictionary!' cited Mr Sedge; and taking hold of the end of the trunk, he pointed to the two lip-like protuberances at its end, that held the ink pad in a very firm grip. He took the pad and pointed to the trunk tips:

'Behold a thumb!' said Mr Sedge and fished in the bag himself for a little note pad on which were prepared some squares of stiff paper the size of passport photographs. Turning the paper pad over, Mr Sedge managed to hold the ink pad on top of it with one hand and took the end of Finta Fanta's trunk with the other.

'Now move your trunk around as I'm directing you and we'll see what we can do.' Mr Sedge manipulated up and down and finally got the upper thumb on the trunk end vertically above the ink pad. He pressed the pad on to it and then made a few prints on the back of the note pad underneath. The first couple of impressions came out as rather incoherent round blobs.

'Tense your thumb a bit,' asked Mr Sedge. Finta Fanta tensioned her trunk tip. Mr Sedge tried again.

'Aah, that's more like it,' he said. 'A bit tenser. Now a bit less tense . . . We'll start from the side this time . . . Oh no, that won't do at all . . . From the top . . . That's it! Got it, perfect! Now two super impressions just like that one on those bits of card here.'

Mr Sedge turned up the prepared squares and made two more impressions. 'Perfect, perfect,' he said; and then performed the same operation with Rumpus Pumpus. Within a few minutes he had four little squares of card all with oblong prints on that were indisputably elephant thumb prints to those who knew what they were looking at; but, more important, were quite credibly human thumb prints to those who did not know what they were looking at. Mr Sedge filed his equipment in the briefcase and turned to more interesting matters with the elephants.

On the path, the newsmen and the elephant unit were starting to get worried. They were wondering if they should shout to Mr Sedge to show himself and beat a retreat while all was still well. But shouting, they thought, had its dangers: and then the sound engineer piped up.

'You know,' he said to the others, somewhat puzzled, 'he's got somebody with him in there.'

'What do you mean?' came in the most senior policeman.

'He's got someone with him,' reaffirmed the sound engineer, directing his long-range microphone precisely along a line towards the elephants and Mr Sedge. 'I can hear him talking and someone's replying. There's too much wood and thicket and probably elephant too, in the way to catch the words: but there are definitely two, maybe even three people talking in there.'

Everyone looked very surprised. 'Knew it all along,' said the policeman again. 'Course they must have been accompanied. Couldn't have got here otherwise. Accomplices hiding up in the bushes: probably animal rights fanatics. And this Mr Sedge, is he for them or against them?'

'We'll soon find out,' said the ITN reporter, shrugging his sheepskin coat up and down his back to rub away the chill of the approaching evening. 'With any luck we'll get in an interview with him before the light goes. It even looks as if it's clearing a bit.'

The reporter had seen the top of Mr Sedge's head appearing over the briar brake and, sure enough, he came out along the path, negotiating the slime with great skill and addressed the waiting group from the far side of the stagnant ditch. Thinking this was going to be the only action metreage of the afternoon, the cameramen had recorded this slithery walk for the benefit of televisual humanity and were considerably shocked at Mr Sedge's announcement.

'The elephants have been positively identified and are quite happy to come and conduct a brief interview with you.' His face was quite straight and he managed to achieve the tone of a junior Home Office minister announcing the statistics of prisoners held on remand in Wales for the preceding six months.

The police sergeant in the elephant unit was about to ask Mr Sedge to just come along quietly, when he realized that the stagnant ditch between them made this a very risky request. Mr Sedge could decide to make a run for it. Although, to the policeman, Mr Sedge was obviously mad, he looked disarmingly sane and he was at a loss what to do. The newsmen were under no such inhibitions and, having already captured on video the potentially comic sequence of gumbooted Whitehall inviting newsmen to talk to elephants, they sniffed an official bungle of the first order and leapt in its pursuit with the instinct of the true newshound.

'We're on our way across, just hold it there, Mr Sedge.'

'Er, no, no,' cut in Mr Sedge quickly, 'er . . . all things considered, it wouldn't do to come on the elephants suddenly with all that equipment. Wait here, please, and I'll bring them to you. You should be able to interview across the ditch quite satisfactorily.'

'Bring 'em out, Mr Sedge, we're ready and waiting,' sang out a newsman, egging on the rounded bureaucrat, as he thought, to make a fool of himself.

But after a short break in which Mr Sedge slithered up the path again and then slithered back into view; coming once more towards the group from the opposite side of the ditch, the newsmen went mad with delight, nearly falling over each other to grab the best camera angles and jostling eagerly, microphones at the ready.

For behind Mr Sedge, in a casual stroll that cared not a jot for slime and slipperiness, for the slime and slipperiness upset it not a bit, came a pair of elephants who, despite their awesome presence, seemed quite unable to hide a certain saunter in their stride, the casual swagger of a man at home walking down his own garden path to meet the beggar at his gate.

'Can you bring them side by side, Mr Sedge?'

'Can you get them to trumpet?'

'Can you give us a quick interview with the elephants beside you?' jabbered the newsmen.

'We'll just jump across and get right in close,' said the BBC cameraman anxious to outdo all comers in the pursuit of public information.

'No, you will not!' boomed a mighty voice from the other side of the ditch. All eyes turned on Mr Sedge; but the voice had undoubtedly come from a place rather higher than his head and with a projection of utterance rather too large for his stature.

The elephant unit and the newsmen stopped dead. They looked at the elephants, now no more than three or four metres away from them, then they looked at each other and then, as if drawn unwillingly by a very powerful magnet, their gaze wandered disbelievingly back to the elephants who waited with Olympian calm until all eyes were fixed upon them.

'This reserve,' said Rumpus Pumpus calmly and commandingly, 'is exclusively designated for *loxodonta africana* and various other species. *Homo sapiens sapiens* has no automatic rights of entry upon it save to observe from the broad paths such as the one you are now standing on. Stay on your side of the ditch, please.'

There was a disbelieving pause. People started glancing sideways at Mr Sedge, obviously wondering how he was managing to pull off this very professional stunt.

'We were given to understand you wanted an interview,' said Finta Fanta a little cheekily and rather coldly. 'We can give you ten minutes, fifteen at the most, right away; and we suggest you get on with it because the light's beginning to go with all this cloud and we don't give you permission to come into our reserve at night with artificial lights.'

The camera- and sound men needed no second bidding and were indeed already hard at it recording all they could. The reporters took some moments to marshal their ideas. Then, confronted with the implacably smiling Mr Sedge and the two elephants, now casually tweaking bits of grass out of the tussocks at their side and occasionally raising their trunks to sniff the air, they finally both spoke together and then, for the first time in their journalistic lives, actually offered the other one to go first. Finally the ITN reporter waded in:

'Er . . . Mr Sedge, what are the elephants' names?'

'Well, I think that's a little rude, if I may say so,' said Mr Sedge, 'asking me the name of someone I'm standing right beside. Ask them.'

Suspecting he was being set up, this was precisely what the reporter had been trying to avoid. He was now on the spot, blushed for the first time in his life; and steeled himself up to going through with the question.

'Er, could I ask you what your names are, please?'

'Yes, of course you can ask,' replied Finta Fanta in a warm and friendly tone, 'but for a number of formal reasons it's not to our advantage to reveal that for a month or so yet. We don't anticipate this will cause too many problems in identifying us, though.'

'Er, no, probably not,' admitted the interviewer and cast around for a follow-up question. 'Um . . . er, are you married?' he managed to ask, racking his brains for the question his viewers would be wanting to ask if they were in his place.

'Oh, really!' laughed Finta Fanta. 'Don't be potty. Surely you know marriage is a uniquely hominid concept. Now why don't you ask us how we got here?'

'How did you get here?' asked the BBC man who had now had enough time to organize his thoughts and began to sense the realities of the situation.

The elephants described how they had swum along the Thames and walked up the River Lee (Lea) Navigation, following plans they had obtained in the previous weeks. The newsmen warmed to the details of the interview and began to treat them like intelligent beings. They zoomed in on the elephants, Mr Sedge being only too pleased to step back out of camera and get out of the limelight.

'But what were you doing in Soho?' came in the BBC man.

'Earning our living,' replied Rumpus Pumpus. 'We're professional musicians and performed regularly at The Splurge. If the police will let you look over the place now, you'll find a pair of trap doors from the warehouse and the light well into the clubroom: we used to trumpet into loudspeaker cabinets through those – quite ingenious, you know.'

'Er, yes, well: and how did you eat there?'

'The fruit and vegetable market, of course. Very convenient. Our colleagues could collect best food by the barrowload.'

The interviewers extracted the full story in its essentials from the elephants and moved on to their escape and the future:

'I'm afraid,' trilled Finta Fanta, 'we can't reveal how we left the zoo. There will doubtless be others who want to leave one day and we don't want to prejudice their chances. Suffice it to remind you that the fence opposite the elephant compound had only a temporary barrier to it during the clay delivery period and we made use of all means available to us.'

'You got out over your wall and through the temporary barrier,' forced the ITN man.

'We made use of all measures available to us,' reaffirmed Finta Fanta.

'And what are your plans now,' he pressed, determined not to be put down. The elephants seized their chance at a free advertisement.

'We're currently looking for a new venue for the band: when that's sorted out we'll be back at our music. We want a summer season somewhere and then it would be nice to put together one or two albums over next winter – maybe even before that.

'Anyway, we have to go now, our colleague Mr Coulisse will be making a statement when he's resolved his difficulties in a few days' time.'

'But!' 'Just a minute!' 'Where?' 'Can you . . .?' 'I say . . .' tried the interviewers. But it was too late. With a sweep of his trunk, Rumpus Pumpus picked up Mr Sedge and swung him over the ditch, depositing him alongside the news-hounds. Then the elephants turned their backs and with their tails swinging idly from side to side, sauntered off to their alder thicket again, to have supper and settle down for the night.

The newsmen then rounded on Mr Sedge and in the tradition of a fair-minded civil servant he accorded them a two-minute interview each, in which he said the same thing to both of them and nothing that wasn't the regurgitated report of the lunch-time news or what they had just been told by the elephants. Freed from the limelight, he made his way back with them to the mobile control unit, handed back his gumboots in return for his shoes, said goodbye to everyone and wandered anonymously off along the tow path, retracing his steps to Seven Sisters Station.

Although it was after seven o'clock when Mr Sedge got

back to the centre of town, he did not go home. He went back to the ministry, was let in by the dead-pan security man and went to his alcove in the open office. He drew himself a coffee and, sitting at his desk, pulled out the passport application 'special' which private office had sent back. Carefully, he endorsed as true likenesses two of the four thumb prints he had obtained, and signed to that effect. He added a note to the docket that the Foreign Office would approve this procedure, written confirmation following that same day.

With a feeling of some satisfaction he took the file and walked through the open office to the far door at the end opposite his alcove. It was a great, silent place at that time of day. One bank of fluorescent lights burned right across at the far side where someone chasing promotion was rushing through an urgent report. Apart from the creak of that man's chair and the sound of his own feet, it was silent in the ministry, the hens had left their run and gone away to roost.

Mr Sedge pushed through the door at the end, out into a brightly lit landing. He took the lift to the eighth floor and went up to the door of the private office itself. As he expected, a few sounds filtered out, someone was still at work there. He knocked and walked in. A very smartly dressed young lady was opposite him, one of the minister's political advisers, fingering her way through a filing cabinet in the outer office, looking for something desperately.

'Oh!' she said as Mr Sedge came in rather unexpectedly. 'You don't happen to know the standard pack number for deportations, do you?'

'Foreign, commonwealth or EEC?' asked Mr Sedge.

'Oh . . . er, EEC.'

'It'll be in the eight hundreds somewhere,' said Mr Sedge, 'unless it's Ireland, in which case it'll be nine hundreds.'

Mr Sedge put his file in the acceptance clerk's in-tray.

From the inner office he heard the Home Secretary's drone recounting his rough handling in the Commons that afternoon. A smooth mandarin attempted to pour honey on his soured feelings. Mr Sedge turned and moved towards the doorway.

'Oh! Thanks. I've found it,' said the young lady. Mr Sedge nodded in assent. She smiled and disappeared towards the inner office. Mr Sedge went back to his alcove and got his coat. He headed for Croydon and, as he left his office, the promotion seeker's chair sent out a long and distant creak as the man stretched and yawned and went back to his report.

The President of the Zoological Society of London switched on the television news with rather mixed feelings. On the one hand things had not gone too badly – the elephants were safe and under surveillance; on the other hand he needed to get them back to the zoo with a minimum of fuss. He judged that after a few days, the animal rights lobby would have made their point and their action would tail off. Public interest, too, would wane: an elephant is after all just an elephant as far as most people are concerned. Once the newsworthiness declined, he could call up a couple of transporters and get them back to the zoo with only a winding up article for the inside pages of most papers.

The news bulletin effectively destroyed such comforting thoughts. After the dramatic announcement that the elephants were sapient beings, there followed the interview, tailed with a comic-looking shot of Mr Sedge being lifted across the ditch by Rumpus Pumpus. There then followed interviews with elephant keepers, animal intelligence experts, ventriloquists, the elephant unit and anyone else who could shed any light on the subject. None of them could really shed any light on the subject but that didn't prevent them from taking the opportunity to have a little light shed upon themselves. One or two eminent zoologists declined to comment and those that did, reserved their judgment on just what was going on. The newscasters permitted themselves a couple of words of witless repartee and then moved on to the serious matters of death and destruction in the world.

The President switched off the television and got himself a stiff cup of malted milk. He settled into his armchair. He looked a bit like an orang-utan with a problem: his cheeks pouched out a bit and his brow came forward, his hand occasionally flapped rather than drummed on the arm of his chair. Absent-mindedly, he lifted his malted milk and drank, slurping it inadvertently like a listless ape. Nonetheless his mind was working hard and well. A dispassionate observer might have remarked that if the zookeeper can take on the appearance of one of his charges, cannot the charges be expected to acquire the characteristics of their keepers? But the question was not posed; and after half the malted milk, the President shrugged off his orang-utanism and nodded wisely with the comfort and regret of a man who has made a decision. The only solution, he had decided, that would please all parties, especially the elephants, was the status quo. Tacitly, he'd support the animal activists, leave the elephants in the marshes, get a pair in from Whipsnade to fill up the empty elephant house and let time reveal what all this hoo-ha about talking and being musicians was to come to.

He finished the malted milk and trotted off to bed with his favourite book. Decisions to do nothing were always very comforting. They combined the resolution of problems with the minimum of inconvenience.

Chapter 18

The following day was Friday and the minister, having no business in the House, spent it in the private office untangling all the pressing affairs that any week always seemed to tie inextricably together. He cut through the Gordian knot of the prison officers' pension entitlement, unravelled the delicate web of custody rules for subnormal adults in moral danger, kicked the tangled heap of unwelcome judgments from the European Court of Human Rights into the limbo of the Custodial Remand Review Committee and, finally, turned with a sour grin on his face to the update on the Walthamstow Marshes situation.

He looked at video recordings of the previous night's news bulletins and smiled wryly at what he assumed to be a civil servant from the press office of the Department of the Environment being lifted over a ditch by an elephant. He checked with Scotland Yard and with the President of the Zoological Society and found there was a consensus, strongly supported by Environment, that things should stay as they were for a week or so, with the elephants being observed from afar. Surrounded as it was by river and railway embankments, the reserve was easy to police. The world's camera crews were set up in Springfield Park which stretched up the hillside across the river from the reserve. Their long lenses captured all the action they wanted: if watching Finta Fanta consume twigs can be called action; and everyone seemed fairly happy.

In the outer office, the acceptance clerk checked through Mr Sedge's returned dossier. He checked with the Foreign Office himself with regard to thumb prints and, reassured, passed the file on to the Private Secretary who looked it through quickly, mastered the problems it presented in a moment and said to the clerk, 'It's really just a decision on nationality so that FO can issue passports, isn't it?'

'It amounts to that,' said the clerk. 'We could be pedantic and make these two go through the full naturalization procedure, but it depends on whether their invitation by HMG to take up permanent residence, in the absence of any other nationality, adds up to *de facto* acceptance as citizens or not.'

'Well, of course, it doesn't,' stated the Secretary flatly. Then, looking closely at the file: 'But then I suppose the fact that we seem to have recovered these people from East Africa . . . there's some kind of adoption certificate here . . . with their permission but specifically for our own benefit, is unusual.'

The 'adoption certificate' was a fine piece of bureaucratic opportunism by Mr Sedge, consisting of nothing more than an ornate bill of lading for the two elephants at Mombasa, written principally in Swahili, but in which 'acceptance' of the cargo had been translated as 'adoption' in the English text. His friend in Environment had managed to find it somehow and it proved a most impressive addition to the file.

The Private Secretary chewed his lips.

'F. Fanta and R. Pumpus,' he said. 'Clean records, held down important jobs at the London Zoo by the look of it – can't seem to get clear of the wretched zoo these days, can we? – Yeees. Doesn't set a precedent of course . . . and they've no citizens' rights anywhere else in the world. Yes,' he said, suddenly making up his mind, 'I'll recommend this one. Does no harm to anyone and gets the file out of the office. Seem to be ill at the moment, too. Hope this cheers them up.'

He scribbled his recommendation on the docket and placed the file in the tray for the minister's final decision.

The minister, meanwhile, having seen the videos, turned his attention to the police side of the operation. He called up Scotland Yard who were able to relay the essential contents of Sergeant Apta Dapta's exploits and findings to the Home Secretary. Questions of worshipful companies and elephants apart, the police job, affirmed the Yard, was a model of detection and surveillance. The Home Secretary's eyebrows rose. Knowing the warm glow that great praise can add to a Commons Statement or to a television interview, he enquired as to who was in charge of the Soho operations and learned the name of Sergeant Apta Dapta. The Home Secretary ordered the Chief Inspector and Sergeant Apta Dapta round to the ministry for an immediate de-briefing.

'In, say, half an hour?' commanded the Home Secretary.

'Half an hour,' replied the Chief Inspector and rang off to go and rustle up the Sergeant.

The buzzer sounded on the Home Secretary's intercom. He pressed the button and a voice said, 'Secretary for Environment on the phone, minister.'

'Put him through,' said the Home Secretary and picked up the appropriate receiver from behind a sheaf of papers on his desk.

'Ah, glad you could speak to me,' said Environment as he heard the line connect.

'What can I do for you?' asked the Home Secretary.

'I've been checking up on my side of this Walthamstow Marsh affair,' he said. 'Obviously what's embarrassed us a bit is that that nature reserve actually was set aside for elephants, amongst other things. What we've found out now is that it was my Order of only a week ago that allowed that – a bit too close to events to be a coincidence, don't you think?'

'Well, I'd have thought so. But you can't be telling me you didn't know what you were doing . . . Heads have rolled for less,' he added, now grinning all over his face as he detected a colleague squirming in his seat at the discovery of a chicken come home to roost in the private office.

But as Environment continued, it was the Home Secretary who nearly squawked:

'Heads roll, indeed,' continued Environment. 'But hang on to yours. That order to protect Elephants in the Marsh came over from your private office.'

'Impossible,' drawled the Home Secretary.

'Not so,' said Environment. 'I've checked and double-checked. It came over in the private papers last Friday with a note saying – I quote – "designating a habitat for this species, which is venerated by a number of immigrants, would materially assist with some immigrant-related problems. The species is known to exist in the UK with up to about a hundred individuals present at any one time. At the moment they have no designated habitat, yet more people are known to have sighted the species in London than any other location." The standard format then goes on to give the Latin name and the named location – Walthamstow Nature Reserve.'

'Well, blimey, old fruit,' said the Home Secretary, 'how could you introduce the Order without knowing it said "elephants"?'

'Because it only gave the Latin name. I thought they were butterflies like all the other species on the list – I hadn't got the faintest what the Latin for elephant was – *horsus hannibalis* or something, I would have thought.'

'Nooo,' groaned the Home Secretary, feeling chilling waters rising to his ankles, 'Nooo . . . the Latin for elephant is elephant, or something very like it. What goes on those lists is the scientific name – about as much like real Latin as English is like Anglo-Saxon. Oh lor, what did they teach you in that school of yours which you went to at vast public expense?'

'Economics,' came the dry reply, slipping now into an accent just recognizably Birmingham. 'Economics and discipline – how to stop your subordinates stepping out of line.'

'I see, yes, how forgetful of me, I'm sorry,' lulled the Home Secretary whose own school had taught obsequiousness in adversity quite as much as Latin. 'But who perpetrated this farce? Any idea?'

'Well, one of my people was asked to send the forms over to your N2 section – so I suppose that's where they must have been filled in. The despatch date has your own office stamp on it so it must at least have come through your acceptance clerk.' There was a moment's silence.

'Right,' said the Home Secretary sharply. 'The hunt is on!' and he rang off, almost simultaneously hitting the button on the intercom to command the presence of the acceptance clerk.

Three floors below, Mr Sedge was busy in his partitioned-off corner rustling around in swathes of brown paper and bits of string as he tore away at the wrappings on a gigantic parcel that had been delivered to him a moment ago. A burly man in a grey overall, barely deigning to speak, had plonked the package before him and shoved a note under his nose to sign. He signed with joy, stood up and handed the man his tatty old chair. The man loped off. His new chair had come! The system worked!

He stood the package near the entrance to his corner and worried off the wrappings with alacrity. What colour would it be? Had the design been modernized? Had the padding been increased?

Mr Sedge was not unaware that eyes from other alcoves and desks in the open office were turning his way. Large packages, delivered to men whose reputation had always been for solid uniformity of performance, threatened to disrupt the pecking order. A little feeling of discomfort ran in the observers and grew almost to outrage in some, as Mr Sedge unveiled the latest model of HMSO chair, with snappy green upholstery and concertina-like rubber sleeves over the springs and swivels. It wasn't exactly private office stuff, but it was a deal better than he'd expected.

'Hmm,' he mused to himself. 'If you don't ask, you don't get: and that's sure enough.'

He put it behind his desk and sat back in its luxury. Across the aisle was a discreet rustle of civil service handbooks. Just what grade was Mr Sedge? And what was that grade's entitlement by way of seating? Mr Sedge smiled, the pecking order was definitely under threat, his colleagues were checking the rule book in preparation for cock fights.

On his pad in front of him, Mr Sedge sketched out when he thought the passport application would come under the Home Secretary's nose. About mid-day, he thought, guessing the minister's work-load from afar. So, if he put the naturalization papers in the afternoon delivery, there was a good chance they'd get taken away by the minister for decision over the week-end. The two sets of papers were so different, he didn't expect the hard-pressed man to make any connection between the two: he might even win on both counts he mused, and rocked himself gently back and forth in his green luxury seat.

The phone rang. A host of possibilities raced quickly

through his mind and he opened his second drawer down, where all his elephant references were stowed.

'Sedge,' he answered.

'Head of Section here,' came the distinctly uncomfortable-sounding voice from the other end of the line. 'Come and see me at once, please.'

It sounded serious. Mr Sedge was quick-witted enough to throw in a tester that would tell him just how serious it was.

'Could you give me fifteen minutes? I've just got an urgent extradition appeal to vet.'

'Come and see me at once,' repeated the voice. Things were serious. Mr Sedge slipped his note-book into his pocket and went to the Head of Section's office.

Now the Head of Section, who revelled in a personal office, in fact a properly partitioned-off corner of the open office, was a civil servant of immense ability whose career was blasted from the outset by the possession of a congenital adventurousness. Perhaps in colonial days he could have risen to be governor of a Pacific island or even an Indian province, but in these latter days he had had to work out his adventurousness as a personnel clerk for an oil company in a very hot place. The very hot place had a tradition of rule by absolute power. The adventurer in him had taken to this like a pirate to his cutlass, with the result that his personnel operation had prospered immensely. So much so, the company had brought him back to Britain in a higher capacity. There, alas, the cutlass had glanced off the shoulders of the democratic tradition, normally being deflected under its own impetus, down on to his own toes. No matter, he had long since been wearing steel toecaps. But after a couple of fracas, he resigned and joined the civil service.

Mr Sedge now knocked at the door to his office. There was a panel of opaque glass in the door and the outline of the man Mr Sedge could vaguely see, moved slightly as he tapped.

'Come in,' said the voice, a little rough but not unfriendly: only angry, only authoritarian.

'Come in, Sedge, and get into that chair.' He indicated the place opposite himself.

Mr Sedge saw the bear-like form with a bearded face and brown eyes glare at him.

'It's a matter of papers sent over to Environment last week from N2, via our private office. Tell me what you know about it.'

Mr Sedge knew everything there was to know about it. So he wrinkled his brow and looked puzzled.

'Environment?' he enquired, concerned but apparently ignorant.

'Yes,' said the Head of Section and let an embarrassing silence fall between them. Head of Section glowered but Mr Sedge managed to maintain a quizzical look. On no account was he going to let Head of Section browbeat him into revealing anything until Head of Section had revealed at least some of his own hand. After all, it might only be that somebody had left off a security envelope or some such detail. The silence ended.

'Some papers went up to private office from this section, N2, for forwarding to Environment. Something to do with race relations,' said Head of Section, starting to twist his lips. This lip-twisting Mr Sedge found amusing; though apparently, Head of Section had found it very effective when dealing with Arabs.

Mr Sedge jumped at the lead he had been given.

'Race relations! For Environment! Yes, I processed them myself. A rare species was to be given a Designated Habitat in order to show respect for a minority that venerated it.'

'Quite so,' snarled Head of Section. 'What species?'

'Oh, my goodness me,' oozed Mr Sedge, now softening into a functionary glow of good-hearted warm-spiritedness. 'Well, I'm not a classicist myself – you see it was just a Latin name to me – an African butterfly, I believe. You know there are sometimes freak winds that blow here from the Sahara, all those thousands of kilometres and deposit red . . .' As he swung into his stride, Head of Section cut him short.

'No,' he interjected. 'Not butterflies. Something else; *loxodonta africana*, in fact.' He stopped abruptly again waiting for Mr Sedge to commit himself, to reveal his guilt.

'Not butterflies?' queried Mr Sedge, resuming a rather put-out quizzical attitude. 'Er . . . moths?'

'Where did you get the name from?' said Head of Section, now feigning an attitude of boredom.

'What name?' said Mr Sedge, stalling for time as his brain raced furiously for the excuse he thought would fit.

'*Loxodonta africana*. Where did you get it from?'

'Oh . . . er, Environment,' said Mr Sedge, suddenly and very firmly, as if his memory had just been jogged. And he saw at once he was pursuing the right strategy. Head of Section perked up on the spot. Here was a circular argument which by its self-contained nature had a sort of life of its own that enabled responsible people to step back from it and not feel too threatened. Even better, the prospect that it was Environment's fault pleased Head of Section no end. A doubt remained, though.

'How is it that Environment gave that to you?'

'I phoned them up and asked them for the correct name of the animal venerated by the Afro-Asian community. My opposite number looked it up in some sort of index and read it out over the phone.' Mr Sedge managed a beautiful, naïve smile.

'Mr Sedge,' said Head of Section with unnatural

quietness, 'do you know how big Afro-Asia is and how many animals are venerated there?'

'I could find out for you,' said Mr Sedge, eyes sparkling with enthusiasm. 'I expect Military Intelligence has got statistics on that sort of thing. Or maybe the Admiralty Handbooks . . .'

'Thousands!' roared Head of Section. 'India alone is bigger than Europe and has more sacred animals than the Ark. When I was in Calcutta . . .' but he stopped himself short and just shook his head. He knew now why he had an office to himself and Mr Sedge only a partitioned-off corner. He knew now why he had cream and brown two-tone filing cabinets and Mr Sedge had only grey ones. Mr Sedge was a good man; thorough, meticulous, precise but he was incurably naïve. He had no experience of the world, no horizons beyond Buckingham Palace and Bognor. Why, men like himself who have travelled the world and rubbed shoulders with more nationalities than old Sedge had even heard of, would always rise to positions of superiority, would always be in command over others and regulate the running of the world. What's more, there was evidently someone like Sedge in Environment: sometimes one had to acknowledge one was surrounded by ignorant fools.

'Thank you, Mr Sedge,' he said. 'Double-check these things next time, will you. You'd better get back to that extradition appeal.' Mr Sedge rose and left. As he opened the door, Head of Section said, 'Oh, and Mr Sedge, *loxodonta africana* is an elephant.' Mr Sedge scurried quickly out and closed the door with a rattle. Head of Section reported back to private office on the phone.

Back in his alcove, Mr Sedge blushed furiously. The fingers in the open office running through the rule books slowed down and stopped. His colleagues had heard Head of Section's outburst and felt vindicated. If one will go sticking one's neck out and ordering new chairs, one risks getting one's head cut off. They enjoyed his blushes as if they were their own victory. They were, however, wrong.

Mr Sedge's flushed countenance was nothing to do with being told off. Tellings off by superiors were a nothing to him now; his heated collar region sweated with relief at the closeness of the shave. Head of Section had not rumbled him, had seen no deeper intentions behind his apparent slip of procedural meticulousness. Where Head of Section was concerned, he had slipped up, he had not done wrong.

Mr Sedge set to work diligently constructing alibis and excuses.

Up on the eighth floor, a porter whose face looked like a model skull made out of a leather handbag ushered the Chief Inspector and Sergeant Apta Dapta from the lift. The two went to the outer door of the private office suite and gently knocked and entered. The acceptance clerk showed them in and led them to the minister's anteroom where they took a coffee and basked in the status of having the minister's ear and attention.

Two-thirds of the way through their coffees they were called in to be consulted by the Home Secretary. They were seated in chairs of a most unaccustomed luxury – Sergeant Apta Dapta couldn't help being reminded of the foyers of some of the better class illegal establishments it was sometimes his privilege to raid in Soho. The Home Secretary, however, was unaware of this comparison and was able to settle down to conversation with great ease.

They covered the police operation to find the elephants, the scaffold-top stake-out in Tyler's Court and the unfortunate crossed jurisdiction with The Worshipful Company of Bell Founders and Organ Grinders. Finally they turned to the continuing investigation which was, of course, now being pursued by Albany Street and the elephant unit. They were obviously coming to the end of the briefing when the Home Secretary asked as a matter of course:

'And there are no other suspects in the case, of course? Once you've been able to talk to Coulisse, the affair should be more or less closed, shouldn't it?'

'More or less,' replied Sergeant Apta Dapta. The others in the seated circle round the coffee table looked in his direction again with sharpened interest.

'There is one individual that Police Constable Monica Sullivan identified visiting the club. He only came once; but he was let in immediately and, from the sound of it, stayed for a rehearsal. Plump chap, thin on top, looked like an office worker – accounts clerk, something like that. We never got a tail on him but he's the only person who could conceivably be a contact with an outside organization – if there is one.'

'Are you likely to find him?' asked the Home Secretary. The two policemen eyed each other and decided truth would be better than bravado. The Chief Inspector answered:

'No. Not if he's an insurance salesman or a shop-fitting rep or something like that. But if he's involved in this lot we might do. You see, the elephants must have taken part in that rehearsal – if we believe all this stuff they're supposed to have said – and he was there at the time. He might have some interest in the elephants and if he follows that up – we'll snap him!'

There was a long pause. The Private Secretary was about to close the meeting but, for once, the Home Secretary wasn't talking and holding the floor. He had his eyes closed and he was thinking. This had a slightly unnerving effect on the policemen who began to smile a little nervously; but then the Home Secretary suddenly said:

'Was this chap below average height?'

'Yes, apparently,' said Sergeant Apta Dapta.

'Balding?'

'Yes.'

'Official, busy, civil service sort of air about him?'

'Could be,' said the Sergeant, now getting interested.

'Put on that video of last night's news,' said the Home Secretary. The Private Secretary quickly obliged; and before long the little group was huddled round the screen in the Home Secretary's office.

They saw the marshes and the reporters and then the interview with Mr Sedge. His image was simply captioned as 'Ministry Spokesman'. As Rumpus Pumpus finally lifted him into the air and the cameras zoomed in to show him in close-up as he swung across the ditch, the Home Secretary leapt up and thrust a finger at the pause button.

'There!' he said. 'Could that be him?' Sergeant Apta Dapta nodded. 'It could, indeed,' he said, 'it could indeed.'

'Ah!' shouted the Home Secretary. 'Environment again! Get Environment on the phone will you, Private Secretary. Good morning, gentlemen,' he said, dismissing the policemen. 'Well done, thanks for coming and I'm glad to be able to help the police with their enquiries for once.' Everyone laughed rather forcedly. 'We'll keep you up to date with what and whom that character is. Stand by to take him in, if you're called on to do it.'

By the time they were out of the office and in the lift, Environment was back on the phone to the Home Secretary, now distinctly on the defensive as the Home Secretary launched into a triumphant accusation of withering force.

'Quite an interesting item on television news last night,

don't you think, old chap?' said the Home Secretary. The studied casualness bit Environment deep in his doubts and apprehensions.

'More of a fun-and-games job for the Metropolitan Police, I would have thought,' said the voice, now unashamedly and gruffly Midlands in its accent. 'That spokesman of yours must have felt a right berk.'

'What do you mean, that spokesman of mine? I'm referring to that spokesman of yours – the man who wrestles elephants single-handed without dropping his brief-case.'

'Oh no, none of your implications here, Home Secretary. My ship's tight you know, sound as a bell. Remember I've got men from Environment posted all round that marsh. They know their opos and I've checked with them, double-checked: and with our PR section too. I've got you there, haven't I? What's more, would you like to know where my men in the marsh said that civil service circus act came from?'

'Well, perhaps that's not necessary,' said the Home Secretary, starting to fiddle with his pocket handkerchief in a rather uncomfortable way, as if he sensed something unfortunate about to happen.

'Oh yes, it is, very necessary,' came back Environment. 'Home Office,' came the delighted Midlands drawl. 'No question about it: Home Office.'

'Well, thank you, I'll check it out, thank you so much. You know, that incisiveness that econometrics brings to thinking does have some uses after all, doesn't it?'

He knew that Environment would fume at this dig without being able to muster any proper reply. And the Home Secretary made sure no reply could come.

'We'll almost certainly have to talk again on Monday. So good of you to talk now. Have a good weekend. Good bye.' And the phone clattered down with considerable relief.

Home Secretary's composure started to turn into panic bustle. But he kept it down, although his pocket handkerchief cascaded down his left breast like icing gone out of control. He hustled his political advisers, his Personal Private Secretary, Head of Personnel and the head security guard, the latter mortally intimidated, into his office. He played the video, jabbed the pause button with poor Mr Sedge suspended manfully above the stagnant ditch and almost shouted to them all, pointing with a trembling finger:

'Who is that man? Who is he? He's supposed to work here and I want to find him. Who is it?'

At that his handkerchief came to his attention as it dropped from his pocket and landed on his shoe. There was total silence. No-one seemed to know who that man was. The Home Secretary realized he was about to sneeze. He drew breath. Drew deeper breath, stooped suddenly; and, whisking the handkerchief from his toe, exploded into it with jowl-reddening force. A kind of fundamental embarrassment hung in the air. No-one quite knew whether to comment on the screen or console the Home Secretary. Then a young, female voice piped up.

'I think I saw him last night.' Eyebrows raised, eyes turned. The young political adviser who had climbed into the private office up the grape-vine of academic honours and party contacts suddenly became a centre of attention. 'I was trying to find a file in the acceptance office. I think it was him came in to deliver a pack.'

'What section was he from,' cut in Head of Personnel, determined to be efficient.

'I don't know,' said the adviser. 'I was looking for an extradition pack and he seemed to know every pack number in that field by heart. I'm pretty sure it was him.'

'Obviously not a top man or we'd know him at once,' thought Head of Personnel out loud. 'I should say he's one of that mass from the open office on the fifth floor – N2 Section, I should think.'

'Leave it to me, minister, I've got him fixed in mind now, I'll have him in ten minutes if he's down there.'

Everyone nodded and was hustled out in haste. The Home Secretary sat back in a kind of administrative apoplexy, called for the routine papers by way of light relief and awaited the report from Head of Personnel.

In his alcove on the fifth floor, Mr Sedge's blushes had subsided. His alibi studies were more or less complete and he looked carefully at his watch. He knew that the minister either made a dash for the constituency with a boot-load of homework between three and four on a Friday afternoon; or else, not wanting to waste time in traffic jams, he worked till seven, taking supper off a tray in his office and then drove out to the constituency with three-quarters of a boot-load of homework. He had a problem: should he put the nationality request into the lunchtime or into the afternoon delivery to private office? To risk missing the minister might mean the elephant affair was too old, too well understood to slip anything through unnoticed at the start of the following week. To get it in too early might make the papers come up for decision on top of the passport applications and spoil both. There was no way round the problem. Mr Sedge heaved a sigh and put the file in the out-tray for internal delivery. His fingers were on it and he tapped the file thoughtfully once or twice, just running through the possibilities in his mind for the last time.

He became aware someone was looking at him closely. No-one stood at the entry to his alcove. He shifted his gaze to the left. There were a pair of grey eyes set beneath grey eyebrows and a wedge of grey hair looking over the top of his screen, just staring. For a second there was silence.

'Come in, come in!' called Mr Sedge with all the *bonhomie*

he could muster; which was, in fact, quite a lot.

For a moment, the forehead just nodded. Then it turned and its owner paced round the screens to the entrance and the tall, stern figure of the Head of Personnel looked in on Mr Sedge. The lips were pursed. The hands were behind the back.

'Come with me, please, Mr Sedge. I'd like a word.' He spoke flatly, softly and without humour or colour. He caused no obvious stir but, as Mr Sedge rose to obey the summons, it was clear this was serious business: Head of Personnel was not to be trifled with – especially when he had bothered to find out your name and used it with such calm effect.

The two men said nothing as they walked the length of the open office: but many eyes followed them. Mr Sedge shoved a hand in his trouser pocket, with fingers very firmly crossed.

They went into Head of Personnel's office. Mr Sedge saw his personal file open on the desk. They sat down and Head of Personnel flicked through the pages of the file.

'A good record, Mr Sedge,' he said casually. 'A very good record. According to this you're an eighteen-carat civil servant, Mr Sedge: no high flying, but then wings aren't given to everyone; no malingering, hundred per cent reliability, you're the kind of man who runs the nation, Mr Sedge, the work-horse of the country's administration.'

He stopped and just looked at Mr Sedge, waiting for a reaction to the praise. But Mr Sedge knew the technique. One lulls the suspect into trusting one by praising his achievements and then hammers him into the ground with some damning piece of evidence or well-prepared tirade. Mr Sedge let the silence become awkward. He wanted to judge what part of his activities had now been rumbled. Somehow he was pretty sure Head of Section had nothing to do with it, or the summons would have come direct from him.

'I'm surprised you'd want to throw up all the benefits of that good service just to become a circus act,' said Head of Personnel.

Mr Sedge smiled quizzically and shuddered within. He hadn't expected to be recognized off the small screen quite so easily, at least not in the ministry. He remained silent.

'You don't know what I'm talking about?' asked Head of Personnel with a tired expression. 'I rather think you do.'

To Mr Sedge, that steel-grey hair, immaculately groomed, scrupulously waved, looked like a block of sculpted french chalk sitting atop the head of the interrogator opposite. Mr Sedge gave up all hope of ever being able to say anything palliative to the sort of person who would walk around with a block of french chalk on his head all day. He plumped for the tactic of ignorance as an opening ploy:

'Well, I'm sorry; but . . . could you just clarify that a little, please,' he asked diffidently, but not unhelpfully.

This time Head of Personnel fell silent. Mr Sedge ventured an approach:

'I haven't been to the circus for over thirty years,' he explained with absolute truth. And with equal truth continued, 'In fact I'm really not sure I agree with circuses at all. I tend to see them as places with a lot of rather dubious animal acts . . . I'm not sure I'm in favour of that. Is the department taking some sort of responsibility for circuses?'

'Come along, Mr Sedge, you must know what I'm talking about. This department has, should have, nothing at all to do with the circus. But as that's the case, why did the entire nation last night see you cavorting in Walthamstow Marshes with a pair of elephants and, what's more, claiming to be some kind of government spokesman to boot? No-one in this ministry has any responsibility for elephants; so what's it all about Mr Sedge, what's it all about?'

'Oh that, yes, I see,' said Mr Sedge in a forlorn voice. 'It was very painful you know, although I tried to put a good face on it. You know I've still got the marks all round the bottom of my rib-cage . . .' And Mr Sedge threw back his jacket and started pulling up the side of his shirt to expose his flanks. In fact, he had no such marks at all but guessed, rightly, what the reaction would be to this.

'Yes, yes, Mr Sedge, quite so, no need to show me, I'm sure it's very distressing.'

From the corner of his eye, Mr Sedge saw the aghast look on the now distinctly sallow face of the Head of Personnel. There is nothing, as he knew so well, quite as horrifying to an administrative civil servant as the sight of bare flesh in the office. Mr Sedge stuffed his shirt back to add to what was now becoming an air of cultivated dishevelment about his person. Head of Personnel was knocked a little off guard by this and began to think that somehow there might be a proper explanation for everything.

'Look, tell me how it all happened, will you Mr Sedge,' he said.

'Well, you see, I had this brief which came up, ultimately from Community Relations, I believe, about designated reserves for animals held in veneration by minority communities; and I had to send some papers over to Environment about protecting the species in Walthamstow Marshes.'

Head of Personnel started to look a bit perplexed at this. But he knew the ways of the Home Office and under certain ministers had been involved in even more unlikely matters himself.

'Well, yesterday afternoon,' continued Mr Sedge, 'I had a call from Environment saying I should formally identify the habitat in the Marsh and that I should be prepared to just explain what I was doing to some pressmen who were over there at the moment. Well, I don't often get the chance of an outside assignment; at my level, you know, it's not to be missed; so I went straight away, thinking it would all be a straightforward formality.

'Well, when I got there, it appeared the whole thing was all about a pair of elephants. So I went through the formality of identifying their habitat and finally . . . well, you saw the rest on the news, I expect.'

Mr Sedge rubbed his rib cage carefully. If truth be told, ran his thoughts, it was a pretty thin story. Head of Personnel would see through it pretty quickly. His only hope was to survive till five o'clock and then get to work on a decent scheme of self-preservation over the weekend. He thought he was about to be dismissed for the moment, when Head of Personnel timed it right to drop his bombshell.

'Was that your only contact with these elephants, Mr Sedge?'

'Why yes,' said Mr Sedge, none the less alerted by the tone of voice.

'Then what were you doing in Tyler's Court, in Soho?' said the Head of Personnel triumphantly.

'Oh my goodness!' whispered Mr Sedge looking utterly flabbergasted. 'You know about that?'

'You've been positively identified visiting the elephants there,' he stated, smiling in triumph. But Mr Sedge had already considered this one, ever since he'd thought the painter might be a police woman.

'Elephants?' said Mr Sedge, apparently bewildered again. He pulled a nervous smile. 'I was surprised to read in the papers yesterday that the elephants had been in that

320

part of Soho. You see . . . there's a young lady I visit there from time to time and . . . well, I'm sure you understand.' Of course, Mr Sedge had in mind his innocent acquaintanceship with Sady McCabe; but he also had in mind the suspicious nature of the minds of civil service Heads of Personnel.

'You can give me the name and address? It can be checked?'

'One reached her through a door marked "The Splurge": a club of some kind, I believe, in an alley off Wardour Street. I'm afraid names you can check up on aren't normally used in that quarter.'

The Head of Personnel could check, and what there was to check would check out. The grey head thought for a moment and nodded with great doubt in mind. But he knew he would get no more and Mr Sedge knew he would live till five o'clock, though next week was less certain.

'Thank you, Mr Sedge,' said the Head of Personnel, suddenly, and quite drily. 'You can go now, but I shall be checking this lot out. If all this turns out to be simple blunder, eventually it can be forgotten – eventually. But if it's more than that: beware, Mr Sedge, beware. Good day, Mr Sedge.'

Mr Sedge got up and made for the door.

'Oh, and . . . Mr Sedge. Tuck your shirt in, will you?'

Mr Sedge tucked in his shirt, making sure the action pulled up his trousers almost to mid-calf. He tottered out, slightly pigeon toed, Head of Personnel shaking his head gravely. After a quick visit to the gents to sort out his dress, Mr Sedge made his way back to his alcove. Lunch time had come and there were relatively few people in the open office. Those who were there ate sandwiches and read newspapers. Once at his desk, Mr Sedge saw that the naturalization pack had been collected. It would be with the minister at any time from now on.

However, up on the eighth floor things had entered what the political advisers know as a routine terminal panic. Routine because it happened every week, terminal because it happened at the end of every week; and panic because, although the minister retained his famed, long-winded lugubriousness, he did so in a manner that set everyone else in the private office racing all over the place as if the world depended on their action.

It was a kind of filing-cabinet steeple chase in which the commanded rushed from drawer to drawer, checking an initial, flicking up a precedent, squaring a decision with policy, wheeling in tray lunches, fending off the ninety-nine suppliants. These came with urgent matters to call on their minister's time before the dangling deadline of the end of the week dropped on them all and smothered the chances of action for another two days or more.

Amongst the heaps of files, bristling with advice dockets, rife with recommendations, fine-combed by functionary fingers in anticipation of the authoritative eye, was one bearing the elephants' passport applications, floating up now through the overburden of other business, needing only the ministerial monica, to fly it to the Foreign Office and certain success.

A clerk bustled sideways in, pushing a trolley with a plate of scrambled-egg-and-mushroom sandwiches, a bowl of fruit, some water, coffee and chocolate biscuits and a prawn cocktail. As it passed beneath his nose, Private Secretary raised his eyebrows slightly: the choice of food by those in a position to eat absolutely anything they cared to order, never ceased to amaze him. The trolley hove to beside the minister's desk and he swung back and put his feet up on an upturned waste-paper basket, grabbing the plate of sandwiches. He set to with a will, throwing open the elephants' file at the same time – using it in effect as a kind of dual-purpose table napkin.

'Mmm,' he mused to himself, gulping some water and then taking another bite, 'I don't think I can have this. Then on the other hand, Private Secretary has approved it. Nice egg sandwich this. I wonder what the prawn cocktails are like in Mombasa. Big prawns I expect. I think they should naturalize in the usual way. No photographs? What is this? Skin disease? Bit more mayonnaise needed really. Perhaps a touch of Tabasco. Are there any precedents for this?' He called in the Private Secretary.

'Look PS, is this thing about these zoo-workers really all right? I mean what are the precedents?'

'None. That's certainly true. I must say I took the view that what created no precedent and hurt no-one could only end up in an extra vote or two for the government of the day. I thought we should rule in favour as a general principle rather than against, if all things were equal.'

'I agree,' said the Home Secretary, 'but something about this one is just a bit too funny. I don't know. I'll come back to it after lunch.' He whacked another file on top of it over his lap and turned to the coffee. A lump of scrambled egg squashed horribly between the two files; but he saw it not.

The next two items were the red meat of real politics. First, autographing a photograph of himself sipping a gigantic mug of prison tea; to be hung on the wall of the new warders' canteen at Pentonville which he'd opened the previous week. Secondly, recommending his best chum at prep school for a knighthood after years of blameless service with the Barristers' and Solicitors' Charitable Trust. In fact, he knew very well, the service had been so blameless the chap didn't stand a chance of getting the knighthood; but the signature satisfied honour: at the very least, it ennobled one's own sentiments.

He then turned back to this bit of funny paperwork from the Foreign Office. He tried to make out the name of the officer who'd prepared the Home Office side of the case. 'Sedge' he managed to read on the cover, followed by the section. He had half a mind to check back with this minion but, since Private Secretary was happy, that smacked of disloyalty. He shrugged his shoulders and bunged the file on to a heap of others on his desk top. He'd leave it till Monday and then decide. Then he kicked the wastepaper basket upright again, got someone to wheel out the remains of lunch, lifting an apple off the tray as it went, and got down to the serious things again.

He checked with Head of Section in N2 to see what had happened about that elephant habitat matter. Environment's fault again; he'd thought so. He asked for a brief memo to be sent up to him at once on how the affair had occurred. He then called Head of Personnel and asked him about the man on the video. He'd dealt with it, said Head of Personnel and was happy that it was all blunder and no conspiracy. He'd found the man in question, an insignificant though hard-working man who'd made a fool of himself for once – a chap who probably kept his head down because he had a penchant for nameless ladies in Soho. He would check it all, but he was fairly sure it was all right. Yes, Head of Personnel would get the details up to him in a brief memo right away.

With a goodly whack, the naturalization file hit the desk of the acceptance clerk in the outer office. He checked it through for completeness without the least regard to its contents. All the formalities were fulfilled. Its precedence marking showed it was fairly urgent, but its security rating was low. On balance, as it looked as if the Home Secretary was going to stay late that evening, he'd better have it sooner rather than later. If the non-urgent work suddenly started to build up, it might frighten him off earlier: and, on the other hand, if the minister got through it quickly, he'd be able to go home earlier anyway.

The acceptance clerk directed the pack to the Private Secretary for a final opinion and the Private Secretary looked it through idly, in the acceptance office, as was often his habit before going into a case deeply. Private Secretary's brows knit. He looked at the circulation order on the front of the file.

'Up from N2?' he queried.

'Yes,' said the clerk, and noted a slant of suspicion in his eyes.

Private Secretary continued to look carefully through the pack. It was immaculately prepared. The evidence, the precedents, the opinions and the recommendations clearly and persuasively presented. But it reminded him of something else unusual he'd done that day. It was reminiscent of that passport application. He asked the acceptance clerk to look it out for him, only to learn that it was with the minister who was himself at lunch in his office.

Private Secretary grabbed the file and went and tapped at the minister's door.

'Arhgharrarrh,' said the minister, and the Private Secretary went in.

'Oh,' said the minister, 'if you'd come a moment ago you could have had an egg sandwich, but I've sent them away now. Like a bite of my apple?'

'Thank you, no,' said the Private Secretary with complete aplomb. 'I've just had a raisin and banana sandwich; very satisfying, raisin and banana sandwiches. I do recommend them.'

'Oh yes,' went on the minister, 'I suppose they ought to be good. My wife seems to live on that sort of thing: brown bread and all that, you know.'

'I do know, Home Secretary, I do.'

'Good. Well, what's that under your arm? Sling it on the pile if you like; I'll try and whip through it by home time.'

'Could I ask you to cast your eyes over it with me now,' said the Private Secretary, 'and at the same time look at the passport application for those two zoo employees.'

'Ah,' said the minister, 'I'm glad you mentioned that. I thought there was something a bit funny about that one. Look at it – oh dear, there's a great blotch of squashed egg on the inside. Never mind, there now . . . mmm. I see what you mean – something odd; and definitely out of the same stable, wouldn't you say?'

The two of them opened the two files, scratched their heads and chewed their lips. 'Same people, same names,' said the Private Secretary darkly.

'You know, when you get down to it,' said the Home Secretary, 'one doesn't know who one's dealing with here – it might be a machine or robots – there's none of that juicy personal detail that these cases normally contain – it's as if they were zoo animals, not zoo workers.'

And the penny dropped. The two of them looked at each other and the Private Secretary made a quick internal phone call.

'Who was the man you questioned about habitat designation earlier on?' he asked the Head of Section. 'I see, Sedge of N2.'

He made another call. 'Who was the man you questioned about the news item?' he asked Head of Personnel. 'I see, Sedge of N2.'

He looked at the minister. 'And who prepared the passport file?' The minister checked the front page.

'Sedge of N2,' he said. And before the Private Secretary could ask any other questions, turned up the page in the nationality file and nodded with grave countenance, 'Sedge of N2. I think we'd better call up Mr Sedge and see what all this is about. Prepare a little reception will you, Private

Secretary, for, say, three o'clock?'

By three o'clock, Mr Sedge had disposed of all the work which the ministry had generated for him and turned his mind to the work he had generated for the ministry. He calculated that if no-one came back to him about the elephants before four o'clock, he would probably be clear till Monday. In that case he would be better off leaving to make preparations at home for the week ahead, rather than staying to fend off more dressing downs from above. Just the same, he was now distinctly uneasy; and when the phone rang just a minute or two before three and Head of Personnel's secretary said in a very dry and commanding voice that he was wanted at once in the small conference room on the eighth floor, Mr Sedge realized he had not beaten the system, and the system was setting itself up to beat him.

As he rose from his desk, he felt as if a protecting hand moved to support and help him. He sensed the naïveties and the non-sequiturs, the ploy of blending incompetence and the air of congenial misunderstanding, were not going to work now. On the other hand, these would be ploys which they would be expecting, these would be the strategies they would seek to lay bare.

Mr Sedge stiffened his back and put on his jacket. He looked round his office: the meticulously ordered filing cabinets, the new green chair, the internal phone list on his desk and the departmental handbook in its time-honoured place. His coffee-cup holder stood beside his pen tray and he looked at it and smiled wryly. Only a few weeks ago, it had been one of those little accoutrements, a personal possession, which in a large and uniform office assumes an importance beyond all reckoning. Yet now he counted it as nothing. He saw that he had made a decision; almost without knowing it; yet without any hesitation or doubt.

He realized he had decided for the elephants and against the ministry. None of these fixtures and fittings, handbooks and instructions, were now really invested with any meaning on his account. There had been a time when he had clung to these trappings for dear life and come in to enjoy them at all hours, for they were his claim to existence; but that time was now gone.

Mr Sedge had come of age. He had grown too big for his alcove. Though those who now watched him as he adjusted his tie and did up his shoes, coveted that corner beyond the dreams of bureaucracy, he, for one, had outgrown it. He realized that now he might be going to his professional death. If they knew all and were so minded, they could charge him with all sorts of terrible things. His career might be over, his pension forever blocked, ultimately to yield only a pittance to a Home Office has-been hiding in a corner of Croydon.

And he smiled. The guiding hand bore him up like a trunk round his rib cage, and he knew that the sideways glancers, for all their conventional wisdom, were dooming themselves to lives like his had been. While he was walking out to take responsibility for his own actions, a mighty wrestle on a Friday afternoon with the mighty ministry.

Seated at a shining table, fumes of righteous vindictiveness rising almost visibly from their heads, sat the Head of Personnel, the Head of Section N2, the Personal Private Secretary and, with them, the acceptance clerk poised to take minutes of their deliberations. Before them lay a pair of files which Mr Sedge was very familiar with; and in the corner, a video cassette player ready to go. They sat licking their lips, waiting for the timid tap on the door that would announce the arrival of the sacrificial victim.

Mr Sedge walked from the lift on the eighth floor and

along to the small conference room. Now he knew what was waiting for him, but chose to reason that a conference room is not an office and one should expect to be attending a conference of some kind. One walked into conferences and took one's place, one didn't meekly tap, expecting an invitation to enter.

Outside the door he set his jaw hard, shrugged his shoulders deep into his jacket and checked his flies were properly zipped up. His hand stretched out above the door handle, he took a deep breath and with a burly, official briskness pushed straight into the room without so much as a by-your-leave.

Head of Section sat up like a ram-rod, initially taken aback. Head of Personnel looked cross and Private Secretary smiled slightly; one point, at least, he thought, to Mr Sedge.

'Sedge of N2,' said Mr Sedge firmly and matter-of-factly. None of the self-effacement that couldn't tell an elephant from a butterfly here. He looked Head of Personnel directly in the french chalk, dropping his gaze to meet him eye to eye. 'Your secretary asked me to come right away,' he said. 'How can I help you?'

Private Secretary answered: 'Sit down Mr Sedge. This is an ad hoc investigation ordered by the minister under departmental rules to look into the conduct of the ministry's involvement with the alleged theft of two elephants from London Zoo. You must understand that, in itself, this is not a disciplinary hearing; though I ought to say that the only reason it isn't, is because we couldn't drum up proper representation for you in time from a staff association. But the findings of this investigation can be used in such a hearing at a later date. Do you understand that?'

By now, Mr Sedge had taken in the array of faces ranged against him, the video monitor to one side and files on the table before him. He replied with great propriety.

'You'll find under the rules that if it's in the department's interests, as decreed by Head of Personnel, officers such as myself can be sent on up to three weeks' paid leave. It's a catch-all clause that's designed for people on the verge of breakdowns and people too embarrassing to have around. I fall into the second of those categories at the moment and I think you should take advantage of those rules.'

Only truth hurts. Whereas one can tell a buffoon that he's an embarrassment and see him squirm and send him off on punishment leave, someone who intends to be an embarrassment and has an air of uncomfortable righteousness about him, not to mention confidence, ought not to be sent on the leave he asks for because it proves he is the embarrassment he intends to be. It gives him what he wants while implying the ministry needs time on its part to sort the case out.

The Private Secretary now gave two points to Mr Sedge, and smiled wryly again.

Head of Section attempted to cut in and save the day. 'Do you realize these files, and the video film we can play on that machine there, could be construed by a suspicious mind to be an attempt to get a pair of elephants naturalized as British subjects – and on the initiative of the government?' It was another statement aimed at making incompetence shudder. The reply made authority blanch.

'I should jolly well hope so,' said Mr Sedge in a confident, jovial and friendly manner. 'That's exactly what I was trying to achieve. There is no doubt about it, those elephants are persons – there's nothing in any act anywhere which defines what biological species "persons" have to belong to. You've read the files and I suspect they were within an ace of getting approval when someone tumbled to the fact that those people were elephants and not humans. It doesn't make any difference; look at the rules, look at the acts, there's not a falsehood in any of it and I intend to see those people with their proper place in society if it means taking the matter through parliament at the end of the day.'

This served as an effective put-down to Head of Section. At last he had met someone whose experience, in some important ways at least, was quite out of his own range of knowledge. It was Private Secretary who came back, urbanely, wisely, with the air of a man who has got to where he was by facing the fact that the most interesting things that go on in any walk of life are the ones that the rule books don't provide for.

'You're on a rough road, Mr Sedge,' he said, 'but if your feeling is right it may not be an impossible one. What you're trying to do is going to make everyone in this ministry look like a right ninny, to be polite about it, and we can't have that. Think what parliament would do to the minister if he gave citizenship to a pair of elephants – think of what the papers would do with that. No, Mr Sedge, for bringing the Service into ridicule, I think we should act on your suggestion of a period of leave and with some kind of disciplinary hearing at the end of it, too.' He had brought the unofficial suspension round to an act that was to the advantage of authority. Its possibility became an option once more.

'Yet,' he continued, 'you may have a point.' Mr Sedge warmed to this unexpected ally. 'The status of animals is an important matter. Things have come a long way from the days when animals meant only dog licences and rabies control. If you want to pursue this outside the ministry, with all your inside knowledge to your aid, you might, after a long time, get somewhere. But, and this is the crux of what I'm saying, Mr Sedge, you have to make a decision. What we've got in front of us here,' and he tapped the files and the smile faded from his face, 'is tantamount to subversion. I suspect it's no-one's plan but your own, Mr Sedge, and that may be what saves you from the law at the end of the day – but it remains an abuse of your position for a personal end that is not espoused by the ministry. For that you must take the consequences, Mr Sedge.'

'I do, I do,' said Mr Sedge.

'So you admit to attempting to obtain passports for unqualified persons?' said Head of Section who was having trouble following the nuances of the arguments.

'Not at all,' came back Mr Sedge, enjoying the chance to adopt a tone that indicated he was in the presence of fools and idiots. 'I admit to raising passport applications for consideration by private office without going through Head of Section – you've acquiesced in that many times before.'

'And to processing fraudulent nationality applications?' went on the Head of Section. Mr Sedge sighed. He looked at Private Secretary and at Head of Personnel. All of them looked at Head of Section in a rather endearing way. The acceptance clerk tapped idly for a moment on his note pad, deliberately staring at no-one at all. Head of Section fell silent. Silence reigned for just a moment or two.

Mr Sedge looked straight at the group of men opposite him: they all avoided his gaze. It was one of the awful situations where authority, to maintain its authority, must act decisively. Yet every course of action open to it was either plainly unjust, publicly unpopular or politically suicidal. Mr Sedge had the ministry over the barrel of its own rule book and the barrel of the undying popularity of animals with the press and populace.

Mr Sedge coughed. 'My mother . . .' he said slowly, 'is very unwell. Er, she's in a nursing home in Bognor and very old, you know. Er . . . would this be the right moment to request up to three weeks' compassionate leave to be in a position to attend to her?'

Private Secretary nodded at Head of Personnel. Head of Section gasped in exasperation. Everyone else ignored him. Head of Personnel turned to the acceptance clerk.

'Minute that Mr Sedge's request for up to three weeks' compassionate leave is granted,' he said. 'The meeting is closed.' The clerk closed his note book and the atmosphere relaxed.

'Time you were going home, Mr Sedge,' said the Private Secretary, 'and I should clear my desk out pretty thoroughly, if I were you. I think there's a good chance you won't be sitting at it again.'

Mr Sedge nodded and left the room. As he went down to his alcove, a surging, raging anger began to well up inside him and take possession of his senses. These walls, these carpets, these partitions; his favourite urinal in the gentlemen's lavatory, his personal coffee-cup holder, his new green chair, all this was nothing but froth blowing off the surface of his great purpose of the moment. In a sudden surge of feeling, he turned and detested these badges of job security; he wanted freedom and honourable status for his friends, the elephants; and his plots and plans had failed. He could only guess, but he was sure things must have come very close. The path of stealth was over now. Things would have to come out and be appraised; pursued outside.

He rushed into the fifth floor open office. It was that moment on a Friday when those who could were starting to drift off and when those who couldn't were desk tidying and housekeeping to fill in the time till they could. Mr Sedge burst through the end door like a bull loosed into a field. He pounded down the aisle between the desks and screens with a positive presence that struck terror into the hearts of civil service man. He looked not to right nor to left but thundered straight into his corner stall where he picked up his briefcase, stood it open on his desk and threw into it every personal item he had. The speed and positiveness with which he did this surprised even himself. Only as his coffee-cup holder went into the little cubic space at the back right of his briefcase did he realize that, in the back of his mind, he'd been rehearsing this moment for weeks.

With all his private goods stowed, he grabbed the current files off his desk top and charged the length of the office again. He burst straight into Head of Section's corner office, knowing he wasn't there, but raising a gasp from other desks just the same, dumped his files in that man's in-tray and returned to his own corner. He grabbed the briefcase, gave one last, cursory glance around the alcove, and breezed out, grabbing his coat on the way from the rack near the door.

As the door swung to behind him, many glances were exchanged between the occupants of the other desks. They had not seen the like before: Mr Sedge upright, positive and dynamic, treating the ministry with the irreverence of a conquering army. And then leaving a full five minutes before he should have. The eyes wandered round perplexed, amused, wondering what it could mean. More often than not, those wandering eyes came to settle after a moment or two, questioningly, curiously, hopefully, on the green swivel chair now resting at an angle to the desk in what perhaps had been, rather than was, Mr Sedge's alcove.

On the ground floor, Mr Sedge brushed past the security guard and out of the office. Clear air, the open street and the need to think. He wandered towards Charing Cross wondering which way to go, what to do. The unofficial disciplinary hearing was behind him now, the ministry in all probability behind him too, and he thought no more about them. He wanted to go to the marsh to let the elephants know how he was doing and what was happening, but all of that seemed too fraught with public spectacle and indecision. He might as well go home, he thought, but felt he should be able to do something, even if it wasn't much.

In truth, the self-contained Mr Sedge was feeling lonely. In his single-handed struggle, he needed a friend; and with this feeling strong inside him his thoughts turned to Henri Coulisse. He wondered where he should have got to by that hour. He bought an evening paper and saw that the elephant affair was already beginning to lose interest for the news. Where the elephants were concerned, nothing new was happening. From an inside page he was able to infer that the Worshipful Company which was holding Henri might complete its arcane deliberations by the end of Saturday. He headed still for Charing Cross. But when he got there, he looked at the station and the taxis outside, and up at the cross standing in front. He stopped and thought a moment. Then he went down the street beside the station to Embankment. There he took the underground for the City and, without much hope of succeeding, went in his loneliness to seek Henri Coulisse, whom, he was sure, would also need a friend in his.

Chapter 19

By mid-afternoon, especially on a Friday, the restaurants and snack bars of the City of London are closed. Mr Sedge, emerging from the underground at Monument, found it a curiously inhospitable place despite the business bustle and the rivers of people flowing towards the railway and underground stations. They were all running like mad to get away, starting the weekend time-trial, the race from the office that owed all its urgency to the simple fact that on Monday morning these people must be here again, heading back to the place of labour, with less speed, but also with greater determination; for their presence here paid their bread.

Mr Sedge was now curiously outside these considerations. He wandered, a detached observer, along King William Street, preferring the breeze and the clouds above his head to the travolator, below street level, that joined Monument station to Bank. At the Mansion House, he didn't cross through to Throgmorton Avenue as he knew that Henri would have no chance of leaving before six or seven at the earliest, if at all. He wandered round the corner to St Stephen Walbrook, planning to sit in the church a while and think the time through. But the church was full of scaffold and being restored and the public were kept out, so he turned back to the streets. In a state of indecision, he wandered through to the Grinders' Hall anyway: around the circus of Bank, in front of the Old Lady herself and behind the Stock Exchange where he soon tracked down the Hall's entrance.

As he was crossing Throgmorton Street, someone crossing in the opposite direction suddenly recognized him, raised his eyebrows and smiled, but made no move to speak. Mr Sedge was momentarily puzzled, then suddenly realized he had been recognized from the television pictures. By this time the man had passed by. Mr Sedge chuckled to himself. The incident somehow rid him of his anger and the disappointment that had accompanied it; a bounce came back to his step and he arrived smiling at the reception window of the porter's lodge at the Grinders' Hall.

A few miscellaneous newsmen were kicking their heels around the entrance; standing, as seemed to be the lot of their tribe, on the pavement, eyeing all comers and pouncing on those leaving for gobbets of information. Mr Sedge knocked at the porter's window. It opened:

'There will be a press release on Sunday afternoon at two o'clock,' said the stentorian porter and made to slide the window closed again. Mr Sedge, however, whipped his briefcase into the gap and stopped the window from shutting:

'I'm not from the press,' he said. 'I'm an associate of one of the Guild members who's deeply involved in the hearing. When will it be over?'

'Hasn't started yet,' came the reply.

'Would you expect the participants to come out this evening?'

'No.'

'When would you expect them to leave?'

'After sunset tomorrow, sir,' came a kind of final reply. The porter turned away.

From what Henri had told him, sunset was likely to

have all sorts of arcane significance for the Company. He took the man at his word and shuffled at his evening paper again to see what time sunset would be. As he was doing this, one of the reporters recognized Mr Sedge and bounded forward to get a few choice words.

'No idea,' said Mr Sedge in reply to the question put to him, 'I've been taken off the case.' The ring of newsmen closing round him, dispersed again. They could see themselves waiting all weekend for a bland statement at the week's worst moment for news. They turned up their collars and Mr Sedge wandered off round the block.

Not quite sure where to go, he turned down an alley and then down another and realized that he must now be directly behind the Grinders' Hall. The wall beside him rose vertically for ten metres or more of smooth stone, yet in the middle of it was a single wooden door of studded oak with the coat of arms of the Worshipful Company set in the centre of a small Tudor arch that formed its lintel.

'A postern?' thought Mr Sedge. And he thought of Henri. 'He'll leave through there,' he thought to himself. 'At least, I'll risk watching it to see if he does.'

He had a day to lose and, walking to the end of the alley, found a small pub nearby that was just opening. He went in to unwind and readjust his thinking and bought a couple of pies and a pint of shandy. He read the paper, several times, and in the course of a busy sequence of mental meanderings, consumed a second pint and read his paper three times more.

The following day he returned; but finding the pub, like most in the City, closed on a Saturday, he hung around, eyeing the wares in the window of a bespoke tailor's and listening to the screech of swifts, newly come from Africa, till day began to die.

The dusk was fast gathering. Mr Sedge went back to the

postern and waited. The lights were on and a few gnats buzzed round them despite the chill of the evening.

It was nearly nine o'clock. About the time when he thought Henri would appear. A key grated in the lock of the postern. A latch clicked and, unsurprised, Mr Sedge found himself face tc face with Henri, who in turn seemed almost to expect to see him.

They shook hands and were about to speak when another pair of hands possessed by a figure emerging from the shadows, descended on to their shoulders. They turned and, in the strange, pinkish imitation daylight of the alley lamps, they saw the imposing figure of Sergeant Apta Dapta, with the outline of Police Constable Monica Sullivan just behind him.

'Gentlemen,' said the Sergeant, curiously unofficiously, curiously curious it would seem. 'I have no power to arrest either of you in this matter but, you see, I want to close my case and provide certain information to the Home Secretary. Would you please come along?'

The two of them, after brief consideration, agreed; and the police led them to their car. They swept silently out into the empty City, finally pulling up in a lorry space outside Smithfield Market; a place where a checking police car caused no comment; and where they had the leisure to stop in quiet and talk.

It was the dead end. Henri was able to confirm everything the Sergeant had learnt from questioning the band and could add very little to it. For his part he was able to tell them what had happened at the Worshipful Company and show them its options were not soft. Mr Sedge recounted the course of ministerial inquiries and their implications for him. The Sergeant and the Constable seemed happy, their files could be closed.

'As you can see,' said Henri, 'we have nothing to keep from you, we'll help you all we can. Can you help us, too?

'How?' asked Sergeant Apta Dapta with a non-committal air.

'The elephants are members of our band. It's their job, it's their means of survival in the world. Can you fix it so that the band has access to them whenever we want it?'

The two police officers looked at each other. 'That should by easy enough,' said the Sergeant. 'I'll arrange it. The Chief Inspector can send a directive to the marshes.'

Mr Sedge and Henri thanked the two police officers from the bottom of their hearts.

'Can we drop you off somewhere?' said Sergeant Apta Dapta. Henri and Mr Sedge looked at each other. They mused a moment.

'Yes,' said Henri, 'The Splurge.'

'The Splurge,' echoed Mr Sedge.

And with a roar, the car engine burst into life and the two outcasts were driven in a certain style back to their first port of call.

As they were dropped off in Wardour Street, the Sergeant jangled something at them through the car window. 'I guessed you'd be needing these,' he said. 'The place has been closed down since the raid. Good luck.' And Henri took the keys the sergeant had so thoughtfully brought along.

They wandered slowly down the alley to the door of The Splurge. The neon sign above it was dark and the whole place had a deathly hush about it that made them feel rejected, uninvited. Henri raised his hand and pushed the key into the lock. He turned it and pushed against the door: it swung open and revealed the black interior; the stone stairs scarcely visible in the night. The police must have just left it as they found it once their men had finished with the premises. The two of them looked at each other and pushed on in. Henri found the light switches and clicked them on. There were a few bits of broken glass underfoot from a drinks bottle that had probably been thrown off the staircase in the struggle. The wreckage of a smashed chair had been kicked into a heap in the corner by the entrance to the warehouse.

'I wonder,' said Henri, and pushed through into the echoey room. After a moment's fumbling round the roller shutter he found the lights. On the end of one flex hung the remains of a smashed bulb; he vaguely recalled a contretemps with it at his moment of departure aboard Finta Fanta. But the other bulb was good and shed a weak light over the empty and voluminous space. Mr Sedge saw him looking intently around. With a whoop, Henri suddenly leapt forward and kicked aside a few old cardboard boxes under the roller conveyor. Reaching in, he pulled out his trombone case and eagerly looked inside.

'Fantastic!' he shouted. 'By the look of it some police hound has just picked it over and put it back where he found it. I thought I'd lost that for good . . . Spare mouthpiece seems to be missing.' They rustled about a bit amongst the debris.

'Is this it?' asked Mr Sedge, holding out the small brass tube with the dome-shaped end that he'd found on the floor. It was indeed. And with the finding of the trombone, their mood changed and they decided to go up and see what the clubroom was like.

At first sight, as they had expected, it was a mess. But once they had pulled up a few tables and put the cloths back on them, a semblance of order returned. Henri fished a key from his pocket: the bar key, and opened up the shop. In the little kitchen they found rice and some tins of food. Before long they had a very passable curry for two laid neatly on the very table where Mr Sedge had so unexpectedly slept. Opening a bottle of wine, Henri poured them a glass each and, raising them in growing good humour:

'To us and to the elephants!' said Henri. Mr Sedge repeated the toast and they set to on a very pleasant meal.

'Well, what do we do now? That's what we need to work out. It looks like the management have abandoned this place,' said Mr Sedge, very glad he'd found a handful of raisins to put in his curry. 'It looks like I'm out of a job – though if they don't give me the boot, I'm not sure I wouldn't resign anyway now. You're a key member of an exploded jazz band, your father's supposed to be in terminal surfeit by now and I've lost my cause with the elephants.' Mr Sedge took another slurp of wine and felt a bit better. 'Drink up,' he urged Henri, 'I think we need a bit of mental release to sort this lot out.'

Henri drank, refilled and, with hunger subsiding and a feeling of security growing in him, he started to muse out loud on their situation:

'You know, we ought to look positively at all this. I've a feeling we've missed a vital point somewhere. Look at my father, for instance, walled up in deadly luxury by that bunch of professional vengeance seekers. By the way, I've fixed things so that he'll survive, you know. He looks at everything as if he's bound to come off worse; that's what all his equiposition is about. He's got ample time for reflection now, of course. Should be a long and sobering experience for him. If someone can be that nasty to him maybe he'll question the basis of his equiposition. It's a way of not being defeated while not tempting fate by winning. But why should winning tempt fate? You've done it, I've done it, the elephants have done it: we've won and we've lost. You can do both. One doesn't prevent the other.'

'It's that vital point you mentioned that interests me,' said Mr Sedge. 'I feel like that, too. As if there's something we could do that would pull the whole situation straight. As I see it, the elephants are the key to everything. Of course, I've pinned my destiny to theirs, so I would see it that way; but I think that they are what made the band distinctive, they're what people are interested in just at the moment. If I'd only been able to get their complete freedom, things would be so much easier.'

'Well, I don't know that their lack of freedom – legal freedom, that is – makes things any harder, does it? I mean, they're not likely to be deported are they? It makes no sense,' said Henri. Mr Sedge nodded.

'True enough,' he replied, 'but being sent to a zoo is the same thing as imprisonment. It's just as bad as deportation.'

'Well, I don't agree,' said Henri. 'You're looking at it from the point of view of legal rights and all that. That's not what counts now. They've gone public – the nation has heard them talking, the world's apparently got a couple of hundred photographers permanently surveying them. Aren't things turning in our direction? Popularity will make them invulnerable, popularity will never let them be taken back to a zoo against their will.'

Mr Sedge sipped at his glass. 'And what about us?' he said. 'Will James Daley want to carry on the band here. Indeed, can he now? And should I look for some sort of admin job as my civil service career reaches its bitter end?'

Henri's mind wandered back over the trial, he munched the spicy rice and wondered what port tasted like in total darkness. The thought made him wince a bit. But locked up in that black hole, he felt, was not only his father but a kind of static tension that had held his past life in motionless anxiety. His brilliant defence, his courage in defying the Worshipful Company, these were the things that were saving him; he must go on, and so must Mr Sedge. Anonymous admin jobs in faceless offices weren't what he should be doing: yet he obviously was a first-class paper tiger – he'd nearly got an elephant a passport and it

took a lot of sheer neck even to get that far. Suddenly,
Henri sat bolt upright.

'I have it!' he said. 'Of course, of course. Where we go
from here is where we are going anyway. You, Mr Sedge
will resign from the ministry and take up an admin job:
but not an anonymous admin job in a faceless office. Oh
no: you will become a manager, the manager of a jazz
band called The Jazz Elephants, and we shall be the
darlings of the music world!'

Mr Sedge was chewing a mouthful of spicy rice. He
stopped chewing. He nodded; he began chewing again.

'I've a feeling you're right,' he said after a savouring
swallow. 'I don't know what it is about this table, but it
seems to be here that all the great decisions of my life are
fated to be taken.'

'If you'll do it,' said Henri, 'we could broach it to James
Daley and the others. I think they'd jump at the chance.
What if I see whom I can contact and take it from there?'

Mr Sedge rocked back in his seat, finished eating and
started enjoying a few sips of the wine on its own. What
did he have to decide? Could he decide now? As he cast his
mind back over the last few weeks and wondered what
decisions he should make, he saw that it all boiled down to
a view of the future. Whether he could in any case
contemplate going back to the ministry, or whether that
course was cut off for him now, no matter what
happened. Not cut off by others, but by his own future.
Was a return to the ministry possible? What were the last
few weeks? A snippet of a life he'd wanted and would
never have; a little cream on the cake of the commonplace;
or was it something new, a passage to a new world?

He cast his mind forward and thought of himself in five
years' time. Would he look back at a part-life of office
existence, essentially marking time until he broke away
into jazz band management? Or would he sit back in his

green swivel chair, happy to have overcome a rough patch in his career and be even more established, even more pensionable than before?

The green swivel chair, that was the crux of the matter. Its curves beckoned to him, its comfort held out caressing surfaces to flatter his status. He would be a kind of king in that open office, and his throne would be a green upholstered swivel chair that gave the status and stance that all his past life had worked towards.

That image floated before Mr Sedge; and Henri wondered what was going through his mind. It didn't seem the moment to ask, so he slowly rose and went to open a tin of fruit salad for dessert and set the coffee machine in motion.

Suddenly Mr Sedge smiled, and smiled very broadly. 'Have you ever been seduced by a swivel chair?' he asked Henri.

'Er . . . not to my knowledge,' replied the trombonist from behind the bar.

'I have,' said Mr Sedge. 'But I see that, like all temptations, when you see them for what they are, they quite lose their attraction. The seductive appeal of a swivel chair is, you know,' and he chuckled, 'the illusion of power. A better place in the pecking order, a sign of being in with the Almighty – the Almighty in the shape of HMSO, at any rate. So it isn't really chairs at all, it's power over minions in an open office; and I don't want that. I really don't. And . . .' Poof! The chair disappeared in a puff of alcove dust. 'I want to manage a jazz band, you know; and if that doesn't work out, well, something very like it. So the answer's yes. Yes, I'll manage The Jazz Elephants. Let's see if we can get the others together on this and launch ourselves big – elephantine big!'

Between them, they pooled their small change and Mr Sedge went over to the telephone. Henri moved the fruit salad on to the table and busied himself with the rituals of coffee making. By the time the filtering was finished, the dessert set and the curry washed up, Mr Sedge was coming back from the phone.

'I've got hold of most of them, and they're on their way here,' he said. 'Apparently the drummer's lost interest and gone off somewhere else – and I couldn't contact Pete Davis. Apart from that, they should all roll up in half an hour or so.'

As it happened, Pete Davis was the first to arrive. As Henri and Mr Sedge were just pouring a liqueur to go with the coffee, they heard the street door bang down below. This was followed by the noise of someone panting up the stone steps and the sound of a rather breathless 'Hello'. And there stood Pete Davis, complete with double bass.

'Gosh, could I have a drink?' he asked.

Like the other two, he had been thrown out of the centre of his universe by recent events and, like them, when the turmoil was over, fell surely back to its centre, the stage where he had worked, the centre of the universe of every performer.

He drew a lager and joined them. One by one the others turned up until, finally, all of them were there, sitting on tables with a coffee or a drink, or leaning on chairs and swapping memories of police custody.

James Daley pulled the gossip into a conference and turned the word over to Mr Sedge. 'I think Mr Sedge has got something to say to us all,' he said, 'by the look of it – at any rate by the look of the news on Thursday night – these have been harrowing times.'

'I would say interesting times – at any rate times of change,' replied Mr Sedge. 'Henri and I have been talking about the band – all of the band, including the two of us now browsing in Walthamstow Marshes. I'm likely to lose my job over all this and, in any case, I'm clear that I don't want it anyway. Henri suggested I should manage the band. I've thought it over and I think he's right. The band needs a manager and if we can literally pull ourselves together at the moment, we should be in great demand. Henri suggested we should call ourselves The Jazz Elephants, by the way . . .' and his words were at once interrupted. The title obviously crystallized the idea that had been at the back of all their minds:

'Yes, of course, of course.' 'Let's get on with it,' came the chorus from the others. 'How'll we do it?' 'I think it's a great idea!'

'It's exactly that "How'll we do it?" that I think we need to tackle. But, can I take it from this that you'd like me to be your manager?' All eyes turned towards James Daley.

'I would,' he said without a hint of doubt. 'Playing is my job, working with music is my job . . .'

'It is,' said Mr Sedge, 'and you should stay in charge because jazz is what we're here for.'

'. . . not working out deals and contracts. I think you'd be better at that than I am. I'm for it.'

Nods and cries of assent went up from all of those present.

'Unanimous?' asked Mr Sedge.

'Unanimous!' they all cried.

'Then let's work out what we're going to do.

'Look, I see it this way: we've got to get a venue somewhere where the elephants can appear with us. Not as exhibits or curiosities but where we can really get into jazz with them properly. Somewhere where the television can get at us and publicize our existence to the world. Now, they're over in the marshes at the moment, so what I'm going to do, starting tomorrow, is go venue-hunting in that area. I'll also tell them somehow what we're up to.

'If we can get a venue sorted out, immediate problems

are over; we've then got to look to the long term. That's what we all need to be thinking about now. What I've got in mind is some kind of really prestigious event. something with lots of credibility and smothered witn important people, dripping with worthiness – you know, a kind of coronation atmosphere. If we can get into something like that we'll be established good and proper and there'll be no turning back. Well, what do you think?'

The others thought; and agreed as far as they had thought about it. The venue certainly was necessary and the continuing work on getting freedom and a proper position for the elephants in society remained the background to it all. The conversation rattled on, ideas came and went and the evening settled to a close.

In his wardrobe, Mr Sedge possessed a pair of shoes which he used in winter walks along the beaches near to Bognor. They were marked 'Masculine Brogues' and always gave him a feeling of outdoor earnestness, a kind of seriousness of purpose that differentiated him from the old dears and children in wellington boots. On that Sunday morning, he put them on again and headed for Walthamstow Marshes, dressed in a tweed suit and carrying a briefcase full of sandwiches. For he anticipated a long day's trudging that must always start and finish, must radiate outward like a set of spokes, from the corner of the marsh where the elephants had their home.

He passed the police control caravan and wandered along beside the Lea (Lee) Valley Navigation. To his right, a green slope stretched up in a very pleasant park. At the top of the slope, he could see the tent-like structures that the long-range cameramen of the world's press had erected to photograph the elephants from afar. Between Mr Sedge and the river ran iron railings that separated the lane he was on from the towpath and the water. Beyond the water was the section of marsh where the elephants lived. If they were to get to a venue in Stamford Hill, or Clapton, the local centres on this side of the river, they would have to be able to cross the stream and somewhere come through the fence. The stream he thought was easy – after all they had come up in it from the Thames – but the fence and pilings of the banks were mostly too difficult.

He left the river bank at the end of the park and climbed the steep hill that rose beyond it. Mr Sedge surveyed Stamford Hill and Clapton – a good two hours' walking – but it was no good. They were minor shopping centres in the anonymous London sprawl. They had their good points and their bad, but there was no chance that there would be a pub or club there that would host a pair of elephants and push them as it must to the media of the world. No, the west side of the marshes was a blank; he would try the east.

From Clapton, he took the train to Walthamstow. From its windows, as he hastily gulped down a couple of liver-sausage sandwiches, he saw the reality of what his map had inferred. The elephants really were enclosed in a quadrangle of land that was bordered on two sides by railway viaducts, on one side by the river and the remaining side by the reservoirs. In Walthamstow, he picked his way along the High Street – a ghastly affair of the slightly-out-of-date modernized by the wholly-out-of-touch – a straightforward shopping street now paved over as a pedestrian precinct, with the traffic diverted around it past the back doors of the large chain stores. It was hardly inspiring territory again, though he went through the motions of approaching the marsh from this direction to check if it would be possible. It was possible, right up until the last few metres. For there, after a pretty walk along Coppermill Lane between the hectares of open reservoirs where one suddenly felt the roof had been taken off London, where cormorants croaked and herons batted their way across the sky in lolling ease, there he came to the point where the railway must be crossed to reach the elephants' marsh. And here, hope in this direction died. The crossing was either through a bridge so low that cyclists had to dismount, or over a level-crossing so unsafe for the slow-moving elephants, its dangers warranted not their risks. Mr Sedge went back up Coppermill Lane a little way and, finding a car park near some isolated houses, where doubtless the water board workers dwelt, went in and perched on the kerb and finished another bag of sandwiches. He looked at the map. His mind contemplated what a hopeless place this seemed to be. The agoraphobic equivalent of Claud Coulisse's immurement. At least Henri seemed confident Claud was going to survive somehow. With those surroundings, he felt distinctly less sure whether the band would.

The only way out was the way they had come in, he concluded, from the south east. Wearily he went back to Walthamstow station, thence to Clapton and from there on foot to the riverside again at Lee (Lea) Bridge Road. From this direction, he confirmed, the arch under the railway viaduct was high and wide: an easy access for elephants to walk to Lea (Lee) Bridge Road along the eastern shore of the navigation. But to walk to Lee (Lea) Bridge Road for what purpose? Mr Sedge, in mid-afternoon, stood at the bridge of the Lea (Lee) Bridge Road and felt helpless. It had all seemed such a good idea the night before; but now, here he was, a jazz band manager in Masculine Brogues in the most jazzless place in London: with his prize trumpeters trapped in a wild life park and his legs aching. It was the aching legs that irked him. The thought of that green swivel chair flashed through his mind. He smiled and looked around him. It would be, he decided, better to have aching legs.

An enormous green building caught his gaze for the first time. It looked like a gigantic latter-day Nissen hut in a rather pleasant shade of pale green. Its semicircular metal structure dominated the skyline; for here in the middle of the marshes all was flat land, football pitches and rough fields. This was an isolated barn of a building. Mr Sedge half thought it would turn out to be an aircraft hangar. Out of curiosity as much as anything, he wandered over to see what it was. 'Lee' (Lea) 'Valley Ice Centre' he read on the board outside. 'I wish they'd decide what this place is called,' he thought. ' "Lee Valley Ice Centre", "Lea Bridge Road", "Lee" this, "Lea" that. I wish they'd make up their minds.'

Curiosity got the better of Mr Sedge. He went in, paid some money for a ticket as a spectator – of what he didn't know – and went and sat in a seat overlooking the ice rink that spread out silvery grey, like a small football pitch before him. A damp, chill draught trailed its clammy fingers across his face. He pulled out an apple and started to eat it. He watched the ice dispassionately.

Some sort of family skating period was in session. Little girls in pink leotards tried to dance to the tune of blaring music that came loud and distorted over the public address system. At the edges, adults staggered and whirled their arms to somehow stay upright on unfamiliar, hired skates. Children fell and cried, got up and fell again. Some sped in effortless ease over the surface of the ice; going where they wanted to, how they wanted to and all in rhythm to the distinctly tinny music up above. Mr Sedge began to develop a certain satisfaction in all this busy activity. Especially with those that did it well. Worth the chilly air and the bruised buttocks, went his thoughts, if the end result was the swooping, bird-like grace which some managed to attain.

After a while, an announcement was made that the ice

351

should be cleared to make way for the local ice hockey club who had an hour's practice session coming up. The families danced and pirouetted, staggered or slithered off the ice and Mr Sedge waited for the booted and padded puck chasers to enter the rink. Instead, however, an enormous pair of double doors opened opposite to the entrance where he had come in and a large yellow vehicle about three times the size of the average dumper truck trundled into the building. The doors were quickly closed behind it to keep the temperature down inside. Part of the barrier surrounding the rink was opened and the vehicle, with a driver sitting high on top of it, trundled on to the ice and started to systematically sweep from end to end of the rink. As Mr Sedge could see, it was evidently some kind of ice levelling device to prepare the surface after heavy use. All sorts of stiff drapery hung around the bottom of the machine and it was evident that the effect was to flatten the surface and take out the skate marks. Mr Sedge started to think. That machine was much the same size as an elephant, all told, and the doors it came through quite large enough to let in Rumpus Pumpus and Finta Fanta without any trouble at all. Now, that music they were playing: it was very tinny and nothing like the quality that The Jazz Elephants could provide. Of course, jazz might not be to every skater's liking but then, they needn't be the only source of music. Indeed, wasn't that an organ opposite with perhaps even a band platform behind it?

Mr Sedge snapped his briefcase closed, took a deep breath and went to find the Manager. This would require some delicate negotiation.

It was late afternoon when Mr Sedge toddled out into the foyer of the ice rink. It had been a tough couple of hours but, with some satisfaction, he went along the towpath on the marsh side of the river. The railway embankment soon came into view, with the bridge through it that led to the nature reserve. There he reported to the policeman on duty, who was turning back all those who wanted to go through to the elephants and, between times, sat glumly on his propped-up motorcycle, occasionally sipping tea poured from a red vacuum flask.

Mr Sedge announced himself and the policeman, who had received the orders Sergeant Apta Dapta had promised to arrange, let him through the brick arch. Mr Sedge wandered on for a few minutes looking for the elephants. After a while, he branched off down a side path that led between small reedy ponds, surrounded by the thrusting green of springtime. He entered a group of thickets and, not knowing which way to go, stopped and looked around. After a few seconds he heard a discreet tooting and walked down a distinctly muddy path towards it. There he found the elephants up to their shoulders in a small round pond, squirting themselves down and rubbing their sides together in a most convivial way.

'Hello!' they chorused.

'Glad to see you. Good to get a whiff of an old friend again,' said Rumpus Pumpus. 'How are things?' and he shot a spout of water into the air and apologized at once as Mr Sedge had to leap back out of the way of the falling cascade.

'How thoughtless of me,' said Rumpus Pumpus. 'What a bore to have to be forever watching out for your clothes.'

Mr Sedge brought the elephants up to date on what had happened. They commiserated with Mr Sedge but were glad of Henri's freedom. The arrangements for the band set their ears flapping in excitement:

'Yes, yes,' said Finta Fanta. 'If we can find a venue near

353

here – if we can – that would be wonderful. At least for the summer we'd be secure and on our way. Is there anywhere? Have you looked?'

'It's what I've been doing all day today,' explained Mr Sedge. 'I must say the local centres round here can't offer what we want. It's inner-urban residential territory really. Everyone goes to The Splurge from here when they want to hear jazz, and it's nowhere near the outside of London where you can find out-of-town venues. But just the same – I think I've got a solution, and very close to here; almost within sight in fact.'

The elephants stopped spurting with the water and began to pull themselves out of the pond. Mr Sedge reached into his briefcase and pulled out a sandwich which he demolished as the elephants shook themselves down on the bank.

'Well,' intoned Rumpus Pumpus, 'what's the possibility you've found?'

'There's an ice rink near here,' he said, 'only ten minutes' walk away, in fact. You must have come past it when you followed the navigation way up from the Thames. Anyway, it's vast inside, bags of room for a jazz band with a pair of elephants. I've negotiated with the Manager to let us perform there. He wasn't too keen at first but in the end I got him to try us for a fortnight. They have family skating periods there about four times a week. We can set up a stage at the middle of the rink-side and give them their music.'

'Not exactly the centre of attraction, star billing in a known venue,' cut in Rumpus Pumpus.

'No, that's so,' continued Mr Sedge, 'but I think it could come to that. I worked out a deal with him whereby we get a proportion of the increased receipts above his average for the session, over the last year. In other words, we'll get most of the money that's coming in because people are coming to see us.

'More important, I think that if it's a success at first we

can quickly dictate better terms and maybe get good offers elsewhere – we ought to get a summer season there anyway, if we're any good.'

The elephants pondered a moment. 'I'm in favour,' said Finta Fanta. 'I'm not sure I know very much about ice skating but I don't suppose that matters.'

'I'm in favour too,' said Rumpus Pumpus, 'but we'll need to keep working at it. I still feel some kind of official status is necessary for us. I suppose protected species status is a start; but from what you've told us, it looks like all hope of becoming persons is slipping away. That's saddening you know, very saddening.'

Mr Sedge sat down on a branch that projected from a stunted tree at seat level. 'Well, the rest of the band has been talking all that over, you know. I agree, in fact we all agree. The hope of getting you citizenship by stealth is dead now; but what we all thought might be the case, is that if we can make ourselves big enough, popular enough, associate ourselves with the rich, the famous and the popular, our demands would become almost undeniable. It's an idea you've mentioned yourself, you know, and I think you're right.

'You know, at the ministry we would get citizenship requests from thousands of refugees and we'd make them wait years, literally years, before we gave them a decision, and that wouldn't always be favourable. Then along would come some writer or underground freedom fighter or ballet dancer or some such hero of the popular press, or darling of the infinitely influential, and they'd be in before most people could fill in the forms.

'The common feature all these people would have is something called prominence. A kind of positive prominence that grants them a welcome wherever they set foot. We're prominent as it is: we're in the news and Henri's in the news in his own right too. What we lack is that cachet, a kind of social acceptance that can suddenly open the doors for us.'

'Give me some idea of what's needed,' said Finta Fanta. 'If a degree of fame isn't enough, what more do we need?'

'Gosh, I don't know,' said Mr Sedge. 'I've never thought so analytically about it before. I suppose it's partly the fact of being acceptable in important company. That's the way it seems to be with the ballet dancers, anyway. It doesn't much matter what one-shop village they come from nor whether they talk any English or not; so long as they're acclaimed by the ballet brigade and watched by royalty and members of government, and shake hands with the patrons of opera houses, all is well. It boils down to a kind of patronage really – patronage by the literary establishment, patronage by the artistic establishment, patronage by the journalistic establishment, patronage by the anti-establishment establishment. It seems to me any of these patronages is just about as good as any other.'

'What about patronage by the sculptural, animal and City establishments?' asked Rumpus Pumpus gravely.

'If we could swing that,' chortled Mr Sedge, 'there'd be no problem. In fact we'd be in a better position than any disgruntled minion of the Azerbaijanian Dance Troupe – and that's a distinction hard to achieve.'

'Well,' continued the bull elephant, now prodding the mud with his tusks in an idle sort of way, 'surely we can, as you say "swing" that one. Are you not aware of an exhibition about to take place in Regent's Park – The Evolution of the Elephant – a sort of sculptural extravaganza sponsored jointly by the Monarch and The Zoological Society of London? Finta Fanta and I know quite a lot about that competition. It takes place in about three or four weeks' time. There are sculptures all over the park already – the nation's art colleges are vying with each other for the coveted prize – goodness knows what it is; money I expect.

'But don't you think we ought to be a part of that? We're the nation's, perhaps the world's, most famous elephants and I think we should be presenting the prizes or, maybe, judging the sculptures for "insight into elephant culture" or something like that.'

'What a good idea,' said Finta Fanta. 'We'd be in with the Monarch, make peace with the zoo. But what about the City? You mentioned the City establishment.'

'Well, Henri, of course,' said Rumpus Pumpus. 'That Worshipful Company of whatever-they-ares ought to be able to come in on our side, shouldn't they? After all, if Henri's father can eat himself half dead for them, they can at least help Henri get established in jazz, can't they?'

'Mmm . . . I don't think the world is quite like that,' came in Mr Sedge. 'Gratitude isn't half as powerful as the prospect of gain with people like that. What's more, I'm not so sure that Henri's father really is in such a bad state. Henri made some comments to me that suggest he's got a few tricks up his ex-liveried sleeve yet. Just the same, they're a powerful interest group, you're right; and if we could enlist them on our side it would only help.'

'Shall we just write to *The Times* like last time?' suggested Rumpus Pumpus.

'You could,' said Mr Sedge. 'You were lucky then; but somehow I doubt that it's luck you could rely on twice. Besides, we've got a certain amount of power to our elbow now. We should be able to get a rôle in that jamboree without acting like complete outsiders. Who's organizing it?'

'The zoo and the Monarch and the Royal Academy,' explained Finta Fanta. 'I suppose if we wrote to the zoo we might be able to get them on our side. The President of the Society, after all, must, technically at least, be rather embarrassed that he's lost us. If we offered him a helping trunk he might be only too pleased to play along.'

'Probably would,' agreed Rumpus Pumpus. 'And the Monarch? I think you've got to go a little deviously there.'

'I should think you have!' jumped in Mr Sedge. 'My old minister was a Privy Counsellor, you know, and I think even he had trouble bending the royal ear at times. Most of it's done through layers of equerries and people-in-waiting and secretaries and goodness knows what other formalities. Mind you, the minister exercised the royal prerogative on all sorts of matters; but in something like this, like us, it'd be the Monarch who mattered.'

They batted the question backwards and forwards and tried to come up with some kind of solution – some way of getting themselves together with all these other pillars of the establishment at the great Day of the Elephant in Regent's Park.

'Look,' said Finta Fanta suddenly, 'it's not just a question of asking for favours, it's also a question of us being able to offer them something. I've got an idea . . .' The little group chatted and discussed and chortled and decried but after ten minutes or so, some answer seemed definitely to have been arrived at. Trunks patted backs, hands stroked trunks and Mr Sedge shook a tusk in appreciation. Something had evidently been decided.

'An invitation?' queried the Monarch.

'Yes, Your Majesty,' explained the equerry. 'From a band called The Jazz Elephants, evidently the elephants who escaped from the zoo a little while ago and have now become part of a jazz band; and the er . . . Lea' (Lee) 'Valley Ice Centre, it appears.'

'I rather like jazz,' said the Monarch, and sighed.

'I'm not impartial myself – in small doses,' said the equerry. They looked at each other across the private sitting room. Great red and gold curtains hung beside the windows and the daylight, pale and pastel, lit up the room with a gentle, melancholy lustre.

'Of course, I can't go,' said the Monarch. 'You know what my diary's like for that day – and most of the other days near to it.'

'Would it be possible to send someone to represent you?'

The Monarch looked slightly askance at the equerry. The equerry blushed a little and looked slightly askance at the Monarch.

'Er . . .' said the Monarch, eyebrows just a little raised, 'would you care to go yourself, perhaps? I expect they want to . . . well, you know the way it is; er, bend someone's ear about something. I'm sure you can handle that and let me know if it's anything I really ought to consider.'

'I should be delighted to attend,' said the equerry, quite looking forward to the event. 'And, I shall be only to pleased to act as your ears in the matter.'

'What!' shouted the Grand Master, curling his lip and looking at the Clerk with an air of outrage. 'He has the temerity to invite me to an ice pantomime in honour of his father! We don't immure people to honour them with circuses! Preposterous! Of course not!'

'I've heard the Monarch may be sending a representative,' said the Clerk, whom Mr Sedge, well briefed by Henri, had been careful to telephone in advance of the invitation's arrival.

'Oh, well . . . what's it all about, did you say?'

'It's from the ex-member, sir, Henri Coulisse, and, er, a Mr Sedge who apparently manages The Jazz Elephants, the band with whom those escaped elephants have joined company – you may have heard . . .'

'Yes, yes, I saw something in the newspaper a day or two ago.'

359

'It seems they're performing for a season at ice shows and intervals in between ice hockey matches and so on. They're also doing one or two Jazz Gala Nights and this particular one is being dedicated to a number of worthy causes.

'By the look of it, Grand Master, the young Coulisse is attacked by a well-earned remorse . . .'

'Jolly well ought to be too!' cut in the Grand Master, reddening in the face and starting to relive recent embarrassments. 'Missing the Burst of Spring! He'll rue that for the rest . . .'

'Um . . . Grand Master,' put in the Clerk, 'I agree with you; but I think the Contumacious Grinder's remorse may be rather more to do with the fate of his father.'

'Oh, well, yes. I see. Mmm, I suppose so. What is this event then, a royal gala or a memorial service?'

'That's hard to say, I think. Having seen at first hand the kind of people young Coulisse associates with, I don't think there'll be much in the way of formal mourning. If you decided to go I think it would be a plain-clothes affair – perhaps with a darkish tie.'

'I see what you mean.' The Grand Master was weighing things up. 'I don't want to go, you know. But then old Claud wasn't really a bad chap, in some ways. Mind you, better men than he have been constrained to ordeal from time to time; so he had nothing to worry about there. What's more, I can't really pass by an opportunity to keep the Company's royal presence up, can I? Yes. I suppose I'll go.

'Reply, will you. I'll come with pleasure.'

'With much pleasure,' murmured the Clerk noting the fact.

'No,' said the Grand Master, 'just pleasure, not much pleasure. We can't let the young Coulisse get away with murder can we, er . . . so to speak?'

One of the President of the Zoological Society's favourite interesting facts from near and far, concerning the animal kingdom, was the existence of pythons' legs. He rather liked pythons, they were a favourite animal of his. Cynics on his staff noted that the President rather liked a good meal and remarked, too, that pythons ate till they nearly burst and then hung around the place in torpor for a month getting ready for the next blow-out.

The President's favourite party trick was to take a private guest into the python room in the zoo, at an hour when the public were not admitted, and reveal the miniature legs which sit in recesses about two thirds of the way along the python's length. Many an extra tenner, earned on the basis of an after-dinner bet, had gone into the zoo's fund on the strength of that little party-piece.

This afternoon it was the turn of the Director of the London Tourist Board who, having spent several very pleasant hours at a remarkably good lunch during which he had promised the funnelling of rivers of continental and American tourists through the zoo's portals, had been persuaded to lay down his tenner over the brandy with the prospect of seeing the President look rather foolish.

Together, the two men staggered along to the reptile house, where, with the Director of the London Tourist Board looking on from the empty public walkway, with a distinctly sceptical stance, the President went round into the python room and started to stroke his favourite snake.

Curly the python, about four metres long all told, and pretty full of good food, was draped over a section of tree at his tail end, whence across the floor for a metre or so and over a log. On top of one tyre-like coil, sat, finally, the animal's head, right at the edge of the tepid pool at the centre of the warm room.

Meanwhile, in the President's outer office his secretary rang the main gate to see if he had come back from lunch yet. There was an invitation with important implications that needed an immediate reply. The main gate said that he had indeed returned and appeared to have headed for the reptile house with his guest. The secretary grabbed the invitation and rushed there at once, knowing that if she didn't manage to catch the President as he went in, there was sometimes a considerable break before he was in a condition to come out again.

But it was too late. She plunged into the half-lit building to see the Director of the London Tourist Board standing with his mouth agape looking into the python tank. From the concourse, the secretary saw the President slowly creeping up on the head of Curly which rested on top of his neck coils across towards the pond. Slowly, the President's hand descended on to the python's head and gently began to caress it. Curly's eyes fluttered. He was evidently enjoying the experience and the President seemed to be humming or singing to the long, spread-out animal as he gradually stroked it further and further down the length of its great dappled body. For a moment, the secretary thought that this was going to be an easy tenner for the President. His hands passed now over the squat, middle body of the great snake. They approached the almost imperceptible slits where the tiny legs were hidden. Curly's head made a snuggling movement, like a sleeper about to change position.

The hand just rocked Curly's body over a bit and, with an expert dexterity, the President drew out the tiny legs and the Director, putting hands over eyes in a sign of disbelief, reached into his pocket and pulled a ten-pound note from his wallet. He waved it at the President who acknowledged victory with a gracious nod of the head and made to take his leave of Curly. But Curly rather liked someone waving at him; and liked the President anyway, so he thought he'd give him a parting hug. With that smooth and deceptive speed which all the great snakes have, his head just arced around and the coil of his upper body perfectly lassoed the President as he made for the door. Two or three more coils slung around him quicker than the President could say, 'Oh Curly, not now, old chap!' and he tumbled to the floor of the cage like an advertisement for car tyres, while Curly, hugging gently in his friendly way, put his head on the President's shoulder and, to the latter's utter resignation, fluttered his eyes and started to go to sleep.

As the President knew, this is a ticklish situation. Curly meant very well and only wanted to be friends. Indeed, were things otherwise, the President would now be on his way down Curly's gullet. But snake-time and man-time are different things. Curly might happily snooze for a week in this position and it wasn't really safe to complain about it too much.

The secretary saw her chance. Going round to the keeper's door, she let herself into the snake compound and kneeled gently in the gravel by the President's head.

'Excuse me,' she whispered, knowing the strictures that might follow from disturbing Curly's sleep, 'but there is an important invitation from a musical group called The Jazz Elephants. They're the ones who are involved with our two elephants you know . . .'

'I know!' hissed the President in a desperate whisper that accompanied a rounding of his eyes like a bush baby's. He stopped abruptly as Curly contracted a fraction in his sleep.

'They've invited you to a gala performance at the Lee' (Lea) 'Valley Ice Centre,' whispered the secretary again. 'You're free that evening, do you want to go? I have to reply this afternoon.' The President's eyes turned upward in a gesture of terrified resignation; but his secretary was quite indifferent to self-inflicted problems of this nature.

'Yes, accept,' he hissed, making a fair imitation of a snake himself, 'and send over the Cannon-ball Shag,' he murmured.

'Cruelty to animals,' taunted the secretary, though not unkindly.

'Precisely,' whispered the President, 'cruelty to human animals – go on, quick,' and he couched his head slowly upon Curly's neck.

The secretary took her leave and walked briskly back to the office. From the strong-box in the corner she took a polythene bag and, unwrapping it, removed a leather tobacco pouch and an enormous briar pipe. The President had acquired it from the snake keeper at the Plymouth Zoo who, in turn, had got the tobacco, Cannon-ball Shag, and the observation that its fumes were a narcotic to snakes, from a well-travelled nautical gentleman in a saloon bar in Devonport. The secretary got the snake keeper to take the apparatus and fuel across to the python house. With a look of resignation, he did so. Before long, a very sad-looking President was lying amidst Curly's coils puffing wanly on the giant briar pipe. After half an hour or so he felt the coils begin to relax and on Curly's lips, he thought he detected just the faintest hint of an oblivious smile.

'They've all accepted!' shouted Mr Sedge in glee. 'Not all in person – the Monarch's sending an equerry. But it's good enough. The event's on.'

The clammy, echoey interior of the Lea (Lee) Valley Ice Centre lost that dampening influence it has at the end of a session. Everyone was pleased and, as the ice machine trundled into the rink through its double doors, the musicians wandered out into the clear sunshine of the warm afternoon, their session for that day over, beaming with anticipation, elephants murmuring with satisfaction.

Mr Sedge explained what would happen at the gala performance. There was nodding of heads and words of assent. Slowly, the party began to wander up the riverside track towards the marsh, chatting as they went.

'Good grief,' said Pete Davis, 'it's next week. Are we ready?'

'Oh yes,' said Mr Sedge, 'we're ready. You've never been playing better and I've never been playing better either. I'm getting quite experienced at handling my superiors. It's an important art and with any luck we'll use it to our advantage.'

They went through the railway arch and gave a familiar greeting to the Lee (Lea) Valley conservationist who now manned the barrier there. He raised it and let them through, turning back a couple of bystanders who wanted to go through too. The elephants' presence had official tolerance now. Their protection being assured by the zoo and the valley authority, with the police presence reduced to just a sergeant and a motorcycle constable in the mobile headquarters unit.

The elephants trailed off to their supper and the others wandered across the footbridge and along the towpath towards the underground station. It was a mild, pleasant evening with the trees in leaf and the promise of summer everywhere. An air of achievement accompanied their footsteps, and an air of anticipation buoyed up their conversation.

'How do you do?' asked the equerry stepping from the large black limousine with the royal flag tightly furled into a neat little black leather cover to show no royalty was aboard.

'How do you do?' asked Mr Sedge and ushered the man

forward through the glass doors of the Ice Centre to meet the President and the Grand Master who had already arrived.

They assembled first in the Manager's anteroom: a sort of plastic and pot-plant kind of place, trying hard to look luxurious despite local authority funding. The equerry was pressed to a drink and asked for a cocktail that sent the waiter into the back room. The back room then went into a panic for five minutes until a phone call told them it was only brandy, ginger and bitters. The waiter then staggered back with the concoction and the equerry sipped it with equanimity. The Grand Master took a whisky, the President some foreign thing that smelt of aniseed; and Mr Sedge finally descended upon them holding a glass of tonic water himself, as he needed his clarity of spirit.

'It's going to be a magnificent evening,' he beamed with a sincerity that overwhelmed even himself. 'First there'll be the final of the London Ice Hockey Tournament and after that, a quarter of an hour of Jazz on Ice. There's then a figure skating final . . .'

The Manager interjected: 'Perhaps you'd all care to watch that from the Manager's Patio while taking a bite to eat. There's a very good little buffet set out, you know. Figure skating is a bit of a specialist affair and it might be better if I can explain what's going on.'

The Grand Master looked as if figure skating would turn him brown at the edges and jumped at the buffet.

'A bite to eat. Yes, of course . . . er, figure skating . . . good, mmm.' The others nodded between sips and the Manager carried on with the programme.

'After it, there's more jazz, then an ice dancing competition and after that a little spectacular of our own with our local champions giving half an hour of ice variety with our own inimitable live music, of course. It should be quite remarkable.'

The Manager droned on a bit and Mr Sedge whipped the steward into pressing second drinks into everyone's hand and, after a couple of comments more from the assembly, third drinks, too. A positive air of enjoyment began to spread through the little party and, before long, they filed off to the specially constructed box by the rinkside. The ice-hockey players finished off their warm-up and made ready for the off.

With great interest, they watched the two teams hack each other to death for about half an hour until one of them was declared the London Champion. And the royal representative, the equerry, handed over the cup to a sweat- and blood-spattered youth who drifted off across the ice in triumph, holding the trophy aloft.

As the team stumbled off the ice, the band struck up on a rostrum constructed above the level of the barriers, on the side opposite the guests of honour. Toes tapped, heads nodded – little in the case of the equerry who had too much dignity to represent – much in the case of the President who now saw in the elephants a pair of animals even more sporting and interesting than Curly himself. Henri trombone-soloed at, rather than for, the Grand Master. Suggestive as that instrument can be, in the lunging provocations of its protruding pipes, the Grand Master appreciated the music but became quite clear that Henri's attitude to him was less than charitable. The musical interlude came to an end.

'Let us to the Manager's patio,' said Mr Sedge, with a grandiose sweep of his arm. 'The Rink Manager can apprise us of the technicalities of figure skating and I believe there are caviare canapés and a bottle or two of Bollinger up there as well.'

At the mention of Bollinger a smile rose to several lips and an alacrity entered the step of the little party that had begun to look wan at the ending of the jazz.

They stepped out of the booming, echoing, semi-cylindrical rink, slightly self-conscious all of a sudden in the quiet that followed the exposure to sight and noise. On the Manager's patio they took up positions from which they could have looked along the length of the ice and discussed the figures, had such been their wont. But Mr Sedge positioned them so that the crowd outside would have believed them observing the figures, then manoeuvred canapé and Bollinger into hand and throat and began the real work of the evening.

'Don't you think it would add to your Day of the Elephant,' said Mr Sedge, suddenly very earnestly to the President and the equerry, 'if you invited the Grand Master's Worshipful Company to take part in the proceedings. I believe the City should be represented, don't you?'

The three of them looked a little embarrassed at this suggestion, as Mr Sedge knew they would.

'You see,' said Mr Sedge, and he indicated the band setting up its equipment for the next session on a gigantic pallet below the panoramic windows, 'that very excellent band already unites the zoo and the Worshipful Company in a most informal way. Wouldn't it be fitting for the formal phalanxes of the Company to do homage to the royal presence with its bells and organs as well?'

A slight twist of the Grand Master's lips and a little throbbing in his temple made Mr Sedge sure he had struck the right note.

'After all,' carried on Mr Sedge, refilling at the same time with Bollinger right and left, 'I don't believe any organization in the country can better the Founders and Grinders at giving the correct due to a royal presence.'

At this, of course, the Grand Master's vanity swelled to the occasion.

'The Monarch, of course,' said the Grand Master with

subservient pomposity, 'knows that I and my Company will be ever glad to render homage where due. I must say the sculpture competition and the Commonwealth festival elements do really need something to give them the musical, what shall I say? . . . er, ballast, fitting to the occasion. Of course, if a military band would rather . . .'

'Oh, out of the question, I'm afraid,' said the equerry rather laconically. 'Too near Trooping the Colour, the Royal Tournament and all those sorts of things. Can't budget for it, you see. Some parliamentarians start asking questions about why money on military music can't be spent on hostels for the indigent. The Monarch is very sensitive to their case. No, if you would make your musical phalanxes available, I would be pleased to make an initial representation to the Monarch for you.' The Grand Master swelled with vainglory in prospect of the honour. 'Though I must add, the festival is a popular one and the public will require moments less formal than handbell and organ are likely to provide, perhaps.'

The Grand Master's face fell but Mr Sedge leapt in at once. 'Surely this is no problem,' he said enthusiastically. 'I'm sure the President would agree, The Jazz Elephants could provide the popular side of the bill, the Worshipful Company the formal homage it is so excellent at rendering.' A look of doubt began to creep into the Grand Master's face. The equerry knew that look of old; the President and the equerry exchanged glances. The President remembered a most satisfactory reception at which the Monarch had cooked up a scheme with him, or so he now firmly believed, which had launched this whole great undertaking. The President leapt into the breach.

'Well, surely, the elephants themselves, in the shape of The Jazz Elephants, should provide the more popular music. Look at them down there . . .' and through the plate-glass windows, they could see the band pallet rigged with drum kit and music stands and evidently ready to be pushed out on to the ice, '. . . this spectacle is the Day of the Elephant, after all; the zoo should have a living part in it. I sometimes wonder if we'll get that pair down there back again; but in any case they're the best flesh and blood input from the zoo that we've got. I'd say let the Worshipful Company handle the ceremonial music and The Jazz Elephants entertain the great public at large.'

'Of course, with Henri Coulisse in the band we'd be well prepared to grant the ceremonial aspects the separate status they need – he'll be most assiduous in keeping the Company's presence apart from that of The Jazz Elephants,' came in Mr Sedge.

The Grand Master snorted, but, nonetheless, saw the point of the comment. Both the Worshipful Company and jazz band would be at pains to separate their activities. The Grand Master need make no concessions to popular music; he would just refer enquiries to The Jazz Elephants. He turned to the equerry:

'I think I'd like you to put forward the Company's offer,' he said, 'to let it be known The Worshipful Company of Bell Founders and Organ Grinders would welcome the opportunity to give formal music at the Day of the Elephant.'

'And The Jazz Elephants for the informal side,' added Mr Sedge.

'Then I'll recommend it to the Monarch,' said the equerry; and Mr Sedge added Bollinger to Bollinger.

'Great Scott! He's fallen!' added the equerry, who had looked beyond the circle to the figure skating.

'Not to worry,' said the Manager. 'It's over now. Jazz and ice dancing next; then the spectacular.'

They filed out of the Manager's suite, having downed their drinks and polished off the fish roe. As they made their way back to their place of honour, the lights went down and a spotlight picked out the glittering band pallet as it was pushed out on to the ice: the elephants to one side of it, the drum kit at the back, Pete Davis thrumming his double bass as if life depended on it, James Daley with glittering saxophone gurgling like a musical drain into the microphone before him; and Henri Coulisse tromboning by the elephants in the greatest living brass in the universe.

The crowd rose to an almighty cheer. Feet tapped, music throbbed, Sady's keyboards tinkled and tonkled and the lights flew and darted off the glinting brass. After half an hour's figure skating the frost can rather get at an audience, so they came on with the full fire of 'Musk Rat Ramble', heating the spectators and igniting most of those who had been preheated by Mr Sedge. '12th Street Rag' got a standing ovation for the trumpet solos and the audience got an ear-flap in acknowledgement. At the end of the fifteen minute interval, the equerry was ecstatic and the President persuaded; and even the Grand Master with a dour glance in the direction of Henri, had to give a grudging acknowledgement that perhaps the band could provide one or two things which the Worshipful Company could not.

The Monarch leaned back and sipped a glass of Bollinger. The equerry declined, making remarks about too much of good things.

'And what do you think they wanted to bend your ears about last night?'

'Oh music, I think,' replied the equerry. 'The Day of the Elephant. Would Your Majesty agree to formal music from the Worshipful Company of Founders and Grinders – the usual regiments are so tied up this time of year, you know; and to informal music from The Jazz Elephants?'

'Are they all right; The Jazz Elephants, I mean?' said the Monarch. 'That boring crowd from the Worshipful

Company can have the honour if they like – give them a chance to get their prestige back after that fiasco in Soho – but these Jazz Elephants, are they, you know, sound?'

'Sound, Your Majesty?' said the equerry, knowing exactly what the Monarch meant. 'Why Your Majesty: greatest living brass in Britain, I should say, if not the world. Maybe I will have a glass after all.'

'Then see that they're there,' said the Monarch, 'see that they're there!'

There was a tinkle of glasses; and each pair of eyes, as they drank, caught sight of a foot, a foot just perceptibly tapping to a tune it would have been indecorous to hum.

Chapter 20

'Time to go,' said Rumpus Pumpus. He stuffed a last bundle of delicious spring twiggies into his mouth and swiped Finta Fanta a cuffing tickle behind the ears. She swayed sideways and gave him a friendly barge; and the two set off towards the Seven Sisters Road.

The marsh was alive with birds chorusing to the day. The sun was well up but, June as it was, it was early yet for Londoners and few saw the elephants start out. The photographers had more or less drifted away from the heights of Springfield Park. Once speech had been proved and the elephants shown themselves quite disdainful of attempts to make them into performing animals, the news value disappeared and the photographers were reassigned to baby pandas and defrocked clergymen.

They waded the river near the mobile control unit and the Sergeant on duty, forewarned by Mr Sedge, waved them through. In single file, they wandered up the river bank along the path beneath the pale green willows. A pair of elephants beside a London river in the pale morning of a still, June day. It seemed as normal a sight as could be, and one that for all the world looked as if it happened every day of the year.

When they came to the hole in the fence that Mr Sedge used for his short cut, they kicked it a little larger and squeezed through to the road on the other side.

Remembering the road maps perfectly as ever, they walked quickly through to the Seven Sisters Road, alarming the odd milkman, getting a hello from the odd postman but generally causing little or no stir at all.

By seven o'clock they were under the railway bridges at Finsbury Park; and well before eight they were in the one-way streets of Camden Town, strolling lightly, unhesitatingly on to the park. Up the slope and across the terracotta bridge, over the Outer Circle and into the park itself where, beside the children's playground, as arranged, they were met by Henri with a jovial cheer.

'Toot toot!' said Henri with a laugh.

'Rootle–oot,' they replied.

'Mr Sedge has managed to get us a tent for the day, over by the back of the zoo. Breakfast is laid out there for all of us and everyone should be there in a few minutes' time. Are you hungry?'

'Moderately,' avowed Finta Fanta. 'We ate well before leaving but a meal is always a good idea after a brisk walk.'

They went up the path to the zoo but did not turn towards its entrance. Instead, they crossed the Broad Walk, sighting groups of clay elephants in the distance, and along the path that tops the embankment immediately parallel to the zoo fence.

'Familiar-looking territory,' remarked Finta Fanta as they started down the slightly sloping path.

'Ah, yes,' said Rumpus Pumpus, 'the Children's Zoo, the tigers up on their hill. And look, they've mended the fence but there's still a great area of bare earth where the clay deliveries were made.'

Their gaze went beyond the bare patch to the buildings on the far side. They were on top of the bank, on the path now, and stood looking at their old home. There was the elephant house with its moat and its compound and there, within the precinct, ogled at by visitors and seemingly resigned to their lot, was a pair of Indian elephants standing, eating hay, with their backs to the crowd. Finta Fanta looked at Rumpus Pumpus and Rumpus Pumpus looked back at Finta Fanta. They held their trunks in the air and sniffed.

'Rhinoceros!' they exclaimed simultaneously and, laughing, turned their backs on the zoo and looked at where Henri was leading them.

A most splendid sight met their eyes. In normal times, from their vantage point, they would have seen a green field stretching from the zoo away down a gentle slope. Green trees clustered in the park at all the limits of the grass; and beyond the trees could be seen the taller buildings of London, visible like towers in a forest. Sometimes they would have been able to sight the cream fronts of the elegant properties surrounding the park; and perhaps just before them, they could have witnessed a cricket match on the mown square in the middle of the field. Beyond this field was the clump of trees around the café and the little art gallery. Beyond that, more grass, more trees, and the woods that bordered the lake which the elephants knew only too well. Yet on this Day of the Elephant, the spectacle was vastly different.

The park side of the path on which they stood was lined with tents. One or two were for special purposes – a base camp for The Jazz Elephants, or for The Worshipful Company of Founders and Grinders – but most were open on the field side as display tents for the various art colleges participating in the sculpture competition. It was a gay revelry of canvas. Every tent, some enormous, some only big enough for an exhibition of twenty paintings around two pieces of sculpture, was coloured differently; from plain white to stripes of red and yellow, stripes of blue and blue; and stripes of green and gold. The Worshipful Company had erected its field pavilion – an awesome edifice of purple and gold, hung with miniature bells that tinkled in the gentle breeze of what promised to be a beautiful day. At the summit of the two main poles, mighty organ pipes reached to the skies: pipes which moaned, as the breeze that promised summer, murmured its message through the true-formed ducts. Yet if one walked between the tents – or through The Jazz Elephants' tent, for this opened both towards the zoo and towards the field – one came out on what might at first sight have struck one as a ground set for a tournament. For here the artists' pavilions lined one side but, to the right, as one looked towards the trees that hid the lake, was the great Royal Pavilion at right angles to the line one had just traversed. So two sides of a rectangular field, the Royal Rectangle, were marked out some hundred and forty metres by one hundred.

The Royal Pavilion was scarlet and gold and, at its centre, had a small grandstand from which the dignitaries of the day would watch various events due to take place in the field. In the front of the grandstand was a dais for speech making and the presentation of prizes. It too was hung with scarlet and gold and bore the royal arms for all to see.

Opposite the Royal Pavilion, a third side to the field was created by tents, open to the public, serving various edible substances of a greater or lesser palatability. Throughout the park, especially near the various groups of elephant statues, were other stands and displays, often sponsored by elephant-bearing countries, entreating their virtues to the royal and public eye.

The Jazz Elephants roistered in their tent. Pete Davis, till now known to them only as a large and modest double-bassist had his back to the elephants as they entered. He was dashing up and down in front of a camp cooking-range that was belching blue flames and popping and roaring at several points, while he threw together a breakfast of brown rice balls and birch twigs for the elephants, and kippers and porridge for everyone else. From the front opening of the tent one could occasionally see a pompous passer-by suddenly turn his head as his nose picked up the odour of the morning and he would then stamp on, slightly bemused.

Finally the band sat down together round a collapsible rustic table, all with their breakfast favourite before them and a coffee filter infusing in front of their eyes.

'What's the order of the day?' said Rumpus Pumpus to Mr Sedge, who had taken up position at the head of the table, opposite the elephants.

'First of all, porridge with whipped cream and brown sugar,' said Mr Sedge, 'then grapefruit, then kippers, then toast and marmalade and finally a banana to finish off with. Apart from that, we've got to get citizenship for you two,' he nodded to Rumpus Pumpus and Finta Fanta, 'get Henri's father out of the wall and bags of publicity for bookings into the next century, if possible.'

'What I don't see,' said Sady McCabe, 'is how you're going to be able to eat the grapefruit between the porridge and the kippers.' Everyone giggled and turned to Mr Sedge again. As he spoke, he revealed an audacious plan to them which they listened to with half-unbelieving ears. Henri remembered the man who had been carried down to the elephant warehouse just a few weeks before. It was certainly not the same man who spoke now. This man was certain, definite, humorous indeed, but by no stretch of the imagination a conforming civil servant in the Home Office. Mr Sedge glanced at Henri, too, and no longer saw a youth trying his hand at jazz; but a young man forging a future and nurturing a past.

The others added their comments, absorbed the plans with their breakfasts and, that done, and hearty thanks to

Pete Davis, they cleared their table and made ready for the day.

Already, people were beginning to gather on the field for some kind of opening ceremony to the great Day of the Elephant. Bystanders, privileged members of the public, wandered up to the open side of the Royal Rectangle. Stewards here indicated they should stand back beyond a line of gold cord strung between knee-high cast-iron stakes, each stake bearing the royal crest. Each of the societies that had a tent around the Rectangle now put out a contingent to stand before it. Half a dozen Founders and Grinders, regaled and regimented stood in line before their tent. The Jazz Elephants wandered out to see what was going on and cast their eyes over the field. Opposite them, several hundred members of the public were ranged along the gold cord, the number swelling all the time. A few policemen patrolled the crowd who seemed a strange mixture of awfully refined people and curiously provocative students. As Mr Sedge explained: the park itself was, in fact, sealed off that morning to all but ticket holders – hence the freedom of circulation within its limits. The general public would be allowed entry from about midday. Up to that time they could come no further than the Outer Circle – the wide road running round the perimeter of the park. Here the Monarch would make one triumphal circuit in an open vehicle before the public, after which all could enter the park and the Monarch would proceed to the zoo for a celebratory banquet with the President and the other dignitaries of the elephant world.

But now ushers placed a band of sculpture students in one place of the Royal Rectangle, and another band of students in another; a few exhibitors together in one area, a few zoologists together in another. Across the field, a central swathe was left clear. At one end it abutted the pavilion of the Worshipful Company and at the other it ran through to the crowd beyond the gold cord.

In the Royal Pavilion, to The Jazz Elephants' right, a certain hustling and bustling was apparent. Dignitaries took their places and ladies in large-brimmed hats turned their best profiles to the most important people. They were anxious to be noticed by those who saw rank in large brims and were skilled at recognizing profiles. The equerry popped his head out of a door somewhere on the dais and Finta Fanta gave him a gentle wave with the tip of her trunk. He gave a smiling nod of recognition and both of them then turned their glance elsewhere to avoid the curiosity of others.

Except for the central swathe, the Royal Rectangle was more or less full of people now, who seemed to be waiting expectantly. Suddenly, in the distance, a dull sound was heard. Rumpus Pumpus wondered if it might be a rhinoceros belching behind in the zoo. He thought they should have been kept better locked away on an important occasion. Rhinoceros always let one down. But the sound came again, drifting in on the light breeze. A smile came to Henri's lips; and in front of the pavilion of the Worshipful Company of Founders and Grinders, shoulders moved back and chins started to rise in pride.

It was the free drone of the Laudatory Assemblage of the Worshipful Company, now walking in fine order from the Outer Circle up the Broad Walk, whence they bifurcated diagonally left across the green to reach the tented space of the Royal Rectangle. Their rate was slow. The laudatory organ was a hundred-piped affair borne on the shoulders of some twenty Founders and Grinders. Its air passed in tubes made of sheep's intestines into the organ at a manifold entry point where some twenty pipes joined to one. From this entry the pipes passed to the individual porters, up inside the arms of their dress tunics, where they bifurcated and passed out at the bottom of each

leg of their belles culottes. From here the flexible ends –
kept supple by long application of neatsfoot oil – went to
the heels of the wearer where they slipped tightly over the
nozzles of his foot bellows.

For each organ porter had, on each foot, a bellows worn
rather like a snow shoe. These sent, with each step,
compressed air to the organ and demanded that play take
place when either proceeding or when marking time. It
made for a rolling, lumberous sort of progress, and its
load was valued high by those in dignity.

It seemed an age to wait; but all waited as this
procession grumbled up towards them. The outlying files
tinkled hand-held clarion bells and the inner files moaned
the Royal Chant to the tune of the laudatory instrument.
Henri could scarcely contain his laughter as the whole
contraption of them hove into view, toiling up the gently
grassy slope like an end-of-the-world machine at a
fancy-dress party.

Finally staggering, puffing, labouring their way up to
the place left for them amidst the assembled mass, now
standing ready to hear the initial royal address, they
shambled into position and, stiffening themselves to
attention as they lowered the organ to the ground, they
gave the gasping deflatory salute as they joined the guards
before their tent in positions of worshipful respect.

A quiet fell upon the company assembled there. The
clear sun shone in the cool air; a moo or two floated over
from the zoo and the Royal Pavilion stood expectant of its
principal occupant, waiting for the opening address. The
bevy of a royal entourage genteelly herded itself out of the
door of the pavilion; and the Monarch emerged to mount
the dais and make the opening speech. Mr Sedge held his
breath.

'Elephants, Lords, Ladies and Gentlemen,' began the
Monarch. Mr Sedge sighed with relief. The sparkling eye

of Finta Fanta caught the sparkling eye of Rumpus Pumpus. 'It has long been known that the universe must contain intelligent life other than mankind; and for long we have assumed that one day a spacecraft somewhere out there, a radio station or some other sensor would contact such beings and make them known to us all. Yet, such is the way of human affairs, the first truly intelligent life which we were able to contact had long been known to us and was to be found here on our own earth: indeed, in the zoo in one of my very own parks.

'How appropriate it is, in the context of today's events, that that life-form should be the elephant. Most of us would have guessed the dolphin or the whale and, who knows, perhaps they will have much to say to us too; but in the event, the first non-human life-form to make contact with us, was the elephant – long admired for its well-known qualities, but now capable of even greater admiration for what we now know about its potential.

'The proof of intellect, at least for us who are only human, was of course the act of speech. Let us not forget that great intellect is possible without speech and yet, such are our human limitations, that only a being able to speak to us in human language, no matter how irrelevant that is in any ultimate sense, appears truly an intelligent being; appears – if I dare to be so bold – as one of us.

'To mark this historic event, for all humanity as much as for all the intelligence that undoubtedly must exist in the universe, I am delighted that Finta Fanta and Rumpus Pumpus have agreed to accompany my tour of the exhibits this morning and to act as consultants to the panel of judges in the great Evolution of the Elephant competition, to be judged today.'

Mr Sedge and the elephants exchanged knowing nods. They listened on. The Royal person thanked all who participated, all who had ideas leading to the day, all who contributed to this international day of elephantine euphoria. All good causes were regally espoused, from conservation to evolution, and a final welcome given to all now present.

At a preordained signal, the Laudatory Assemblage slipped into its bellows shoes, raised organ and proceeded forward out of the Rectangle. At the same time, the Monarch descended to the steps from the dais and took up position in a gold, silver and ormolu-covered jeep that crept off at walking pace, behind the Assemblage, towards the first group of statues in the field beyond the cricket ground. Rumpus Pumpus and Finta Fanta slipped in behind the jeep.

They staggered away downhill and to the right, in the general direction of St John's Wood. In the midst of the grassy plain stood the first group of sculptures to be judged – a *moeritherium* group apparently browsing in the middle of nowhere.

Despite being double life size, the *moeritheriae* looked like a troop of Eocene pigs seeking pannage on a cricket pitch. The various judges walked around the little group, making notes and pointing out the strengths and weaknesses to the Royal personage.

'Imagine being descended from that,' remarked Rumpus Pumpus.

'Much more like ascended, I should think,' said Finta Fanta. 'It could only have been half a metre high.'

'Just the same,' joked the President, '*moeritherium* could have made similar remarks about the amoeba. Ultimately, all of us are descended from that.' The Monarch looked sideways at the President; but said nothing.

For a few minutes, everyone talked to the sculptors, then made their polite goodbyes and the cavalcade moved on to the next group. This was none other than an *amebelodon* group by students from Liverpool. The beast had a certain resemblance to a conventional elephant in so much as it had a trunk and short tusks; and it had an elephantine head, except that its ears were hippopotamus-sized. The distinctive feature of *amebelodon* was the projection of the teeth in the lower jaw to form a mighty bone shovel that stuck out nearly as far as the end of the short trunk.

The bevy rounded on the *amebelodon* atop the slope that led down to the lake. The Monarch descended and passed pleasantries with the Liverpudlian sculptors who had created the group. Sir Danvers Panter prowled round the four statues with the look of a surgeon seeking the zip. The President wandered round with an admiring smile:

'Very good, very accurate,' he said in a low voice. Bobbing to pass under the legs; for these, at double life size, were now considerably taller than Rumpus Pumpus or Finta Fanta. The President waxed quite enthusiastic to Sir Danvers Panter and moved towards the short trunk of the adult female of the group. Her jaw shovel touched the ground and the trunk curved up above it.

'So accurate, one can just imagine it routing for roots in the Miocene woodland,' said the President; and took hold of the trunk as if to shake it like a hand. It crumbled to dust at his touch. Losing balance, he toppled against the mighty foreleg: it broke at once. Sir Danvers proffered a helping hand. The President took it and pulled himself upright, but, in doing so, brought Sir Danvers head first into the *amebelodon*. The President, his back momentarily to the group, started to dust himself down. On the other side of the sculpture the Monarch and entourage talked to the sculptors. Rumpus Pumpus and Finta Fanta looked on aghast: for Sir Danvers' involuntary tumble set off a kind of chain reaction in the dried clay of the group. The head, probably weighing half a ton, fell off, fortunately missing Sir Danvers, but immediately disintegrating into a vast cloud of yellow dust that rose like a fog into the air. The head fell on to the legs of the male, which immediately broke into dust in the same way, bringing *amebelodonian* bodies down, one upon another, in a kind of rushing, bumping sound that made everyone look up. The little circle of onlookers stepped back from this foul-looking argillaceous smoke only to see, after a few seconds, a khaki-coloured shape, that must have been Sir Danvers Panter, making his way out of the dust and rubble in a fair imitation of a yeti in a sandstorm.

Polite goodbyes were made to the sculptors and the party moved on.

'Inappropriate use of materials,' murmured Finta Fanta. Judges' heads nodded and notes were made. Sir Danvers coughed along beside them like a desert ghost. The little procession henceforward kept their distance and contrived to quite ignore the sartorial plight of Sir Danvers. The Scottish *palaeomastodons* were an obvious candidate for high honours. The scale made them something like the size of a modern elephant and so instantly credible to observers in a way that the towering six- and eight-metre-high mammoth mountains were not.

The judging party arrived at the *amebelodon* group that bevied near the refreshment booth. A most touching display. The Monarch was obviously relieved to have a grain of humour to allude to in the way in which the mother *amebelodon* seemed to be calling her two children on, with excited stance and majestic sweep of the trunk, towards the nearby stall. The two youngsters seemed to be looking up to their gigantic mother, a full four metres high at the shoulder, and saying with pleading sympathy, 'Ice cream! Ice cream!' Father *amebelodon* was bringing up the rear with a cross expression on his face something like, 'What do you want ice cream for? There's going to be an ice age soon.'

Suchlike considerations amused the sculptors and the royal group as the professionals made their judgements. They moved on and saw the 'Plastic Money for Plastic Arts' T-shirts proudly on display by the next group, that appeared to be quite unusual in its concepts. As the bevy rounded on the towering sculptures, Sir Danvers hung back cautiously, but not a little in awe of the animals, and the elephants whispering serpentine advice to the panel, through trunks placed carefully towards the right people at the right time.

The intercom on the Home Secretary's desk buzzed, and the voice from the secretary told him Sergeant Apta Dapta was on the phone. For a moment he had no idea who the Sergeant was. The secretary explained it was the officer involved with the elephant case, whom he had seen several weeks previously.

'He says you asked him to get in touch if there was anything important and he says it's vitally important,' said the secretary.

The Home Secretary made noises of annoyance, realized he was doing nothing very vital and told the secretary to put him through.

'Yes, Sergeant,' said the Home Secretary.

'Good morning,' said the Sergeant. 'I thought I'd better contact you direct. You asked me to, if anything important arose. I'm afraid this elephant and City Company business is going to turn into the scandal of the century. Not just red faces in the City boardrooms, maybe the demise of the monarchy too.'

The Home Secretary sat up and stopped thinking about his lunch menu. This all sounded a bit uncomfortable. That Sergeant didn't look like the sort of man to make trouble. On the other hand, he did look like the sort of man to pursue justice to the ends of the earth – to the City of London and the ends of The Mall at least. He looked in his diary and saw nothing that couldn't be rearranged.

'Come round straight away. I take it you've decided to leave the Commissioner out of this for the moment for some good reason?'

'Quite so, Home Secretary. I can't really tell whose side anyone is on. You're the only person deeply involved but at the same time far enough away from actual events not to have a personal interest in their outcome – except to do the right thing . . . I'll be round directly.'

They rang off and the Home Secretary was left with a deep feeling of unease. Some chord in the midst of his mind had already resonated a warning note over the affair of Sedge and this Coulisse fellow. The Norman Conquest was good stuff, and its traditions somehow rang true to the kind of society he was trying to uphold. But yet this wasn't the eleventh century. No matter how much he wished it was, no matter how much the mantle of power that claimed the inheritance of millenia sat elegantly on his shoulders, the dress and the man beneath must be a man of today. No matter what the history, history was the record of people in the past doing unheard of things for the first time. Somehow, he felt, the practice of innovation, though being aged itself, had sanctioned perhaps the misdeeds as well as the great deeds of the present. He told the outer office to get his favourite sandwiches and whatever Sergeant Apta Dapta had eaten on his last visit, tidied up a couple of letters and waited for the secretary's buzz. It came. The Sergeant was waiting to come in.

The Home Secretary got up and motioned the Sergeant to the seat in front of him. For a moment they looked at each other and then the Home Secretary said:

'Best if you get straight to the point, I think. By the sound of it, I hope you're mistaken. It is possible to go over the top on cases of a strange nature like this, you know.'

'You can judge that, Home Secretary,' said the Sergeant, leaning forward and looking genuinely worried. 'That Worshipful Company, bulwarks of tradition that they be, are in the business of discipline through ordeal and have managed to get royal support to do it.'

'Now just a moment,' replied the Home Secretary, 'I can't believe that. Before any accusations are made against such venerable institutions we have to be quite sure of the facts.'

'I am sure. A Mrs Coulisse was put in touch with me – the mother of that Founder and Grinder whom the Company came to get during our Soho raid. She wanted to know if she had a right to her husband's gold watch.'

'I don't follow.'

'He was wearing it when the Worshipful Company sentenced him, in the place of his son, at their court a few weeks ago.'

'They're entitled to their disciplinary procedures.'

'But I don't think they're entitled to inflict insanitary solitary confinement with a diet of alcohol and old meat. It all came out in this discussion over the gold watch. She wanted to know if she had a right to it – he got it for twenty-five years' service at General Catastrophe apparently – because he was wearing it at the trial of Henri, the son. The son and father exchanged places for the purposes of the trial, it seems their rules allow that – and the son was convicted, so the father suffered the penalties. Now, none of us seems to have really followed this because it was all wrapped up in obtuse bits of Latin and so on: but it seems that the penalty for not being a good boy in the Worshipful Company – contumacy they call it – is to be bricked up in a wall until you've eaten your way through half a ton of food. Since the son was accused and the son has obviously gone free again now, no-one thought any more about it. But the true result of letting that

Worshipful Company have its petition approved at a Privy
Council meeting . . .' The Home Secretary blushed and
suddenly realized he was not an impartial outsider to the
affair any more '. . . was to allow them to close ranks
against someone they seem to have wanted to cast out of
their City cabal. Not that there was a plot, you
understand. They just can't stand people who rock the
boat and they wanted the young Coulisse out of the way.
Their medieval mumbo jumbo allows them to shut people
up in walls if they fail in their duty to the Company, and
they wanted to do that to him. But it looks as if he
outflanked them – knew their law better than they did and
turned the system against his dad.

'Of course, I questioned him on all this after the trial.
But I was more concerned with the elephants at the time
and, when he said his father had been immured till purged
through ordeal, I thought it referred to some punishment
long since commuted to expulsion from the Company. So
did everyone else: but it looks as if that's not the case.

'Anyway, Mrs Coulisse wanted her gold watch. And
it's pretty sure the gold watch is in her husband's pocket in
the fourth niche of the Western Bastion, on the sixth floor
of Grinders' Hall in the City of London. I didn't let on
what the law thought of these revelations but, I think,
Home Secretary, we have a kidnap victim, a crime and a
culprit; and it might just be the moment for a police raid
on the Hall of The Worshipful Company of Founders and
Grinders.'

'Just a moment,' cut in the Home Secretary rapidly.
Visions of embarrassing parliamentary questions, accusations of laxity, suspicions of self interest flashed before
him. The Privy Council, with him within it, had
sanctioned the Founders and Grinders' action. He was just
about inculpated with the rest of them. 'Let's think a
moment. Let's take it that all your assumptions and

deductions are right. You send a bunch of blokes up to the City and find someone lurking in the wall. Awful, absolutely awful. I'll tell you straight, I'm a Privy Counsellor and I was there when the Soho raid was authorized.' The Sergeant's eyes went up to the ceiling, he felt he'd let himself into the thieves' den. 'But,' and the Home Secretary tapped the table and smiled at the Sergeant, 'my money doesn't come from politics, you know. The worst I can do is lose my job. I don't want that to happen but you're in luck; I'd rather lose my job than my honour. So if the worst comes to the worst, I can take up a few directorships and go and farm the family patch in Suffolk.

'No, don't worry about me. I'm worried about the royal involvement. If you're right, this lot brings the establishment crashing down. Dishonouring the Home Secretary is one thing; but the Home Secretary setting up the Monarch for the sake of some imagined old-boy network is quite unacceptable. This has got to be resolved, Sergeant Apta Dapta – clearly and above board, too – but not publicly. At least, not in the glare of the subversionary media: they'll turn an ordeal into a revolution.'

'I cannot prevent the law from taking its course, Home Secretary,' ventured the Sergeant.

'No, nor should you. Nor should I. But I think we should be able to prevent it going beyond our misdeeds, if any, and those of the Worshipful Company . . . if any.'

They sat in silence for a moment. A secretary came in with a trolley of sandwiches. Being a perceptive person she felt the atmosphere, still, like the eye of a hurricane; left the trolley and went out. The men served themselves silently. Then the Home Secretary said:

'Has anyone seen the condemned?'

'No. But I've been able to ascertain that the man was walled up all right. He's certainly not come out: and that was a month ago he went in.'

'Good grief. Is there even a chance he's alive?'

'Just about none. I suppose you never know, though. One of my men got stuck in a drain for three weeks, once, observing a nightclub. He survived.'

'Well, we've got to know for sure, and we've got to keep the Monarch out of this. What do you say to this?' And the Home Secretary put forth a plan.

The Clerk sat in his room at Grinders' Hall, crossing some t's in black ink on yellow vellum. The phone rang in his drawer. He drew it open and put the receiver to his ear.

'Clerk,' he said drily. Vocal dust avalanched down the mouthpiece.

'Home Secretary,' came the reply. The Clerk stayed silent for a few moments.

'Home Secretary,' repeated the Clerk. Not as a question, not in disbelief but as a kind of nonplussed non sequitur. He had no idea what to say.

'No, I'm the Home Secretary,' said the Home Secretary, starting to enjoy life again. 'You're supposed to be the Clerk.'

'Clerk,' said the Clerk. Not as a reply; but as a confession.

'I've asked the police to come round and check that your recent condemnation to ordeal was properly conducted,' said the Home Secretary, matter-of-factly. 'A Sergeant Apta Dapta from the Metropolitan force will be with you shortly.'

'Oh no, no, no,' trembled the Clerk in fear. 'The Grand Master would never allow it. He's attending to royal duties today. Perhaps you could ring again tomorrow. Goodbye.'

But he didn't put the receiver down fast enough and the Home Secretary was back at him before he could move the earpiece out of hearing.

'He's at the Day of Elephant,' debunked the Home Secretary. 'And I'm a Privy Counsellor and affirmed your permission in the Council to restore your contumacious Grinder. I'm sending this man as a personal envoy. The City of London Police will know nothing about it . . . unless of course he finds an offence has been committed, then he'll be obliged to act. He'll be round in a couple of hours. Now, do you know of any offences you might like to co-operate about?' There was a choking silence. Then the Home Secretary added, 'Of course, concealing evidence is a very grave matter, you know. If my envoy here finds any evidence of that, that will be quite a scandal in its own right.' The Clerk choked back his mounting discomfort.

'Oh, of course, no, no there's no evidence of anything to conceal,' he said. 'Er, goodbye.'

'Fine, goodbye,' sang out the Home Secretary, putting down the phone, and looking back to the Sergeant. 'I'd say he's entered into a state of blind panic. Time to go and see what it's all about.'

The Sergeant nodded and rose. Both looked knowingly at each other and said a rather formal farewell. It was apparent to both that a crisis was at hand.

The Sergeant went back to the police station and called up his man at the Day of the Elephant. He needed Coulisse to be taken in and to lead them to the point of immurement. He was not going to risk the Clerk unwalling niches that he knew to be empty; or full only of the bones of medieval martyrs.

Henri was watching the return of the judging party. The royal jeep was making its way sedately up the grass slope towards the Royal Rectangle before the pavilions. Polite conversation was passing between its members and Henri realized with some amusement that an elephant, by virtue of its long, dirigible trunk and very sensitive ears, had no need to be beside the person it was talking to. The elephants were conversing quite happily with the Monarch, who was seated in the back of the open-topped vehicle, while beneath their trunks walked the other members of the party passing pleasantries amongst themselves. There was a kind of studious conscientiousness about the way in which Sir Danvers' much-dusted state was nobly ignored. The party drove in behind the Royal Pavilion, Finta Fanta and Rumpus Pumpus peeling off to take up position beneath the dais in the Royal Rectangle. The Rectangle itself was filling with people again to hear the speeches and the judges' verdicts.

But Henri, watching from in front of The Jazz Elephants' tent, suddenly felt a presence at his side.

'Ah, Mr Coulisse,' said a policeman who had apparently come through the tent from the path behind, 'I must ask you to accompany me on a little journey: a small matter concerning your father. You're needed to help the police with their enquiries, you know.' A distinctly unco-operative look passed across Henri's face, so the policeman turned the pressure up a little.

'Now, of course, should we find some misdeed had been done and you refused to help us investigate, you might be thought of as an accomplice, mightn't you? And that wouldn't be very healthy, would it?'

Henri needed a moment to think. Well-laid plans were being threatened here and so he feigned a measure of co-operation to clarify what was going on.

'You're an Albany Street man, aren't you officer?' he asked, as if confirming something to himself.

'That's right, sir,' he said, 'the very same who first investigated the loss of those elephants there. I suppose you wouldn't have anything to volunteer on that subject, would you?'

'Oh no, not at all,' said Henri. 'I've no idea how they got out in the first place. You'll have to ask them.' The policeman coughed and politely refrained from this line of questioning.

'If you'll just come with me, please. I've been asked by the highest of authorities to ask you to accompany me to the City; and so we'd better be on our way, hadn't we?'

Unknown to the two of them, Mr Sedge had also come through the tent and, having overheard the conversation, now intervened.

'Excuse me, I'm afraid I couldn't help overhearing you, officer. Er, but I'm afraid you'll have to wait a while. I don't doubt that high authorities are behind your request but you must take my word for it that yet higher authorities will be exercised to overrule yours. In fact, step into the tent a moment and we may come to some accommodation.'

They entered, and the constable saw at once that something was afoot. The other members of the band had evidently followed Mr Sedge into the tent and were poring over a document laid out on the table. It wasn't really certain whether they were serious or mirthful. It was the unbelieving atmosphere of a gigantic try-on.

'We are about to petition the Monarch,' explained Henri, 'on precisely the matter that you are concerned with. If I go with you now we cannot arrive more than half an hour earlier that we would anyway. If we present our petition, it may be granted and we shall all go under royal warrant.'

The constable was a bit mystified by all this; but the royal park was in his area and he knew to treat royal prerogatives with a healthy respect.

'Why don't you stand guard at the door of the tent,' suggested Mr Sedge. 'Everyone will believe you are on official duty and you can watch all our capers to your heart's content. If we lose our attempt you can always take Henri to the Hall as you'd planned, anyway. I think it would be best.'

The policeman had decided already that half an hour could do little in the life of a dead man, as he put it; and resigned himself to the spectacle of some dubious undertaking.

He saw the dignitaries of the day gathering in the Royal Pavilion to his right. Before him, the crowd was filling the Royal Rectangle; but not thickly enough to create a crush. Numbers had been well controlled.

Right in front of him, the Laudatory Assemblage of The Worshipful Company of Founders and Grinders shambled itself into a semblance of order and the organ bearers slipped on their bellows shoes ready to hoist organ and praise. At a sign from the Organ Master, the Assemblage began to mark time, bringing a certain rhythm to the proceedings and providing air for the organ. A long, peaceful moan came from the musicians, preparing the crowd for the formalities of speeches. Below the dais they could see the elephants standing one on either side of the central platform and, in the pavilion, all the judges ranged in their seats; Sir Danvers now looking well brushed but definitely a little dust-worn. The Monarch came regally to the dais and acknowledged the musical homage. The notes died wistfully away, the organ was replaced on the ground and the Monarch stepped back to allow Sir Danvers, as chairman of the judges, to take the dais and deliver the judgement.

Sir Danvers was the soul of boredom. He droned on about anatomical exactitude and the high standards of many of the exhibits. He took modern sculpture to task for not fitting to the rigours of the environment. Finally, after a drawn-out praise of modern youth that set most of the sculptors in the crowd yawning with indifference, he got round to the presentation itself.

Third prize went to the *amebelodons* by the ice cream stall. 'A touching representation of prehistoric family life,' is how Sir Danvers put it, adding a note that this was just the sort of thing lacking in most art today. No-one quite knew what that meant but it seemed a good enough phrase; the journalists certainly scribbled it down, anyway. Six callow-looking youths in ill-fitting suits went up and received their cheque and certificates from the Monarch, who shook hands, beamed and sat down again.

Second prize went to *moeritherium*, the pig-sized group on the open field. Sir Danvers went on and on about physiological conformity and the virtues of exactness. After all this, five young sculptors from East Anglia came and took their prizes and all waited for the winners with baited breath.

The second *amebelodon* group began to get excited. Shuffling their feet about amongst the other contenders near the front of the crowd, it was obvious from their behaviour that they thought they had won. They wore combinations of bow-ties, jeans and dinner jackets, their one common denominator being the 'Plastic Money for Plastic Arts' T-shirts. Sir Danvers circumlocuted, the President prodded him from behind. It went against the grain to give a prize to someone who showed every sign of being original in thought and innovative in presentation. The President slapped Sir Danvers gently on the back; a cloud of dust went up. Rumpus Pumpus and Finta Fanta raised their trunks to his ears and whispered to him to go ahead and announce the agreed winners. With almost a scowl on his face, Sir Danvers breathed the name of the plastic artists and they rushed up on to the dais and took their booty and glory with as little decorum as they could possibly get away with.

Once they had been encouraged out of the royal

presence, the Monarch stepped forward to make a polite speech to close the royal proceedings for the day and declare the general jamboree open. But hardly had the Monarch taken the dais than a roistering fanfare rang out from a most unexpected quarter. Rumpus Pumpus and Finta Fanta, at the foot of the dais, raised their trunks and, with the full volume of the music turned mercifully towards the crowd, trumpeted a fanfare that the Monarch, with great aplomb, made look as if it were entirely expected and the very thing that should happen at that very moment.

From The Jazz Elephants' tent, Henri answered the elephants with a trill on the trombone. The Founders and Grinders standing near him looked aghast. Many of them didn't know what a trombone was and one or two of them almost broke ranks to take him in chains, as they usually tried to do when they met him. But they didn't have their chains with them.

The elephants replied with a final crescendo; and forth from the tent stepped Mr Sedge with a dark blue velvet cushion on his hands; upon it a scroll and behind him came the other Jazz Elephants; Henri, now without trombone, to the fore. At the same time, Rumpus Pumpus and Finta Fanta raised their trunks to the side of the Monarch's head and whispered something that brought a royal smile to the regal lips. So that, when a bevy of security men rushed forth to shuffle The Jazz Elephants away, the Monarch in person signalled them to desist and let the group come forward; the security men hustling themselves away between the tents to stand in readiness upon events.

'Not though there be no other failing to declaim petition upon no monarch but to yourselves as majesty before us,' began Mr Sedge with the usual battery of self-cancelling negatives that began petitions of this kind, 'we however so declaim petition and claim boon by right of service, and by misdemeanour of another now held arraign before you, namely of two titles and a liberty.'

Only the Monarch seemed the least bit happy about all of this, apart from The Jazz Elephants, that is. The police and security men wriggled most uncomfortably in their shoes and the Grand Master of The Worshipful Company, standing in pumped-up pomp before his Assemblage, seemed bursting with rage at the temerity of other musicians to impinge upon his ears. Furthermore, he had heard language of this kind before. It had an uneasy reminiscence of a certain hearing of the Grinders' Court; a case of Coulisse, he thought again.

James Daley, not really being a prime mover in the process of petitioning, hung back by the policeman who apparently stood guard over The Jazz Elephants' tent.

'I hadn't quite bargained for this sort of thing,' said the policeman, 'and, in any case, what's it all about? Might as well be shouting Latin at each other as far as I'm concerned.'

'It's a petition,' said James, 'a risky business, dug out of some archive or other by Henri and Mr Sedge. From the look of the royal face there, they got the elephants to persuade the Monarch to hear it – during the judging drive, I expect – and it looks as if the Monarch is going along with it all.'

Indeed it did. Mr Sedge and Henri were alternately reading from the parchment and kneeling in a variety of abject stances preordained by law or, more important, tradition. James, who had been briefed on what was going on, translated the tradition into meaningful language for the policeman.

'You see, Henri Coulisse as the envoy of his father, can petition as a member of a Worshipful Company even though he has been expelled in his own original person. That's what all that bobbing and scraping they're doing now is about – it's the ceremonial expression of being another person other than who one is.

'They're trying to sort out the very problem you want Henri to accompany you to the Grinders' Hall about: the ordeal of his father.'

Mr Sedge at full height, which was somewhat less than that of Henri who stood at his side, made a formal, stentorian request in some convoluted interrogative that rather seemed to please the listening Monarch. The royal head nodded and a formal gesture of assent was made with the hand.

'Is it all over then?' whispered the policeman.

'No,' replied James. 'They've got through the preamble and the Monarch has given permission to present the petition proper.'

'Why don't they get on with it?'

'I thought you people at Albany Street were used to royalty. This is the real thing, you know, not one of those quickie political decisions that's made today in a secluded room and delivered unchallengably to parliament before an unshakeable majority in the House. This is persuasion of the first order. Displease the Monarch and you're dead . . . so to speak.'

'Anyway, what's Coulisse asking now?' As the policeman spoke, Henri was going through a bit of elaborate mime that accompanied Mr Sedge's reciting.

'It's the crux of the whole thing,' said James Daley. 'He throws himself supine on the ground and asks to be struck by fire from above rather than be denied the permission of his Monarch to redress the grievance of an entombed man. I mean, he's asking if he can go and get his dad out of the wall, dead or alive.'

'Oh . . . I see. And what's he doing now?'

'He has right of accompaniment by three free persons – and . . . this, too, has been granted.'

The policeman frowned. 'Sounds like mumbo jumbo, this bit.'

'Er, jumbo jumbo, anyway,' quipped James. 'He's naming the two elephants as free persons to accompany him – what you heard was their names, heavily Latinized, and inserted in the petition as the free persons to accompany the aggrieved party – Henri of course – in the getting back of his father. It sounds as if the unstoppable Mr Sedge, our ever-competent manager, is to be the third member of the party.'

The Monarch's head turned to the President of the Zoological Society, as Mr Sedge and Henri now went down on their knees in a posture of abject importunity. The President smiled and made, as near as he was able, a dignified gesture and word of final assent. The Monarch's assent followed.

As these last words were being uttered, the Grand Master of The Worshipful Company of Founders and Grinders, rampant before his Assemblage, became scarlet of face as if boiling to the point of explosion. He understood perfectly well that he and his Company were being held in arraign before the Monarch for the immuring of Claud Coulisse. But he also knew that the plaintiff had only to bring the defendant before the Monarch, and state his case in proper plaint, for the petition to be good. But yet farther, no defence was possible without counter-petition and in proper order at the time of complaint. If the form was wrong, the counter-petition failed . . . and he didn't know the words. Even the Clerk was back at the Hall dusting his tomes. There was no reply.

Just before the Monarch signalled assent to the petition, there was a pause like the toppling-over time before the gunshot that starts a sprint race. Assent was given. It was as if the starting gun had sounded.

The Grand Master exploded.

'Ground instruments!' he roared like a bull bellowing before the charge. 'Return and defend premises!' There was a jangling, clattering, cacophonous disharmony of bells and bellows as the instruments were dropped from hand and foot. The organ let out a dying gasp as its bearers kicked off their bellows shoes and altogether abandoned steadying it as it stood. Had it been at shoulder height, doubtless the organist would, in due course, have been buried with full honours of the Company.

Bell and Organ Masters braced themselves up like a pair of ageing PT instructors. With the Assemblage more or less in order behind them, they raced out of the Royal Rectangle in the direction of the Marylebone Road, with all the energy of a hundred metres dash. It quickly degenerated into a long distance event, where a couple of virtuosi who had shed pagodas and tunic tops were followed by a straggling rabble of the unfit sons of gentlefolk, straining to save honour in the face of muscular strain. Last of the horde, beefing and bumbling along like an advertisement for high blood pressure, was a very red-in-the-face Grand Master, trying to give incomprehensible orders to stragglers, as he straggled and gasped himself.

But if, for most people present, the break for freedom was an almighty surprise, for The Jazz Elephants it certainly was not. The reaction was wholly expected. At once, Finta Fanta grabbed Henri round the waist and plonked him on her neck, while Rumpus Pumpus did the same with Mr Sedge. Amid shrieks and, by now, not a few cheers, the elephants broke into a genteel stampede and thundered after the fleeing medievalists like Hannibal routing the Romans.

'Eh! What's this?' said the Albany Street policeman to James Daley, with great indignity rather than surprise. 'You said we'd be able to bring them along afterwards. Now Coulisse has got away.'

'Hardly,' said James. 'They're all heading for the very

place you wanted to take them to anyway.'

'What, Grinders' Hall?' said the policeman.

'The very same,' confirmed James Daley. And the policeman turned his back to mutter rapidly into his personal radio which, in turn, sent Sergeant Apta Dapta, back at his police station, dashing for his car and heading for Grinders' Hall as well.

The traffic in the Marylebone Road is always bad, usually it's awful, and that day it was, in any case, worse than usual. At least on that day, the crawling motorists had some entertainment to lighten the boredom of inactivity. Those waiting at the traffic lights at Park Square, just a little further along from where the elephants had first made their acquaintance with Sergeant Apta Dapta, were suddenly treated to the invasion of the Red Army, or at least the scarlet army. Suddenly, the road was alive with liveried bodies diving in and out among the cars, trying to nobble every taxi in sight. Desperate men in search of a taxi will go to quite extraordinary lengths. The three or four vehicles without passenger, that happened to be at the cross roads, were instantly filled with panting liverymen, six or seven to a cab, promising exorbitant sums for rapid delivery to the Hall of The Worshipful Company of Bell Founders and Organ Grinders. Naturally, not all these cabs were facing in the right direction; so that one or two of them, drivers motivated beyond legality by the hope of personal gain, attempted U-turns at the junction. They swapped carriageways and turned broadside on to the traffic with much tooting and use of hazard warning lights; with the result that the standing traffic jam in the Marylebone Road stood even stiller than normal, with congestion turned into positive indigestion.

However, as the vehicles tried to work out how to unstick themselves, a hooting of another note was heard coming from the direction of the park. Two mighty elephants, mounted by two mighty jockeys, were striking terror into the hearts of passers-by. Through Park Square they came, on the pavement, pedestrians scattering like pigeons before cats; out into the traffic, considerably slower now, weaving their way around cars and buses, lorries and motorbikes, with great dexterity. With equally great dexterity, they broke free of the jam and headed east towards the Pentonville Road, legging it in great heaving strides; that kind of elephantine soft-shoe shuffle that eats the kilometres without the indignity of downright running.

One man, however, was reduced to the indignity of running. The Grand Master, pagoda askew, dress balls a-jangle, belles culottes streaked with the dark traces of sweat emanating from the intimate places, stumbled near exhaustion after his Assemblage, to find them in various states of sardine, squashed into taxis, which, in their turn, were jammed at the cross roads.

Even the Grand Master, now his very status was at stake, could rise to the occasion in his own way. He staggered into the middle of the cross roads and, righting somewhat his head-gear, and unfolding himself from the stoop of crippling breathlessness, took on the role of traffic policeman. In that rig, he might have been anything. But somehow he got the vehicles to follow his lead; shot a taxi off in this direction, turned a lorry into Park Crescent, budged a bus and a few cars and got the east-flowing lanes clear. Nothing more was his objective. He snatched at the door of the last taxi full of liverymen and managed to bundle himself in on top of all the others inside.

The ragged convoy of taxis set off after the elephants in disorganized pursuit. Not being vehicles in a strict manner of speaking, the elephants quickly increased their lead over the pursuing liverymen. The taxis, at least to a minimum extent, felt obliged to stop at traffic lights, while the elephants, using their special status and the full advantage of surprise, stormed on, crossing junctions and lights regardless of their condition and generally getting a jovial wave or two as they did so.

By King's Cross station the elephants were five or six minutes up on the liverymen; but after the hill up the Pentonville Road, and the lengthening distance between lights, the gap was down to two or three minutes by the time they passed the Angel.

Down the City Road slope, and Henri and Mr Sedge urged on their mounts to faster and faster efforts. A pair of taxis with jeering Founders and Grinders passed, tooting their scorn on sewn-in organ pipes. They scented victory: the exclusion of the petitioners from the Hall in the City. No monarch may tread there without permission. The writ of no monarch runs there without consent. A consent not ultimately to be denied but, perhaps, a consent to be delayed, delayed long enough to save a face.

But joy! Old Street roundabout was as clogged up as ever: the taxis stuck like liquorice in an allsort. The elephants shuffled past, overtaking the taxis outside the Salesian Mission and negotiating the roundabout at the approach to Moorgate. From there, Henri and Finta Fanta took the lead and soon dived through Finsbury Square, now certain to arrive before the traffic-bound liverymen.

Through the lanes of the ancient City they went and round the corner to the final approach. And there, the Hall of the Worshipful Company! And there on its steps, Sergeant Apta Dapta and Police Constable Monica Sullivan! Scooting along the Embankment from Westminster, they had beaten everyone to the door.

The Sergeant began to raise an authoritative hand towards the oncoming elephants. But royal right gives mighty courage:

'Follow us, follow us!' shouted Henri and Mr Sedge. The two law officers jumped to one side as Rumpus Pumpus charged the main door of the Hall at full tilt. There was an almighty splintering of wood and a couple of bumps as bits of surplus masonry fell to the ground. The elephant stopped, then continued through the archway that had held the great double doors. Mr Sedge slid nimbly off as Rumpus Pumpus entered the premises. Henri also dismounted as Finta Fanta climbed the steps. But she then turned to face the street, not following Rumpus Pumpus over the splintered wood and fallen doorposts. Mr Sedge took the two members of the Metropolitan Police by the arm and brought them towards the doorway as they regained their composure.

'Follow me up to the immurement. Come on, follow me! Half the wretched Company is in pursuit, driven here by maniac cabbies spurred on by unbelievable bribes.'

'I'll watch the entrance and discourage pursuit,' said Finta Fanta, flicking a very heavy spar across the steps with her trunk, just to make the point. With that she turned her back to the doorway and faced the narrow road – a formidable deterrent to pursuit.

The Rumpus Pumpus group had not been gone five minutes before the first taxi screeched round the corner and came to a halt before the doors. They arrived in strict order – the biggest bribe first and the smallest last. So, naturally, the Grand Master himself was the first to tumble out of his cab and run up the steps to the Hall. But with a gentle flick of her tusks, Finta Fanta sent the mighty spar that was lying at her feet down the half a dozen or so steps in front of her, in a deep resounding banging and crashing towards the oncoming Grand Master. Of course he saw the spar, half a ton of uncontrolled wood, coming bounding down the steps towards him; and leapt effectively, though far from nimbly, out of the way. He turned a kind of pasty-white colour at the narrow escape; and retreated aghast when Finta Fanta added a triumphant trumpet blast to the banging wood. Other taxis now screeched in. Liverymen piled out and hesitated in milling mobs behind the Grand Master, while several cabbies honked and shouted for their fares.

'I don't like the look of that elephant,' quailed the Bell Master trying to avoid Finta Fanta's eye. The Organ Master, a little more enterprisingly, tried to sneak a passage past Finta Fanta's left flank with half a dozen or so of his acolytes in tow. Finta Fanta, however, would have none of it. Her trunk took the poor man by the shoulder and fairly spun him round, so that he staggered down the steps like a spinning top jumping down from level to level in unsteady rotation. The followers dared not to follow further and retreated, turning their attention instead to the solace of their leader.

A small group of seven others tried to storm in on the elephant's right flank while she was turned away from them. They forgot those all-hearing ears: and with an agility scarcely to be credited to such a large animal, Finta Fanta thrust her right foot backwards and made the leading Founder quake in fear as her sole nearly pinned him to the wall.

'You shall not frustrate a just petition, nor shall the law be circumvented by your antics!' shouted Finta Fanta, taking up a menacing stance before the portals once again. All shrank back, none dared to try again.

In this heavy-breathing pause, it was the Grand Master himself who suddenly realized the solution. 'To the postern!' he called. 'I have the key. To the postern!'

The liverymen raced up the side alley as fast as their legs could take them, looking over their shoulders to see if pursuit was underway. It was. But not from Finta Fanta who rightly judged she would have little chance of reaching the postern before them. The pursuit was by a couple of unpaid cabbies shouting for their fares.

'Come back, you taxi drivers, come back!' called Finta Fanta with amused, though inescapable, authority. 'Payment is at hand.'

And with that she wheeled round and snaked her trunk in through the window of the porter's lodge which was just inside the arch of the fallen doorway. The taciturn and irascible porter was just picking himself up from hiding below the level of his window; a position he had adopted when the door had fallen in. He suddenly felt the tight grip of a trunk around his waist. Bodily, he was lifted through the window and presented with sacrificial dignity to the pack of baying cabbies.

'This is the gentleman who settles fares,' explained Finta Fanta nonchalantly and, leaving the trembling man to face his fate, turned and went through the doors herself to follow the others to the immurement.

By now, Henri, Mr Sedge, Rumpus Pumpus and the police officers had reached the sixth floor and were fast approaching the fourth architrave in the Western Bastion. There had been some quick discussion as they raced up the steps, as to whether Rumpus Pumpus could be too heavy for the structure of the building. They had, however, taken heart in the stone pillars and the wide, high, stone staircase and concluded, albeit hastily, that one elephant would not undo that which had stood for a thousand years.

The same thoughts crossed Finta Fanta's mind as she pursued them upwards. Occasionally, she caught small grating sounds and heard little clatters of rubble falling, as she hastened through as gently as was elephantinely possible. Soon she heard the noise of the others above her. She would quickly rejoin them.

Henri rushed up to the niche when he arrived and began searching furiously at one end of it. He seemed to find something that encouraged him. He ran his fingers up and down the mortar that joined the new masonry to the old. Suddenly, the digits lighted on something and bent, as if pulling a splinter from the flesh of the wall. The splinter came out, and out, and out, then stopped. It looked remarkably like a ten-centimetre nail sticking straight out of a wall. Henri grabbed it with his full hand and gave it a sharp tug. Something gave way and a long, pointed piece of wire came out, about forty centimetres long. It was, unmistakably, a knitting needle.

'Great, great,' said Henri to himself, 'airholes!' Then, turning to the two police officers and Rumpus Pumpus, said: 'Quiet. Listen very carefully. Tell me if you hear anything.' Henri scratched the wall and they all listened. There was no sound. Rumpus Pumpus snaked his trunk up to the place where the knitting needle had come out.

'I smell wine,' he said quizzically, 'or something very like it.'

'Shhh!' said Henri. They all listened again. Henri knocked on the wall. They listened. And then they all heard a faint tapping from inside. Henri tapped; the tap came again.

'Where is it from exactly?' Henri asked Rumpus Pumpus, whose ears were spread out like radar dishes, and could have heard a mouse a kilometre off.

'Just there,' said Rumpus Pumpus, pointing with his tusk to the very corner of the wall, by the joint where the knitting needle had come out.

'Bust the wall in there,' said Henri, pointing to the other side of the niche and standing back.

'All right,' said Rumpus Pumpus. 'Free persons to the rescue.'

At this moment Finta Fanta reached the top of the stair

and turned towards the voices. Rounding the curve of the passageway, the group came into sight and she looked on enthralled. Rumpus Pumpus took a step back and eyed up the wall seriously. He remembered briefly that concrete slab in the zoo and judged the angle of his tusks carefully. With a lunging movement, he stepped forward and jabbed his tusks against the masonry. There was a deep, hollow banging sound; and the building shook. The wall visibly trembled and puffs of mortar left the joints; but the masonry stood.

Rumpus Pumpus pulled back again. Placing both tusks at a slightly lower angle he thrust again. This time the wall gave way.

'Thank goodness,' breathed Henri. 'Fifteen of sand to one of mortar. A bribe worth every penny.'

There was a rumbling crash as stone and mortar fell in. The police gasped. Henri crowded in through the dust past Rumpus Pumpus' head. A hole the size of a door had appeared; and in a moment, everyone was reeling back in disgust.

'Oh! Ah! The smell! Aah! Blimey!' escaped the lips of the onlookers. They recoiled before a blast of port-sodden putrefaction. A kind of dreadful mixture of port, rotten meat, sewage and sweat. The blast hit Finta Fanta and she trilled with dismay.

'Eeeh! The charnel house!' she called; and backed a few steps, before curiosity, as it did with all of them, gained the upper hand and pressed them closer to the hole. Henri, the most highly motivated, was the least deterred and leapt into the niche through the gap, disappearing at once from the sight of the others.

Almost at once they heard the sound of Henri vomiting amidst the stench that flowed from the niche. For his part, Henri was at first overcome with nausea and saw nothing but blackness. Then his eyes adjusted and he saw in the corner, with his mouth near the holes that had been painfully bored with the knitting needle through the weak fifteen-to-one mortar, just as Henri had intended, the half-prostrate figure of a man. He was covered in muck, port stains and the remains of month-old mutton sandwiches. There was no movement; and even in the half-light the man's face seemed pale. Was Henri looking at a corpse? Yet there had been tappings. He stretched out a hand and touched the cold, white cheek. There was a dank feel to it, yet it seemed not quite completely dead. The eyelids flickered. The eyes screwed up as if confronted with the full glare of the midsummer sun. Two pale, port-stained, grubby hands went up before Claud's eyes.

'Alive!' called Henri to the others. 'Alive! Weak; but alive.' Claud murmured something Henri could hardly hear. Gently he approached the frail shape.

'Yes, Father,' he said, and listened again as Claud whispered something in his ear.

'There's . . . there's,' murmured Claud. 'There's . . . an old . . . mill by the . . . stream . . .'

'Alive!' called Henri. 'Alive and blind drunk! Come on, Pater!' And he heaved the paternal mass more or less to its feet and with dragging, pulling movements humped his father to the hole.

'. . . Nellie Dean . . .' mumbled Claud, audibly now. Hands reached through the hole to prise him out and Claud looked up at the faces staring at him. 'Aaaah!' he shrieked, almost deliriously, as he saw the two elephants, 'Delirium tremens, oh no! Delirium tremens!' and he slumped into the powerful arms of Police Constable Monica Sullivan. She slung him over her shoulder in a fireman's lift, and the party turned at once and made for the staircase again.

'Stop!' rang out a shout from behind them. 'In doom of fealty, I command you to stop!' The Grand Master, dragged along, borne up and pushed forward by his acolytes, ran breathless, exhausted, on to the scene and into the pursuit. It was Claud whom they wanted, believing him to be dead, the evidence they must take and hide, the face they must save.

'Run for it!' yelled Henri.

'Go ahead!' shouted Finta Fanta, 'we'll delay these characters a bit.' And the two elephants turned on the pursuers. The corridor in the bastion was only just large enough to allow the elephants to turn. As Rumpus Pumpus swung round, a couple of the more agile liverymen dodged between his legs and tried to circumnavigate Finta Fanta. But she would have none of it, whacked them soundly across the shoulders with her trunk and sent them scuttling back the way they had come to rejoin the now tattered but still colourful band of regrouping liverymen under the direction of the Grand Master.

'Time to put a meaningful barrier between that bunch of jackanapes and us in the real world,' said Rumpus Pumpus. With a well-aimed kick, he snapped through the pillar and part of the buttress that formed one of the niches at his side. The corridor shook as a few blocks of stone fell and a scatter of gravelly bits shot out in the direction of the liverymen. With the other foot he did the same thing on the other side. Finta Fanta thought she saw the ceiling sag. She did.

The elephants stepped back and Rumpus Pumpus took the rose-carved boss in the middle of the old vaulted roof with the tip of his trunk. With a deft, strong movement he ripped it down and backed away from the scattering of rubble that littered the floor. The ceiling trembled, seemed to jam solid for a moment and then, with a horrible crash, came tumbling, stone and mortar, to the floor.

The gap let an odd, spritely beam of spring sunshine

into the old medieval corridor, thick with the fog of dust. It was like a collision of worlds, one old and listless and decrepitly cruel, the other young and joyful and invigoratingly real.

The pile of rubble was certainly an obstacle, although not an insuperable one. Rumpus Pumpus turned tail and followed the others who were now well down the stairs and getting more distant at every second. The liverymen held back, unable to see properly in the flying dust and debris; but prevented more by the clear light that illuminated the powdery air like a white curtain, than by any physical barrier. They stopped and gasped at the meaning of events and, when their presence of mind returned, started to creep feebly forward over the ruins of their ancient hall which they felt now to be lame, imperfect, somehow shown up as a contrived shell without a real body inside.

Rumpus Pumpus, too, was on the stairs now and followed the others down as swiftly as he could go. Finta Fanta, a floor or two below, still proceeded with a certain caution. Rumpus Pumpus, in his haste to catch up, shunned care and thundered down at all speed. The very building felt the passage. The Clerk in his study felt the trembling and heard dully the noise. Something big was going on, he thought, very big. He was frightened and stayed in his study.

At the foot of the stairs, Rumpus Pumpus caught up with the others. As they all surged out through the splintered doors, the third flight of stairs from the bottom also crashed in ruins, cutting off any liverymen who had braved the crossing of the rubble heap, from any immediate pursuit. They passed the gatekeeper, who cowered back in his gatehouse, ruffled and timid, like someone who has recently been in a fight over money, and lost. Down the steps they progressed and there in the warmth and the sunlight, they halted a moment and brought themselves into order for the coming procession.

The Sergeant went over to the car and opened the rear door. With a kind of liquid expertise that comes only with great practice and enormous natural talent, Police Constable Monica Sullivan poured Claud into the seat, where he flowed into a semi-reclining position with a look of great contentment on his face. The police car led them out of the narrow lane into the thoroughfares and ways of the City; then to the City Road, Marylebone and Regent's Park.

From some of the windows of the Hall of The Worshipful Company of Bell Founders and Organ Grinders, a pallid face here, a fearful eye there, saw them go. A kind of silent hopelessness settled over the Worshipful Company's premises. One by one, from its doors and exits, members left, changed back into the normal clothes of City men, mingling quickly with the passers-by and losing themselves in the outer world like fingers fitting back into a glove. In his office, the Clerk heard a deadly silence invade the air. Sometimes it was punctuated by the distant slamming of a door, sometimes by the thump of some falling masonry and the sound of a rubble slick following. He sat in uncertain fear.

Suddenly his door opened. In came the Grand Master carrying a gigantic silver dish laden with mutton sandwiches. Behind him came the Bell and Organ Masters carrying between them a case of old port. They passed through the Clerk's office to the Grand Master's. This man held open the door and let the port and its bearers through, then turned in after them. He looked at the Clerk.

'We are not to be disturbed,' he said to the Clerk. 'We are never to be disturbed . . . not ever . . . not ever.' And he closed the door; and the Clerk heard a cork pop. Glasses tinkled. The Clerk got up and went out. The glasses were already tinkling again. He wound his way to the robing room and changed into civilian clothes. With a slow, sad step he left by the postern, switching out all the lights upon his way as he went.

Half-way up the hill to Angel, along the City Road, the Metropolitan Cattle and Drinking Troughs Association had thoughtfully placed a granite bath for the thirsty equines of London. Though the horses have largely disappeared, the trough is still there and recent rains had filled it. The elephants, with Henri and Mr Sedge mounted, passed by, led by the police car at a brisk but even pace.

'Whoah!' called out Henri. 'Time for my father to have a shower, if he's to present himself to the Monarch.' Henri spoke to Finta Fanta. She went over to the trough and took a trunkful of water. Police Constable Monica Sullivan wound down the back window of the car and Finta Fanta put in her trunk. She gave a sharp burst of spray into Claud's face. He awoke and, with a little encouragement, staggered out of the vehicle. Finta Fanta water-jetted him down at the side of the road; and with a bit of hard work from the team he looked, after five minutes, at least like a sort of well-to-do tramp and not like an underprivileged corpse.

They bundled him back into the car and continued the steady progress back to the park. The police car led, waving other traffic out of the way and dissolving traffic jams with masterly authority. As they went, Henri and Mr Sedge discussed tactics as they tickled the elephants' ears, and the elephants discussed tactics with them as they pulled their legs with their trunks. In the car, Police Constable Monica Sullivan radioed back to the park. Messages were passed to the Albany Street men, the

Home Secretary was kept informed and, at a succulent luncheon where the Monarch sat beside the President of the Zoological Society of London, a waiter, dressed impressively in black, presented to the Monarch, on a silver salver, a note bearing news of events. A wry smile spread across the Monarch's face and a sprightly little conversation took place between the two leaders of the occasion. There were some words and knowing looks, some passed notes and changing plans. A course was missed out and speeches were cut to mere formalities. The luncheon ended and the master of ceremonies announced that the company would reassemble at the Royal Rectangle for an important addition to the day's events.

As the Monarch had left for the lunch, the public had been let into the park to peruse the statues and the stalls participating in the fringe events: the carnival capers that were being put on by the various nations and groups that exhibited throughout the park.

When the new message came from the Monarch, the Royal Rectangle was cordoned off and cleared of the public again. The remainder of The Jazz Elephants had been entertaining the crowds, less a trombone and two trumpeters, of course; but successfully nonetheless. More for fun than anything else, Pete Davis and Sady McCabe had been trying out some vocals in rehearsal and, without the brass, tried them out for real in the Royal Rectangle. 'Yes Indeed' had gone down well, with James's saxophone a pretty good substitute for the absent brass. Pete and Sady sang and played together; they looked at each other and at James, their eyes sparkled and the drummer brushed away: this was going to open new repertoires once they had properly worked it out. They finished 'Blueberry Hill' and retreated into their tent.

The good and the glorious reassembled in the Royal

Pavilion. The invited reassembled in the Royal Rectangle. Outside the Rectangle crowds of the public assembled, curious to see what was about to happen. Then, from behind them came cries to clear a passage. A toot or two from a car was heard. People turned to see who was trying to stop them looking on in peace and comfort; and their gaze remained averted as they saw what was coming.

From across the grass approached the police car, headlights on, at a walking pace. Behind it, the elephants mounted by Henri and Mr Sedge, acknowledging the surprise and the applause of the crowd. Marshals cleared a way for them and they drove forward on to the Royal Rectangle. They picked their way round the dumped organ and the discarded bells. The elephants trunked their mounts to the ground and, joined by the rest of the band, all of them stood before the dais, the police car at their side and the dignitaries of the land before them.

The Monarch took the dais and, to the Monarch's left, the Home Secretary showed his face; called in through the agency of the police and rushed to the park in the ministerial limousine.

'You may account for yourselves,' said the Monarch.

'We four free persons,' began Henri, 'deliver up to you no body, but the living person of my father, Claud Coulisse. By your prerogative, by grant of freedom, delivered into your service by us your servants, free men and women all.

'By thanks to your police with help provided, we declare no lasting grievance, and thus no grievance whatsoever done, and ask only one favour.' Everyone paused; all eyes were on the Monarch.

'Ask,' said the Monarch.

'Our petition and our task was proper only to free persons. You have empowered us to go and, as free persons, we went. Yet two of our number, Rumpus

415

Pumpus and Finta Fanta, having yet the mission and the accolade of free persons from yourself have, apart from that, but its form and not its formalities. We do but ask that you confirm reality and confer citizenship and passports upon these two named persons.'

The Monarch was stunned for a moment. Then smiled. Then the President stepped forward and whispered to the Monarch. 'These elephants are persons: none others are. It may be, none others ever will be. Conferring this upon them can set no precedent and . . . it'll get a dirty great problem off my shoulders.'

'Granted,' said the Monarch with a smile. 'My Home Secretary will administer the details.'

The Home Secretary gritted his teeth, for once was speechless; and then he smiled, too.

And with bows from all to all, Claud was delivered up into the service of the Monarch, who released him at once from his obligations as a restituted body, and sent him back to General Catastrophe where he equiposed claims as before; but did it a little less precisely and a lot more quickly, so that he gained promotion to the board and was rather surprised at himself.

As the Monarch quit the dais and the entourage followed, the crowds closed in on The Jazz Elephants; not just the elephants themselves but all the members of the band. News cameras and reporters descended on them like butterflies on to buddleia and the elephants, seeing their comrades sorely jostled, lifted them on to their backs and made their way sedately to their own tent. They grabbed their instruments and went to the Royal Dais, beckoned thence by the equerry to set themselves up just there. The band struck up 'That's A Plenty' and the crowd roared and cheered. The cameras turned and The Jazz Elephants, before all that swaying, shouting mass, revelled in the publicity and saw, already, the bookings come piling in.

Mr Sedge slipped away from the playing and organized a press conference at a nearby hotel for early that evening. They were on the way; and they would write their names in large. The elephants trumpeted and Henri tromboned. In each others' eyes they saw satisfaction and freedom; and set to their music with gusto.

Over in the zoo, the animals heard the noises. Some looked on curiously, others squawked or shrieked or sang along. But two great rhinoceros blinked and snorted and didn't know what to make of it. Finally, they belched; and wandered behind the rhino house, bleary-eyed and amazed. They slowly shook their heads and groped for a mouthful of fodder. They wondered why anyone should go to such trouble of making music, when all a body needed was a few strands of hay inside a walled-off enclosure.

THE PLASTIC TOMATO CUTTER

Michael Curtin

Mr Yendall, one of life's great snobs, watches with distaste from the sanctity of his gentleman's outfitters as the 60s sweep away his social certainties on a tide of Beatlemania and unisex boutiques. Helping Yendall to narrate the gripping Irish madness of *The Plastic Tomato Cutter* is Tim Harding, 'black Protestant' ex-Trinity man of debatable parentage, who is currently operating a company called Fagenders to help people stop smoking (though he's rather fond of a puff himself to be perfectly honest). Harding is also a member of the Society of Bellringers, a very odd assortment who gather and peal at the Redemptionist Church, and he is so enamoured of a local beauty called Cecelia Sloan he can hardly see straight.

Yet this is that rare love story which is really about bellringing and snooker – particularly how men came to play the game on television wearing waistcoats. While he is at it, the inimitable Michael Curtin takes a hard look at tackiness and tradition, loyalty, plastic, religion and the taking of glorious chances.

'Lunatic yet gripping entertainment'
Literary Review

'The effect at first is of tuning one's radio into the middle of a garrulous Irish soap opera ... Curtin's is a wit that touches the heart'
Daily Telegraph

'A brilliant imagination and an almost lunatic sense of humour'
Irish Times

ABACUS
0 349 10314 3

ANIMAL DREAMS
Barbara Kingsolver

Animals dream about the things they do in the daytime,
just like people do. If you want sweet dreams, you've got
to live a sweet life. So says Loyd Peregrina, a handsome
Apache trainman and latter-day philosopher. But when
Codi Noline returns to her hometown, dreamless and at
the end of her rope, Loyd's advice is painfully out of her
reach.

Animal Dreams is a powerful story of courage in an exotic
southwestern landscape. At its center are Codi, her sister,
Hallie, and their dispassionate father, Doc Homer. When
Hallie leaves for Nicaragua to join the fight for social
justice, an aimless Codi returns to Grace, Arizona, to
confront her past and face her ailing father. What she
finds is a town threatened by a silent environmental
catastrophe, some startling clues to her own identity, and
a man whose view of the world could change the course
of her life.

Blending flashbacks, dreams, and Native American
legends, *Animal Dreams* is a suspenseful love story and a
moving exploration of life's largest commitments. With
this work, the acclaimed author of *The Bean Trees* and
Homeland sustains her familiar voice while giving readers
her most remarkable book yet.

'*Animal Dreams* is a rich, compassionate book filled with
political and personal horrors and the hope and magic of
everyday life. In this original, engrossing fictional world,
Barbara Kingsolver examines the nature of evil and
innocence, and the very real way mythology can affect a
people, a culture, a family, as well as a woman in search
of both her future and her past.'
Alice Hoffman

ABACUS
0 349 10270 8

☐	The Plastic Tomato Cutter	Michael Curtin	£5.99
☐	Animal Dreams	Barbara Kingsolver	£5.99
☐	The Scissor Man	Jean Arnold	£5.99
☐	Generation X	Douglas Coupland	£6.99
☐	Rose Reason	Mary Flanagan	£5.99
☐	The Beautiful Screaming of Pigs	Damon Galgut	£5.99

Abacus now offers an exciting range of quality titles by both established and new authors. All of the books in this series are available from:

Little, Brown and Company (UK) Limited,
P.O. Box 11,
Falmouth,
Cornwall TR10 9EN.

Alternatively you may fax your order to the above address.
Fax No. 0326 376423.

Payments can be made as follows: cheque, postal order (payable to Little, Brown and Company) or by credit cards, Visa/Access. Do not send cash or currency. UK customers and B.F.P.O. please allow £1.00 for postage and packing for the first book, plus 50p for the second book, plus 30p for each additional book up to a maximum charge of £3.00 (7 books plus).

Overseas customers including Ireland, please allow £2.00 for the first book plus £1.00 for the second book, plus 50p for each additional book.

NAME (Block Letters) ....

....

ADDRESS ....

....

....

☐ I enclose my remittance for _____

☐ I wish to pay by Access/Visa Card

Number | | | | | | | | | | | | | | | | |

Card Expiry Date | | | | |